HOPELAND

TOR BOOKS BY IAN McDONALD

THE LUNA SERIES

Luna: New Moon

Luna: Wolf Moon

Luna: Moon Rising

IAN McDONALD

HOPELAND

TOR PUBLISHING GROUP
NEW YORK

HOPELAND

Copyright © 2023 by Ian McDonald

A Tor Book
Published by Tom Doherty Associates / Tor Publishing Group
120 Broadway
New York, NY 10271

www.tor-forge.com

Tor® is a registered trademark of Macmillan Publishing Group, LLC.

Library of Congress Cataloging-in-Publication Data

Names: McDonald, Ian, 1960– author.
Title: Hopeland / Ian McDonald.
Description: First edition. | New York : Tor, a Tom Doherty Associates
   Book, 2023.
Identifiers: LCCN 2022040598 (print) | LCCN 2022040599 (ebook) |
   ISBN 9780765375551 (hardcover) | ISBN 9781466847651 (ebook)
Classification: LCC PR6063.C38 H66 2023 (print) | LCC PR6063.C38
   (ebook) | DDC 823/.914—dc23
LC record available at https://lccn.loc.gov/2022040598
LC ebook record available at https://lccn.loc.gov/2022040599

Our books may be purchased in bulk for promotional, educational, or business use. Please contact your local bookseller or the Macmillan Corporate and Premium Sales Department at 1-800-221-7945, extension 5442, or by email at MacmillanSpecialMarkets@macmillan.com.

First Edition: 2023

Printed in the United States of America

0 9 8 7 6 5 4 3 2 1

In memory of Enid

HOPELAND

THUNDER IN OUR HEARTS

1

Love falls from the summer sky.

It is twenty-three minutes past twenty-two and London burns. Flames roar from the shattered windows of a Brixton Foot Locker. White skeletons of torched Citroëns and Toyotas lie broken along Wood Green Lane. In Enfield a barricade of blazing wheelie bins defies police and riot-dogs. The Turks of Turnpike Lanes, baseball bats ready, form a phalanx between their shops, their cafés, their livelihoods and the voiceless roar of street-rage. Jagged teeth of bottle-smash, car-crash windscreen-sugar, bashed-in shutters. Scattered shoe boxes and a single flat-screen television, dropped on its back, face shattered by a fleeing foot. Waltham Forest to Croydon, Woolwich to Shepherd's Bush, riot runs like molten lead from BlackBerry to iPhone, Nokia to Samsung, flows down into the heart of the city, to Islington, Sloane Square, Oxford Circus.

'What are you doing here?' the woman in the TfL vest asks the young man stepping from the train. White, wide-eyed, a coxcomb of red hair flopping into his eyes. Tweeds two sizes too small, brogues, a leather bag slung across a narrow shoulder. A thin, unworldly thing caught out of time and space: a fawn in a foundry. She and this fey boy are the only people on the Central eastbound platform.

'I'm trying to find Meard Mews?'

'Meard Mews?'

'Yes. It's around Broadwick Street somewhere. I think.'

'Are you out of your head?'

'I am at Oxford Circus?'

'Did you hear what they said? Avoid inessential travel?' The woman in the hi-viz holds up her BlackBerry. 'It's kicking off up there.'

Subterranean winds whip shoe-dust, rattle chocolate wrappers across the tiles and carry the rumble from the street, at times voices, at times a soft, surging roar. Crashes. Splinterings. The sounds swirl through the tubes of the colossal instrument that is Oxford Circus station and the young man looks up, antelope eyes wide.

'Can you help me?'

'Exit 7,' the woman says. 'Please be safe up there.'

'I have a charmed life,' he calls back up the platform.

He emerges into riot. Hands shy rocks, bricks, pieces of smashed litter bin and bus-timetable off the shutters of Nike's flagship store. Every hit on the swoosh raises cheers. He ought to slip behind them into the narrow ways of Soho but the sight, the sound, the smell of anarchy are so contrary to everything he understands about the city that he lingers a fascination too long. Mob radar registers him. Mob turns. Mob sees him. Pale, tweeded. A bag over his shoulder. Effete. Elite.

His hand goes to the leather satchel, soft as kisses from age and love. The same satchel once accompanied his great-uncle Auberon as he pursued sensitive misdemeanours in Lycia and the Dodecanese. These men can take it from him. These men can do whatever they want. Flesh is so much more satisfying to rattle rocks from than clattery steel. Flesh can cry and bleed. Four men break from the group and move towards him, shards of street furniture in hands. He backs away. Glass cracks under the heels of his brogues. He stands in a shard-crop field of smashed bottles, car-window sugar, shop glazing.

The sky beats with sudden noise. A television news helicopter comes in low and hard over the roof of Debenham's. The swivel camera hangs like a testicle from the helicopter's thorax. It turns above Oxford Circus, seeking newsworthy shots. Mob looks up, poses: its CNN moment.

He spins on broken splinters and vanishes into Soho.

The narrow, tight streets open onto a parallel world. Soho ignores helicopters, breaking glass, rattling shutters, jeering voices, the fact that this is the year 2011. Soho life moves as it ever has, shoaling in sushi restaurants. Chinese buffets, coffeehouses, corner bars. Lads in plaid shorts and Havaianas stand loud-drinking on the pavements. Young women smoke in cut-offs and summer shoes. Televisions play live rolling feed of the riots. Amy Winehouse sings how love is a losing game.

He pauses to consult his phone. Google doesn't know Meard Mews.

'You want to be careful with that,' a street drinker calls. 'Someone'll have it off you.'

'I'm trying to find Meard Mews?'

Shrugs. Giggles.

'Meard Mews?' The glass collector flickers his fingers over the phone screen. 'Map doesn't show it, but it's there.' A tap on the glass.

Meard Mews is a shoulder-wide crevasse between two brick walls, crowded with pungent shadows. He flicks on his phone torch: heaped black refuse sacks, cardboard pulped by rain and feet. Reeks of August rot, garlic, over-heated cooking oil. Kitchen chatter. Radio gaga and Soho beer piss. A set of black double doors, the email said. There are three such doors in the narrow passage.

He buzzes the intercom on the first door.

'Crumble?' he asks.

'What?'

'Crumble. It's, uh, a club.'

'Fuck off.'

Sirens, amplified by the brick trumpet of Meard Mews. Next door, next intercom.

'Crumble?'

A long stream of swift syllables in a language he does not recognise ends in a dead intercom. To the final door.

'Hello, I'm the music.'

'What love?'

'The music. For Crumble. I'm playing a set.'

'Never heard of it love.'

'It could be small.'

The voice calls someone out of the range of the intercom. 'Sorry, nothing like Crumble round here love.'

'This is Meard Mews?'

'Yes.'

'I got an email to come to Meard Mews. A black door.'

'Not here love.'

The news helicopter passes overhead again. He taps up the promoter's email again.

Then love falls from the summer sky.

2

'Hey hi hello?'

He stares at the intercom on the final black door.

'Here. I'm up here.'

The light from his phone scampers up the walls, over the barbed wire and broken glass embedded in cracking concrete, along the gutters. And strikes a young woman's face above the rotted brick parapet. Her skin is light brown, her cheekbones sharp, her face freckled, her eyes green, her hair held back by a Nike headband.

'Maybe turn the light off? You're blinding me.'

'Oh. Sorry.'

'How much charge have you got?' the woman calls.

'Uh?'

'On your phone.'

'About eighty percent.' A fire escape ladder drops to the street. Shoes descend first. Such shoes; soft, like gloves for the feet. Then he sees old-school skater tube socks with the proper red, white and blue bands at the top. Next, Adidas capri tights; three-striped, hole in the back of the thigh. A backpack over a crop top. Light, tough fingerless gloves. Around her left forearm, a phone in some kind of harness. The woman descends with equilibrium, momentum, glory. Angels descend like this on their ladders from heaven. Angels of Soho.

'Bluetooth me.'

She crouches in the alley, her face lit by screen-shine. She swipes a finger. His phone plays a small snatch of the music he would have performed at Crumble: a notification. The package had arrived.

'Accept it. It's safe. If this goes dead, I'm dead.'

'What?' he says.

She peers over his shoulder and taps the app. His screen fills with a map of Soho, bisected by a vertical translucent green band. 'Yes,' she hisses and snatches the phone from his hand. A jump, a vault, a grab and she is half-way up the fire ladder on the opposite side of the street.

'My phone!'

She turns on the ladder and throws a tablet of glow down to him. Her phone. As he holds it in his cupped hands like a sacrament, it drops into power-saving mode. Five percent. He switches it off.

'Recharge it,' she shouts. 'It'll find me.'

'What?' he says again, and 'Wait . . .'

A moment is all. Seize it. At some point in eternity random quantum fluctuations will re-create this universe in its every detail and this moment will present itself again. Myria-years are too long a wait to redeem unrequited desire.

He pulls himself onto an industrial trash bin. The fire escape is a stretch but he is skinny and lithe. He swings his satchel behind him. The soles of those gecko-grip shoes are vanishing over the parapet above him. He winces as he scrapes toes on brickwork. These are handmade brogues.

She is a rooftop away already, crouching against the air-glow of Richmond Buildings like a superheroine. The higher lights of Soho Square hang like a sequin curtain behind her.

'I'm coming with you.'

'You can't.'

'But you're in trouble.'

'What?'

'You could die.'

'What?'

'You said, "if this goes dead, I'm dead".'

She shakes her head.

'Not literally. Dead. More like . . . look, I haven't the time. I'm in a race.'

She is fleet, but he follows. Those light roof-ballet shoes barely touch the asphalt, the splitting slates, the moulded leads. His brogues run sure. She flickers across the Soho rooftops like low summer lightning. He is the small thunder in her wake. In the lee of a flaking chimney stack she stops, hands on thighs, breathing deep. He arrives beside her.

'That's tweed,' she says, surveying him.

Victorian men scaled Alps in tweed, he is about to say, but she is running again, down the sloping roof slates to a brick parapet overlooking a narrow alley more a punctuation between buildings than a thoroughfare. She stands on the edge, shifting her weight from foot to foot, judging distances. The *no* is in his throat as she steps back, finds her balance and makes the short, strong run. She jumps. She seems suspended over the dark void filled with Soho heat and the odour of Thai food: the sole still point in the seething city. She lands with a crunch on the tiles, crouched, finding her balance.

'A race against whom?' he shouts across the gap.

'My kynnd,' she calls back.

'Your what?'

'Kynnd Finn. And did you say "whom"?'

He measures up the gap. Run in, launch, the landing, traction: all against him. For him: the Grace. He makes his run, throws himself over the street, lands hard, pitches forward, breaks his fall with his hands.

'Gods,' she whispers.

'So.' He dusts off his grit-pocked hands. 'Race against whom?'

The sky behind the woman is wreathed with yellow, sodium-lit smoke. Sirens weave a web of alarm. 'Listen. There's a thing I can inherit. Something so rare and magical you wouldn't believe it. Finn also has a claim to it. So: We race. First one to bring it to life, keeps it. We start at opposite ends of a line that runs through London.'

'Like a train line?'

'No shut up listen. A map line. Zero degrees eight minutes two point one two seconds west. Me in Streatham, him up in Muswell Hill. If we stray more than twenty metres off the line, it's game over.'

'Even, people's houses and private property and things?'

'Shit on private property, tweed-boy. I had to swim across the Thames. There's a wetsuit in the backpack. It's a bit stinky.'

'You put a wetsuit on in central London?'

'And took it off in front of a dozen pervs. I got the river, Finn got Euston and the West Coast Main Line. So, if the line says run over the roofs, jump over alleys, I run, I jump.' She turns to show him his phone shining from her left arm. 'GPS. The Arcmages are watching. Now, I got a race to win?'

'I can be useful,' he calls as she works her way up the roof, fingertips brushing the slates.

'Really, tweed-boy?'

'Really. I have a charmed life.'

It's true, and more than true. It is the defining truth in his twenty-four years. It is why the doors in Meard Mews hadn't answered to Crumble. It is why the rioters on Oxford Circus sniffed, growled and moved on; to bring him here, to this rooftop. And she won't turn him away. The Grace will always favour the Graced.

'Well come on then.' And she is along the ridge tiles. He follows on her heel.

A small crowd talks and drinks outside the Nellie Dean on Dean Street. Intent on their blunt gossip, their blaring laughter, they never look up. Half the universe is unseen, like dark matter. A city burning ten streets away, women slipping into wetsuits, a spandex superheroine and her tweed-and-brogue sidekick running the ridge tiles, like a quirky sixties spy-show cancelled mid-first-season: dark energy.

The girl checks a red pin on the appropriated phone.

'He's fast.'

'How far is it?'

She flicks her chin towards Soho Square. 'Carlisle Street.' She drops to a high porch and peers down into the street.

'Five, six metres.'

'There's a fire escape down that side.'

'Off the line.'

'Not to me.'

He takes the forbidden fire escape and descends to the Dean Street drinkers. 'Um, could I ask a wee favour?' The Grace can never be summoned or commanded. It is a shine. It goes out from him and touches hearts made wide by beer and summer and the drinkers help him drag a picnic bench across the street, upend it and position it under the drop point.

'What's it now?'

'Maybe three metres.'

Now the drinkers see the girl on the porch and they are in an adventure. She turns, lowers herself over the edge of the porch, hangs from the lip, drops. She hits the slope of the bench, skis down into the street and is across the road, over the bonnet of a tight-parked Peugeot 205, down an alley, up an industrial bin, then a wall, then a fire exit to a high coaming.

'It's that free running thing, isn't it?' says a skinny bloke in a plaid shirt.

He watches her striped socks vault, jump, climb out of his life up among the crumbling chimneys and the rooftop weed-smoking dens, chasing her prize beyond price.

The Grace is not cheated so easily. He is not tied to her strict desire line. He can go anywhere in this city. So: up Dean Street to Carlisle Street to Soho Square. With the last of the power in the girl's phone he summons the app and faces north, the direction of the other racer. The kynnd, whatever that is. There, moving against the groups of drinkers headed for the earlier tube, the safer bus. Early twenties, tall. Damn fit. Olive skin, prominent nose, gazelle eyes. Dark waves of thick, glossy hair. He wears the same Adidas capri tights as the girl. Same shoes. Same socks. A hydration backpack over a compression top, grippy fingerless gloves. The defining glow of a phone mounted on his left forearm. His wide eyes are turned to alleys and fire escapes and rooflines. Eyes on the prize. *And that is how he misses it,* the Grace whispers in the chambers of his heart.

At full speed he runs into Finn. They go sprawling to the street.

'Sorry sorry.' He helps Kynnd Finn up. A moment of legerdemain. 'You okay? I think this is your phone.' And the trick is done. 'I'm so sorry.'

Finn slips the phone into the armband and runs on, eyes on the top of the city. Now the final act.

Finn glances at his left forearm, as he must. Glances again. Takes the phone and shakes it.

He sees the moment the life and hope run out of a man. He sees him go to his knees. He hears a thing he hoped never to hear again, a man howl as if his bones were wrenched through flesh. In the name of love, he has done the worst thing in his life.

He walks away from the scene of the phone-switch. On Finn's stolen phone he can easily locate the Prize. This battered street door leads to a courtyard. There is a fire escape. Of course. Before he climbs the ladder in his inappropriate footwear to a flat roof he makes sure to switch off the purloined phone. Seal the crime. Across a few metres of abandoned barbecues and bottle-smash rises a stained-glass cupola, patterned with branches and leaves like a Tiffany lamp. At the four corners of the roof stand slender metal pillars, twice his height, each capped with a metal sphere the size of his head. Are those arcane markings etched into the roof lead beneath his feet, or the hieroglyphs of pigeon shit?

The stained glass is old and carbon-greasy, etched fragile by decades of light pouring through it. He peers through the panes. Glow and shadows. He sits and leans his back against the dome to wait for the girl to come up the long, strict way dictated by the line. Columns of smoke rise against a sodium sky. Sirens and shouts. The city growls, sullen and disobedient. The helicopters have flitted away to districts more newsworthy.

A gloved hand comes over the parapet. A second hand reaches. He is there to offer his own hand.

She stares up into his face. She is exhausted, eyes sunken, face jazzy with sweat and dust, nails chipped.

'What?'

'I knew another way in.'

She takes his hand and clambers onto the roof with the last of her strength. She sees the glass dome and every muscle tightens.

'Oh my God.' She freezes. 'Am I . . . is he?'

'He didn't make it.'

'You saw him? Finn?'

'His phone . . .' He thinks about the truth. Truth and Grace are not necessary lovers. 'His phone died.'

'I win,' she says simply and because the words cut no night, speaks them again, speaks them to the heedless city. 'I win!'

The phone on her forearm flashes a four-digit code. She squats to turn tumblers on a lockbox beside the dome. Inside is a ring bearing two keys. She unlocks a section of the dome, opens a panel and steps inside.

'Come on then. You need to see this. You need to.'

3

A metal staircase curves down into a large room occupying the top floor of the building. Mythologies dwell in the walls: deities, spirits and djinn peep from sprays of foliage, blousy blossoms, orgies of fruit and roosts of bright-plumed birds. Beaked beasts, jewel-eyed reptiles, demons and many-armed godlets, hammers and axes and drums. Glowing blue crowns and tiaras of sparks, wrist-bracers and rings of might; power arcing from god to god in a circle of lightnings.

He pauses on the spiral staircase, enchanted.

'Zeus, Indra, Astrape, Thor, Xolotl, Thunderbird, Set, Raijin. I'm not so familiar with the sub-Saharan ones.'

'Frank Brangwyn,' the young woman says. She flicks on a bank of creamy Bakelite switches, crumbling with age. 'Private commission. This place goes way back. They're kind of valuable.'

'This is the prize beyond price?' he says.

'No,' the girl says. 'This is.'

She unfolds the second key from the ring and unlocks a box in the floor. Inside: a set of gears. A loop of chain runs from the cog-train to a pulley in the ceiling. She hauls. Links rattle through wheels, meshed teeth tick. A circular hatch in the centre of the parquet floor splits into triangles. A rounded metal dome pushes the wedges up and apart. Up on the staircase he clutches the rail in dread and delight. If a giant city-killing monster robot had been built with a cock, it would be the steel bell rising out of the floor. The knob ascends, beneath it a slim pylon.

'This; what is this?'

'Never seen a Tesla coil, tweed-boy?'

Then he spots the man hiding among the thunderheads and jungle fecundity, a prim Victorian in a high collar, neatly coiffed and moustached, with a sly smile and quick eye amongst the thunder-gods. Nikola Tesla, the Serb mage of electricity, greatest of all.

'Be useful,' the young woman calls. 'That handle.' She points with her chin. She has a fine pointy chin. The crank is set in the opposite wall to the chain. He clatters down the cast-iron steps to the handle. He cranks, she hauls. Wonder happens. Aged machinery creaks, shakes off years of rust and disuse. The zenith of the dome opens in a tiny starburst of night. Gaps appear between the metal ribs. Slowly and with a great din, the separate petals retract and descend into the room beneath.

'This is real!' he shouts over the racket of gears and guide rails and ball-bearing trains. A curved triangle of stained glass lowers before his face.

'Realest thing there is, tweed-boy,' the girl yells back. The coil rises above ceiling level. 'Electromancy! I loved this place as a kid but the way it worked Finn went here and I went to Tante Margolis in Spitalfields. I always envied him.'

'I have no idea what you're talking about!' he shouts.

The dome has retracted. The Tesla coil has risen above roof level. The young woman throws a sequence of bolts to lock the coil in place.

'You ready for this? Do you want to see this?' Lightning crackles in her eyes.

Cables and conduits cover the third wall, fuses and junction boxes and trips all wired into one big knife switch, an honest-to-Godzilla monster-movie Baron Frank-N-Furter raise-the-casket-into-the-lightning switch, with a red handle. And she throws it. Her hands go to her mouth in awe of her own daring. The building throbs to a pulse of power. The brow of each god and daemon and angel and tesla in the walls blazes with flames of St Elmo's fire.

The girl bounds up the spiral staircase. The backpack holding her stinky wetsuit bounces on her back. Clutching his satchel to his chest, as if his heartbeat could ward off chip-killing electromagnetic fields, he follows her to the roof. He brushes the handrail and yelps, stung by small lightning. High above Soho the head of the Tesla coil flickers with electric fire.

'This is mad!' he shouts to the girl.

'Greatest mad!' she shouts back over the hum of power.

And the Tesla coil explodes in lightning. Blue-white plasma bolts to the pillar on the south-east corner of the roof. Arc-light sears his retinas. Lightning skips from metal sphere to metal sphere, flickers and dances, finding new paths through the air, never the same from moment to moment. He stands breathless with excitement and exhilaration in a pavilion of lightning. A stray bolt might strike him to ash; he would not care. He is a squirm of carbon, a triad in eternity. The woman stands ecstatic, crowned with electric fire.

'Who are you?' he shouts.

She throws open her arms, a Tesla Angel demanding the city's adulation.

'I am Raisa Peri Antares Hopeland!'

Pedestrians on Carlisle Street stop and look up, cars halt on Soho Square. Pedicabs pull up, their fares step out to stare.

'Maybe you should . . .' he says. 'The police . . .'

'Not yet,' Raisa Peri Antares Hopeland says. All storm gods concur: wielding lightning is very moreish. She crosses to the eastern side of the roof overlooking Soho Square. 'They have to . . . Yes. There! Oh man, look!'

North-east of east, lightning flickers among the towers of the City of London.

His hair rises, his scalp prickles. Awe, pure and old. She has called something ancient and mighty out of the east of the city, something that has slept long and now wakes alert, wild, undiminished.

'The Arcmages recognise my claim,' Raisa Peri Antares Hopeland says. 'I'm an electromancer.' Her dark skin shines electric indigo; her cheeks, her eye-hollows, her hair crawl with fire. A helicopter clatters low over the roof, turns above Soho Square. 'I should shut it off now. I'm getting noticed.'

She descends to the electromancer's study between helices of St Elmo's fire that flicker up and down the handrails of the spiral staircase. The lightning dies. Chains rattle, the coil descends. He feels chilled and exposed. The energy that sent him over Soho on psychogeographic leylines has run to earth. The nighthawks and the street-curious resume their journeys, all but one who lingers after the rest have moved on; a tall, athletic young man in sports top, tights, tube socks, looking up. He watches him turn, walk, then jog, then run into the city.

The helicopter rises straight up, banks and beats east.

She is not in the great room. He looks for her along the halls and down the stairs of this flat that seems bigger than space-time permits. He catches the sound of running water. Light around an ajar bathroom door. Sports gear and grip shoes and sweat socks on a tiled floor. The wetsuit is a sloughed neoprene selkie-skin. His heart turns, aroused; he has always wished that his was a life that wore wetsuits.

'Is it okay if I crash here?' he shouts through menthol and lavender and the noises of small private pleasure that humans make under running water, the last memory of the wet womb. 'It's, well, I was supposed to have been in a club tonight.'

'Sure. Loads of beds here.'

'Amon Brightbourne,' he calls from the hall. 'My name. Amon. Brightbourne.'

She is singing *Back to Black*. Amon retraces his steps to the landing and locates the bedroom that smells least of old men. By the green light of a bedside banker's lamp, he works along a history framed on the walls like an Egyptologist deciphering dynastic lineages. An entertainer lived here. Playbills for the Palladium and the Hackney Empire; the headline stars proclaimed in 96-point Playbill: ten acts down, among the 36-point dog acts and comedy jugglers; Sir Karageorge, the Electric Knight. A round-faced man smiling in a hood and suit of chain-mail. He wears a smart Tesla moustache.

Photographs now: the Electric Knight in a soft, smart suit, neatly knotted tie, cufflinks, posing with other old-time acts. A petite woman singer who looks like a primary school teacher in a wonderful fifties Empire-line dress. A woman, taller, brasher, in a fantabulous ballerina frock and high-spiring beehive do. Old comedians: a balding guy in horn-rim specs. A smaller one beside him with silvering hair. A tall gangster-faced man in a fez. Another man in a suave trilby hat and raincoat whose features need rinsing and ironing. Showgirls in gloves and silver shoes and feathers. Stage shots, capturing lightning from a coil onto the tip of a lance. Lightning arcing between chain-mail gloves. A stage crackling with arcs exchanged between two coils. Shots from what looks like a television studio with sixties singers. Amon recognises Cliff Richard because his mother still believes he smiled at her from a television screen. A tautly young Bruce Forsyth with scared-looking civilians in what must have been some kind of game show. Now the stage again—with rock bands. Here is the Electric Knight, older, dapper moustache grey, with a man dressed as a giant flower; here with Ozzy Osbourne baring teeth and popping eyes and throwing shapes with his fingers; here on a raised dais, casting streamers of raw electricity over a three-piece with a weedy, long-haired bass player and a muscular drummer behind the largest kit Amon has ever seen. Rick Wakeman in a silver cloak behind a battery of keyboards, with knights in armour on ice. After that, blank wall.

The bedsheets repulse Amon Brightbourne so he lies on the quilt. Over the bed hangs a small, strange device: a gimbal hanging from a light silver chain. Inside the gimbal, free to spin, a five-pence-piece-sized mirror. He has no idea what it does but it radiates no ill vibes and is so delicately mounted it spins when he blows at it so he treats it as a charm.

Imagined footsteps in the hall shock him awake time and time again. She is never there. He lacks the courage to go in search of her, in case she never was there and the night's magic is just cinders. While Amon Brightbourne settles into twitching sleep, London burns. Teenage males fight through the corridors and waiting rooms of King's College Hospital. The Brixton Currys electrical store is stripped. Here lies the skull of a dead Tesco. In Woolwich the Great Harry pub blazes. Rioters finger-paint slogans on its walls in its own ashes. Helicopters and dogs; burning cars. Foam upholstery makes such pretty flames. He wakes in the night, paralysed, not knowing where he is, convinced that some momentous, terrible event has occurred and that when the light comes again he will see a world changed, changed utterly. It has. Love has fallen on him.

And the morning does come and he calls her name—her full, preposterous, wonderful name—and, receiving no answer, he again searches the apartment. She is gone. The kettle is warm, she's moments departed and he takes heart in that as he makes coffee from the jar of Nescafé on the peeling worktop in the yellowed melamine kitchen. He climbs up to the electromancy studio. She has retracted the coil. On the centre of the hatch in the floor she's left a sheet of paper. On it: a map, an address, a date four days hence, and the words *Come get ur fon*.

4

He hears the music from across Wandsworth Common, Trojan dub-beat over the huff of runners and the moan of electric trains through the cut. Early-autumn leaves blow across the paths; the air feels soiled and oily, dusted with rage and smoke from London's lunge of anger, coiling back into sleep like a snake. Amon Brightbourne's step quickens. Work is done and he is free.

Four dawns. Four sessions between Karageorge the Electric Knight's sanctum and here.

Shoreditch: five A.M. First grey gloaming. The tall windows of a warehouse loft thrown wide, people high on morning. The little pitch-bent pleadings of his music scurrying among their feet. Had he dreamed his night of lightning? He is given a sofa to sleep on, Wi-Fi to squat on and an invitation to session at another private party.

Stoke Newington: an abandoned stationery warehouse, security sheeting opened with angle-grinders while police eyes were turned to Lord Riot. Amon is too young to remember the shining years of rave—that had been his father's terroir—but these things circle. We can't dance to this, they cried. Except we can.

Croydon: London lacerating its own arms. Ghosting around soft blowing ashes and the glowing skeletons and springs of looted sofas to a high glass apartment, playing a dozen trust-fund kids on wireless earbuds. They never know that none of them move to the same beats.

Rotherhithe: headed for breakfast and a place to spin away Sunday until it is time to see Raisa in Wandsworth. 34a Dorling Avenue. Google knows every number on Dorling Avenue except 34a. Amon Brightbourne grew up with places that didn't want to be mapped, but he can't rid himself of the fear that she has used his own deception on him: left a faery misdirection. Come get ur fon, come get mugged. Satchel clutched tight to chest, he takes a rusted-open park gate onto Dorling Avenue. He wanders under gracious plane trees. The big Edwardian terrace houses exhale unconcerned dilapidation: old Toyotas and battered Volvo estates parked half on the pavement, bikes hung from railings, styrene fast-food boxes swept into the gutters. He walks past 33. Number 35. Walks back. Number 35, Number 33. There is no place between them to put a Number 34, much less a 34a.

'You right mate?' A black face calls from behind the wheel of a Ford Focus van. A skinny white van mate grins up from the sagging passenger seat.

'I'm trying to find 34a Dorling Avenue.'

'You going to the Starring?'

'I'm looking for Raisa Peri Antares Hopeland?'

'You are then.' The man beams. 'We can be a bugger to find if you ain't been before. I'd give you a lift but it's literally up the end of the road.'

The van turns down the alley at the end of the terrace. The two men wait at green double doors. Amon hears voices, smells barbecue smoke. Dub waves over him. A neat ceramic plaque beside the door declares 34a.

'It's not round the front, see. It's round the back. Of everything.'

The driver punches a keypad and the green doors open. Amon Brightbourne steps into paradise.

Pairi Daeza. Old Iranian: a walled enclosure. Through Akkadian and Elamite to Greek: paradeisos, and Latin: paradisus. The abode of bliss is a walled garden. Milton's Eden was an enclosed paradise. Hieronymus Bosch's Garden of Earthly Delights was bounded on either side by creation and damnation. At some theological junction paradise moved from the natural world to the supernatural. Paradise became heaven, infinite in extent, yet contained. Further up and further in; Aslan drew the Pevensies from the wreckage of Narnia into successive heavens, each paradise larger and more paradisaical than the one that contained it.

Amon Brightbourne stands in a great garden guarded by houses. Yards, lawns, patios and decks. Mossy herringbone brick paths wander into small green delights: Buddha-haunted bamboo groves and secret suntraps, tiny amphitheatres, raised-bed vegetable gardens, a trellised vineyard, summerhouses and belvederes and barbecues and Ottoman-style divans around firepits. He glimpses chickens. Towering dub thumps from a raised wooden platform at the far end of the great garden, glimpsed through the branches of the three lime trees at the heart of the hidden place. Hammocks single and double have been slung between their trunks and their branches are home to bird boxes, bat boxes, wind chimes and tree decorations that twinkle as they spin. Water, for there is no paradise without water: a fountain-noisy grove to a garden deity and a netted-over koi pond built from railway sleepers; more affably, outdoor Jacuzzis and inflatable paddling pools. On the lawn stand junior football nets and B&Q gazebos. Blankets and cushions and folding chairs lounge across the grass.

The garden is as crowded as a small free festival; one of those impromptu festivals that are about who's there, that die whenever mobile phone companies move in with brands and badges. Football shirts, crop top, beer bellies. The season's cut-offs and leggings. Plaid shorts, saris and suits. Havaiana feet. Glorious silly heels. Ages and skins. Some black some white, most both. Like her.

Children.

This is why paradise is better than heaven. There are no children in heaven. Here are children's voices, colours, dartings and stillnesses and suddennesses, chasing each other down the brick paths, kicking and throwing things, wailing and hitting each other, intent in their own private dances to the riddim, jumping up and down and squealing with sheer delight in the spray from a garden hose. Tricycles, balls, Dora the Explorer lunch boxes, Happy Meal toys trodden into the sward—pain-mines for bare feet—dolls and Transformers and Sylvanian Family members.

There's a tree-house. Of course there is; railed-off platforms and ladders and staircases. Through the leaves he glimpses a movement of kingfisher blue, eternity blue. Blue as E minor 7. Blue and heart-red.

The van driver claps a hand on Amon Brightbourne's shoulder.

'We'll sort you, mate. I'm Jacob Sirius. This is Demetrios Denebola.'

One tall, one squat, they steer Amon by crazy-paving and plank-walk and decking to the foot of the tree-house. The kingfisher blue is a dress, the heart-red tights and improbably matching shoes. Ruby slippers.

'Hey!' Jacob bellows. 'Raisa Antares! Someone to see you!'

The blue and the red flurry, leaves part and she looks down over a wooden rail.

5

Hands on the waist of her best favourite only dress, she looks down from the first gallery of the tree-house at the hoped-for guest. The Starring booms and rolls around her.

'Still rocking the tweed, I see.'

'Amon,' he stammers. 'My name is Amon Brightbourne.'

And still so skinny. Still so wide-eyed. Still calling up to her from down there. Has he changed his clothes? Does he have any other clothes? Has he eaten? She throws the Number Three rope ladder over the side and climbs down. Only Hopelanders who've grown up around the back of everything can do this in heels.

'You've got my phone,' he protests. She beckons. Come with. The beer lives in a paddling pool slushy with melting ice. She uncaps a Red Strip and she sticks the bottle into his fist.

'When did you last eat? Karageorge's, right?'

To the tables around the rim of the great garden, where backyards and patios grade into greenery. She takes a samosa from a middle-aged Caribbean woman—Kynnd Patience—at a trestle table piled high with the deep-fried pastry triangles. Behind her on the house wall is a plaque: 34a.

'Eat.'

He wolfs it down like a man who hasn't seen food in four days. He sprays greasy pastry flakes down the front of his cute tweed jacket.

His eyes widen at the spike of chilli, then lower into a frown.

'Is this foie gras?'

Kynnd Patience smiles hugely.

'It's placenta.'

On to another pop-up kitchen, another 34a plaque. Two young women in salwar kameez from the Bristol Hearth offer golden pakoras on a paper napkin.

'Is this placenta too?'

'Oh yes,' says the older girl.

She moves him onto a third patio, a third 34a plaque and a third table,

crewed by a lightning-thin young kynnd in an improbably white shirt offering rounds of baguette thickly spread with paté.

'Would I be right in thinking that's placenta?' Amon Brightbourne says.

He's getting it.

'You would.'

Amon eats, nods. 'Hint of sage?'

The man beams.

'Sage is the herb for offal.'

'Is everything placenta?' Amon Brightbourne asks. His beer is done.
Raisa takes him around a screen of bamboo and through a crease in space-
time she's never been able to work out in the years she's lived here, and
they're back at the beer bath.

'Well, it is a Starring, and it's a big organ,' she says, placing a fresh bottle
in his hand. 'There's barbecued stuff. And always cake.'

'Cake,' says Amon Brightbourne. Along another path through the bamboo and they're on the other side of the garden where metre-long skewers
grill over an oil-can barbecue. 'How did . . .'

He's cute when he's baffled. A group has gathered around two men
squatting under an awning: Kynnd Marco and Kynnd Patterson. Raisa
never liked them much. Always a deal going on somewhere. Boxes of
trainers lie at their feet. Each box has a Foot Locker price sticker on the
end. Money leaves hands as fast as hands can find it.

'Xboxes and flat-screen TVs in the van,' the older man, hairless, face
like an unkind Muppet, calls out. 'Get in early for Euro 2012 and the
Olympics.'

'Did they loot . . .' Amon begins. She touches her finger to his lips.

'If you don't want it, don't buy it.'

From the lawn come the high-low shouts of children playing and the
sharp plastic spang of an over-inflated football being kicked. Teenagers
show each other their phones. Old people laugh in folding chairs, glasses of
wine perilous in the armrest cup-holders. Names and greetings.

'Is everyone kynnd?' he asks.

'And a star.'

She spirals him back to the beer pool which never seems to get any emp-
tier. At the Buddhaed heart of a small turf maze she's offered a toke. She
draws deep, coughs. She's never been much of a smoker. He waves it away.
They recline awhile on a garden divan with people who seem to work in

the media and are trying to decide whether the riots signal the end of the world, the end of innocence, the end of middle-class smugness, the triumph of middle-class smugness. All agree it is poor taste to flog loot at a Starring, though the deals on Xboxes look tasty.

'Stars too?'

'All stars.'

'So what is a Starring?'

She should stop teasing the boy, spinning him out and around like spider silk. Today nothing can be denied her. Today she is the brightest star among the Emanations. Arcmage of the Great Coil of Soho. She lays her finger to his lips again.

'I got to go. Get ready.'

'What?'

'For the Starring.'

'Don't leave me.'

'Whatever happens, accept it. Lisi will look after you.'

'Lisi? You've still got my phone?' Amon calls as she walks away through another fold in the garden.

The bottle is taken from his hand. In front of him, squinting up into his face, stands a kid, ten, eleven, brown-skinned, green-eyed, great-haired. A stripe of blue sunblock highlights each cheekbone. Amon struggles with gender, makes an arbitrary assignment. Who is she, where has she come from?

'Come with.' The kid is fast and well-camouflaged. Amon manages to follow her. Like the Soho house, this Wandsworth garden seems larger than its available space. A shaded, sweet fig grove. A firepit that might double as a handy temple. A rattling palisade of banners and wind socks. He catches up with her by the raised vegetable beds.

'Who exactly are you?'

'I'm exactly Lisi Priya Sirius Hopeland,' the kid says. 'Now come on.'

The party—rave, protest, rally, coven?—seems to be flowing towards the north end of paradise.

'So, Raisa is your sister?' Amon hesitates. 'Mother?'

The kid deals him a stare that stops worlds in their orbits.

'Raisa is my kynnd.'

'Like . . . Finn?' Amon ventures.

'Finn is kynnd too,' the kid says. Amon is no more enlightened. 'He's Soho and me and Raisa's Spitalfields. Now come on. The Starring's about to start.'

Amon resists the tugging hand.

'Why will no one tell me what a Starring is?'

Lisi frowns again. It is her most expressive face.

'You aren't Hopeland, are you?'

She leads him through the carrot and corn to the front of the stage where the crowd gathers. Lisi hauls Amon up to a thin, fifty-wise woman in a floaty handkerchief dress, sheer calf-length leggings and much metal around her ankles and wrists and face.

'This is Tante Margolis,' Lisi says. The woman offers a hand to Amon Brightbourne. The Grace prompts him to touch proffered fingers, dip his head. The woman smiles, charmed. 'Grand Primary of the Order of Electromancers,' Lisi continues. 'My caregiver. Sort of.'

'Amon . . .'

'We know you,' Tante Margolis says. 'Raisa told us everything.' The dub DJ ends his set. A thin teenager comes up onstage, lifts an electric guitar from a case, slings it around her neck, trips harmonics up and down the frets. 'You coming to Spitalfields tomorrow? We're moving it. It's a bit of a palaver. Be sober. Hangovers and high voltage: not friends.'

The guitarist strikes four blasting E major chords.

'It's starting,' Lisi says. 'You want to be at the front.'

Again, the guitar calls the people. Amon glances around. He has lost Tante Margolis, affable Jacob, spooky Demetrios. Lisi pulls him to the edge of the staging. A third time the guitar calls. So close to the stacks, the sound is a physical, visceral thing.

'Is this the Starring?' he shouts over the reverb.

'It is, Amon Brightbourne,' Lisi says.

'You hear me?' the dub DJ shouts into a radio mic.

And the people say *Yay!*

'Said, you hear me?'

The people yay again, with heart.

'Hail and well-met, stars. Great day! A new star!' The biggest yay yet. 'In a moment we're going to name our new star, but first, be joyous! Raisa Peri Antares, star, come on up!'

Again, the musician rips a fanfare from her guitar. Crowd-roar carries

Raisa from behind the stacks onto the stage in a flash and dash of red and blue. She raises her arms like a cup-winning footballer.

'Raisa Peri Antares, I got a new name for you,' the MC shouts. 'From this day on, in the presence of the Hopeland nation, you are Raisa Peri Antares Arcmage of Spitalfields, guardian of the Great Coil of Soho!'

And Amon Brightbourne finds himself roaring with the assembled Hopelands. Raisa struts the front of the stage, bowing and air-punching and blowing kisses. She is radiant. She is electric.

'That's me some day,' Lisi shouts. 'I'm the next . . .' She stops speaking. The crowd falls silent in an instant. The guitarist cuts her reverb. Finn is on the stage—from where, how, no one can tell. He is dressed in a skinny grey suit, too short at ankle and wrist. White shirt, top three buttons undone; winklepickers. Unshaven, hair tied back. He grabs the MC's microphone.

'Is Amon Brightbourne here?' he asks. 'I heard he was invited.'

'Finn,' Raisa says. Finn has seen Amon in the front row.

'You've got something of mine. And I got something, but it's not yours.' He takes Raisa's phone from his inside pocket and holds it up. 'Is it?' He fixes Amon with a raven glare. 'Is it!' Feedback sets the crowd wincing. Jacob is up on the stage, Demetrios behind him.

'Whoa whoa whoa whoa whoa kynnd,' Jacob says. He is a head shorter than Finn but no one in 34a Dorling Avenue's paradise garden doubts that he could crush universes in his fists if so provoked. 'Kids here. Okay? Kids here.' He points a finger at Raisa, who had been about to speak. She takes a step back. Demetrios closes up on Jacob's shoulder. 'This is a Starring, kynnd. Okay?' He gently takes the radio mic from Finn's hand. Finn grimaces, sets Raisa's phone on the stage and stalks off. The assembly parts before him like dust.

'Okay, let's remember why we're here,' Jacob says, returns the mic to the DJ and nods to the guitarist. She picks up a chugging reggae offbeat. The MC stalks the stage.

'Stars!' Back and forth, a slip-beat skip now. 'Stars!' Guitar and MC knit the kynnd back together again. 'Make light!'

And Amon Brightbourne is blinded. He blinks through dazzle. Stage and crowd are lit by tiny spots of moving light; a daylight glitterball. In Raisa's hand, in Lisi's, in Tante Margolis's, the MC's hand, in the hand of the girl guitarist, Jacob and Demetrios and every guest in the great garden, is a short chain from which hangs a small gimbal. Inside the frame, a mirror spins. The same device that hung over Amon's claggy bed in the keep of the Electric Knight. The tension, the ill of Finn's anger is dispersed. Amon hears the air sing. All is full of light.

A young woman comes onstage. She wears a baby in a sling. *I've eaten your placenta,* Amon realises as the leopard-light plays over her. She holds the baby high over her head. A cheer goes up. The baby kicks but does not wail. The mother walks the stage, infant held high, showing it off to the mirror-spinners.

'A star! A star is born!' the MC bellows.

Another cheer.

'Constellation of Los, Aldebaran ascending! Passive, sensitive and warm. Shy and private; always knows what's going on—no fooling Aldebaran: secret keeper of the family. You are Kisi Kufuor Aldebaran Hopeland.'

Cheers and tears. The lights go out. Amon blinks again. The mirror-chains are put away. Kisi Kufuor Aldebaran is crying now.

'What happened there?' Amon asks. Lisi presses forward to greet the new baby. She gives him an over-the-shoulder shout.

'We have our own religion!'

6

Kisi Kufuor Aldebaran Hopeland sleeps in a swaddle of blankets in a hammock beneath the many-decked tree-house. A fingernail-sized mirror on a chain hangs over her face and tiny fists, catching the city-shine breaking through the leaf canopy and spinning it across her closed eyelids. High above Amon Brightbourne and Raisa Hopeland talk quietly. The Starring ended so late it's early. The police would have come about the noise but no police have ever found the way in to 34a and anyway everyone in the street was at the party. Now she sits knee to knee with Amon in her favourite place in the Hearth: the topmost crow's-nest in the fore-dawn.

Raisa says: 'You swapped phones.'

'I did. Yours for his.'

Raisa leans back on the divan seating.

'I'm not sure how I feel about that.'

'I wanted you to win.'

'You're far too honest.'

She should be furious with him. She can't find the anger. It would be like being angry with a dog that's eaten your Starring Day cake. And there was cake. And a lot of it. It didn't taste right. Nothing tasted right, meat cake toke, after Finn's interruption. She sets his phone on the cushion between them.

'If I give you his, can you get it back to him?' Amon says.

'That could take awhile,' Raisa says. 'And he's probably out of London. Gone back to the Alderley Hearth.'

'I don't understand anything that's going on,' he says and it's so plaintive it's adorable.

'Ask me.' She curls her legs up on the divan, kicks off her red shoes.

'Okay: well, Lisi said you have your own religion.'

'Sort of,' she says and sees from his face this is not the answer he wants. 'Everyone is a star. Well, no. Everyone *has* a star. It's not astrology. Stars don't rule us. They're more like parts of ourselves. They're not souls or spirits. They're Emanations. They have their own system. They don't need prayer, but they like acknowledging. They can be in places, or buildings, sometimes animals or people, or weather. Does this make any sense?'

'As much as any of them,' Amon says.

'They're most easily seen in mirrors,' Raisa says. 'They like places where their earth and ours rub up against each other.'

Raisa takes her coin-sized mirror from around her neck and sets it spinning with a tap. Little lights.

'This is a yata. Look.'

He leans forward, peers, shakes his head, peers deeper. The yata spins to a stop.

'Nothing,' Amon says.

'You wouldn't. You're not a Hopeland.' Raisa slips the yata around her neck.

'What am I supposed to see?' Amon asks.

'Emanations. Maybe.'

'Like . . . angels? Gods?'

'Nothing like that. They're not gods. They don't need belief,' Raisa says. 'It's a praxy. Not a doxy. It's a thing to have. Karl-Maria Lindner thought we should have our own religion to keep the family united. You can believe in other gods as well, or none, but this is ours. Look up.'

She touches her fingers under Amon's chin, feels his thrill of tension, gently tilts his gaze up into over-London.

'What do you see?'

'Not a lot.' London poisons its sky with light. 'A couple of planes. Bigger stars. At home the stars are like handfuls of scattered jewels.'

She could kiss him for that. Her fingers insist he keep looking skyward.

'Understand this, understand us. We're like them. Scattered stars. Connected into patterns. Constellations. Put them together, they have a story. Like you see the Great Bear and Cassiopeia and they have histories and legends and old dead gods. We got our constellations. Enion the Mama, Ahania the Leader of the Starry Skies, Enitharmon and her guitar. Our histories and legends. We are a constellation, the Hopelands. We're connected by lives and loves. Lines and histories. Relationships. As below, so above.'

Her fingers slip from Amon's chin. She looks into his eyes. His gaze flits away, bat-shy. *Come on, tweed-boy. If you got up on the top of London, you can look for the Emanations in my eyes.*

Connect.

Then he stammers, 'I brought you a present.'

'Not traditional at a Starring but I like presents.'

He sets his satchel next to his phone and takes out a MacBook, small, satin-soft.

'I'm sort of a musician.'

'Sort of?'

'I am a musician. I make music. It's like party music you can't dance to. Well, sometimes you can. People like it. It makes them cry and feel cosmic.'

'I'd like to hear music that makes me cry and feel cosmic,' Raisa says.

'It doesn't like crowds, just a few people, played kind of low so you can barely hear it, like it's playing only for you, right inside you. The best audience is maybe me playing it to just one other person.'

'I'll be that one other person, Amon Brightbourne.'

Amon's hands shake as he moves Raisa's hair, slips the audio buds into her ears. He opens Ableton, plugs the Push pad into the MacBook. The pad is a chessboard of buttons, each connected to a sound clip.

'I mix in real time,' he says. 'Every performance is bespoke.'

An edge of arcing light outlines the east. Bird calls to bird across Wandsworth Park: the blackbird, sweetest singer first; then the robin; next the wren, the King of the Birds. Chaffinch, warblers; thrush, finch and dunnock until the trees ring.

'In Brightbourne, where I come from, the dawn chorus is overwhelming,' he says.

The voice that sings in the dawn. He touches the play button. Raisa Hopeland's eyes go wide, then close. The music takes her.

7

Raisa hurls the ancient Volvo through courts and closes, avenues and alleyways. The heel of her left hand rests on the horn, eager to declare her opinions of any other road-user. She turns onto Tower Bridge Road. Hand hits, horn shouts. A cyclist wobbles out of her path and veers into the bus lane.

'Where you belong, hipster!' Raisa yells.

'Don't you think that's a little excessive?' Amon Brightbourne says. He sits in the passenger seat, eyes wide with dread, satchel hugged close.

'I love bikes,' Raisa says. 'I had a job as a Cycling Advocacy Officer. What I hate is hip bastards. Fixies and Macs. I get them in the coffee shop. Wi-Fi hogs.'

'I use a Mac,' Amon says. 'Sometimes in a coffee shop.'

She turns to Amon.

'You're not hip. You're a young fogey.'

'I'd like it if you kept your eyes . . .'

'Who's driving, tweed-boy?'

She hauls a cassette from the glove box and jams it into the car player. *The Boy in the Bubble*'s accordion riff wheezes out. Every car over a certain age has a cassette of *Graceland* in the glove box.

'Soundtrack to my childhood,' Amon says. 'We had this old Saab; Mum would put it on and me and Lorien would sing while she tried to get us to miss a note by steering into the potholes. We had a lot of potholes in the drive.'

'Days of miracles and wonder, tweed-boy,' Raisa says and she tells Amon about another place like Graceland: Hopeland. It is a family, also nation, also community, also culture. It has many homes; it has no home. It is scattered across the world, mirroring the stars of the night sky. It is boundless like the night sky for it never stops expanding, like space-time, as new lives are born, adopted, fall, drift, leap into it with a whoop and a cheer. It is easy to join and difficult to leave, like a religion. Unlike a religion the difficulty in leaving is not coercion, or guilt or the price of apostasy; it is because no one ever needs to leave. Once you enter Hopeland you can travel all your days through this constellation of lives, making and breaking and reforging relationships, and never come to the end of love. And they cross the Thames, sacred stream, to the slinky Soweto guitar of *Diamonds on the Soles of Her Shoes* and blare their way up Commercial Street and right into Fournier Street. The crane is already deploying its stabilisers. Spitalfields has turned out, from the landlady of the Ten Bells to the imam of the Masjid on the corner of Brick Lane. Tracey Emin, Dan Cruickshank, Gilbert and George. Cranes are always worth watching.

No-nonsense in hi-viz yellow, Lisi waves the spectators back and shifts police cones. She beckons Raisa in behind the crane.

'You're going to hit . . .' Amon murmurs. Lisi slaps the hood, the Volvo bounces to a stop. Fuck parking. Look. Look!

The Tesla coil gleams on a wooden pallet on the back of the truck.

'Shouldn't you take the keys?' She holds up an indicting hand. Enough, tweed-boy. The coil draws her, as if its power were magnetic, not electrostatic. Shine of copper, glint of primary. Varnish and mahogany and steampunk brass. The Soho coil is an old beast from deep time, created long before it was drawn into the constellation of Hopeland, before even the Electromancers gathered in a Huguenot weaver's loft in Fournier Street. Karageorge maintained it came from Belgrade, wound by the hands of Tesla himself, but he, entertainer and old trouper, was a notorious bullshitter. Raisa climbs up onto the truck and reaches up to run her hands over the golden glans of the secondary. She cries out, snatches her hand back. Tracey Emin, Dan Cruickshank, Gilbert and George, the imam of Brick Lane Mosque, the landlady of the Ten Bells hiss in consternation.

A shock.

Not electric. She would not have survived that, not from this coil. Ghost fields resonated with the electrolytes in her blood. Waters calling to waters, salts to salts. Lightning to lightning. As within, so without.

'I'm all right,' she tells the crew. 'Lift 'er up.'

The crane operators bring the jib in and lower and lock strapping. Raisa jumps onto the lifting pallet and wraps a hand around the webbing.

'Health and safety,' the flatbed driver mutters. The rest of the crew stare at him. Tracey Emin, Dan Cruickshank, Gilbert and George, the imam, the landlady, the other rubberneckers in Fournier Street stare at him. He is not Hopeland.

She lifts a hand. Engine noise, slack taken up; then the Tesla coil, Raisa clinging to the strapping, rises up from the cheering crowd. She waves, she grins, blows kisses as the crane lifts her high, higher, highest above the roof-lights of Arcmage House.

Raisa ascending.

'Come with,' Lisi tells Amon Brightbourne which, it seems to him, everyone in this family/constellation/cult/coven has been telling him since Raisa hey-hoed him from Crumble Alley in Soho. Before he can protest Lisi sweeps Amon through a crazy-angled front door into a tiled front hall, up a curving staircase onto another, then another through a high-ceilinged laboratory, up another staircase to a library, up again past another laboratory, this one hung with copper spheres and glass bubbles and then, just as it seems the house can contain no more up to go to, onto a precipitous companionway to a door that opens into light and air and views that take Amon's breath away. The top floor of the Fournier Street house, the old weaving loft, is roofed and walled with glass. He cannot but wonder. To the north Georgian panes look across a shadowed garden to Shoreditch and the towers and cranes of the Olympic Park. To the south the tombstone loom of Christ Church and the lurching banalities of the City dominate the skyline. To the west Tante Margolis waits seated on a high wooden chair.

'Welcome to Arcmage House,' she says. She wears loose silk pants and a wraparound top. Heavy copper bangles. Amon has no dress code for how a Grand Primary should turn out but she looks every thread the part. She gets up stiffly from the chair. 'Bugger this.' She crosses the room to a handle in the wall through which Lisi and Amon entered. 'We need to do something about those stairs.' She kicks the handle.

'It's too stiff for me. Or I'm too stiff for it.'

Lisi moves to an identical crank handle across the room's long diagonal. 'And one!'

Lisi and Amon heave the cranks. Amon's creaks a millimetre. He throws his whole strength into it. The wheel turns. Chains take up slack, turn gears and worm-screws. Paint flakes snow down as the roof splits from prow to stern. Hinged ribs fold the glass neat as a shop awning. A moment's resistance—a new mechanism coming into play—and floor panels flip open, the roof folding flush to the glass walls and creaking down into the hidden spaces. The air smells of old paint and chamomile, which Amon has always thought of as the smell of windows. The glass clicks home. Amon stands under open sky. City sun anoints him. Birdsong, sirens, aircraft engines, train boom weave around him. He's high, the crane boom and the steeple of Christ Church rise higher.

A walkie-talkie scratches on Lisi's hi-viz.

'Here she comes.'

'Careful,' Tante Margolis warns Amon as he peers over the edge of the house into Fournier Street and the upturned faces.

'It's all right, I'm charmed.' He remembers a video of the Beatles playing from the roof of the Apple Records headquarters in Savile Row. Auberon claims he was there, at a fitting with his tailor. Great-Uncle Auberon claims to have been at many of the past century's key moments. The Beatles were tired of each other. Apple was music then.

Raisa ascends towards him, waves as she passes. She flies high over Spitalfields. The crane driver nudges the boom controls, careful not to set his load swinging. Raisa drifts over the roofline to the centre of the floor.

'Okay stop,' Lisi commands into the walkie. 'Lower away.'

Raisa steps from the descending Tesla coil, an archangel touching foot to Earth. She bounces to the Fournier Street front and raises her arms. Adulation greets her. With poles and careful chivvying, Raisa, Tante Margolis, Amon and Lisi lift the Tesla coil from its pallet to its place on the thunder-floor. Lisi sends the pallet back down and she and Amon close the walls and roof over the shining coil, potent with sun-gold.

In Soho the coil was hidden, buried in the architecture, a hooded hawk. In Spitalfields it crowns the house, completes a geomantic trinity with the titanium minaret of Brick Lane Mosque and the spire of Christ Church. The women check the coil, careful fingers working the wires, testing the circuitry. Raisa hooks it into the house's steampunk power supply. Amon imagines he hears a colossal sigh—from the coil, the house, the Arcmages, or Fournier Street? Or from the Emanations, those things glimpsed in mirrors?

The three women glance at each other.

'Test?'

'Test.'

'Test.'

And Raisa strips off her top, slips off her shoes, steps out of her pants. Under her coil-shifting clothes she wears a sports base layer, clingy and flat-lock seamed.

'Enjoy the view while it's there, tweed-boy.'

Amon blushes as he tries to conceal a tweed hard-on. Lisi opens a chest and hands around old leather welding goggles while Raisa opens a panel in the wall and hauls on a chain. A dummy clad in chain-mail rises from below. Tante Margolis slips on a pair of gleaming black shades. Raisa suits, boots, coifs in silky mail as the sun goes down in defeated carmine pennants and banners behind the city's towers. Goggles on.

'Primary on,' Raisa says. She steps on a yellow-and-black-chevroned floor switch. Every hair on Amon's pale arm erects. His scalp prickles, his skin crawls. The air smells of funfairs. The house hums with electricity from basement to chimney. Iron banister spindles, brass stair rods, crawl with St Elmo's fire.

Lisi pushes Amon's goggles down.

'UV,' she whispers.

'Secondary,' Raisa says and stamps the green floor button. The coil ignites. Energy crowns around its bronze head. Amon finds he is holding his breath. Universal forces have been summoned here. Raisa steps to the coil and lifts an arm. Power leaps to her fingertips. Electricity rages: the roaring coil tries to imprison her in a cage of lighting. She takes arcs in her hands and turns her palms to each other. A searing blue bar of electricity connects them. She forces her hands together. Ball lightning blazes in her grasp, then she loses control. Her hands open, the lightning zigzags upwards into the flickering corona. Raisa kicks the yellow-and-black switch. The power dies, the coil goes cold. She tears off her armoured cowl.

'Can't even do fucking ball lightning!' Raisa holds up her chain-mail hands. 'Finn can juggle five balls of lightning.'

'He trained on this coil,' Tate Margolis says. 'He knows it. You don't. Every coil has its harmonics.'

Harmonics.

'Could you put the coil on again?' Amon asks.

'Again?'

'Please.'

Tante Margolis nods. Raisa armours up and stomps on the foot-switch. The coil re-awakes with a throb of power that shakes Fournier Street from

Commercial Street to Brick Lane. Amon holds up his phone. Ultraviolet scorches his face, he smells the salt-sun-sear of his own skin.

'Why am I doing this?' Raisa shouts from inside the cascade of arcs.

'B flat,' Amon shouts back. He beckons her forward, through the electric waterfall. She dances in lightning. 'G. E when you open your arms. Then D Mu Major.' He flicks his phone into an inside pocket. 'I've got enough now.'

'You recorded . . .' Raisa shouts.

'Coil music. The sound changes when you move through the field. Everything has music.' He shakes his head. 'No, that's not quite it. Everything *is* music.'

'Coil music,' Raisa says. She hits the switch. Amon blinks away afterimages.

'I could use more recordings but I've enough to make a start.'

'Lisi, the Volta Room,' Tante Margolis declares, whipping off her UV glasses. 'You're staying.'

The Grace stirs and turns inside him.

Amon grew up in rooms with names so he knows that they retain a piece of every life that has passed through them. A smell, a discomfort, a divot in the bed, a rub of worn paint, a lingering aura of joy. The Volta room occupies the second-floor Fournier Street front of the house. From the sets of shallow wooden drawers that line the wall facing the sleigh-bed Amon concludes it had a previous purpose but it's been a bedroom long enough to gather flotsam: The top of a toothpaste tube. USB cables. A long-tined comb. A sports bra. An illustrated copy of de Sade.

Constellations, she said.

Like the room in the Soho house—like his own, lost home, Brightbourne—pictures fill the walls. Tante Margolis with her coil at a drag-race track. At a flat shingle bank with mushroom-like concrete pagodas in the background, somewhere on England's weird east coast. Raisa—he thinks—young, androgynous, grubby between two police; Raisa, older, in clingy silver space suit and boots and bubble helmet just big enough for her hair, posing with a silver plastic ray gun. Tante Margolis at the Millennium Dome. Amon follows the photographs until he comes to a wooden door. Of course he opens it, onto the library (a library, it's quite possible Arcmage House has many libraries, in multiple dimensions), and an elderly black man, wiry, grey salting his hair and neat beard, looks up from a table strewn with documents.

'Oh sorry,' Amon stammers.

The man beams. He wears heavy-framed glasses and a yellow hi-viz tabard stamped with London City Airport logos.

'Not at all.' He extends a hand, which Amon takes. 'Didn't get a shock. So you're not a paduan.'

'I'm a musician. Amon Brightbourne.'

His eyebrows rise over the heavy frames of his glasses.

'Raisa's help from above.'

'More like below.'

'Griffith-George Rigel. Known as the Vault.' He indicates the oak shelving, the ladder circulating on tarnished brass rails. 'Historian of Hopeland, Archivist of the Impossible. We write history faster than I can archive it.'

'I can see there's a lot of it.'

'This? This isn't even all the history of the Electromancers. And they're just one tiny constellation. I got twelve storage units down the Beckton full to the rafters.'

'You don't live here?'

'I got a pacemaker, kynnd. I shouldn't even be working here. Every time they fire that thing up, I think my time's come. I got to incorporate the Karageorge material before they sell the Soho house.'

'Oh,' Amon says. He only stayed one night beneath the glass pleasure dome but the news of its sale feels like losing a wonder of the world. A collapsed Colossus. The last silverback. The Taj Mahal turned into a KFC.

'London's insane expensive, kynnd. Even the cheap seats we occupy.'

'The Brangwyns . . .'

The Vault looks up again from his papers and smiles.

'You'll do well.' He gathers a sheaf and shoves them into an accordion file. 'Them muriels're going to be a whole new storage headache for Griffith-George. No one thinks about the archivist, but I'm the keeper of souls, kynnd.' He tucks the accordion file under his arm. 'I'll be all night on this and I got a red-eye out tomorrow. Anything you want to know, ask me. One warning.' He looks over his glasses. 'Don't fall in love with my family.'

A noise behind him distracts Amon. When he looks back the Vault is gone. Raisa peeks into the library.

'Oh hi.'

'I met . . .'

'The Vault. Yeah yeah. Tweed-boy,' Raisa declares. 'It's a nice night and I'm too charged to sleep. Fancy another top-of-the-city adventure?'

8

Satan had an architect and his name was Nicholas Hawksmoor.

Born 1661. Possibly. Nottinghamshire: East Drayton. Or maybe Ragnall. Schooled: not known; schooled certainly, with talent enough to be taken as clerk to a Justice in Yorkshire, then to London and the practice of Sir Christopher Wren.

Uncertainties: loose joints in biography, into which legend can seep.

Certainties: that he was the ablest and most ambitious of Wren's apprentices.

That he was commissioned in 1711 by Queen Anne to oversee the construction of fifty new city churches.

That only twelve of these churches were built, and that only six are wholly from the mind of Hawksmoor.

That his six churches are unique in English architecture—in church architecture. That they are aggressively classical, disturbingly formal. Cubes intersect, golden sections nest, columns, bays and galleries proceed by numerological resonances. Some say the foundations of his architecture delve far beneath the Greeks, to the Dionysiac architects who designed the Temple of Solomon in its hermeneutic beauty—that the god they glorify is not that of Christ but one older, darker, more dreadful. A stepped pyramid inspired by the Mausoleum of Halicarnassus stands over St George's Bloomsbury. Perched atop, no cross of Christ, but King George I as world-conquering classical hero. An Egyptian obelisk crowns St Luke's Old Street: above the plain box of the lost St John's Horlseydown stood a tapering column, topped with a weathervane in the shape of a comet. A pyramid rises in the churchyard of St Anne's Limehouse, engraved with an All-Seeing Eye. Stand on the steps of Christ Church Spitalfields—Hawksmoor's greatest work—and your spirit is cowed and vertiginous, as if the massive façade might fall forward and annihilate you. Hawksmoor said that he wanted to create architecture of Terror and Magnificence.

That he did. God is dead, his churches declare. The eternal truth is the cold hum of entropy, the drone of a universe winding down into thermodynamic equilibrium. The cosmologists' god.

St John's Horleysdown burned in the Blitz. Its weathervane comet was saved and displayed in the Museum of London. Over the years a significant number of visitors, on encountering the comet, have been overcome by dread, terror, horror. None can ever say why.

Architecture and emotion. Place and psyche. Into the gap between the uncertain and the uncanny creeps myth.

Iain Sinclair, Bard of Hackney, is the first psychogeographer to explore Hawksmoorland. His 1975 essay *Nicholas Hawksmoor: His Churches,* from the collection *Lud Heat: A Book of the Dead Hamlets,* reveals a message in those churches. Alignments, orientations, locations. Oppositions and architectural contrasts. Patterns. Dots joined. A triangle here, a star there. New constellations drawn on the map of London: the seal of Set, Egypt's god of chaos, disorder, storms. Deserts and violence. Strangers and foreigners.

Peter Ackroyd, biographer of cities and rivers, in his novel *Hawksmoor* transforms the architect into Nicholas Dyer, church-builder, murderer, occultist. Dyer sacrifices human lives to create an architecture of the anti-Enlightenment. Dyer rejects the ideal of human progress through linear time. Dyer-time is a circle, finding harmonies and resonances in the twentieth century through ritualised murders investigated by Detective Sergeant Nicholas Hawksmoor. The worm Ouroboros bites its tail. Satan has his architect.

In *From Hell* Alan Moore, Shaman of Northampton, plants a phallosphere of obelisks, tombs and Hawksmoor churches into a pentagram with St Paul's Cathedral at its centre, the divine feminine chained and buried by eternal patriarchy and sealed in by walls of occult energy. Within this unholy star, Jack the Ripper carries out his obscene sacrifices to the man-gods. Geography becomes architecture, mind made stone. Resonances ascend through time, Moore insists, and also ripple into the past, like backwash running down a beach. So the mythologies of late-twentieth-century psychogeographers rewrite the past in which they are rooted. Who's to say that Nicholas Hawksmoor did not indeed plan a Satanic architecture for London that was never completed? Funding cuts, as ever. Place becomes psyche, story becomes history.

9

Bridges, great domes, churches, birds: these have hollow bones.

By the bobbing light of an LED head-torch, Raisa leads Amon Bright-bourne through the space inside the wall of Christ Church Spitalfields. Plaster blisters burst as they brush past and mark their clothes with chalky dust.

'Tight here.'

They turn sideways, feet splayed at ten to two, shuffling, heads dipped to avoid breathing the dust of stone and bone.

'Low here.'

They duck into a tunnel half Raisa's height and edge forward in a squat crouch. Cobwebs crown them. A few handspans of stone away smokers outside the Ten Bells exhale pale plumes into the still air, pizzas whir by on the backs of mopeds, hi-viz police patrol the tense post-riots night. Don't think about becoming wedged in this crack a stone's width and a universe from help. They won't hear you.

'Through here.'

Raisa's voice echoes: open space ahead. Her light illuminates the foot of a staircase tight as DNA.

'We're under one of the columns,' Raisa says.

Churchyard gate to crypt steps to a narrow side door to a secret passage inside the walls of Hawksmoor's great church. Round the back, inside the walls. She leads Amon up the tight stairs: Wee Willie Winkie. Her hair brushes stone.

'Head down.' Amon ducks under a low arch and joins her in the or-gan loft. Viewed from the nave the great organ of Christ Church is the angel of music; a central spire of open diapasons and bourdons between two wings of quints and aliquots, each clutching a crosier of prestants and gemshorns. Gold, mahogany, warm ivory. Seen from the rear catwalk it's a favela of ropes, stops, pumps, flues and reeds and wooden shelves stacked with unused pipes. Dust and bird shit, furniture polish and old zinc patinas. Creaking planks and fragile ladders.

'Biggest Georgian organ in the world,' Raisa says, sending her headbeam dancing up the smooth organ pipes. 'Keyboard goes down to bottom G. Is that really low?'

'It's really low.' Amon gazes up into the city of pipes. 'I play church organ. I taught myself keyboard on the old Brightbourne harmonium. I auditioned for the local churches but they turned me down. I think my music might have been a bit . . . trancey.' He touches the satin-soft metal. 'Oh, I would love to spend time with you, glory. Learn your voices and intonations. Draw out your secret music.'

'Maybe not tonight, tweed-boy,' Raisa calls from the turn of a wooden staircase up into the tower.

'That's reasonable,' Amon says and together they spiral up into the spire of Christ Church.

At the top of the final ladder a hatch opens to a small rectangular chamber beneath the dunce cap of the spire. Three masonry arches form each side of the space; each centre arch is slatted openwork. In the centre of the chamber stands a tall wooden box, hinged and bolted.

Raisa draws stiff bolts, pulls chains. Window slats rattle up. The merest of evening breezes cools dust-sticky sweat.

'Watch,' she says and goes up on tiptoe to open the bolts on the top of the tall box. She removes the lid, then the side panels. She imagines Amon's surprise, then remembers her own when she discovered the Tesla coil hidden at the top of the steeple of Christ Church. Weirder than any weirdness Hawksmoor stuck on top of his churches.

'So that other lightning,' he says. 'When you said the Arcmages . . .'

'Tante Margolis came up here and fired up the coil.' Raisa touches the shaft of the primary, tingles to a small thrill of remembered lightning. 'You can still smell it. If you got the nose.'

'I have to ask the obvious,' Amon says. 'What's it doing here?'

'Defending the east,' Raisa says. 'There are four coils under the care of four Arcmages: North, South, East and West. This is the Coil of the East. Tante Margolis is Grand Primary; Arcmage of the East is Kynnd Hope

Achernar. She's some kind of sub-minister here. I don't know much about how Christianity works.'

'She's a minister and a Hopeland?'

'Like I said, you can believe in other gods, or none. Praxy not doxy.'

'Defending the east against what?'

Raisa swings to the window on the west and the lights of the City.

'Against that. That's death. It wants to roll over everything. Make everything like it. We hold it back. We bind it tight, here where it comes from. This church, Kynnd Hope will tell you, there's nothing Christian about it. Its foundations are built into an old plague pit, but the roots go deeper than that. Way deeper.'

Raisa sits on the ledge, legs dangling. Fifty metres below night people throng Commercial Street. She pats the stone, daring Amon. He squeezes down beside her. Brogue heels scuff bird-shit limestone.

'Now listen. I got a story for you.'

10

RAISA AND LIGHTNING WOMAN

I was kissed by the Lightning Woman. In Epping Forest. I lived there awhile. When I was seventeen. I kind of went feral. Lived in the woods. Twenty kay from Marble Arch. You can do that in Epping. It's like the slashed edge of London. The city opens and wild things get in. It's bigger than you think. The further in, the bigger it gets. People moved in during the Blitz and can't get out. They went deep. I never went that deep.

When I was a kid I loved being a kid. I grew up in the Wandsworth Hearth and I was the happiest kid. Then I became a girl and I didn't like being a girl. It was difficult. Effort. I had to think about things. Take things under regard. When I was a kid I could do anything. Be anything. When I became a girl, all I could be was a girl.

And I was supposed to move into the Girls' House. I hung on as long as I could. In the end I went. I hated Girls' House. Girls, living together. What made anyone think that was a good idea? Police and bitches, all the way down.

I stuck it for two years then I moved out of Dorling Avenue, moved up to Epping and walked out under the trees until I found one that welcomed me. It was a big oak—thousand-year oak. Epping's long but thin: all the weird lies on the long line. You won't find that tree if you walk the short line, across. So I was close enough to the car parks to see the lights from the doggers but they'd never find me.

I built a bash under that big oak. Plastic sheets, gas cooker, all that. The leaves were thick; not one drop of rain ever wet me. Got bugs though, bugs, sap, lichen. Four hundred types of insects live on English oaks. I know a lot about oaks. I thought forests might be the thing for a while.

Everything is for-a-while with me. I never stick at anything.

The Forest Gate Hearth would look in and make sure I was all right, had water, food. I'm pretty sure they had security up as well. Some of the Forest Keepers are kynnd. I never had no trouble. Like I said, it's where the wild things go. I was halfway to being moss when the storm struck.

You smell a big storm first. Comes out of the roots, the soil, the spores.

Then you hear it; everything starts to move; leaves, then little twigs, then the branches and by the time the storm hits whole trees are moving and creaking and it's like you're inside a wave bowling you over and over and over. That happened to me. Down in Cornwall. We were in the sea and this wave came over me and next thing I was in the middle of it, bowled over and over and over. A storm in a forest is bigger because you are part of it. The storm is in you. Then it goes still. Like waiting. And you hear the thunder and every tree, every plant, every leaf, every fungus is shining. You see the life.

I went back to the bash. Shouldn't have done that. Oaks and elms are lightning trees. I sat there under my black bin liners and the sky went crazy. The forest, it went crazy too. I saw things in the flashes. Tall things walking. Then my tree took a hit. The air exploded! Just blew my bash, my stuff away. Never heard anything so loud in my life. Light. Blazing light. And more than light. A woman, made of lightning. She turned to me. Her lips moved. She bent down, her face to mine. The light! I could feel my skin curling and crisping. But no pain. Her lips touched mine, then she pulled back like she was going to say something. Then flash! Gone. I should have burned there. The tree channelled the lightning around me, down its branches, kept me in a bubble in the heart of the storm.

The Forest Keepers found me raving. Raving. About the Lightning Woman. Shock, they said. Trauma. Hypothermia. They got me to A&E. One of the Keepers, she knew. She'd seen her too. Something not ours. A new Emanation.

I wouldn't go back to Girls' House. No no no. Well, they said, then where can she go? Then old Tante Marco Betelgeuse said, This is easy. She has the lightning in her, can't you see? Send her to the Arcmages. The what? I said.

I'd wanted to go to the Soho house because it's in the middle of things but Finn was already there and Karageorge didn't want to take on another paduan at his age. Tante Margolis had time and space. So I came here.

The thing about stars is they never stop moving. Constellations change. Bits can get left behind. Bubbled out. The Electromancers have been around longer than the Hopelands. Bombs were falling when Grand Primary Annaliese Godin met Kynnd Satcheverel. They were sheltering. There're deep tunnels down there. They fell in love in deep tunnels. And the Arcmages turned into stars.

Grand Primary Annaliese started working with the War Ministry: Department of Spook. They'd never call it that, official, but everyone did, private.

They called in magicians, artists, shrinks, set-builders, crossword-setters—anyone who could mess with the enemy's heads. Electromancers. Kynnd Annaliese had done opera before the war. Wagner. Spears and storms. They thought it might work with Germans. Never got to try it, though it would have looked the proper shit. She met another Tesla coil artist: this twenty-year-old who'd like walked from Serbia towing his coil on a cart. Well, that's the legend. She took him in as paduan but he didn't want to spend his days keeping the darkness in a lightning cage. No, he was a showman. So they split and he took over the old Soho apartment and put his own magic into it.

Which you seen.

Karageorge stayed kynnd—no one ever stops being kynnd, though they may forget they are—and between them they trained up the Electromancers. Never many. They have to have the lightning, you see. I got it. Finn got it. Tante Margolis got it and Tante Annaliese saw it in her way back in the seventies when it was bleak and the dark was high and it looked like the line of Arcmages of Spitalfields might break. I didn't. We bound it tighter. Like lashing one ship to another. But hey! She saw my lightning, and she saw Lisi's too, and the coil still stands here, keeping London.

I tell you this; everything I've done, everything I know, is to see the Lightning Woman again and at last hear what she has to say.

Raisa's lower legs are numb, the nerves behind her knees compressed by bending over limestone lintels. It's much later than she thought.

'Come on then, Amon Brightbourne. School-day tomorrow.' She gets to her feet, kicks out the stiffness. She pulls bolts back, drops shutters, fastens up crating around the coil. 'Let's go, tweed-boy.' She extends a hand and hauls Amon to his feet.

'One thing,' Amon says as she starts down the ladder. 'Raisa, what did you mean, when I became a girl?'

11

Raisa is long gone baristaing to the early workers of Spitalfields by the time Amon Brightbourne wakes from white sleep. Strange beds, strange energies, the miasma of Christ Church (does a secret Tesla coil stand at its summit, did he sit there with his brogues hanging fifty metres above Commercial Street?). Most of all Raisa's line dropped like a flake of limestone dislodged from the face of Christ Church.

When I became a girl.

Lisi's school term is weeks off but she's busy with washing machines and tumble driers. Tante Margolis talks on the phone with what sounds like (judging by her answers) solicitors.

'Breakfast?' Lisi asks. Amon takes coffee. 'For breakfast?' Lisi's disdain is cold and hard. She makes good coffee.

'Maybe you should be the barista,' Amon says, attempting levity.

'I'm eleven,' Lisi says.

Amon takes his good coffee up to the library, where he hopes to remedy his broken night in working through the samples of coil music. He finds Griffith-George among document boxes, file cases, magazine holders, stout manila folders straining at elastic bands, plastic storage crates, bundles of letters tied up with musty string, peeling briefcases, school satchels, wallets, valises. Books, ring-binders, fan-fold cases. Papers bound, papers stacked, papers piled, papers folded: sheets of A4, printouts, curling photographs. Long tongues of foolscap. Handwritten journal pages, flow charts, family trees. The Ark of the Covenant is surely here, under a pile of papers next to the Palantír of Orthanc.

He clucks and tuts Amon's coffee away from his fragile documents. After ten minutes of Amon sipping his coffee, he says, 'That coffee's stone cold. So what do you want?'

'Raisa said something to me last night. She said, when I became a girl.'

The Vault looks at Amon over the top of his glasses.

'What did she mean?' Amon asks.

'Some join, some adopted, some born,' Griffith-George says. 'Let me tell you a story. And that story may lead to another story, and another, and then you might get somewhere.'

The Vault came to England from the island of Montserrat with two treasures. The first is a claddagh ring, passed finger to finger from its first bearer Proinsias Joyce of Galway, sent under indenture to Barbados in 1632. April Griffith took it from her finger and slipped it onto her son's at the airport as he prepared to leave three hundred and forty years after his ancestors arrived. The second and greater treasure is visual memory. See a thing once—place, face, object or page—and decades after he can recall it in supernatural detail. The face of the official who stamped his passport when he arrived at Heathrow immigration. The markings of his landlady's cats at his first lodgings on Greencroft Road. Every article of clothing worn at his tenth birthday party. He leads groups of Montserratians exiled after the volcano on memory-walks through the streets of Plymouth, the buried capital. It is still the capital, though only ghosts walk there now.

Griffith-George, heart turned out to the world, landed in 1972 and found a job. Found job after job. Bus driver, baggage handler, fueller, dispatcher; always in the hi-viz industries. In 1987 he was among the first crew at the new London City Airport and has remained since. On the ramps and aprons he met and fell in love with Desiree Therese Arcturus Hopeland. Arcturus, he said. That's a star.

It is, she'd answered.

He turned the heart in at their Fastening in the Beckton Hearth. She took the claddagh and placed it back on his finger, heart turned out. That's not our way. There were years, there were children, the Fastening dissolved but Griffith-George Rigel remained a Hopeland, for Hopeland never ends.

'Raisa Peri Antares: Let me see. Born 16th June 1988, King's College Hospital and put up for adoption. Both parents, I can't see them. Ailsa Canopus and Chloe Centauri adopted her in August. All their children have been adopted. We adopt as many as are born. Great Lindner's notion. So we don't become too inbred. We're a gene river not a pool. Starred September 23rd, 1989. Don't ask questions, Mr. Brightbourne. Questions are rocks. They obstruct the memory.' Griffith-George frowns, then a smile dawns. 'I see her! In a silver dress. Spangles. Short. Glossy tights. The tip has come off the heel of her left shoe. Her hair is pulled back. Silver there too: glitter. Glitter eye shadow and lipstick. It's winter. Let me see.' He turns his head to the left. 'Winter solstice 2008. Wandsworth Hearth. It's cold. Braziers lit all over the garden. She's talking with Donna Capella and Jean-Claude Castor. I walk past, she looks at me. She thinks she should recognise me. She's nineteen.' A tilt of the head. 'It's 2004. Carmen Sirius's Speedforth. We are at the Sitges Hearth to praise a soul's returning to the sky. Yatas turning. They're there among the moving lights. I'm not sure how they come to be there. Let me see. Ah. Carmen Sirius had been fast with her parents. There they are, Ailsa and Chloe.' He turns his head to the left. 'Raisa stands apart. Fourteen. They're frightened. Soon they will go to the Girls' House.

'It's 1998. I'm hot. There is cool cool Guinness in my hand. Dew on the bottle, the label is peeling. Wandsworth. Lot lot lot of faces. Let me see. There! Big big big. Shorts, shoes, shirt. All big. Hair everywhere. Someone has a hose and Raisa is running through the rainbows. Nine.'

Griffith-George opens his eyes.

'It's a gift and a curse.'

'You said *she* and then you said *they*,' Amon says.

'I did, yes,' Griffith-George says. 'And now you got another question but all I got is two hundred and twenty thousand Hopelands and their histories, heartbreaks, hopes. That's where you'll find your answer.'

12

London is pre-eminently the psychogeographer's city. Each district possesses a behaviour and a personality. Time snags in the foot tunnel under the river at Woolwich: minutes become hours, hours minutes; tales are told of time-vortices, time-doubles. The corner of Old Bailey and Newgate Street has a gloomy, doomed demeanour, haunted by the Black Dog of centuries of imprisonment, torment and despair. Clerkenwell is the enduring heart of radicalism and revolution, the spirit of King Mob. Spitalfields has always had a pilgrim soul and laid a migrant's table.

1686. Gaston Godin of Nantes arrives in Spitalfields with his wife, his three children and his skill. The old fields and market gardens of St Mary Spital have been laid out into streets for Irish and Huguenot silk weavers, a craft the English lack. Behind him in Nantes, dragoons loot Protestant homes, enforce bayonet-point conversions and where none succeed, slaughter Huguenots. A century of religious tolerance is ended because Louis XIV's magnificence is offended by religious beliefs not his own.

By 1726 the shuttles of Gaston Godin's sons fly across the light-filled loom-loft of their house on Fournier Street. Forty years later, their own sons watch John Doyle and John Valline, weavers by trade, hang in Bethnal Green for riot. After a century, French imports have resumed and domestic prices collapse. Spitalfields weavers are regular and spirited rioters. Richard and Paul Godin have long since moved out of textiles. As silk fades, the tall, generous weavers' houses split and degenerate into slums. New feet arrive on the streets and see in these rookeries the perfect opportunity for another low-rent, light-hungry trade: tailoring. Pogroms drive persecuted Jews across Europe to the web of streets in the shadow of Christ Church. Patterns in time. Nerves and memories. Voices calling across centuries.

Huguenot church becomes Wesleyan chapel, becomes Grand Synagogue. Will become the Jamme Masjid. Will become something else as the Bangladeshis move out and Somalis, Eritreans, Ethiopians move in. Will forever change, world without end, and remain the same.

1: INT. LECTURE ROOM ROYAL SOCIETY - NIGHT
1891. Lightning: indoors! Terror and wonder on the faces of the DELEGATES in the tiered seats. The DELEGATES are without exception well-dressed Victorian men. Blue flickering light.

CAMERA moves across the faces of the spectators. Among them is CHARLES GODIN, pale and enthusiastic in his early twenties. Lightning reflects from his eyes.

CUT TO: the lab bench at the front of the lecture hall. On it stands a TESLA COIL. Behind it, NIKOLA TESLA. He is the master, the magician. He lifts a wand and an electric arc dances to it from the coil. Joy lights up his face.

NIKOLA TESLA
You see lightning, gentlemen. I see electricity transmitted anywhere in the world! Broadcast power! That is a power to shape the future.

2: INT. LECTURE ROOM ROYAL SOCIETY - NIGHT
Moments later. The demonstration is over. DELEGATES surround TESLA, bombarding him with questions. CHARLES GODIN tries to push in.

CHARLES GODIN
Mr. Tesla! Mr. Tesla!

Exasperated, he runs up the steps to the main door.

3: INT. ROYAL SOCIETY ENTRANCE LOBBY - NIGHT
CHARLES GODIN is on the great balcony as NIKOLA TESLA enters the lobby, still mobbed by DELEGATES.

CHARLES GODIN
Mr. Tesla!

NIKOLA TESLA looks up.

CHARLES GODIN

Mr. Tesla! Your coil . . . how may such a thing be built?

NIKOLA TESLA lifts his cane to point to CHARLES GODIN.

                    TESLA
You, sir! What is your name?

                    CHARLES GODIN
Charles Godin, Mr. Tesla!

                    TESLA
You, I can educate.

4: INT. FOURNIER STREET - NIGHT
Five men, one woman gather in the weaver's garret of the Godin house. Storm: lashing rain, lightning among the chimneys
of London.

A visibly older CHARLES GODIN stands before a TESLA COIL
that dominates the rooftop salon.

                    CHARLES GODIN
Thank you for braving such a vile night. Duke Donnerblitzen.
The Three Storms. Lady Lightning. The Astounding Smith and
Jane.

Acknowledgements from each as they are named.

                    THE ASTOUNDING SMITH
The Astounding Jane sends her apologies. Clients . . .

                    CHARLES GODIN
Of course.

(BEAT)

We have worked wonders, we have summoned storms, we have
harnessed lightning. Thousands have been awed by our shows.

We command the forces of the universe. In the end, what do our talents amount to? Spectacle. Entertainment.

Lightning flashes behind Christ Church tower.

CHARLES GODIN

My friends—my fellow Tesla devotees. I want to be more than just an entertainer.

FIRST STORM

Why scorn entertainment?

SECOND STORM

Our business is sound.

THIRD STORM

We have a royal command performance.

CHARLES GODIN

Hear me out. Not for a moment should we turn our backs on our public. We educate as well as entertain. But we can do more than juggle ball lightning. Tesla himself is building a device that will draw power from the Earth itself and transmit it across the whole globe. We control this power, we need to look further, higher.

LADY LIGHTNING

'We'?

CHARLES GODIN

I propose a society—a guild if you will—of practitioners to explore the potentialities of the Tesla coil.

LADY LIGHTNING

Will it cost?

CHARLES GODIN

No cost at all, my dear lady. Only dedication, and commitment.

(Beat: lightning flash.)

A name. What's in a name? Inspiration, authority, awe. We must sound . . . awesome.

DUKE DONNERBLITZEN
The League of Extraordinary Gentlemen!

LADY LIGHTNING
Extraordinary Gentle*folk*.

CHARLES GODIN
No. Too many syllables. Lightning . . . More, much more. Lords, ladies . . . no no no!

None of the titles he mutters inspire him. THE ASTOUNDING SMITH opens his mouth.

CHARLES GODIN
Hush!

He 'thinks' conspicuously.

CHARLES GODIN
I have it. Oh, I have it! Arcmages. Like the wise Magi of old. My dear friends, I give you the Arcmages Guild, wizards of the next century!

EVERYONE
Arcmages!

Apartment 6
Thurngasse 8
Wien
3rd March 1919
My dearest Ana-Lena,
    Forgiveness, they say, is the heart of Christianity. I hope you are a

better Christian than I and find it in your heart to forgive this letter, and my course of action. I understand if you cannot.

I must call an end to our engagement. This will come as a dreadful shock. I am abrupt, I am despicable—and at the end a coward. By the time this letter finds you I shall be embarked for London. I have not left Wien to flee you, or the consequences of my decision—my reasons are sound, professional. I shall lay them out below, not that I imagine they will convince you, not that I dare offer excuses.

I can imagine the shame of our parents, the outrage of our society, the concern of our private circles, yet that concern that masks prurient curiosity. Gossip will fly around the gables like swallows. Ana-Lena, I do not think you will be heartbroken. We both know that our betrothal was always dynastic, never romantic. I like to think I have spared us the ghastly marriages of our parents.

You will ask, why this, why now? The war, which some see as a humiliation—an empire of fifty million cut down to five, Old Austria to end as a province of Germany—I see as liberation. As possibility. The old order has crumbled; there has never been a greater opportunity to build a new one! Surely now is the time for new ideas about how a society might be made healthier, deeper, better. I am but one voice among hundreds clamouring for a hearing in the new Constituent National Assembly—social democrats, nationalists, socialists, Bolsheviks, old imperialists. Voices with nothing new to say. Not one word. A rump nation, they bellow. I say not small enough. Cut cut and cut again until Austria is no more than cantons, then dissolve those cantons into peoples. My ideas are radical yet deeply transformative. Simply listen and we will have a better world, a world of care and compassion, where generations may be nurtured and better futures built.

So, London. As you know, I have been corresponding with a number of free-thinkers and social theorists, among them the esteemed Mr. H. G. Wells. I have found a ready reception for my writings, and an open invitation to lecture and tour. Fertile ground: it seems my endless family may grow from English loam.

There is no future for me in this dead city wrapped in a gilded shroud, Ana-Lena.

And alas, there is no future for us, either. There never was, I think. Marry well, Ana-Lena. Marry better. Marry a man full of wit and life and love and without a thought in his head. It is the thoughts that kill.

Forgive me if you can.

Karl-Maria

13

Ladder to shelf to desk, Amon Brightbourne moves across the library of Arcmage House while the stern gnomon of Christ Church counts morning into afternoon. Hundreds of metres of books and documents and records but he is always able to put his hand on what he needs, as if guided.

14

A SALON IN FITZROVIA
The drawing room of the GODIN SISTERS' Maple Street apartment: high-ceilinged, bay-windowed, spacious and welcoming. Dark outside, it is five nights to midwinter. The room is decked with boughs of evergreen and holly. A fir tree hangs upside down from the ceiling, roots notably exposed. CORA, AMELIA and AVELINE GODIN entertain a party of distinguished guests: JOHN HARGRAVE, H. G. WELLS, KARL-MARIA LINDNER, the BISHOP OF ST ALBANS.

AMELIA GODIN speaks with KARL-MARIA LINDNER and a small circle of guests.

AMELIA: You are the most terrible, blasphemous man, Dr. Lindner.

LINDNER: Forgive me, Miss Godin. I meant no offence. I merely . . .

AMELIA: Oh, you dear man! Never apologise for theory. We're dreadful pagans here. Even the bishop.

(BEAT)

Especially the bishop.

(Polite amusement)

A modern religion for a modern age, that is rather thrilling. Don't you think? Gods of cars and trains. Zeppelins and ocean liners. Very fast gods. Noisy, petrol-powered gods!

WELLS: You sound like one of those Italian Futurists.

AMELIA: Oh no, Mr. Wells. They support that ghastly Signore

Mussolini. How could I adore a man with bandy legs?

HARGRAVE: But this is our entire problem—our malaise.

AMELIA: Signore Mussolini? A nine-day wonder.

HARGRAVE: No no, Miss Godin. These . . . machine gods. They should serve us; rather, we serve them. They have made us inhuman.

BISHOP: Like Mr. Čapek's *roboti*?

WELLS: Mr. Čapek's *roboti* proved all too human.

AMELIA: John, your answer to everything is a healthy dose of outdoorsiness and folksinging.

HARGRAVE: You must admit, we have become fatally alienated from nature.

AMELIA: Woodcraft, darling. Whittling. You make your own cloaks.

(BEAT)

Now, Dr. Lindner: Your idea of a private religion does appeal. Polytheism is such a robust creed. Rugged. Natural. To be serious, don't you think that with so many gods, well, the danger is that everyone can believe what they jolly well like? Where is your community's new unifying spirit then?

DOROTHY GODIN arrives at the group.

DOROTHY: Orthopraxy, not orthodoxy.

LINDNER: I beg your pardon?

DOROTHY: Conformity of practice, not belief. Enforced belief is no belief. It's obvious. Know another's belief? Impossible. Agree practice and everyone has a common bond. That's how it works in the church. Doing, not believing.

BISHOP: Actually, Miss Godin . . .

DOROTHY: *Dr.* Godin, Bishop. Now, Dr. Lindner, I have thoughts on your lecture. Might we talk?

She leads him into the window bay.

DOROTHY: Polytheisms, all well and good. Have you given any thought to *pantheon*?

LINDNER: My inclination is away from the Mediterranean and Scandinavian mythoi. I've always found Hinduism attractive. The venerability, the energy, the diversity . . . the idea that the numinous both cascades down and ascends the pyramid of the divine . . . The staggering epochs of sacred time . . . Monstrous, and at the same time, magnificent!

DOROTHY: Yes, quite. I think you'll find that in polytheism as in many things, Blake was centuries ahead of us.

LINDNER: Blake?

DOROTHY: William Blake. Poet, artist, polymath. Visionary. The prophet of Albion.

LINDNER: Ah! Yes. You have a . . . book . . .

DOROTHY: My sister has "books", Dr. Lindner. *Novels*. I have a *thesis. A Tree, Filled with Angels: The Ecstatic Writing of Blake, Coleridge and Julian of Norwich.*

LINDNER: I regret I'm unfamiliar . . .

DOROTHY: Of course, you're unfamiliar with it. I commend Blake to you. A firmament blazing with divinities. Gods, demigods, demiurges, demons and emanations. Spirits of place and time that touch not just mortals, but the land itself. Tharmas and Urizen, blazing Los and lustful Orc. Golgonooza and terrible Entuthon, Hand and Hyle, Coban and Quantock. The Four Zoas! The daughters of Albion!

CORA GODIN cuts in to take LINDNER by the arm.

CORA: My sister's book is rather long, Dr. Lindner, and crushingly dull.

DOROTHY: Thesis! Thesis!

CORA links arms with LINDNER.

CORA: (whispering) A little like my sister.

(BEAT)

Now, this Sunday evening at the Conway Hall, there is a talk. Dorothy Gildernew will expound on Clifford Douglas's theory of social credit. I very much want to hear that talk. I very much require you to accompany me, Dr. Lindner.

She steers LINDNER across the room.

DOROTHY: (from across the room) I must invent a system or be enslaved by another man's! I shall not reason and compare, my business is to create!

(Excerpt from transcript of the lecture by Karl-Maria Lindner to the Lunarian Society, September Full Moon 1928)

. . . This is my issue with Freud. His psychology—the psychology of the primacy of sex, guilt, repression, transference, Oedipal rage, the dubious forces of psychoanalysis—is precisely what you would expect in a repressed, guilt-ridden, paternalist society like Vienna. Like this country—for all your English Exceptionalism, you are no different from us Austrians!

Freud puts the cart before the horse, as you say. Man is a social creature; if we are to understand the mind of man, we must look to society first. Freud mistakes particular social norms for universal psychological truths. He fails to subject his analyses to analysis in the context of a wider society and so condemns us into individualism, egotism, narcissism.

Freud reduces us to collections of individual neuroses. If we have neuroses—a diagnosis I by no means accept—it is because our society is neurotic—maladjusted, deformed. Yes, deformed. Imagine a society free from the constraints and repressions that stunt our emotional, psychological lives. Imagine how our loves, our relationships, our families and friendships, our inner loves, might flourish!

Imagine no more! Such societies exist. I have visited them, I have lived in them, I have studied them and I have found in them many institutions and practises with the potential to transform our drab, oppressive lives.

For many years I made a close sociological study of the societies of Polynesia—Samoa, Tonga and Ava'u; most assiduously, Ava'u. Ava'u is a small archipelago of coral atolls some three hundred kilometres north of Tonga and the same south of Samoa. It was settled by the Lapita people at the same time they colonised Tonga, nine hundred years before Christ. Its language and culture are strongly connected with those island groups. The population of the three islands of the archipelago totals twenty-two thousand, seventy percent of which inhabit the main atoll of Ava'utapu. The maximum height above sea-level is eighteen metres, though some minor outlying atolls lie lower. The main economic activities are fishing, market-gardening and tapa-mat manufacture. Government is by hereditary monarchy; the royal house of Tu'i has been in power since at least 1777 when the islands were first mapped by Captain James Cook, who named them the Maundy Islands after arriving at Ava'utapu on Holy Thursday. The islands were part of the Tongan thalassocracy between the thirteenth and fifteenth centuries. Since then, it has been a remote, conservative Polynesian culture, resistant to colonial politics and capitalist exploitation in ways that Tonga and Samoa have not. I attribute this to the strength and enduring nature of Ava'uan cultural practices. The Ava'uan people are among the most mentally healthy in the world. In their islands, our industrialised ills of depression, ennui, alienation, isolation, feelings of worthlessness and futility—all of Freud's neuroses—are unknown.

(An interjection expressing disbelief.)

I exaggerate but a fraction, sir. There will always be instances of individual mental disorder. I have made a deep study of this culture and there are palpable, demonstrable advantages over our so-called civilisation.

The recent Great War proved beyond doubt that western civilisation is in decay. The heart of our society—all our societies—is sick. Not the sickness of individuals, amplified by statistics into cultural disease, but disease of our concepts of society, family, individuals, of our roles and responsibilities. The previous century was the century of the nation-state, empire, capital, false religion and psychoanalysis and what did it achieve but bring us to the brink of complete and utter destruction in a war that spanned the globe from this city to the archipelagos of the South Pacific? Surely such horror will have taught us never to repeat such insanity? Surely we have the wisdom to learn from our mistakes? I fear not, not while we let the social foundations of that war still stand, foundations that may again be built upon.

(Murmurs from the audience, some of appreciation, some of apprehension.)

The nation-state is a diseased thing. It is arrogant and domineering; it accrues power to itself at the expense of its people. It is aggressive, regressive. It demands the rights and affections of a human being without the constraints or responsibilities. It has no sense of society, only competition with other nation-states. It has no morality, only what will further its own ends. It is dangerous. Worst: it is unnatural.

From my work in the South Pacific, I have derived an optimum size for a nation. The ideal nation comprises somewhere under five hundred thousand individuals. Larger than that and the personal ties of individuals to others, to families, to groups and institutions, are too weak, too remote, too abstract. The distances between us grow too great. The seats of power are too high. Hierarchy pulls away from accountability. Power inheres. The ideal takes over from the real. True, physical relationships become subjective beliefs. The actual nation—and I draw here on the North American Aboriginal concepts of tribe-as-nation—becomes abstract nationhood, becomes alienated nationalism. Nationalism becomes competition, becomes aggression, becomes hatred of what is not the nation. Becomes war.

There is beauty in the small. There is honesty in the local. There is strength in community. In family. I learnt this truth on the atolls of Ava'u: that a family can be a nation, a nation a family. Our notions of family are too small, too weak, too concentrated on biological parenting, on the binary, on all the quatsch of Freud's Oedipal posturings. On what I call the "nucleated family". In Ava'u family is extended family. It takes an island to raise a child.

I am not blind to the negatives in island societies. They war upon each other. They carry vendettas and grudges down generations. How to avoid sectarianism, factionalism, tribalism? How to negotiate the deep human desire for me-and-mine over you-and-yours? After years of study, analysis, thought and theory, I have a solution.

Split nation from territory. I advocate non-geographic nations. Families across borders, across oceans. This is not an unfamiliar notion to us. Consider the Communist International, which some of you support. Consider the fraternities of ancient seats of learning. Consider secret societies: the Masons, the Rose Croix, the Theosophist and ancient Dionysiacs. Consider the oldest and perhaps most powerful of non-geographical nations, the Catholic Church. Now imagine something greater. Something nobler. Imagine enormous families, tens—hundreds—of thousands of seeming individuals connected by marriage, adoption, generation, care, duty, devotion—scattered. Dispersed. To the eye they would look like stars across the night sky. They are connected, there are lines between them and if we draw those lines in our minds' eyes, we see shapes appear, monsters, heroes, demons and gods. We see not stars, but constellations!

The Open Family Community
From Wikipedia, the free encyclopedia

The Open Family Community was a short-lived experimental residential community that existed between 1930 and 1934, based on the social theories of Karl-Maria Lindner, who arrived in London from Vienna in 1919 and was active in the Free-thought, Social Credit and Utopianist movements of the 1920s. The community was founded in 1930, fourteen months after it was proposed at the First Utopianist Convention[1] at the Conway Hall.

The community occupied Hopeland House near Braintree in Essex, the 19th-century residence of the Gurney family (now Four Wheels Good! Off-Road and Paintball Centre). Membership peaked at eighty-five residents, with another forty (estimated) in 'constellation' relationships, living outside the main community, in accordance with Lindner's theories. Lindner himself lived in an open relationship with Cora Godin[2], though personal and philosophical tensions between them led to the schism of the community in June 1934[3]. Lindner and a group of sixty community members took the name Hopeland and moved to a new centre in South London.[citation needed] Godin led a rump community for a further four years, after which it disbanded to become a naturist and vegan colony. Members briefly included composers Gerald Finzi and Harry Partch, illustrator Edward Ardizone and folk-dance collector Mary Neal.

See also
Kindred of the Kibbo Kift
Constellation Family
Social Credit Movement
The Godin Sisters
Kinship

References
1. Facsimiles of the Minutes of the First Utopianist Convention are held in the Museum of London and British Library.
2. Savage, Joanna. *These Electric Girls: The Godin Sisters and the Fitzrovia Set.* Warwick University, 1987.
3. "Residents Rejoice as 'Free Marriage' Community Quits." *Braintree and Witham Times.* 26 October 1934.

(some) Lands
By population
Prathet Thai (Thailand): 70,000,000
Poland: 38,000,000
Switzerland: 8,750,000
Ireland (all): 6,800,000
Scotland: 5,454,000

Aotearoa (New Zealand): 4,800,000
Eswatini (Swaziland): 1,160,000
Iceland: 367,000
Hopeland: 221,000
Greenland: 57,000

15

Now Amon sees Raisa as the Vault sees them, in baggy shorts and shirt and too big shoes, nappy hair, running through rainbows.

The Hopelands understood the old truth about children. They made it the keel of their culture. Children are the true humans. In Karl-Maria Lindner's psychology children are not embryonic people, seeds of psycho-sexual maturity waiting for the wash of hormones to blossom. Adults are the flowerheads of children. Kids grown tall and complex. Every adult was a kid.

When Raisa said *When I became a girl,* she spoke the profound Hopeland truth. Kids are what they are, can be whatever they want to be. Become whatever they wish to become. Change and change back again. Flow, weather, play, experiment, indeterminacy are the child-nature. Kids are pure potential.

Among the Hopelands, adults can be women, men, asexual, multiple gendered, trans, all the rainbow of being, all the showers of pronouns, adjectives, identities, bodies and senses of self. Kids are kids. Primal humanity. Boy one day, girl the next, lion the day after, city-killing robot, space-witch, pet cat, a comet across the sunset sky.

Frocks, smocks, big T-shirts, shorts in all weathers and Wellington boots. Long hair, short hair, glitter make-up, mud, war paint.

One day a call is heard, a scent caught, the prickle of another season salts the skin. Kid becomes girl, boy, other. Genders. Sexes. Sex. Adult love. Anything the adult body can be. But the kid always knows this is a loss, a fall from grace into mere embodiment. Angels spiral down to earth to crystallise under its gravity, harden under its sun, lose the multivalence of the divine. A kid never forgets when they were everything.

When I was a kid I could do anything, she said. Be anything. When I became a girl, all I could be was a girl.

On the cheap, many and slow boats from Ava'u to Trieste, Karl-Maria Lindner developed his social theories. In the archipelago pubescent boys left the extended family house to their own adjacent lodge where they lived until adulthood. They were expected to keep it clean, keep themselves clean, never be less than immaculate in public, observe evening prayers and turn up for dinner in the great house every day. Other than that the boys were free. Amon Brightbourne, alumnus of an all-boys grammar school, remembers heads stuffed down toilets, clothing stolen, locker doors glued shut, ritual spittings: the thousand callous humiliations of dudes in close company. He remembers the bravado, the dirty talk, the constant status plays, the ceaseless competition for minuscule movements up and down the hierarchy.

Boys together are disgusting.

Raisa says, girls are no different.

Karl-Maria Lindner appropriated the Ava'uan concept and in the Open Family Community, the first Hopeland, set up both a Boys' House and a Girls' House. A simple binary. Raisa clung hard to her kid-self. Biology and social convention forced decisions on her she did not want to make.

Amon's heart cracks and drips for that glorious, everything-everywhere kid in the Wellingtons and the big clothes, leaping through rainbows. There is no greater betrayal than growing up.

No house for them, so Raisa built their own house, under plastic, christened by lightning under the heart oak of deep Epping. A house where they could be all the things they once were. Until they met Lightning Woman.

'Learn something?' Griffith-George asks. He gathers up his papers, stuffs his accordion file that seems able to swallow all history. The shadow of Christ Church has passed over the house and west light slants through the tall windows.

'Enough,' Amon Brightbourne says.

'Understand it?'

'No.'

'Still.' Griffith-George tucks the file beneath his arm. He looks up. Amon hears it at the same instant. Feet on the wooden staircases, running. The library door bursts open. Raisa rushes in like a Special Forces team.

'Fuck!' she shouts. 'Fuck fuck fuck.'

Every book seems to rise fizzing from its seat on its shelf, pages separated by static.

'Finn's challenged me. Says I stole the Tesla coil. There's going to be a trial.'

16

(From the Hopeland archive, Sherguard Personal Storage, Beckton)

Transcript of the afternoon session of the Electromantic Court, Coil Chamber, Arcmage House, Fournier Street, 19 August 2011.
Bench:

Kynnd Siorcha Sirius Coombes Hopeland, meteorologist and weather presenter, RTÉ. Coil of the West.

Kynnd Dave 'Thor' Vega Oliver Hopeland, SFX designer with metal band Lord Onyx. Coil of the North.

Kynnd Rev. Hope Achernar Oyedepu Hopeland, curate of Christ Church Spitalfields. Coil of the East.

Kynnd Jean-Jacques Polaris Gauthier Hopeland, electromancer with Les Machines de l'Île, Coil of the South, is unable to attend due to performance commitments. In his absence, Kynnd Melora Cassiopeia Margolis Hopeland, Grand Primary, recuses herself as chair of the Court to take his place.

Recording and transcription by Kynnd Margolis.

Kynnd Oliver's tea and bourbons supplied by Kynnd Lisi Priya Sirius Hopeland.

There being a quorum and both parties consenting to arbitration by the court, hearings commenced 09:30 with Kynnd Finn Mikael Hamal Hopeland.

. . .

14:00 Court resumes after lunch and Kynnd Oliver's eighth cup of tea. Testimony of Mr. Amon Brightbourne.

Kynnd Oyedepu: You are Mr. Amon Brightbourne, a musician? Of no fixed abode?

A B: Currently living here.

Kynnd Oliver: Musician?

A B: I'm a bespoke DJ. Custom micro-music. Nano-ambience.

Kynnd Oyedepu: This is in the notes, Dave.

Kynnd Oliver: Which page?

Kynnd Coombes: Page three.

Kynnd Oliver: Ah, right. I kind of speed-read. Give me a mo.

He reads.

Kynnd Oliver: Your dad worked with the KLF?

A B: He made samples for Bill Drummond. You've heard them.

Kynnd Oliver: *Justified and Ancient?*

A B: Yes.

Kynnd Oliver: Which bit?

A B whistles a riff.

Kynnd Oliver: That was your dad?

A B: That, and 3 *A.M. Eternal, What Time Is Love, Last Train to Trancentra*l, all those. The Orb, early Orbital, Sunscreem, Dario G. Hundreds of samples. The licenses keep Brightbourne—that's my family home—running.

Kynnd Oliver: Impressed, sir.

Kynnd Oyedepu: So, Mr. Brightbourne, could you tell us the events of the night of the 12th of August?

Mr. Brightbourne: I was at Oxford Circus station and it was kicking off . . .

Kynnd Coombes: Maybe cut to when you swapped phones with Kynnd Finn?

Kynnd Oyedepu: Allegedly.

Kynnd Coombes: Allegedly swapped phones with Kynnd Finn?

A B: Right. So, I'd helped her down the big drop into Dean Street. She had to stay on the line. I didn't so I went up to Carlisle Street. I still had her phone, and I saw Finn . . .

Kynnd Oliver: Whoa whoa whoa whoa. I haven't a fucking clue what's going on here. You helped her what?

A B: I asked some people to help me with a bench so she could make a safe drop down into Dean Street.

Kynnd Oliver: I'm a middle-aged man with a long history of recreational drug use, mate. How did you have her phone?

Kynnd Oyedepu: Dave, we went over this in Kynnd Raisa's statement.

Kynnd Oliver: We did? Right. Her phone.

A B: She asked me for my phone. On Meard Mews. Hers was short of power. I gave her mine, she installed the app. She gave me hers.

Kynnd Oliver: Right, you swapped phones with Raisa first.

Kynnd Oyedepu: Deposition 2, page 1, Dave.

Kynnd Oliver: Lisi, could I get some more tea? So, you're carrying Raisa's phone.

A B: Which was low on power. And if the app dies . . .

Kynnd Coombes: Then that runner is out.

A B: I was on Carlisle Street when I saw Finn.

Kynnd Coombes: How did you know it was him?

A B: He looked like a runner? Phone the same place as Raisa's. Everyone was looking down; he was looking up.

A pause while Kynnd Oliver drinks tea.

Kynnd Oyedepu: Go on, Mr. Brightbourne.

A B: I sized him up, then ran into him. Knocked him down. While I was helping him up, I switched his phone out of the mount and switched in the phone Raisa had given me.

Kynnd Coombes: To be clear, you took Kynnd Finn's phone and gave him Kynnd Raisa's phone. Which was about to run out of power.

A B: That's correct.

Kynnd Oliver: So you made him lose.

A B: I did.

Kynnd Coombes: Why did you do it, Mr. Brightbourne? You had no skin in the game, why get involved?

A B: Raisa asked me to help her.

Kynnd Coombes: At Meard Mews. This was five streets away, and you followed her across the rooftops. Did she ask you to do that?

A B: No, she didn't. She told me several times she didn't want my help.

Kynnd Coombes: You involved yourself without her consent.

A B: She needed me to get down into Dean Street, like I told you. She left me behind on Dean Street.

Kynnd Coombes: Would you say that was a clear indication that she didn't want your help anymore?

A B: That's one way of looking at it.

Kynnd Coombes: But you persisted.

Kynnd Oyedepu: We need to be satisfied that your help wasn't pre-arranged.

A B: I don't understand.

Kynnd Oliver: That you didn't conspire.

A B: Well, if it was a conspiracy, it's a pretty random conspiracy. I don't think you can ever disprove it. You have to trust.

Kynnd Oliver: That's true. Have we any more questions? I'd like to get this wrapped up by three. The cricket's on Sky.

Kynnd Oyedepu: No more questions from me. Siorcha?

Kynnd Coombes: I need to understand this. Why, when she told you she didn't want your help, did you keep helping her?

A B: Okay. All right. The truth. Because I was smitten. That's like an auld boy's word. It's right. Like being hit.

Kynnd Coombes: By what, Mr. Brightbourne?

A pause.

A B: By Raisa. Don't tell her this.

The Coils smile.

Kynnd Oyedepu: I think she knows.

Kynnd Coombes: Thank you, Mr. Brightbourne.

Amon dozes on the green fainting couch to an ambient drone of his coil music. It grades smooth his anxiety that he betrayed Raisa, soothes his fear that his adventures in love and lightning end here. Then his door opens, Lisi looks into his room and says, Come with me.

She leads him by an unsuspected spiral staircase to a secret door that opens onto a narrow gallery on the upper level of the Coil Chamber. Beneath a plaster ceiling of cherubic Zeusettes and Thorlings, Amon settles beside Lisi on the iron grating. The Electromantic Court is in session. To hand down the verdict the three Coils wear capes of office; splendid high-collared, Doctor Strange cloaks, red adorned with appliqué silver lightning bolts. Very Ziggy. Amon rather fancies one for his next nano-gig.

Tante Margolis sits on the Grand Primary's high chair. Carved wooden lightning bolts form her halo. She records the session on her laptop.

Raisa and Finn sit facing the Coils. Raisa wears the blue dress and red tights from the Wandsworth Starring. Also rocking blue is Finn, in a Soho-tailored suit fashionably worn two sizes too small. He is prettier, thinner, more bruised than when Amon saw him, sprawling on Carlisle Street, betrayed.

'The Electromantic Court is in session, 19th of August 2011,' Arcmage Oyedepu announces. She wears an Anglican collar under her cloak. Dave Oliver is in a T-shirt for his band. He has tied his hair back in a silver clasp and a mug of tea stands in the ring it has scorched in the library table over the course of the hearing. Siorcha Coombes is gymmed and foundationed, screen-stylish in Ruby Kobo.

'Why wasn't I invited?' Amon whispers.

'I invited you,' Lisi says.

'We've reached a verdict,' Arcmage Oyedepu announces.

Judge Oliver takes a sip of tea.

'We're unanimous in this,' he says. Heads nod.

'We find that Kynnd Raisa was significantly aided by Mr. Brightbourne,' Arcmage Coombes says. 'Not least the substitution of Kynnd Finn's phone with Kynnd Raisa's dead phone. We're satisfied that this contributed to Kynnd Raisa's victory.'

Up in the ironwork, Amon Brightbourne needs to spew. Finn is out of his chair, face Jesus-bright. Dave Oliver waves Finn back into his seat.

'However,' Arcmage Oliver says. 'However . . .'

'The task was almost impossible without help,' Rev. Oyedepu says. 'When we set it, it was expected others would be involved. That's the Hopeland way. We draw others in.'

'However,' Dave Oliver repeats. 'However . . .'

'There is an issue of consent in Mr. Brightbourne swapping Kynnd Finn's phone for Kynnd Raisa's,' Siorcha Coombes says. 'Help must be asked for. So we find that Kynnd Finn was unjustly obstructed.'

'With these considerations, we've reached a verdict.' Dave Oliver takes a senatorial draught of tea.

Fingers tighten. Electricity is wild in the room. Finn leans forward, fingers pressed into prayer. Raisa uncrosses her ankles.

'To award the coil to either party would not be just,' Rev. Oyedepu says. 'Our judgement is that Kynnd Finn and Kynnd Raisa compete again.'

(simultaneously) Kynnd Finn: 'What?' / Kynnd Raisa: 'Are you fucking insane?'

'It wouldn't be fair to ask you to rerun the race,' Dave Oliver says.

'Five nights from now, on the twenty-fourth of August, we will convene the Four Coils,' Siorcha Coombes says.

'And you will fight,' Hope Oyedepu says. 'A duel. Of lightning.'

17

The in-between mornings break high and clear. City and nation kick and prod through the wreckage of the recent riots. The crash of a comfortable old order leaves no black box, no clarifying words from the cockpit. The state settles its scores, the media hunts motives, reasons, blames. On Fournier Street, the combatants prepare.

Raisa and Finn take turns practising on the Soho coil. The house crackles with power. Hammer-Horror arc-light illuminates the attic workshop. The landings shake to big beats, new musics, cracks and pops and small thunders. The high, clattering house feels crowded and restless. Arcmage House is big enough to contain worlds in its wainscotting but not so big that Amon can avoid meeting Finn in the library, the kitchen, on the stairs. There's hurt, there's anger, there's something more Amon can't identify.

On a morning when Griffith-George has come in from the Beckton Archive and spread his material on the library table, Amon asks.

'Finn?'

'Finn Mikael Hamal Hopeland,' Griffith-George says, looking down into his memory vault. 'Born 13th May 1987, Stockport, Cheshire. His birth mother is from Lebanon. Fostered by Duncan Mira and Nancy Spica of the Alderley Hearth, June 12th, 1987. Subsequently adopted. Starred November 18th, 1988. Alderley's not one of the great hearths. Only been there once. I remember collapsing farm buildings, pavilions and shipping containers. Woods and hollows and folk-stuff. Smelled dank. Everything knitted. Not for Finn Mikael Hamal Hopeland, he turns seventeen and he's down to Manchester. He studies video art, theatre lighting and sound design.

'Can't see this too clear but this is how it must have happened. I know Kynnd Karageorge is touring up in Manchester with Iron Maiden. Kynnd Dave is recently graduated from paduan to Arcmage and is taking over the music circuit. Finn is rigging lights: they meet, they turn the boy's head. Karageorge says, I got a place for a new paduan. Finn Hamal turns up in Soho soaked through by a summer storm. Everyone knows that bit of the legend. And that's the bottom of the box, kynnd. That's all that's in the Vault about Finn Mikael Hamal.'

Amon asks Lisi at the big kitchen table.

She looks up from her bowl of soup noodles.

'Oh that's easy. They had a thing.'

'But they're, you know . . .' His stomach turns. 'Brother and sister.'

'No they're not,' Lisi says.

'They're related,' Amon insists.

'They're kynnd,' Lisi says.

'And that makes it all right?' Amon says. Finn comes into the kitchen, opens the fridge.

'Finn . . .' Lisi starts. Amon kicks her under the table. *You're dead, kid,* Amon mouths to her.

'What?'

It's not about you, she mouths back.

'Can I be your second?'

Finn finds a bottle of water.

'Sure. Why not?'

Lisi gives a squeal of pleasure. When Finn has returned to his praxis, Lisi kicks Amon back, harder.

'It don't mean anything,' she says. 'Really. Kynnd is kynnd. And it's not like it lasted long.'

Movement through the garden, the back door opens and Raisa arrives in the kitchen.

'What lasted long?'

'You're early,' Lisi says.

'I quit,' Raisa says. She slings her bag onto the big table.

'Barista?' Amon asks.

'It's just coffee.' She slips off her street shoes, pads sock-soled to the enormous double-refrigerator that is the kitchen's sole concession to modernity. 'Anyone can get a job in coffee. Any time.' She leans into the blue light. Amon buckles with desire. He knows his enemy now. Jealousy.

'Oh yes.' She curls back around the refrigerator door. 'Tweed-boy. You're my second.'

His heart could burst.

18

Lightning calls lightning. The morning of the duel breaks yellow and tense and so thick Amon Brightbourne feels as if small demons have wedged a wardrobe into his sinuses. London cowers under a boiling sky. Hot winds carry dust and litter from other worlds. Tempers crackle, road rage seethes. Up-rushing masses of hot moist air strike ions from each other, building mega-volt static charges. By evening the thunder-gods have raised their black anvil of cumulonimbus over the City towers.

All day Lisi has run up and down stairs, in and out doors, down and back up streets, armoured in hi-viz, moving cars, warning residents, laying out cones and sealing off Fournier Street with film set tape. It's the standard Hopeland trick. The police have been told it's a superhero movie. *Lightning Girl and Thunderbolt Boy.* Film shoots, like hi-viz yellow, bestow invisibility. The residents of Fournier Street, who know their neighbours and their small, necessary lies, all turn out. The Arcmages put on a good show.

Amon has rehearsed rehearsed rehearsed the few and simple instructions Raisa gave him. Foot-switch for power, foot-switch for music. Kill-switch. Step in, step out. Thor's hokey-cokey. He practises again and again and again, fearful that through some minute omission, calamity might fall.

Jean-Jacques Polaris Gauthier, Coil of the South, arrives on the last flight into London City, the small plane lurching down between micro-bursts. He slides into Fournier Street in Tante Margolis's dismal Volvo, pulls on his robe of office and steps into the basket of a cherry-picker to join his kynnd in a rooftop duel of lightning.

'Hoods up, stars. Weather coming,' warns Tante Margolis.

Electromancers' robes of office are famously weatherproof, and well insulated.

Finn enters Christ Church—the legitimate way, with the curate's keys—climbs the tower and unshutters the Spitalfields coil. He works the old rituals and rubrics: polishes its brass head, tightens its horror-movie bolts and switches, dusts the co-primary and secondary. It is not his native coil; he must learn its songs. He strokes it, makes it proud and battle-ready as a fighting cock. Lisi hauls his armour to the organ loft. He strips down to base layer, mails up. A coin was tossed at noon; Raisa won and chose home turf.

'Give me a hand with this,' she orders Amon up in the rooftop studio.

He holds back her hair as she pulls on a black balaclava, folds in stray curls, tucks it into the neck of her compression layer. Her face is a pure heart.

'You look great.'

'I look like a Lycra gimp,' she says.

Her armour arrives up in the dumb-waiter. Amon helps her dress in chain-mail pants, vest, boots. The sparksuit is supple but heavy; armoured-up Raisa will almost double her weight. He understands the physics now; the charge flows across the surface of mail, link to link, insulating the woman within and allowing the wonderful bolt-casting feats of electromancy. He tries to imagine thousands of volts millimetres from his skin, cocooned in power.

Raisa takes a swift, shuddering nervous breath.

'Let's go, tweed-boy.'

He cranks open the roof. The panes fold into the slots. Arcmage House stands open to the night. The hot wind that runs before a storm flaps Amon's slim trouser legs, tugs at the narrow lapels of his jacket. The coil stands inside the new wooden frame Raisa had the kynnds Jacob and Demetrios build for her.

A shout from the street, a lurch that sends its passengers clutching for the safety rails, then the cherry-picker lifts the four Coils in their robes of judgment high above the rooftops. A vanguard wind snatches at their cloaks. They seem perilously exposed to the coming storm but if anyone knows thunderstorms, it is the electromancers. Fournier Street is solid with onlookers now, there is a light in every window, and a watcher.

Tante Margolis lifts a walkie-talkie and points it at Arcmage House. It is some moments before Amon discovers she means for him to pick up the receiver.

'They're ready in Christ Church,' Tante Margolis crackles.

'Two minutes here,' Amon says, then realises he has to push the send button, and so has to repeat.

'Gear me up,' Raisa orders. Amon slides on the gauntlets. She halts him before he pulls the chain-mail hood down over her head. She kisses him.

'For luck.'

She is smoky, sweet, charged, sharp. She tastes like Hallowe'en.

'For love,' Amon says.

Raisa settles the cowl onto her shoulders. She climbs the wooden rungs to the platform at the top of the frame. She stands astride the coil's head.

'We're ready.' Amon waves to Tante Margolis in the cherry-picker bucket. Dave Oliver raises an arm. A flare arcs over Fournier Street. Thunder rolls on cue. How metal.

'Okay tweed-boy,' Raisa orders from atop the Tesla coil. 'Primary ignition.'

Yellow black for primary. Green for go. Two new foot-switches. White for audio. In serious red, SCRAM. He stamps on the ignition button.

Raisa catches fire. Her light burns Amon's face. He steps back, then remembers his goggles.

Raisa raises her arms and metre-long bolts snap from each fingertip, forking and reforking into fractal feathers. She lifts a foot and a writhing column of plasma connects it to the platform. She throws back her head and lightning blazes from each eye. Raisa laughs, blazing with her own power. A cheer goes up from the street. Thunder answers from behind the palisades of the City.

The walkie flashes.

'Round one,' Amon yells through the white-hot sizzle of electricity. 'Bolt!'

Limned in were-light, Raisa turns on her platform to face the Arcmages.

A duel of lightning is no haphazard, Sturm und Drang thing. Electromancy is a praxy, discipline failures end in electrocution. There are rules. There are formalities. Over four rounds, each contestant will compete in the three main theatres: bolt, ball and beam. The fourth, final round is freestyle. Each Electromancer will show their mastery. Take lightning where it's never been before.

'Hit it Amon,' Raisa shouts. Amon stamps the green floor switch. The secondary blazes, the sound system rattles rooftiles from the masjid to the Ten Bells. Big beat, three A.M. Ibiza; the tunes you bang out when the crowd is lit and loving. Raisa folds her armoured hands across her chest, dips her head. The rhythm builds, a simple beat accelerator. On the resolve she jumps, throws open her arms and becomes Lightning Woman. Swings her arms downwards and seems to rise out of a pyramid of bolts. Brings her hands together in a clap of thunder, snaps her fingers. Flings throbbing bolts to the conductors in the four corners of the sanctum. Forms twin loops with fingertips and thumbs and fire running in rings around them. Opens her hands and bolts hurdle Fournier Street and cling to the lamp-posts, the gutters, the chimneys and television aerials.

And gone.

Amon blinks, blinded, deafened by small thunders and big beats.

Raisa scissors a thumb across her throat. Amon hits green. Cheering from the street pushes through the susurrus in his ears. Looking down he sees a hundred mobile phones held aloft, applauding with screen light. In their cradle the Arcmages confer.

'That was amazing . . .'

Raisa presses a mailed finger to her mailed mouth.

A muted peal of thunder plays an entr'acte.

The tower of Christ Church glows. Fournier Street oohs. The glow intensifies into hard blue glare. It bursts into waterfalls of bolts: each of the lantern windows a cage of lightning. Beats: the fake film crew in-stalled a proper South London sound system in the street and the shining bars of the prison of light pulse in time to a swelling beat. Amon knows the tune. It's a mid-set favourite of the Shadow Proclamation, who ses-sions two before him in all-nighters. It's never sounded so good. Amon glimpses an arc-lit figure weaving between the high windows. The mu-sic builds: the silhouette somehow expands the glowing bars until the steeple dances with arcs. The music stops. Amon waits for the pick and kick. Lightning stabs from each of the four windows, bolts five metres long, pulsing on and off in time to the music, growing with each beat: ten metres, twenty, thirty. Forty. The full nave of Christ Church. Then across Commercial Street to the market. Vaulting the church gardens, over the roof of the Ten Bells.

Lightning calls, lightning answers. The waiting storm looses its first bolt to the top of Heron Tower.

'Fuck,' Raisa says.

Darkness.

Fournier Street takes a breath, then breaks into an oceanic roar. Amon finds he is cheering with them. The walkie flashes.

'Judges are in!' he shouts to Raisa. 'Kynnd Raisa. Coil of the North, eight. Coil of the West, seven. Coil of the South, eight. Coil of the West, seven. Total, thirty.'

'He's got me beat, Amon,' Raisa says. 'I know it.'

'Kynnd Finn. Coil of the North, eight. Coil of the West, seven. Coil of the South, eight. Coil of the West, eight. Total . . .'

'I can do sums,' Raisa snaps.

'First round to . . .'

'Just hit that beat. On cue.'

Amon's face is hot with hurt and arc-burn.

'Round two.'

Ball. The most exquisite of the electromantic arts and the most diffi-cult. Generations of kitchen wizards and domestic alchemists sought the secret of ball lightning, that self-sustaining form of lightning mysterious as ghosts; like ghosts, imbued with almost-life. Only the Arcmages have learned, over long decades, the summoning and command of these djinn.

Raisa brings her palms together. A beam of plasma leaps the twenty-centimetre gap, so bright it illuminates Raisa's features through her cowl. On cue, Amon boots up the show music. Raisa's hands sculpt secret signs and rubrics, warp space-time and energy, fold flux-lines, weave them to-gether, trap them in a magnetic cage. Amon's breath catches as white light flashes to blue and a sphere of sapphire floats between her palms. Amon's breath holds as Raisa opens her hands as if she holds an iridescent hum-mingbird there. The ball lightning hovers like a grail above her supplicant palms.

Raisa turns her palms outwards and gives the lightning-ball the soft-est push. It drifts towards the south-east conductor, accelerates down the charge gradient. Raisa sends an arc to each of the cardinal conductors in turn; the ball dances from pillar to pillar to pillar, drawn from charge to charge. The plasma boils and spits, furious at its confinement. Raisa lifts her right hand, her left manipulating electrical fields, summons the ball to her. She tosses it, high, and down in a sizzle of trailing sparks. Higher, spinning it with flickers of fingertip electricity. Highest. Raisa bends for-ward to catch the ball lightning on the back of her neck.

The approaching storm hurls a javelin. The bolt breaks Raisa's delicate balance of electrical fields, the ball lightning rolls down over her head, skitters across the floor to the parapet. It teeters on the edge then drops screeching into Fournier Street. Spectators scatter. The ball lightning fizzes back and forth across the cobbles, then explodes with an ear-ringing crack and puff of ozone.

'Shit,' Raisa says.

'You were great,' Amon says.

'Don't be nice. I was not great. Ball is my weakest discipline.'

'Maybe Finn will be shit.'

Finn is not shit. Finn rocks ball lightning. Finn conjures two spheres. Finn stands in the east window of the tower and ostentatiously juggles the two balls before sending each of them on a tour of Christ Church, chasing each other along the roof-spine, bowling back along different gutters. Finn's wizard-hands cajole his lightning babies up the side of the tower as if he is reeling in quicksilver fish. He merges the two balls into one, leans out into empty space over the nave and throws it up. It runs up the steeple to perch on the cross atop the finial golden ball. A snap of the fingers and it dissolves into sparks.

'Fuck,' Raisa says. 'Fuckety fuck-fuck.'

Amon knows better than to tell her the scores.

'I'll take him in the beam,' Raisa declares from her tower of lightning. 'Beam is mine.'

Raisa snaps her fingers. Creation-light burns between them. Amon hits the music button.

Metal pours into Fournier Street. Thunder deities are solid metal: They signal their approval with the closest bolt yet. Two seconds later the crack rolls over Raisa's soundtrack.

Raisa holds up her closed fists shoulder width in front of her face. She opens her palms and again blazing plasma jumps between them. Amon shields his eyes. The Arcmages' faces are lit white as pages from a hotel Bible.

Raisa lifts her hands to her ears and the beam seems to go through her head. Now she dips and weaves, sending the white beam from her mouth, her eyes to the conductors around the studio. Arc-lit faces in the windows across Fournier Street watch open-mouthed.

The second finger-snap.

Amon throws her the Staff of Lightnings. This is the element of the duel he has feared the most. Raisa is charged and he is a terrible thrower. Raisa catches the staff, a sectioned metal pole a metre long. She holds it horizontally before her and the staff becomes a line of blazing plasma. Raisa twirls the staff like a majorette, a wheel of sparks, then spins the staff into the air. Bolts snap between spinning staff and fingers. Raisa catches the staff. Holds it up and it is a spear. She turns her spear to the four quarters and plasma blazes in turn to the corner conductors. The spear goes up into the air, crowned with power. Raisa catches it two-handed and wrenches it into two parts connected by a chain. She spins the nunchaku, one hand to another, over the elbow, around her back, her neck. White plasma blazes every time it passes a conductor. Raisa weaves plasma bolts so fast they fool the eye and merge into a burning cage.

Amon feels concussed with excitement. The faces of the judges are blue ecstasy.

A third time Raisa's electromantic wand spins blazing up into the air; she catches it, throws it to Amon, jumps. Can electricity defy gravity? She hangs airborne for longer than the curvature of space-time surely permits, comes down on the final power chord in a crouch, one knee bent, the other kneeling, one fist to the mesh, the other blazing power.

Iron Man pose.

The roar from the street is ploughed under by lightning, the thunder one second behind. One kilometre and closing. Fists pump in the Fournier Street windows.

Raisa is still kneeling, panting in her heavy armour. She turns her mailed head to Amon and he knows she is grinning. Somewhere Amon hears the walkie-talkie pass the baton to Finn in his tower. Somewhere there are bolts and beams and rays of light, like a Glastonbury Saturday night, like Martian fighting machines. Somewhere defiance is flung in the face of the eastering storm. All he can see is Raisa struggling to her feet. He aches to help her, steady her, touch her. To touch her is death.

Again, the walkie-talkie. Amon recites the scores, never taking his eyes off Raisa as she hauls her metal-shrouded body upright. She's won this round. Of course she's won it.

The final round. Freestyle. If she wins this, it goes to the casting vote.

She beckons. Amon snaps the Velcro straps around the final prop and lifts the pole. This is the hard stuff. He closes until he can feel the hairs on his hands stirring, erects the pole. It fights like a snake, caught by the gusting storm. He lofts it, Raisa snatches, battles it against the wind, slots it into the holes cut into the frame. St Elmo's fire licks the shaft; the tip coruscates with micro-lightnings.

'You ready?'

'Hit it.'

Amon stamps the white button. Raisa claps her hands—an explosion of lights. And dances.

Her music. His music. The coil music. It shakes coil and dancer, house and street, earth and heaven. The storm stoops close to listen. So entranced is Amon by the strangeness of his music playing wild that he almost forgets the performance that Raisa pulls out of the coil. She seizes the pole, swings around it, kicking bolts from her toes to the cardinal conductors. She hauls herself to the top of the pole—Amon boggles at the upper body strength—and hangs inverted. She opens her arms and arcs dance across the floor. Slides, spins, pulls herself up. She is pole-dancing a Tesla coil.

A heavy wet drop hits Amon's face. Fat spatters stain the floorboards.

Rain and Tesla coils.

'Raisa!'

When storms drop rain, they drop it all at once.

'Raisa! You got to stop!'

She is a dance of light, a vortex of fire, a Catherine wheel of power.

'I have to scram!'

Each raindrop is as weighty and warm as lead. Raisa swings and the storm answers with an opening salvo. The thunder arrives on top of the flash. No distance, no time.

'Raisa!' If the full storm catches her up there, charged, she will burn. Water runs down Amon's face, from his long fingers. A curtain of rain advances across Commercial Street. Raisa looks up into the face of the storm.

'Scram the coil!'

Amon's foot hits the red button. The power dies as the rain hits Arcmage House. Amon Brightbourne's tweeds are soaked through. He combs hair from his eyes. The rain tastes of salt and wet and places high above the earth. Raisa leaps from the platform to land heavily on the floor. She rips the cowl from her head.

'The roof!' she yells through the rain-hammer.

Amon dashes half-blinded by rain to the handle. Slat by pane by window, the roof closes. Out on the cherry-picker the Four Coils have pulled up their capacious hoods. The downpour chases spectators back to their doors and cars. The glass panels meet and seal. Raisa tears off her gauntlets and runs to the steaming coil, caressing its curves, stroking its windings and still-warm transistors.

'Oh baby baby . . .'

Amon stomps the button and his music dies. He heard something inside it, under it. Other music. He opens a windowpane and leans into the rain. Music pours from the belfry of Christ Church: growling, humming, restless, twitching. Bass shakes the rattly Huguenot windows; the treble sets the raindrops shivering. Christ Church sings. The bell tower windows flicker with coil-light. A dark silhouette dances from arch to arch, arms moving to the rhythm: a conductor.

Finn has turned the coil into a musical instrument.

Sorcery, bewitched-Amon thinks. Electric music, musician-Amon answers. Amon recorded the sounds of the coil; Finn plays it in real time. Tuned thunder. The storm answers with a creation-flash and world-rending crash. Amon lets the rain punish him, grinning like in ecstasy. No DJ, no producer, no cosmic-scale gig or intense quartet can match this thunder-music. Futures open before him. Finn and Amon. He sees himself composing suites for lightning and ambience; a double concerto, a fugue for storm and electronica.

'Listen to this!' he roars into the roaring night.

Raisa joins him at the window. In the rain.

'Fucker,' she says. She has shed her armour and her saturated spandex presses close to Amon's dripping, creaking tweed. 'He's got a roof.'

'Listen,' Amon yells. 'Have you ever heard anything like it?' She hasn't. The Arcmages clinging to their swaying cherry-picker cage haven't. No one has. That's how everyone knows that Raisa has lost. She makes lightning dance. All dance aspires to the condition of lightning. Finn makes lightning perform against its nature, takes its roar and turns it to song. He has blown electromancy into the twenty-first century.

Lightning thunder strike, on top of them now.

'He has to stop!' Raisa shouts.

White blinding light; a blast like the world splitting. A threnody of car and house alarms. From St Mary Axe to Allen Gardens Spitalfields is dark. Mobile phone torches waver behind Fournier Street's windows. A fresh flare climbs from the cherry-picker to light up the Arcmages, rain-soaked Batmen in their hooded capes. Sirens to west and east.

'What?' Amon asks.

'He got hit,' Raisa says. She snatches the walkie-talkie from him. 'Finn. Lisi. You all right?'

Another flash and crack; the storm has passed and drives east to intimidate Stepney and Mile End.

'Finn! Lisi!'

Emergency lighting stammers into life. The Arcmages descend through the rain. The downpour stutters, slackens and the walkie crackles.

'I'm okay.' Lisi. Amon can barely make out her words. 'Finn's okay. Sort of. The coil's gone.'

Raisa bolts to the sanctum door.

The walkie flashes a light. The Arcmages wish to speak.

'Raisa!'

Fast feet on the stairs.

The Coils deliver their verdict. Amon hears the front door of Arcmage House slam and leans out over the drop far beyond sense and safety.

'Raisa!'

A running shadow on rain-wet cobbles.

'You won! Default! The coil is yours!'

She never stops, never looks back.

'You won,' he whispers.

19

After Raisa's return from Christ Church.

After Finn and Lisi limp in smelling of charred hair and ozone.

After Tante Margolis and Rev. Oyedepu go up the tower and declare the Christ Church coil dead.

After warm towels and dry clothes and capes dripping in the hall.

After the muted celebrations by candlelight, the off-chill champagne, Finn polite and hang-headed, after he makes his good-nights.

After Raisa says that she's knackered and heads off with a candle and the Arcmages have gone out in search of electricity, Bangla food and beer because judging is exhausting work.

After Amon and Lisi have been left in echoing anticlimax in the kitchen: Amon Brightbourne announces, 'I'm going too.'

'Where?'

'I want to look in on Raisa.'

'Why?'

Amon hears suspicion.

'See how she is.'

'She's knackered. That's how she is.'

'I just want to . . .'

'She needs rest.'

'I need to . . .'

'Leave her, Amon.'

Amon lifts a candle. Goth-handed, he lights his way up the staircases and landings to Raisa's room.

'Raisa?'

No answer. He cracks open the door, shines his candlelight through the slit. Behind him he hears Lisi's voice calling his name, climbing stairs.

'Raisa?' He opens the door. 'You asleep?'

Light. EDF restores power to blacked-out Spitalfields. Raisa lies foetal on her bed, spine turned to Amon. She wears panties and kneesocks. Nothing more. Curled around her like punctuation, abdomen to vertebra, is Finn. He is naked, magnificent. His mouth is open. He and Raisa lie sleeping like lost fairy-tale children. They breathe in innocent synchrony.

Amon looks until he can bear the sight no longer. He turns, pushes Lisi aside, rushes down the staircases, useless candle held high under the electric sconces. His satchel, which holds what is left of his world, is in the kitchen. Still damp. He pulls the front door behind him and makes his way up Fournier Street to the high windows of the City, and the greater city, and beyond them all, to Brightbourne.

20

The lane hadn't been there the other three times they came off the sharp junction at the sign for Broighter Glen Picnic Area, nor the gates (iron, scabbed and rust-blistered) and certainly not the young woman sitting on the stone stile beside those gates.

The woman waves down the Volvo. An unnecessary identification: her red hair, pale freckled skin, luminous eyes are the colours of Brightbourne. Where Amon is the cock pheasant, she is the greenfinch; rural hues, outdoorsy style. She buys her clothes in supermarkets, on monthly shops, with loyalty points.

'Sorry I'm late,' she says. 'Were you going round long?'

She has an accent. Lisi and Raisa now realise that Amon has an accent; every word he ever spoke was accented.

'It can be tricky, finding us,' she says, getting into the back seat without waiting for an answer. 'You need someone to show you. The first time at least.'

The Volvo turns through the iron gates and crunches onto pot-holed gravel.

After the storm cleared eastwards.

After the rain dried from the cobbles.

After the Arcmages took the cherry-picker up to salvage the saveable from Christ Church tower.

After the Do Not Cross tape was rolled up and the traffic cones were lifted and the *Lightning Girl and Thunderbolt Boy* security folded their hi-viz tabards.

After the Spitalfields Trust's engineers completed their inspection of Hawksmoor's steeple and an unseasonal chill in the air raised eyes in Brick Lane and Commercial Street to the sky, as if a cloud had covered the sun.

After Finn rolled out of Raisa's bed and out of Arcmage House, back to Dorling Avenue, to life after lightning.

After all this, days after, Lisi said to Raisa, 'Go to him.'

'I can't.'
'You hurt him.'
'I didn't mean to.'
'Yet you did.'
'He didn't understand.'
'That doesn't matter.'
'You're very old for your age.'
'Go to him.'
'I don't know where he is.'
'I do.'
'I can't.'
'He loves you.'
'You don't know that.'
'I do.'
'How could you know that?'
'I'm on Facebook with him.'
'Fuck off.'
'He loves you, you hurt him. You owe him.'
'So where is he then?'
'He's home.'
'That place . . .'
'Brightbourne.'
'Take the Volvo,' Tante Margolis said, drifting in for coffee. 'I don't need it.'
'You ganged up on me.'
'So if we did?'
'Okay. Not on my own, though.'
'Deal,' Lisi said. 'I'm the contact. So: Brightbourne.'
'Brightbourne.'
Only then did Raisa realise that Amon lived on another island entirely.

Raggedy rhododendrons yield to dark fir woods. Browning conifer needles carpet the drive. It seems too long to fit into the triangle of country round which Raisa and Lisi steered, lost, three times. As if Brightbourne lay on the crease of a map flattening and unfolding as they drove along it.

'*Lost Acres*,' the woman—Lorien, younger child of the demesne—says. 'It's a poem. By Robert Graves. When the Ordnance Survey mapped the country whole bits got overlooked. Like folding the edges of a piece of paper together. Landscapes got left out, hidden away. Brightbourne's like that.'

From close, muffling fir forest into straggling broad-leaf wood. Vistas open—they drive up the western side of a shallow wooded valley. Lisi leans forward.

'I hear something.'

Lorien smiles.

'Stop the car.'

Raisa pulls into a passing space.

'Turn the engine off! Can you hear it?'

Between rushes and dashes of birdsong and the colossal susurrus of a high wind stirring the trees hides a swelling and ebbing in snatches and tantalisations: chimes and bells, tinklings and fat-bellied xylophone tonks, glissandos and scurrying fugues.

'Is that Amon?' Lisi asks.

'No, no,' Lorien says. 'That's the Music.'

The Music accompanies them up the drive, heard then unheard with every bend, every opening in the trees. Raisa glimpses a glitter of glass, grey roof, a scrap of scrubby parkland, a gleam of water. Brightbourne is a coy house. Lorien directs the Volvo down a right fork at a stone arch that opens onto a yard of decaying outbuildings. The car swings around an elbow of rhododendron and there it stands; a three-storeyed, generously windowed, seventeenth-century box with thuggish additions—a Georgian ballroom annexe leaning against the east wing as if wheedling a loan, a massive Victorian porte cochère above the front door, ludicrous as a black eye. Shy of grandeur but strong-boned, Bright-bourne leans back into the close-shouldering woods. The arrangement of the windows with the outsized covered porch gives the house a look of permanent surprise, that it has been discovered at mischief after four hundred years.

Grey cloud hung over the drive from the ferry port, yet the house stands in a pool of sunshine.

'The Golden Place,' Lorien says.

And people wait in that sun on the apron of weedy gravel before the porch: a middle-aged woman with a grey streak in her hair; an elderly man, eagle-nosed, very upright; and Amon Brightbourne.

21

Nine o'clock, UFO Terrace: fireworks, says the handwritten invitation pushed under the bedroom door. Dress.

Dress, Raisa Peri Antares Hopeland discovers, means a chest at the end of her bed and the key in the invitation envelope. In that chest, soft wonders. Things that smell of time and old perfumes, other bodies, five A.M. waltzes. Raisa slips on a 1920s drop-waist silk flapper dress, daringly short even for the twenty-first century. Kitten heels, piratical swatches of pearls. She combs up her hair into a glowing aura.

'Hot,' she declares.

Oohs as she opens the French windows of the ballroom and steps onto the terrace.

'Great-Great-Gramma Euterpe wore that at the 1922 debutantes' ball at Dolby's in Mayfair,' Amon says. 'There's a picture of her in it, up on the Infanta Staircase.' Amon Brightbourne wears a kiss-soft velvet smoking jacket. Cravat, sharp-creased dress pants, dancing pumps. This fancy dress helps navigate the scratchy distance between him and Raisa. Everyone wears the uniform of the unfamiliar. He senses, like the warmth of the ebbing day from the flagstones of the UFO Terrace, that time will turns things true.

'Why UFO Terrace?' Raisa asks.

'Auberon was into UFOs in the seventies,' Amon's mother says. Morwenna, chatelaine of Brightbourne, in 1950s Dior New Look: full skirt, peplum, crop sleeves. 'Ancient astronauts, Erich von Däniken. He built an orgone accumulator to summon aliens to the landing site he cut in Broighter Wood.'

Lorien hands Raisa a gin and tonic in a heavy, nubbly crystal goblet.

'He got bored with it pretty quickly. Lysander dismantled it for the Music but the terrace is still a few degrees warmer than the rest of the house.' Lorien wears a floral Liberty print, self-conscious and uncomfortable in fine clothes. Lisi and Great-Uncle Auberon rove out in Broighter Wood across the valley, stalking the undergrowth like pyrotechnic tigers in the easy alliance of old and young, setting off rockets with glee. The air on the UFO Terrace is huge with insect voices, last light clings to the northern hills. A whoosh and a jet of sparks streaks up from beyond the bourne. A rocket bursts in a pop of falling stars. Another, then another, then three in quick succession, detonating softly above the leaf canopy.

'Auberon has a theory about fireworks,' Lorien says as the rocket fire becomes a small barrage. 'They are the art most like a human life. An act in three parts. Spark, ascent, detonation. Accensione, salire, detonazione. In some the salire is long and slow and the detonazione brief but beautiful. Rockets are like that. In some the salire is quick, but the detonazione is long and fades out slowly, like a Roman candle.'

'Auberon made the theory up and stuck some Italian around it to make it sound wistful,' Amon says. 'He just likes fireworks.'

The far woods sparkle. Brief bright burn. Whistle and pop. Star shower.

'I don't think so,' Raisa says and her eyes glitter with reflected sky-rocket. 'I don't think so at all. Life is lightning.'

The last stars fall. Dark figures move on the bridge, moments later Lisi and Auberon come up the river steps to the terrace. Auberon is rural in tweed ratting jacket, random hat and sporting an ashplant; Lisi wears duck boots, a short black Biba dress, sequined and beaded.

'I like this place,' Lisi says. Her knees are green and she smells of rank weeds, smoke and gunpowder. 'I'm glad I made you come. Raisa, you can see them. You don't need yatas. The woods are full of them. Everywhere, but if you look too hard . . . You know.'

Great-Uncle Auberon follows her stiff-hipped onto the UFO Terrace.

'Fierce hungry business, pyrotechnics,' he declares. 'I shall coddle some eggs. Light, proteinaceous and easily digestible. You find you sleep differently in our country than in the east. Miss?' He holds open the French window and Lisi, Lorien and Morwenna return to the ballroom. Raisa and Amon remain among the spooks and the moths and the orgone-powered saucers.

'Can I tell you something, tweed-boy?' Raisa says. She twists her glass, a tell of discomfort.

'I'm not in tweed . . .'

'I never could see them. I spin the mirror and it's pretty and I never see nothing. I do it. Doing's the thing, ain't it?' She turns to him. 'Amon . . . what you saw . . .'

He closes his eyes.

'You're here. I'm here, you know?'

He lifts a hand: too much.

Raisa's eyes widen.

'Oh! I heard it again. What did Lorien call it?'

'The Music,' Amon says and she hears the capitalisation.

Raisa goes up on tiptoe, drawn upwards by sprays of bells, half-heard chimes and glissandi.

'It's like it's coming from . . . I don't know. Where is that? Oh. It's gone.'

'It's never gone,' Amon says. If not gone, then moved to another plane and in the silence neither he nor Raisa have anything they dare say. Amon shuffles in his patent dance pumps.

'Do you fancy Auberon's eggs?'

'Not really. I'm kind of tired. Long drive and I never tried sleeping on a boat before and it weren't good.'

'I'll come with you.'

A hand on his arm.

'Don't come with me.'

'You might get lost.'

'I got here all right.'

'Yes, but it's different getting back again.'

Raisa lets Amon guide her and though her path is identical to the one she took making her entrance, the doors seem to open onto different rooms. Here is a moon-lit study, here a morning room decorated in cyanide-green cockatoo wallpaper, and in the dining room she catches a vignette of Auberon cracking an egg into a copper chafing dish while Lisi, Morwenna, Lorien watch, ghost-lit by the blue glow of spirit-burners, like spectators at an eighteenth-century experiment into phlogiston. Raisa grew up among the continuum distortions of the Wandsworth Hearth and Arcmage House and she's quite sure she's not taking the same way up the monumental Infanta Staircase she took down. Images of Brightbourne's children watch from the walls, dolorous seventeenth-century Planters, Georgians in nursery smocks and coiled ringlets, Victorian boys in pink.

Amon points out Blazing Bob Brightbourne, avid promoter of rural boxing, a five-year-old in a buttoned-up powder-blue skeleton suit and frilled collar. They stop for Nicholas Saviour Brightbourne, duellist, Dublin gadabout and founder member of the Hellfire Club, in nursery frock and necklaces to turn the jealous eyes of faeries. Raisa stops on a small unexpected sub-landing in front of a painting.

'And this, Amon Brightbourne?'

Night. A ghost moon. Atkinson Grimshaw trees lift dark branches against a green sky. The view from the ballroom. The French windows stand open. A young boy steps from the terrace into the house, peeking and shy. He is clad only in a golden halo so bright it throws shadows across the foreground. His eyes are pale yellow. In the house's half-light Raisa thinks his eyes are slitted like a cat's.

'That's the Brilliant Boy of Brightbourne,' Amon says. 'He's a family apparition.'

'That is one creepy kid,' Raisa says.

'Your room's here,' Amon says. He opens a door Raisa has not seen before into her sag-floored, wood-scented bedroom. 'Sleep well.'

'With that thing outside? I wake up and see Sparky, I come out shooting.'

'He only appears to the oldest boy of every generation,' Amon says.

'Only boys,' Raisa comments.

'Since Crispus. In 1788.'

'And did he appear to you, Amon Brightbourne?'

'He did.' The stairs creak, as if the children in the walls were talking. The house sighs out the heat of the day and settles like a weary dog.

'And did he do anything, or did he just appear and shine at you?'

'He brought the Grace,' Amon says and before Raisa can ask *the what?* he's off another way down the Infanta Staircase and the eyes of the children of Brightbourne aren't following him. Not at all.

22

East-light wakes Raisa too early. She follows the music to Amon at the half-grand piano in the ballroom, MacBook balanced on the lid. His left hand strikes jazz chords. Men intent are beautiful things. Raisa watches Amon shake his head, try another chord, turn it into an arpeggio. Nods, samples it. Light streams through the amber-leaded windows, graces him a blinding halo. Over a century it has bleached the hand-painted Chinese bird wallpaper almost to invisibility. Generations of Brightbourne children have attempted to restore the faded aviary with everything from crayons to poster paint to felt-tip pens.

On silent bare feet, Raisa comes up behind Amon and touches his neck with her lips. He starts as if shot, knocking the MacBook onto the piano keys with a clang of discords.

'Sorry!' She's not. 'Whatcha at?'

'I'm trying to get a clip I recorded on the phone to work on the piano.' Amon's left hand picks out another arpeggio. He pouts in displeasure. Raisa slides onto the piano stool beside him.

'Clip of what?'

'Do you want to know?'

'Go on.'

'I'm trying to get something I heard in the music.'

'The . . . stuff out there?'

'Finn's music. From the coil. That night.'

'Oh.'

She slides off the piano stool.

'I need to get this done. If I don't, it's gone. If you want to come back later, I will have something. If you want to hear it.'

'I want,' Raisa says.

Then the light dims, a true cloud covers the sun and the breeze carries a waft of the other music into the ballroom; faint, haunted runs of the bells that swing beyond the walls of the universe.

'You should hear that Music too,' Amon says. 'You can't understand this place unless you see it. Ask Lorien to take you. Bring Lisi along. She'll like it.'

With every step along the river path the Music grows nearer. In this shallow valley, Raisa's sense of Brightbourne being askew in time crystallises. Time clings in the damp shade beneath the scrubby willows, eddies in the burn, pools behind the shallow weirs.

Lorien parts a screen of buddleia, loosestrife and ivy to expose a green door in a wall of soft, crumbling Victorian brick; sun-shy, moss-colonised, slippery. Raisa makes out some kind of building in the fecundity.

'I come and see it most days,' Lorien says.

An unseen movement—a drop, a surfacing—sends ripple-rings across the water. Lorien takes a small key from the pocket of her jeans.

'I hate locking it, but all it takes is some lads getting in. They break anything they don't know.'

She opens a green door in the mould-stained brick wall.

'Oh!' Raisa says, and Lisi: 'Whoa.' They stand in a low-ceilinged brick chamber. Ivy overgrows the small windows; the interior is all shadow-light and leaf-dapple. Damp air smells rich with mould and decay but the first, dominant impression is ringing. Chimes, tinkles, tiny bells, plinks, clinks, tinks. Glissandi, peals and tocsins, drones and chords. Wheels of sound circle; themes play point and counterpoint. Behind the tintinnabulum runs the conversation of restless water. Clicks, drips, trickles, gushes and rushes and jets. Sprays and gurgles: lively and innocent and joyful.

After the sound and odour come humidity and spray. Raisa tastes fresh water on her tongue, feels it mist her face and bare arms. She and Lisi laugh at each other's hair, silvered with webs of dew. Last, as eyes adapt to the dank gloom, comes motion. Wheels spin within wheels, drive belts fly and cogs and cams turn. Movement begets music. Hammers rise and fall, cams rotate, pin cylinders turn, valves open and close. Turbines whir, ballcocks rise, cisterns empty and fill-pipes tip and everywhere water gushes from jets and nozzles. Raisa hugs herself with delight. She stands at the heart of a beautiful water-powered music machine.

Lisi traces a drive belt to a series of step-down gears. With her finger she follows the drive chains to a small hydraulic glockenspiel and a set of tuned bells.

'Careful,' Raisa says. 'Fingers.'

'There's something else in here,' Lisi says. Raisa joins her to peer into whirring machinery. A second mechanism is at work, of clever cams and cycles of gears. Part hydro-sinfonia, part water clock. Raisa tries to follow the narrative of cogs and rachets and drives. The nested mechanisms are as intricate as a watch.

'What does it do?' Raisa shouts over the gushing and chiming and whirring.

'You're in time!' Lorien shouts back. She takes Raisa's hand. Raisa snatches Lisi's fingers away from the spinning cogs and hand in hand in hand they go ducking under pipes, sliding around humming turbines, stepping over chuckling flumes. Lorien edges them around a sharp-toothed gear set.

A gear ticks over. An escapement starts to spin. Cams engage, concentric disks of pinwheels shift to a new alignment and rise to strike a sweet, melancholic, twilit theme from a set of chimes. The melody lifts above the singing, ringing orchestra, slowly fading as the power in the drive-spring ebbs and the pinwheel descends back to its passive position. The new voice falls silent, the escapement is stilled. Back along the chain of consequences, the hidden mechanism clicks to a new alignment. A single, unseen piccolo bell chimes. A weight on a chain ratchets up a notch.

'That's a thirty-year measure,' Lorien shouts. 'I've never heard that before. No one's ever heard it before. I'll be fifty by the time anyone hears it again. Then again when I'm eighty. Twice. There are yearly measures, five-year measures, ten-year measures. I've heard all those. Some still turn up to hear them, on the new year, the leap-year measure. Solstices and equinoxes. I'm looking forward to the fifty-year measure.'

'What do you mean?' Raisa asks. Lisi slips and ducks between the mechanisms like an explorer in a temperate rainforest. Lorien moves to point up to a cog-train. Inner wheels fly, the outer wheel moves with imperceptible slowness, a peg creeping sub-millimetrically towards a trigger switch.

'It'll take fifty years for this to run through and play its tune,' Lorien says.

'Slow music,' Raisa says.

'The slowest.' Lorien swings under a girder and beckons Raisa into a cubby walled with chain drives. They stand breath close in the ringing spray, oiled metal links whirring past them. 'See that way up there? That's the hundred-year measure. Ten of those measures and the Music is played through.'

'A thousand years?'

'The Music will play for a thousand years.'

Lorien looks up into the wheels within wheels, the theme within themes, the cascading chimes and bells. Her face is bright with love.

'Isn't it wonderful?'

'I can hear it shifting,' Raisa says. 'So slow it's like it's hardly happening.'

'But it does,' Lorien says. 'And it never repeats. What you're hearing is as new to me as it is to you.'

'I love it, but I can't hear all of it. Even a tiny part of it. I'm too small. All of us is too small.'

'How does that make you feel?'

Raisa closes her eyes. Spray dews her eyelashes.

'I think I'm a little scared. Sad and happy at the same time. Sad for everyone who'll never hear it end. Happy because it says, five hundred years and I'm still playing. Eight hundred years, I'm still playing. A thousand years . . .'

Lisi dodges between nozzles, ducks under escapements to the central iron catwalk. T-shirt and baggy shorts are drenched, her big shoes squeak on the metal, her hair sags under the weight of moisture.

'I'm inside a clock!' she shouts. 'Made of water!'

'You're soaked through,' Raisa says and feels the chill of the sunless building on her wet skin. Lorien opens a door Raisa had not seen onto a flight of slimy concrete steps that lead up the steep side of the small valley to the feeder pond. A stone bench stands in a window of sun, inviting pause, conversation, warmth.

Raisa frowns at the sun. It is not where she left it. They came up the Broighter Burn as soon after breakfast as Hopelands and Brightbournes could agree. The sun now stands over the crumbling chimneys of Brightbourne, throwing west-light into the hidden valley.

'How long were we in there?'

'It does things to time,' Lorien says. She sits between Raisa and Lisi. They drip agreeably. 'You listen a bit and when you go back into the world, hours have passed. Whole mornings.' The Music is distant now, further than the old brick hydro-house beneath them that contains it, folded into the scuttle and laughter of the river. Lisi swings her feet, enjoying the arc of drips from the toes of her drenched trainers. 'Mum's chatelaine but the Music is too much trouble for her. Most things are too much trouble for her. So I take care of it. And the house. I do so love Brightbourne. The Golden Place.'

'Why doesn't Amon look after it?' Lisi asks. 'He's the musical one.'

'Oh he can't,' Lorien says. 'He'd break it. Or the house. He can't help it. Lysander could only build it a few weeks at a time. He'd stay as long as he could, then go away, come back, do it again.'

'Why?' Lisi asks.

Sun reaches deep into chill and Raisa shivers.

'It's to do with that painting, isn't it?' she says. 'The Brilliant Boy.'

'Has Amon told you about the Grace?' Lorien says.

'No.'

'Then I won't. That's for him.'

'Lysander?' Lisi says, like a breeze clearing a cloud from the sun.

'My grandfather,' Lorien say. 'I never met him. I barely knew Hadley—Dad: he kept coming and going. Lysander was the oldest, then Auberon—he's eighty in November—then Great-Aunt Hippolyta—she's in France, she hasn't been here since before I was born. Lysander was born in 1929. He had music in his bones. It's in all the boys. Lysander studied composition with Michael Tippett at the London College of Music. After he graduated he took a motorbike along the hippy trail long before it was the hippy trail. There are pictures on the Fragrant Landing of him in Kandahar. He's very good-looking. He drove to India, lived on an ashram before it was fashionable. He was interested in Hindu theories of space and time, cycles of creation and destruction and rebirth. The Indian pieces around the house are from him. Most of it's not good but there is a brass elephant I love a lot. Then he went to San Francisco—Oakland—to study with Steve Reich. He was doing stuff with loops and phases and cycles.

'Lysander developed a theory of time. We don't look at time right. We're chronologically lopsided. We can think about millions of years in the past but not millions of years in the future. We can think about the age of the dinosaurs, or the Romans, but we can't push our minds two thousand years ahead, let alone millions. We can't see it, so we can't think about it. It's not there. We can think about the time when we were not, but we can't think about the time when we will not be. Lysander had this idea of making something that we could imagine going forward, like a thread let out into time that we could follow to the future. If there was something we could say would be there at a definite time to come, and have a connection through the years to our time and our lives, then we, now, might be able to think about time right. We wouldn't be so short-sighted and short-term.

'He wrote a piece of music: a set of variations that takes a thousand years to play through. A thousand years. Can you imagine that? That's what he wanted, for people to imagine that moment when the last note plays and the Music is over. What if there's no one to play the music? Who could organise performing a thing like that, over a thousand years? Like, from the time of the Vikings to now? A piece of music longer than the entire history of Western classical music. So much time. So he had his second idea, which was to make it so it wouldn't need people to play it. The Music would play itself. How could you build a machine that would run for a thousand years? Winds stop blowing, you can't rely on electricity and people, well, you can't trust people. But water flows day and night, year in, year out, and here he had his power source—the Broighter Burn has never failed. And he had the place in the old hydro-plant. He hired clock-makers, jewellers, hydraulic engineers, antiques restorers, percussionists and water diviners. There are lots of pieces of old lawn mower and parish hall pianos in there.

'It took Lysander fifteen years to build. On and off. He opened the sluices at twelve thirty-three on August 26th, 1981. There were more reporters than neighbours. There were pieces in the papers, north and south, even London. There were crews from the BBC and RTÉ. Ten days after, he was killed on his motorbike, right at the main gate. Run over by a milk tanker turning left. He stayed too long. Lysander is gone and Dad is gone and Amon is gone. The Music still plays.

'I look after it. De-gunge the nozzles, oil the gear wheels and cams. Watch out for rust. Rust is the enemy. There's a clever double-cog system so the Music will keep playing on the second cog while you clean the first. And the water's never dried up. It's from deep inside the hill. People who know about the Music sometimes call by when there's a change or a new measure. Or just to make sure it's still playing. There's never many of them. I open the place up and let them take a look and a listen. They can stay as long as they like. See?'

The peat-dark water of the Broighter Burn chuckles over the weedy-green lips of the sluice into the whirring, ticking machinery of the Music to gush out in a thousand springs and freshets bearing time away downstream. The sun is behind trees now, lower than it should be. Shadows have fallen onto the bright seat, Raisa and Lisi are cold and clammy and Auberon lights candles in the ballroom's golden windows for the evening's revels.

23

They go to the woods at twilight. Brightbourne's lights twinkle through the trunks; the close space under the leaf canopy is dense with bird voices. The air lies heavy, a great stillness made of hundreds of small, almost imperceptible turbulences that bring one sound close, then another: the dumb roar of a modded hatchback out beyond the walls of Brightbourne, a shriek of fox-fury, snatches from Auberon's gramophone DJ set, wisps of the Music.

'Where are we going?' Raisa asks.

Amon extends a hand.

'To a hidden place.'

Raisa takes his hand. They push on into the trees, crushing rank late-summer weeds beneath their feet until the lights of the house are lost. The dark canopy opens to stars. In the small clearing stands a temple, a ring of Doric pillars topped with a cupola: Irish rural Palladian. Neglected for years, the space is rewilding. Browning late-summer ferns rustle on the wind-breaths. Stands of purple loosestrife nod feathery seed-heads. Brambles thorn the low sanctuary wall and send tendrils out across the stone flags. Leaves of other autumns gather under the benches. Generations of Brightbournes and other stealers-in have left names and dates and other evidence of their purpose in the soft, honey-coloured stone. Raisa runs her fingers over the scratchings. Old loves.

'This is . . .'

Amon lays a finger to Raisa's lips. Old leaves stir.

'Ssh,' he says and places buds in her ears, setting each with care and precision. He taps his phone. Music floods Raisa Hopeland. By moth-light Amon reads her face: the movements of her lips, her eyes under their lids, the hesitation of breath as she tumbles over a chord transition. The flinch in her features, the pulse in her throat, the folds in her forehead as he hammers her with relentless four-square kicks and brutal bass stabs against a wall of digital squawk. The glints of water-shine in the corners of her eye when out of a long death-march drone he summons the platinum trumpets of the army of Elfland, universes away.

And Amon Brightbourne is a voyeur. A manipulator. A thousand times he has done this in the after-clubs and early-morning parties, slipped on the headphones, pressed play and watched joy as private and intimate as prayer. The music he gives her is all his emotions and incomprehensions and experiences since the night she called down to him from a roof in Soho. There is lightning and placenta pakora; there are mirrors and riot; there is betrayal and a haunted church and an oak tree. Amon has sampled ten thousand sources before but never a life. She hears Raisa Hopeland as a hundred clips, looped and sequenced and mixed for her and given back to her.

She slips the buds from her ears.

'I heard what you did there, Amon Brightbourne.'

'I'm sor . . .'

Now she lays the silencing finger to his lips.

'All that?'

She lifts the finger. Permission to speak.

'And more. The music can only hold a tiny part . . .'

'Shh. Don't talk.'

She silences him again, this time with a tiptoe kiss.

'Oh,' says Amon Brightbourne.

'It was a kynnd thing. He was hurt. Amon, it didn't mean . . . It don't mean.'

'And did that?'

'You have to trust it did.' With one dancer's move she pulls her tank top over her head. 'And this does.'

She quickly disposes of the sports bra. Her breasts are small, with flat nipples and large wine-dark areolas. With a wiggle she kicks off shoes, slides down leggings and pants. She is wearing the tube socks. Amon could detonate with want and joy. She turns, she poses in the soft darkness, butt and socks, socks and butt and a sly, coy smile.

Shoes off, socks off—hopping on one foot; it looks stupid but man-socks are stupider—Amon tries to kick off his skinny trousers and boxers without tripping over them. Men should undress from the bottom, by Auberon's rules of sex. Sling away the jacket, peel off the shirt. Naked. His nipples feel raw and sensitive and unmagnificent. She turns to him. Her pubes are a neatly trimmed exclamation mark. He has ginger balls. Comedy genitals. And he isn't good at sex, she might expect things from him, tricks, put things in places he doesn't know, want things that freak him out a little. She might have had lots of lovers and know everything and make him look like a country fool. Her butt quivers as she moves. Her skin is dark, her hair the night sky. And the socks . . .

Fuck it.

Lisi parts rhododendron leaves. She dares not breathe. The slightest noise could betray. She ventured into the woods on rumours of UFOs and strange Emanations. She is dressed in a sixties zebra-stripe minidress and a pair of pink Doc Martens. Excellent UFO-hunter's gear. The wood is loud with unhuman voices. They lead her, by crack of branch and sting of nettle, by sweep of bat and scratch of bramble until they become human voices. Lisi holds herself still. Human voices, not speaking words. The old rhododendron invites her in.

Raisa and Amon in an old temple. Raisa on top, riding hard. Her eyes are closed, her mouth open. She does not look pretty. Amon underneath is downright ugly. Lisi has spied on many kinds of sex: None of it is ever pretty. It doesn't look exciting or arousing. It looks uncomfortable and difficult. It looks kind of repetitive and boring. She has seen people she knows and loves made ugly and unlovable by fucking.

'Yes,' she whispers to the unhuman voices, the circling Emanations, the UFOs and the distant carillon of the Music. 'I did it!'

24

'I saw Brightbourne,' Raisa says. She sits naked on the late-summer stone, knees pulled up. Her socks are no defence against the night chill. Amon sleeps curled on the floor of the temple. Men can sleep anywhere. It is a mighty power. Raisa has tucked his jacket under his head for a pillow. Men look so vulnerable naked; all their sensitive, delicate sex bits turned out and presented to the world. She drapes his shirt over him.

The sex was awkward but good. Good sex straddles devotion and abandon. Amon had the enthusiasm and inexperience of the near-virgin. Raisa taught him enough tricks to seem clever but not blasé. Amon had cunning pianist's fingers and an instinct for finding music.

'The house was gone, Amon: the house was a shell. There were things in the sky. Trees grown up over everything.' She could never see the Emanations but images have always come to her. Too much to call them visions: they are shots, impressions; illuminated by flashes of lightning. 'And I saw people. People like all the stars in the sky. So many people. And the Music, I couldn't hear the Music.' Bells from outside time hear her and wash over her. 'There was no Music, Amon.'

She pulls on her pants and tank top. She feels cold, uncomfortable, vulnerable and afraid. Her vision clings like night-dirt. She should wake him up soon. He's going to hurt in the morning, on hard stone.

'Amon, you should you know. I never been anything. I never done anything. I never stuck.' Burlesque dancer. Online marketer. PR for an ARG start-up. Word-of-mouth brand ambassador. Stage manager for a variety show. Logo model for a dance-music label (catsuit, ray gun, silver boots). Tour guide. Charity mugger. Crayfish trapper. Cycling Advocacy Officer. Dog-walker. Coffee barista. 'I never finish anything. I move on. One job, one place, one life to another. You got deep time. You got the next thousand years playlisted. I got people. Amon Amon Amon . . .' She hardly dares speak. 'I saw the time when the Music stops. I think it's starting now. We're falling apart. We're angry with the old stuff but we got no new stuff.

'What if we put us together? Hopeland and Brightbourne. Us. My family. You do things with time. We do connections. What if it isn't just music that lasts a thousand years, but a family? A thousand years: ten thousand years. You can see the stars move in ten thousand years. New constellations. That got to be long enough to get us past the things that might burn us. A Hopeland could hear the final note of the Music.'

The wind rises. Leaves rustle, some fall. Summer ending. A shard of Music brushes Raisa's skin. Ten thousand years. A Starring in the year 12,011. That is a thing to work for. How to even take that first step on a ten-thousand-year march? Who is she, a minor star on the edge of a vague spiral arm of the great Hopeland constellation with a notion and a Tesla coil?

The edge of the world is a soft grey line pierced by the black boles of Broighter Wood.

'Amon, you hear any of that?'

Amon rolls over, reaches for her, pheromonally guided. Raisa shifts away from him with a laugh.

'Clothes on, tweed-boy. We're done for this night.'

25

She comes around the hydro-house to a cascade of bells, takes the moss-slippery steps, sure-footed with sexual energy, across the UFO Terrace to the drive, around a pothole that she is sure wasn't there yesterday. A figure, batwinged in a wide white sundress, flaps like a bird from the top of the carriage porch.

'Come and have tea!' The figure waves a flask in one hand, a cup in the other.

'I need a shower,' Raisa shouts.

'You fucked Amon!' Morwenna roars. Starlings rise from the lawn.

'Excuse me?'

'You've fucked Amon!'

A dog-walker at the far end of the lawn pauses.

'Lisi told me,' Morwenna continues at weather-affecting volume.

'Lisi?'

'The only way you're going to stop me is to come up and have tea. I loathe the expression "we need to talk", but we do.'

Raisa can find no obvious way to Morwenna's preview on top of the porch. She might have levitated or portalled. In the little glassed coachman's room, Raisa notices a suspicious shine on a brass knob on an innocuous, white-painted wall panel. Behind, a spiral staircase. On the roof are two folding chairs, a flask and morning news burbling from a radio. Raisa takes the offered seat and Morwenna pours tea. The radio softly dissects the causes and consequences of the English riots, as they are now called, and debates the legacy of Amy Winehouse. News from another country.

'He does need it,' Morwenna says. 'A decent fuck. I did fear for him.'

'That's what I am?' Raisa says. 'A decent fuck?'

'More than decent, from what I heard. She is such a natural little spy, your sister.'

'She's not my sister.'

'Yes, she tried to explain that too. I need you to believe that whatever I say, I am not your enemy. Garibaldi?'

Morwenna offers Raisa a packet of biscuits. The chatelaine of Brightbourne accessorises her white sundress with matching floppy hat and enormous, white-rimmed sunglasses.

'What's this about?'

'Love, dear. The only thing anything is about. I know you're fucking him. Do you love him?'

'What's this to do with you?'

'You've seen the Brilliant Boy.'

'The creepy-ass painting. Amon saw it.'

'Amon did see it. That's the tragedy.'

Amon, Lorien, Auberon and Lisi have emerged to study the hole in the drive. Lisi squats down and drops a pebble into it. They lean forward to listen.

'The story is this,' Morwenna says. 'Isaiah Brightbourne built the house in 1685. One hundred years later Crispus Brightbourne extended it to add the library, the dining room, the new kitchens, the ballroom. Crispus was a Brightbourne through and through—brim-full of dreams and visions, no attachment to any sense of reality. He ran desperately over budget and creditors were pressing. He decided to stake house and estate on a cut of the cards. One cut, high card wins. One cut with each of his creditors. How eighteenth century. A week before the cut, Crispus had a moment of clarity when he realised the odds. Fifty-fifty, heads or tails. Seven cuts . . . He wandered the house, unable to sleep, haunted by what he had done. The night before the wager, he was sitting in the ballroom delirious with exhaustion when he saw a glow light up the room. At first he thought it was the dawn. By the clock it would not be bright for hours yet. Outside on what is now the UFO Terrace was a brilliant golden light. Then he saw that the light was a boy about ten years old, shining like the sun. The boy opened the window and stepped into the room. Crispus couldn't move from the chair. He wasn't scared—the apparition was too strange and marvellous. This was no ghost. This was a visitation. The radiant child stood in front of him, smiled and touched his hand. Crispus felt peace and well-being he had never known before. All fear and dread vanished. Then the apparition turned and walked through the fireplace.

'The next day the parties to the wager arrived. A card table was set up in the ballroom. The rector and the local magistrate were witness. Each checked the deck, shuffled, and set it on the table. In each case the creditor cut first. Then Crispus cut the cards—once, twice, three times. Each time he won. Four times, five times, six times. Crispus won every time. The seventh cut. His creditor drew a King. Surely luck must desert Crispus Brightbourne now. He cut: the Ace of Hearts. And by the agreed rules, aces counted high. Seven times Crispus Brightbourne gambled and seven times he won. The account is in the Lissan parish archive and the Tyrone County Library. He saved Brightbourne. Within the year Crispus had left Ireland. Strange accidents befell the house. The ignorant said it was the envy of the devil against those who would try to claim his luck. Nonsense. Crispus Brightbourne was touched by the Brilliant Boy. He doesn't manifest to every generation. To those he does, the Brilliant Boy is a sign that luck will always be on their side. We call it the Grace.'

'Amon said he led a charmed life,' Raisa says. Out in the drive, a decision has been reached. Lorien and Lisi head to the stable-yard, Auberon hails the dog-walker and strides out to meet her, Amon passes under the great porch without seeing Raisa above him.

'It's true. Those visited by the Grace—always first born, always male—are blessed. They will always land on their feet. But there is a price.' Lorien and Lisi return with a wheelbarrow and begin to fill the pothole. It swallows a lot of gravel. 'I married a Brightbourne.' Morwenna refreshes Raisa's teacup from her tartan flask. 'Hadley was everything Amon is, and more: energetic, romantic, brilliant, mercurial. I loved him. How could I not? The Grace seduced me. And because of the Grace I live here now in Brightbourne and Hadley is in Berlin, and Barcelona, and Goa, and Stockholm. Always far from his home and his people. They have to leave, you see. The house can't withstand them. Look at Lorien filling that hole there. It appeared overnight. A piece of the guttering fell off two days ago. The day Amon arrived five slates slipped from the west roof. There will be other slates. Bigger holes. Larger bits of gutter. Amon understands the rules. The house can tolerate him for a month, maybe six, seven weeks, then he must leave. He's been here a week and look what's happened.'

'It's an old house,' Raisa protests. 'Bits fall off.'

Lisi and Lorien tramp down the gravel and wheel their barrow back to the ruined stable-yard.

'Oh, how can you be so obtuse?' Morwenna exclaims. 'It's not the stupid house. It's you. It's everyone. The Grace has a price, and the price is the happiness of everyone around him. Bad things happen to them so good things happen to him. They're luck vampires. And it will be you. If you stay with Amon, he will destroy everything you know and everyone you love. Every relationship will disintegrate, every happiness will turn sour, every hope will be ground to dust. And in the end, he will destroy you. And he will bounce along through it like a balloon filled with light and love and grace, and your life will be ash.'

'Bull. Shit!' Raisa yells. Starlings rise from Brightbourne's uneven roof. 'Bullshit! You don't want me around your precious son.'

'And that's what I said to Hadley's mother.' Morwenna tops up her tea. 'In this same place. A whole life ago. She was jealous. She had made it up. We were different. Love would conquer. I would be the exception. I wasn't. I raised Amon and Lorien in this fucking house alone. Maybe three times a year Hadley swans in from fuck knows where and I am so happy, so stupidly happy to see him. I love him. It's such a terrible trap. So I have to ask you: Do you love him?'

Raisa surges from her chair, paces the low-walled rink of the porch.

'This is such shit!'

'You haven't answered the question. Do you love him?'

'I fucked him!' Raisa shouts. 'Ain't that what Lisi told you? I fucked your golden son.'

'Yes, but do you love him?'

Raisa sees the flocking of birds, the shiver of turning leaves, the evolutions of clouds, the parade of shadows across the hill. No charm, no oracle, no advice.

'No,' she lies.

'Then it's easy,' Morwenna says and Raisa knows that she sees the lie. 'Get in your car and drive away and don't ever look back. Forget about us and our little tragedy.'

'But Amon . . .' Almost she says what is in her heart.

'Amon is Graced. Amon will always fall on his feet. Amon has a charmed life.'

Raisa turns on Morwenna. She should rage, she should curse and damn, she should scorch the trees to the ground with her hurt. But this is a middle-aged woman in a folding chair and rage is futile. A house destroyed, a people dispossessed and the Music silenced. Raisa has seen her future with Amon Brightbourne.

'Fuck you. All of you.'

Morwenna calls as Raisa steps through the open window onto the Infanta Staircase.

'One favour.'

'Why should I?' She stops, hands on the paint-peeling frame.

'Don't tell him. He doesn't know about the Price.'

Raisa turns.

'You are the worst people.'

'Hadley and I, we understood the Grace and the Price. We agreed that, if the Brilliant Boy came, Amon would know about the Grace, but not the Price. How could he live, knowing the Price?'

'I saw your house in ruins,' Raisa says. 'I saw it burned down to the ground.'

Then she steps through the window into the dark house. On his balcony the Brilliant Boy seems to stand proud from his painting, hovering in his halo.

Raisa flings the bag onto the bed.

'Pack. Two minutes.'

Lisi's room—the Aubade Bedroom—is in the south-easternmost corner of the house, furthest from the ebbs and surges of the Music, fullest of the dawn light. Lisi is the most leaden of wakers. At Brightbourne she seems solar powered, driven out from her duvet to explore dew-heavy lawns, the gently transpiring woods, the cacophonous dawn chorus. She has strolled, chatting incessantly, with the dawn dog-walkers, briefed Morwenna in the kitchen over coffee on her kynnd's sex-life, filled in a hole in the drive and dressed in a Vivienne Westwood from the trunk at the foot of her bed. Which Raisa now notices.

'Get that shit off you.'

'No.'

'Okay, keep it on. We'll send it back when we get home.'

'Home?'

'We're leaving.'

'No.'

'We are.'

'I'm not packing.'

'Right then.' Raisa finds a supermarket bag and stuffs it with Lisi's things so full it rips.

'I'm not finished here.' Lisi folds her arms and parks defiantly, solidly, on the broad Georgian floorboards. 'Auberon wants to show me the reso-nators, and Lorien knows where the badgers are and I still haven't seen the fireflies.'

'I ain't got time for this.'

'Me neither. I'm staying.'

Some children tantrum, some sulk like lead, some complain. Lisi's gift is immovability. When her mind is set, her will creates its own gravity field. Lisi is a black hole.

'Well I'm going.'

'You go.'

'I'm not coming back for you.'

'Don't need you. I can make my own way.'

'See you.'

'If you see me.'

Raisa turns, flips up the cowl of the cropped hoodie to hide her tears.

'Might live here,' Lisi calls from the bright window and Raisa looks back from the car to see her limned by the sun, a brilliant child.

Hood up, she drives the dreadful Volvo full tilt up the drive, rejoicing-cursing every jolt and crack, bang and lurch. Don't look back. Never look back. If she looks back she will see them standing over the house vast and silent as clouds. She's never seen them before, doesn't believe in them, and she knows that this is a moment of holy manifestation, as she also knows she will see him standing beneath them, smaller than a tick and if she sees him she will only imagine his face and she could not bear that, because he would not understand, for now she knows with the sincerity of stone that everything Morwenna told her is true and that this, a family sundered, a heart broken, an innocence betrayed, is the Price.

VONLAND

26

The great migration has travelled for four generations. Voyagers arrive from the sky onto headlands and coves and mountains. In old-growth forests they breed. Die. Send their children back to the sky: onward. Even they will not see the final destination. That lies two generations and millions of deaths ahead.

Vanessa cardui found on every continent except South America and Antarctica. The European painted lady butterfly migrates fourteen thousand kilometres from tropical Africa to the Arctic Circle. North by north-west, generation by generation. Up to a billion may take wing at once. The butterfly clouds are sometimes so large they appear on flight radars.

Atmospheric state of the North Atlantic, early October 2011, in the morning of the Anthropocene. Turned strange by shifting climate patterns, the hulk of Hurricane Ophelia lurches east by south-east. Storm warnings from Finisterre to Brest. The rotting storm draws lesser winds to it, whipping them into yelping frenzy. Cold, fast air sucked in across Belarus and the Baltic strikes central Scandinavia like a fist, snatches up two hundred and fifty million painted lady butterflies in early migration and slings them across the Norwegian Sea. A storm of butterflies bears down on Iceland.

Rain has beaten Vonland for two days. In the afternoon of the third day the wind strengthens, whipping the steam plumes from the power plant horizontal, rattling the polytunnels, but Vonland is lashed fast as a deep-ocean schooner. With nightfall the rain pauses. The wind shifts. The weight of sky is prodigious. Vonland hunkers under turf and stone, corrugated iron and plastic and waits. Gusts snap at loose tiles and frayed polythene, shriek in the power lines. The geothermal plant pipes a demon lament.

The storm raises its fist. The updraught sweeps a quarter of a billion painted ladies ten kilometres high and flash-freezes them. Storm fronts rear and surge. Butterflies drop and rise, again and again, each time adding a fresh layer of ice to their wings. The weight becomes too much for even a force-ten gale. The storm dumps a quarter of a billion ice-butterflies on southern Iceland.

Raisa stretches on her air mattress. The air is polytunnel tropical, the grow-lamps tuned to full-spectrum and she basks naked in the warmth and simulated sunlight. On each side the cannabis stands high as an elephant's eye. Every breath shines with THC. Squall sleet makes a drum from the curved plastic. Raisa loves being inside the storm yet sheltered from it. This plastic tunnel is not so far from her vagrant bash under the lightning oak of Epping Forest. A fist of wind booms and bellies the sheeting.

Her comfort is an illusion. The next blow could send the roof flapping away to the ice of Mýrdal. I need an hour under the lights, Raisa insisted as she stepped out from under the turf eaves, hood pulled tight against the steepening rain. Every day. Since arriving in Vonland she has been tired, nauseous, unable to concentrate, her skin maddeningly itchy and her face freckled with a dark mask of pigmentation: the ills of light-deprivation. Vitamin D, lovely, Tante Jebet said to Raisa. Our skins don't work properly in this pale place. Vitamin D and synthetic sunlight.

Rataplan of rain now. Raisa shivers. The gusts are stronger, more chaotic. The polytunnel booms. Raisa sits up. She heard a distinct crack. A wing of torn polythene flaps in the wind, large enough for storm-fingers to grasp and tear.

A thing from the storm lies on the ground.

Raisa pulls on Ugg boots and investigates.

A butterfly in a pool of water.

She looks up. Rain spatters her face. Wind reaches in, scrubs skin with cold. The triangle of loose plastic tears ten centimetres further.

'Fuck,' Raisa whispers.

She scoops up her coat—quilted, high-collared, ankle-length—and wraps it tight. One hand holds the coat closed against the storm, the other wrestles the door shut behind her. Wind is the hardest tenant to evict. She slips, slides across the sodden grass towards the frown of the house's low eaves. She is a wick of warm brown skin in the howling dark. She throws back her head to roar at the storm. Her coat flaps in the gale, her head swims, her balance reels. The wind would spill her, roll her like a rag ball.

The itching. The nausea. The sudden freckles around her eyes. The feeling that she is insulated from reality inside a dozen quilt-coats, that she can't wake up. She understands them all.

It's not seasonal affective disorder.

The sky opens and drops a quarter of a billion butterflies on Raisa Peri Antares Hopeland.

Tante Jebet sits on the right side of the stove, Tante Hulda on the left. The stove is purely cosmetic; the house is heated by volcano but stove is home and seats on either side are as set and immutable as geology. Tante Hulda faces the kitchen, Tante Jebet the door. So it is Tante Jebet who calls out 'Better my love?' as the wind shoves Raisa through the porch door with one eddy and with the next sucks it shut behind her.

'How are the tunnels?' Tante Hulda asks as Raisa storms past to her room in a squeak of synthetic soles. 'Did you leave the lights up full?'

Raisa whirls.

'Yes. I left the fucking lights up full. Yes. There is a rip in the fucking roof and it'll be up on the glacier by morning. And yes. I'm fucking pregnant.'

27

THE STORMTALKER'S TALE OR HOW RAISA PERI ANTARES HOPELAND CAME TO VONLAND

She drove that Volvo as if it were fuelled by demons. Whipped it, beat it, cursed it. Steered it into every bump and pothole. At the end of the drive she skidded to a heavy stop, sending up berms of gravel. Right was the way back into the world that, twenty days ago, had been clear and brightly lit. Hopeful, loud, crowded. Long before she called down into Meard Mews for the skinny kid in tweeds to lend her his phone, the Grace was blessing Amon, steering him into the stellagraphy of her family, breaking her world apart atom by atom.

Hopeland goes on forever.

She turned left.

When she looked in the mirror, she could not see the gates. The trees, the demesne wall were unbroken. Brightbourne was closed to her. She would never be able to find it again, until someone opened the way.

The leftward road led up the eastern side of Broighter Glen. Already clouds were gathering. The land beyond Slieve Gallion opened onto high bog sepia in September rain. Raisa chose every westward turn. She realised she had crossed an international border only when she found petrol priced in a different currency. They took her English notes anyway.

On the porch of a rural bar where she stopped for a pee and a bag of Tayto, she smelled ocean. Iodine and ozone and the vast, gathering strength across a three-thousand-kilometre fetch. The water-road might lead where the earth-road could not.

Graceland was still in the cassette player. She pushed it in, waited for the Soweto guitars and drove the Volvo to the edge of the island.

A convoy of refrigerator trucks indicated a town of note. The way turned at the head of the sea-lough and she saw masts. She passed utilitarian packing plants, stark shipping warehouses. Diesel and fish in the air vents but ocean underscored everything. Strong deep-water trawlers in reds and whites, occasional blues. Never greens. Sea is blue and earth is green. It is dangerous to scorn the demesnes. Raisa pulled up in the sea-front car park and walked out to the boats.

Ocean Harvest.

Pelagic North Star.

Norfish Orion.

Pleiades.

Los Ascending.

That last was no constellation marked on any star-chart.

Raisa slipped between the lobster creels, over the hawsers and around the bollards, through the bales of ripped netting and past the beeping, reversing forklifts stacked high with fish crates to find a better angle on the boat. A blink of blinding light from the bridge: a tiny mirror hung from the radio handset, turning in a draught. Fishers in shabby hoodies and waterproof trousers worked at whatever employs trawler-kynnd in port. Raisa skipped from ship to ship, stepping over the water to *Los Ascending.* The fishers stared long, hard, cold at her. She took the yata from the pocket of her gilet. The spinning mirror sent Killybegs' afternoon light across the deck. The captain appeared on the flying bridge.

'It's customary to ask permission to come aboard.'

Raisa flushed hot in embarrassment.

'Permission to come aboard Captain.'

Her yata flashed light into the captain's eyes. He was a berg of a man, north-bitten, massive enough to command his own weather.

'Put that thing away. I am Jónþór Jónsson Saiph Hopeland. Who are you?

'I am Raisa Peri Antares Hopeland.'

'Why are you on my ship, Raisa Peri Antares?'

'I want to go with you.'

'Do you know where we're going?'

'Where are you going?'

'Vestmannaeyjabær. Do you know where that is, Raisa Peri Antares?'

'I don't,' Raisa said. 'There's kynnd there.'

Captain Jónþór Jónsson Saiph smiled.

'You have a passport? And money? I am not free, even for kynnd.'

'I have a passport.' She'd imagined she needed a passport to get into Ireland. She didn't, but she had it. 'Don't have money.'

'Get money. We sail at six.'

The teenager crewing Donnelly Motors' car lot gave her three hundred euros for the Volvo, though it was not hers to sell. Volvos were popular with vets and farmers. You could get two beasts in the back.

She ejected *Graceland* and slipped it into her bag.

She spread her notes before Captain Jónþór, who took one hundred and returned the rest.

'Iceland is expensive.' The engines fired.

'Iceland,' Raisa said.

Los Ascending drove out of Killybegs' harbour, crossed the narrow bar into Donegal Bay. Sickness came with deep blue water. Raisa moaned and rolled on her mattress in the corner of the crew cabin. She had been instructed not to get in the way, not to bother anyone, to speak only when spoken to and never, except by captain's permission, to come to the bridge. Seasickness made that easy to obey. The crew brought her Dramamine, Benadryl, Marizine and scalding green tea. She took the lot together and spent eighteen hours gaping in wonder at the paint blisters in the ceiling and imagining them the citadels of a fantastical space empire, casting herself first as a star princess, then a rebel fighter, then both simultaneously. The comedown was savage but her sea legs were firm enough to take her on deck.

Here she met Ocean. Ocean overwhelmed her. Ocean admitted no equals. It rejected Raisa's questions. It was pure surface. It had no sound, no music. Its colours it took from the sky: gun-barrel grey, flecked with white. It had no shape except the constraint of gravity and the whip of the winds across its surface. *Los Ascending* rode northward on train after train of sharp, white-capped waves. Raisa crossed the pitching deck, steadied herself on the rail. She wanted to look beneath that perfect surface. Ocean did not permit that. She felt the depths, the strata of water darkening until the last photon of sunlight was swallowed. She had watched the horror movies that were deep-ocean nature documentaries. Nightmares haunted the dark, stalking, waiting, luring. Whale-corpses sank to the abyssal plain and fed squirming ecologies of maw-worms and death-prawns. Down there, beneath her feet. She knew you were not any more drowned in a thousand metres of water than in one. Yet she dreaded the deep. She feared the loneliness, a solitary soul sinking like a whale to the basement of the planet. A sea-going kynnd once told her it could take up to forty-five minutes to drown. A long time to spend staring at the dwindling light. Ocean made her, this boat, any ship, an atom. Ocean was not majestic, not awesome. Those were human conceits. There was nothing human about

Ocean. It was neither oppressive nor generous, hostile nor quixotic. It was chemistry, pure and blind.

She crossed the deck to look to windward. Clouds piled layer on layer driven by rising winds into a black wall. *Los Ascending* ran before a storm. Captain Jónþór had lingered too long on the A Coruña Seamount hunting shy hake for the markets of Vigo. A trinity of unravelling hurricanes was arcing across the western approaches and he knew well the name of that part of Galicia: Costa da Morte. If he ran far and fast he could make port before the storms merged and closed the north-east Atlantic. Far and fast burn fuel. Killybegs was the last depot before the volcanoes of home. One stop, three hours. And Raisa found the one ship with a yata in its window.

An hour after dark, three hundred kilometres north-west over the Anton Dohrn Seamount, the storm broke upon *Los Ascending*. It took the ship up, shook it like a dog with a rat and threw it far across the Rockall Bank. Raisa careened from one side of the cabin to the other. The crew caught her, steered her back to her berth. She clung to her mattress, eyes wide with fear. Nothing held firm. The universe was broken into whirling tossing shards. She was too terrified to vomit. Here was death. Here was a window smashing, a hatch tearing loose, water flooding in, filling up this steel box. Here was electrocution as a generator shorted out and the ship went live. Here was a metal ship sinking stern-down at fifty kilometres per hour. Here were her hands, her face pressed against the glass, staring at the dying light.

The hull boomed, every stanchion and hawser and mast shrieked. Then lightning lit up the cabin.

'Shit,' a crew member in hi-viz orange said. A steel boat on an open sea; the radio masts on her gallows the highest point for five hundred kilometres. Thunder, louder than the slam of hull into the wave-hollow.

Raisa looked.

'Five kilometres,' she said. The windows lit blue-white again. The following thunder split the sky, louder, closer. 'Get me out there.'

The crew stared.

'I need to talk to it.'

Lightning, with thunder almost on top of it.

'Two kilometres,' Raisa said. *Los Ascending* hung on the edge of the wave trough. An Icelandic fish-processor swung down from her bunk to her locker and threw Raisa a pair of waterproof dungarees.

'Haven't time,' Raisa said.

'You will freeze.'

Another crew-member threw her his waterproof. A big Ivorian crew-man pulled on his own jacket and snapped a lifeline to Raisa's waist.

'I will go with you.'

The Icelander clipped her own lifeline to Raisa's belt.

'Talk to it.'

A yellow hard hat was clapped on her head. It took four people to open the hatch. The wind slammed it back against the bulkhead. Raisa leaned forward into tearing wind, searing rain. Lightning froze a nightmare sea. Waves stood taller than the gallows. The working deck surged with foaming sea-wash, the gunwales pouring. Storm water threatened the high lip of the cabin hatch with flood, then *Los Ascending* pitched bow-up into the next roller and the water sheeted back across the deck. Rain blinded Raisa. She staggered into the wind. Her crew kept tight hold of the lines. Each aerial and mast blazed with St Elmo's fire. Lightning dead astern. Thunder a breath behind. Raisa's safety lines almost tugged her off her feet as the crew braced. She closed her fists. Fear the wind, fear the mountainous waves, fear the seaworthiness of Icelandic stern trawler construction, fear the sea-keeping of *Los Ascending*'s engineer, fear the sea-wisdom of Captain Jónþór, maybe. Fear the lightning? Never.

Raisa raised her fists, shoulder wide, shoulder high. *Los Ascending* crested the wave, surfed a moment. As the ship pitched Raisa brought her fists together. The lightning without touched the lightning within. Raisa shivered. Her belly tightened. She found a word on her lips and spoke it.

'Pull me in!' she yelled. Her two storm-wardens dragged her backwards through the hatch. The entire cabin rushed to dog it tight before the tsunami of water breaking over the rear of the ship inundated them.

'What did you do?' Icelander asked.

'I spoke its name.' In the ions in her blood, in brain fluid polarised to the charged sky, she had heard the lightning's name and called it. The lightning answered. The coffee mugs safe behind their rails threw unnatural stark shadows onto the kitchen cupboards. Silence in the cabin. Everyone counted heartbeats.

'Three kilometres,' Ivorian said.

'Is it . . .' someone started and was silenced by the rest of the crew. Again the lightning and the thunder.

'Five kilometres,' Raisa said. No one spoke until the next thunder. Seven

kilometres. No mistake. The supernumerary had sent the lightning howling back into the open ocean.

'Stormtalker,' Icelander said. The crew mumbled it. They understood
the power of names.

With dawn the gales cleared and *Los Ascending* drove north beneath a
sky of such intense infinite blue it refuted the possibility of clouds. Under
the noon sun Captain Jónþór turned his ship under the shoulder of Eldfell
into the narrow harbour.

Captain and crew lined up on the working deck to shake Raisa's hand
as she shouldered her meagre kit and steadied her land-legs. Icelander gave
her an envelope of notes.

'It's an expensive island,' Ivorian said.

Captain Jónþór had a note with a name and a road intersection.

'You'll know it,' he said.

Raisa started towards the customs post, then turned back. She held up her
phone for all to see, then lobbed it into the dark water between ship and berth
with a showbiz heel-flick. The crew applauded. Then she sprinted around
the harbour to the ferry terminal, euphoric on new steps in a new land.

As Captain Jónþór said, she knew the place when she saw it. Spirits of
steam from a hidden valley. Above, moss, grass, stone. That goldening in
the low sun was a glacier. The bus driver advised her to move. Vonland was
deceptive, always further than you thought and the weather was turning.
Raisa could smell it as the bus drove off east; air drawn in from the ocean,
a heavy cyclonic warmth, rich with moisture.

It was further. Each bend of the track across the toes of a volcano turned
onto another, each ridge hid a higher one behind it. The sky had closed and
it was raining hard by the time she came to the valley of the steam plumes.
Not geysers, as Raisa had imagined. Not dragons. White steam whistled
and fluted from the stainless-steel flues of a geothermal power plant. The
air hissed, stiff with sulphur. A rosette of polytunnels glowed pink in the
raindark. Steep turf roofs covered sturdy A-frames standing side by side like
a card-house, stone lean-tos low and gruff as Bronze Age barrows, eye-blink
dormers. A wooden cross atop a gable end: a church here.

'Hello!' Raisa hailed. No answer, no movement. No human sign. The
rain was punishing now. Raisa pulled her thin windcheater around her and
went calling among the constructions.

'Hello?' She opened a polytunnel door and reeled, then grinned at the whack of THC. The turf-roofed church held further wonders. From the door she saw tall, narrow planes of light, turning in stone-scented gloom. Her eyes grew dark-wise and she saw that the phasing planes of light were mirrors, each taller than Raisa, suspended from the church's roof beams and turning in subtle, directed draughts. Yatas. Raisa glimpsed herself in the slow-moving mirrors; herself and herself and herself. Infinite Raisas.

Sudden light blinded her. She saw two silhouettes in the doorway, one tall and wide in a loose robe, head wrapped in folds of fabric, the other small and wiry in close-fitting garb.

'Hello?' A woman's voice. English-speaking, Swahili-accented.

'Oh, hello. I just came in.'

Silence.

'I'm Raisa Peri Antares.' She fumbled for her yata. The Emanations that didn't exist had not failed her yet. 'Hopeland.'

'Hopeland,' said the larger woman.

'Hopeland,' said the smaller figure. A woman's voice, Icelandic-accented. The two figures turned to each other. An unspoken communication passed between them. They turned back to Raisa.

'Welcome to Vonland, kynnd.'

28

The roads reopen in the morning and Tante Jebet and Tante Hulda prepare
The Vehicle to take Raisa to Dr. Rósný in Vík, twenty kilometres away. The
Vehicle is an outsized cab bolted to a truck bed welded to an oversized all-
terrain six-wheel chassis powered by a massive battery bank in its belly. Tante
Hulda built The Vehicle as she built the geothermal plant that powers it
and the polytunnels that sustain Vonland. In her short time since her storm-
bird crash landing into Vonland, Raisa has pieced together the story of this
volcano-powered skunk oasis and its chatelaines. Hulda was a geothermal
engineer consultant on a borehole in Kenya's Rift Valley. Jebet was a teacher
and part-time preacher in Eburru primary school. They met; geysers erupted.
When Hulda's work was done and steam whistled from a calliope of new
piping, Jebet went back with her to a land where their love would not offend.
Jebet missed the children, missed the teaching, missed the preaching, missed
the light most of all, but received from Hulda a family, a nation, a name,
a star, new gods and a hidden place in a hot-water valley at the foot of the
Mýrdalsjökull ice cap. They have been together for twelve years and their rituals, their formalisms of speech and conduct, their firm-set customs remind
Raisa of her Spitalfields neighbours Gilbert and George.

The two Tantes insist Raisa ride in The Vehicle's rear seat. Hulda drives
grim-faced with concentration, cajoling her contraption around boulders
washed out by the storm, through flood streams. Suspension is agricultural;
Raisa jolts so hard on the track out of the valley she fears her pregnancy
may not make it to the highway. Tante Jebet rides serene in the passenger
seat. She is a tall woman of the Kalenjin, with strong cheekbones and a
high forehead. Raisa has never seen her in anything other than full-length
white dresses that supernaturally resist grass and mud. Vonland is generous
with both. Hulda curses her cranky vehicle down the flooded track. Jebet
radiates nobility.

On the road Hulda opens up the engines. Best speed is sixty kilometres
per hour. Raisa rolls her eyes (unseen), sighs (unregarded) and slumps back
in the seat (uncomfortable). Seeing her bag, she remembers her farewell to
the last family car she travelled in and fishes out *Graceland*.

'Got a cassette player in this thing?'

'Radio only,' Hulda says and flicks it to a spoken-word station. Other road-users raise a finger from the steering wheel in the universal greeting of the rural highway. Tante Jebet waves like royalty. The Vehicle is down to ten kilometres per hour by the time they top the pass to Vík, a small, smart town sheltering in an amphitheatre of sheer cliffs from the Atlantic. Low cloud smothers the cliff tops, lending the town the aspect of a model in a box. A prim tin church on higher ground reinforces the quaint. The clinic stands lower on the same rise, The Vehicle slows to a crawl on the climb.

'I'd be quicker walking,' Raisa says. The Tantes will have none of it.

The Vehicle labours into the car park on the last few electrons. Jebet enters the clinic like a Solomonic Queen, Hulda scurries in with an extension cable. The Vehicle can charge off any domestic supply.

'How long will it take?' Raisa asks.

'Nine months,' Jebet says with surprise.

'The car,' Raisa says.

'About the same,' the clinic receptionist says.

Longer than the wait to get Raisa processed and accommodated into Dr. Rósný's practice. Longer than the wait for Dr. Rósný to wedge Raisa into her appointment diary. Longer than the urine tests, the blood tests, the samples and the results. Longer than it takes Raisa to agree to a pregnancy plan, leave contact details and read the English-language leaflets.

Raisa goes to the coffee machine. Hulda holds up the leaflet *So: You're Pregnant!*

'What does it say?'

'No coffee, it says,' says Tante Jebet.

'It doesn't say that,' Raisa says.

'Alcohol, drugs, stimulants,' Tante Jebet says. 'And what is coffee?'

'We will prepare you a special vitamin mix,' Tante Hulda says.

Raisa clumps back to her seat to sulk. Pregnancy so far has been a massive turd. The light on the charger remains stubbornly red.

Longer than an autumn day in South Iceland. Longer than it takes for all the patients to arrive, be seen and leave. Dr. Rósný pulls on her hat and coat, makes her farewells and still The Vehicle isn't charged.

'I have to close up,' the receptionist says. Hulda and the receptionist talk long and low in Icelandic. Raisa does not understand the words but the voices are serious. Both parties break off satisfied. Wonder: the charge light is green.

Heating, lights, top speed: Pick any two. The Vehicle's batteries can't sustain all three. It takes an hour to rattle back through the dark to the turn to Vonland. Raisa holds her breath. She can only tell where she is going by the small surges and retardations, the micro-accelerations of her body as Hulda negotiates the track. The night is so intense she can smell it. Then she hears the song of the geo-plant, and the glowing rosette of Vonland comes into view.

'It's the skunk,' she says. 'What you were talking about with the receptionist. Isn't it? Buds or resin or what.'

'Oil, lovely,' Tante Jebet says.

'We grow pharmaceutical-grade cannabis for export. Some things need cannabis,' Tante Hulda says as she brings The Vehicle in to the door. 'It is illegal in Iceland.'

'Health care is not cheap,' Tante Jebet says. The Vehicle pulls up in front of the porch. Lights flicker on. 'Now hurry inside, lovely, for the night is dark and we must have soup.'

29

THE MAN WHO LOVED BOOKS

A kynnd once blew through the Dorling Avenue house: a man who was a great writer, a greater reader but the greatest book-lover. His way with books was this: he would recognise the imaginative, the wide-eyed, the divinely discontent, the horizon-watcher and then target them with precision-guided books. *Norse Mythology* on the toilet cistern. *As I Walked Out One Midsummer Morning* on a chair under the awning. *Emma* by the coffee machine. For imaginative, wide-eyed, discontent, horizon-watcher Raisa, *Finn Family Moomintroll* on a stand where umbrellas and outdoor shoes were kept.

This Finn Family, with all its complexity, diversity, openness and generosity, was their family. They hissed at Moomintroll for his pomposity, cheered Moominmamma for her resourcefulness, berated the Snork Maiden for her girliness, yelled in ecstasy at Little My's fierceness, were silent with wonder at Snufkin the super-tramp for his pilgrim soul. They loved the parties in the deep woods, the dress code of Hemulens, the hibernation through hateful times. *Moominland Midwinter* appeared on the shelf by their personal breakfast cereal and they loved more the idea of waking up from hibernation and finding another world inside your house, one that you never knew existed. They shook with horror as the comet threatened the creatures of Moomin Valley, then turned away for the depths of space at the last moment. They voyaged with Moominpappa and the endless journey of the Hattifatteners, set sail with the flood-theatre of *Moominsummer Madness*. Then *Moominvalley in November* arrived on the landing windowsill next to their bedroom that overlooked the paradise garden. Here was the melancholy—they did not know it as such, then, but enjoyed the sweet sadness they could not explain—but where was the hope? Where was the Moominhouse, with its porches and miradors and balconies, the arched bridge over the river, the blue pear tree? Where were the Moomins? Everything was decaying, ending. There were no more books. At age nine Raisa ran hard into finality. Nothing went on forever. Not Moomins, not books. Not people. Not them.

Moominvalley in November killed the reader in Raisa Peri Antares Hopeland. She never trusted books again.

30

This house, this Vonland, is the Moominhouse. Her room is a wood-panelled cabin, boards smooth and imbued with perfumes of smoke and time. Her bed is a closet. When she climbs into it, it feels as adventurous and secure as a sleigh. The high sides will hold her come storm or eruption. The doors are painted with flowers, and morning light falls in dusty planes through the gaps between the planks. When she sits up after riding through the night in her dream-sleigh and throws open the shutters, she can see through her small gable window clear to the edge of the ice.

This morning Raisa wakes far before the light. She dresses quick and warm. Layers. Light, wickable. Hiking leggings with side-pockets for maps and tech. One backpack, small. She knows the house well enough to equip herself without lights or noise. The outdoor boots Tante Hulda bought her. A stick. Already she has trebled the weight on her back. A hat. Her hand hovers over the Mongolian herder's hat. Fur and flaps and fabulousness. Sense opts for the beanie, though it kills her hair.

She hesitates over a note. A swift deep breath and the words are down on the To Do Today pad. The front door cannot be closed without a boom of doom so she rests latch against strike-plate and steps away.

The fore-dawn air is clean and fresh as meltwater. Raisa sparkles to the touch of mountain cold, exhilarated to be abroad and purposeful before the sun. Her face glows. The eastern sky promises a clear, bright day. She finds tones, harmonics, patterns in the geothermal plant's chorus.

The polytunnels shine both night and day and by their light she navigates to the track. She plants her hiking pole firmly in the dirt. Where to go? She might follow the flown polytunnel sheeting up to the volcano. Be blown by the memory of wind. That flight leads to high ice and she is not ice-ready. She sets up the track still rilling and runnelling as the hills drain. She looks back from the first turn, the one from which she first saw Vonland, then steps away from the track, away from Vonland.

After the exertions (mental, physical, emotional, spatial) of the expedition to Vík, Tante Hulda and Tante Jebet rise so late and so overdue for their coffee ritual, then breakfast ritual, then second coffee ritual, then the exciting planning for a baby a baby a baby, that it's eleven thirty before they find Raisa's note.

> THIS IS DOING MY HEAD IN. GOT TO GET CLEAR.
> I'LL BE ALL RIGHT.

Raisa follows the sun path, keeping its warmth to widdershins. She follows sheep tracks out of Vonland, skirting the western ridge and crossing the gravel outwash plain by the bridge. The river runs beneath it swift and grey as doubt. As early as the trail permits she turns inland to the higher country under the breath of the ice. This open terrain thrills, she can see for miles miles miles. Grass and stone, stone and grass. The going is slow and racking. That grass covers fields of stones scattered by old eruptions. Some are as big as small cars, some the size of sheep, most large enough to turn the careless foot, to require a glance down for every step.

Birds stream over her. Populations are in motion, summering flocks returning south; incomers arriving out of the high north. She stops, shields her eyes as a delta of swans whoops over her, wings whistling. Arriving? Departing? Passing through? She crosses a plain of tussock grass at the lower end of a small tarn and geese take wing on every side, necks upstretched. A hosanna of honking. She cowers, covers her head. She crosses the meadow beneath a raucous sky. The geese drift east in flights and squadrons until they are lost to sight and hearing. Abandoned.

With the sun at its highest and southernmost she runs into her first major obstacle: a river sated on storm water. On other—lesser—streams she found crossing places within a few hundred metres and picked her way over, hiking pole thrust firm into the riverbed gravel, stone to stone. The truth she learnt from her time in the woods: look after your feet. Keep them clean, keep nails neat and skin unblemished. Above all, keep them dry. She cannot cross this stream safely, let alone dry-shod. Not here. Upstream the river may be narrower but the spate will be faster and the sides steeper. Downstream the flow will have been joined by other feeders but the bed will be wider and shallower. She turns downstream. Storm-flow has undermined the banks and piled small boulders along the riverbed. No sure footing here. Even the tributaries are a longer jump than she likes. Lips of coarse wet grass overhang the steep sides. As she watches, a chord of stream-bank cracks and slides into the fast-flowing water. The water run pushes her south.

Thirst prompts her to refill her water flask. She had not imagined Iceland in October could be so hot, so sweaty. Must be climate change. Raisa drains the flask, fills it, takes off her hat to pour water over her head. Ten minutes later she stands at the side of the road. A sensitivity on her right heel has become an insistence. Turn left and she can be back at Vonland in an hour. Sooner if there is a bus or a ride. Right will take her on a westward loop around the island until she returns hundreds of kilometres later to this crossing place. Before her the river frays into silver braids on a grey gravel shore. Bronzed spikes of sea-grass, a far platinum ocean. She walks three kilometres of black volcanic sand before she finds a place to ford the river. Her hiking pole probes the shallows. Water laps at her boot seams but they are stoutly sewn and she crosses dry. She finds a low gravel berm to sit and ease off her boot and layers of socks. The sore has stuck to the wool. She dabs the scab with water to loosen it. She grimaces. The blister is a crater of raw pink flesh, gently seeping. She tears away the loose caul of blister-skin and wipes the crusted blood from the rim.

'I'm not going back,' she tells the sore.

She eats a handful of dried cranberries and nuts and is ready for adventure again.

Ten minutes west she comes across the wingless, windowless fuselage of an aeroplane. A figure stands on top of the cockpit, arms outstretched. Photo opportunity. She puts as much distance between them and her as she can. Westward again and she comes to the Skógá. This river she cannot ford and she backtracks three kilometres of black sand to the road bridge. Her heel is a star of red pain now. She strikes inland, on the far side of the river from the tourist road to the falls. As soon as she can she turns onto old packhorse tracks. The sun is in her eyes now and she wishes she had brought a peaked cap rather than a beanie. More than that she wishes she had thought about where she was going to camp for the night. She has three hours of daylight, one of which she will spend making her camp and prepping food, another one in finding a safe location for that camp. She has an hour of westering at best and this land does not promise shelter. Her blister blazes now. Every step is a swear and a grimace and it is sundown by the time she limps to the scarp where the Eyjafjallajökull highland breaks to the coastal plain. Car headlights sweep the highway. She can see clear to the lighthouse at Dyrhólaey. The air is of that breath-taking clarity that promises hypothermic cold. Houses cling to the foot of the scarp. Any of them would open its door to her. They could be on the moon. She can't make the descent in this condition, in this light.

This is not Epping. There is not a KFC within half an hour's walk. There are no friendly doggers in the Honey Lane car park, no Forest Keepers leaving her water and food. If something goes wrong out here she might die. Never be found. Human tibias among the sheep bones. Ribs mingling. Skull bowled about by tiny foxes.

It is imperative she find a camp for the night. It's full dark now, and she doesn't know the terrain.

'Fuck!' she shouts, berating her stupidity. 'Fuck fuck fuck fuck fuck!'

Among the echoes one returns changed. She turns in its direction and 'hello?'s. The call comes back with depth and resonance. A hollow sound. She traces the edge of the hollowing in the rock face by her fingers. She calls again. More than a hollow, a true cave.

Don't bears live in caves?

Stupid. No bears in Iceland. She lights a match anyway. A narrow entrance curves to her left out of the range of her little light. Which burns out. She calls again. The acoustics tell her this cave goes way back. She doesn't need way back. She needs enough room to unroll her mat and bag. The floor of the cave is flat, clean. Almost neat. Swept. People have been here. No sex or drug litter. She wouldn't want to roll onto a syringe in the night. She makes her bed, sits, removes her boots as gently as she can. Rolls back with a yelp of pain. She should go back. Walk out with the dawn, down past the houses to the road, hitch a ride, beg a flight back to London. Train to a train to the station in Wandsworth Common and from there it's a kick through the autumn leaves to Dorling Avenue where the hidden doors will open and she will be received.

She can't outrun what she carries. She doesn't know who the father is. It could be Finn. It could be Amon. And if there is the slightest chance that she might bring the Grace into Dorling Avenue? A beautiful, complex culture torn to pieces and scattered. In the six weeks she has known Amon Brightbourne she has wrecked her kynndship with Finn, lost Lisi to the seduction of the Music and broken the continuity of the Arcmages. It may be too late. She saw Brightbourne fallen.

'What am I going to do?' she shouts.

Light blinds her. A voice speaks. Icelandic. She throws up her arm to shield her eyes. The voice speaks again, in English.

'What are you doing here?'

'Your light, awful bright,' Raisa stammers.

The light weaves and goes to the ground, casting its beam up the wall. A man stands in the cave mouth.

'Why are you here?'

'Don't you come near me!' Raisa shouts. 'Get away from me!' She kicks out with a blood-crusted sock. The man steps nimbly back.

'Please, I will not harm you. This is my land. Why are you here?'

'I needed somewhere to camp.'

'This is a private place,' the man says. 'It is not open to the public.'

'I'm sorry.'

'You can't be here.'

'It got dark . . .'

'This is not for tourists.'

'I'm not a tourist!' she shouts.

The man picks up the torch again and sends the beam to her face.

'You're the new one. From Vonland.'

'I'm Raisa Peri Antares Hopeland.'

'Yes. You came in on Captain Jónþór's boat.'

'You know an awful lot about me.'

'This is gossip season. And you're pregnant.'

'Fuck's sake!'

The man sets the torch down again and crouches to extend a hand.

'I am Tryggvi Oskar Gunnarson.'

She takes the hand.

'You should not be camping out,' Tryggvi Gunnarson says.

'In my condition,' Raisa says. 'Yeah yeah.'

'I have beds. We're a guest-house.'

She's tempted. Like Jesus. Central heating, hot food. A bed the size of a motorway service station.

She has thinking still to do.

'I want to stay here.'

'Really?'

'Please.'

'If you must. Can I get you anything?'

'No.' She's sure she can smell her heel now. 'Well, sort of. Have you got any plasters?'

'At the house yes.'

'Could you, bring them up? Please?'

From kidhood she has worked the big-eyes plead with one hundred per-cent success. Tryggvi Gunnarson sighs and returns twenty minutes later with a box of plasters and a plastic box of pasta bake.

'Has fish,' he says.

'I'm good with fish,' she says and eats with her fingers. The food is warm and has fish and is quite the most magnificent meal she has ever eaten from a plastic box. She is conscious of Tryggvi Gunnarson watching her eat. He is still watching as she tends the blister. The rim of black blood has an inner meniscus of crusty, dried white serum.

'You sleep here, but please be careful. We don't let tourists in for good reasons.'

His light bobs off down between the rocks. Raisa unpeels a plaster and applies it to her blister. Medicated bliss. She plunges into her sleeping bag, pulls the hood tight against the night-haunts and sleeps.

31

(From the Annals of Dicuil, ca. eighth century CE)

Look far, north—north-west
Ocean high and breath is ice.
White the waves and white the mountains.

Brother to seals I am,
The walrus, the sea-duck;
The great whale is cousin to me.

No works of man pollute.
No smoke of fire taints.
This land slips fresh-made from God's hand.

On these green heights
No sheep graze.
The faithful are the flocks and herds.

This forest my cell now.
These leaves my missal.
Starlings shout praise, the sea-duck my bell.

Alone I live, alone I die,
Unseen, unheard, unremembered.
The northern fox will gnaw my naked bones.

The eye of God sees
Bones in the earth,
A stone altar, a forest where no leaves fall.

32

Light wakes her. Dew pearls the sleeping bag. Her breath hangs. Every muscle and joint is wire and rust. The foam mat, so yielding, so accommodating, changed in the night to Torquemada's iron bed. Raisa struggles upright. Low cloud blows in mist-tatters across the cave mouth. There is a flask. It wasn't there last night. Someone was here, watching her sleep. She opens it, sniffs. Coffee. She pours a capful, stares at it. Sets it down. She can't.

She crawls out of the bag. A sour stab in her right heel reminds her: blister. Blood has seeped through the plaster. She peels it off and prepares a fresh application. She'll go nowhere on this foot today. She squats, bounces, trying to pump some warmth and motion into her muscles.

She came to the cave in the dark and so never saw the guardian of this hidden place. Where the cave curves away into the scarp, a trefoil knot of leaves, bound together by a sun-circle, has been incised into the rock. Raisa traces the figure with her fingers. This is Tryggvi Gunnarson's treasure. This stone blessing watched over her sleep. Her eyes adapt and she sees edges of light and shade deeper in the cave. She shuffles forward. Designs cover the walls, the roof. She crouches in her own shadow and cannot see clearly. She takes the matches from the pocket of her hike leggings, makes light. Raisa cries aloud, falls backwards onto her ass.

Trees. Trunks on the walls, branches woven together above her head. A forest in the stone.

Her breath shakes with wonder.

The cave is four metres deep, the floor smooth and free from debris. At the rear of the cave is a small flat rock. On the wall behind it four linked trefoils form a cross. To its left is a rock-cut goblet in partial relief, to the right an oval disc. Above stand three figures, little more than wedges with heads, hands and feet. One carries a smaller wedge marked with a simple cross. The centre figure holds a staff, the head crooked into a coil. She lights another match. Then another, another another until only three remain.

Match-strike. Birds perch in the trees that cover walls and roof, plenteous as fruit, tails merging with the branches in spirals and braids. Between the trunks, animals. It requires a second match for her to work out what they are. Tiny foxes. Those things with the big tusks: walruses. Seals. Arching salmon. Spouting whales.

In the moments it takes the final match to burn down to her numb fingers she sees creation. She puts away questions and suppositions and submerges herself in the presence. She feels this place has been waiting in the dark for her. She did not come here. She was brought. She is washed by holiness. Time has no meaning in the matchless dark until a cramp forces her to change position and catch sight of the light of the world. The mass of the present is ended. She glances back at the forest in the rock. This is not a representation of heaven, not the paradise garden, but this Earth.

The sky clears from the south-west, the low cloud shreds like tattered pennants and whips away. She packs up her camp and within ten steps of the cave mouth finds the track down to the foot of the scarp. Her heel burns but the trail is so easy she does not need her hiking pole. Wet grass soaks through her leggings. The path leads to a sprawling house and barns. Tryggvi Oskar Gunnarson waits at the door.

'Saw you coming a long way,' he says.

She hands him the coffee flask.

'I have questions.'

'Please come in,' says Tryggvi Oskar.

The kitchen is wide and light-filled, painted pale earth tones and sage green. Raisa takes a chair at the long table.

'My wife.'

'Torfey.' She pulls off outdoor boots, hangs hat and coat and takes a seat opposite Raisa. 'You slept up in the cave.' Her English is better than her husband's. She pushes a basket of rolls across the table. 'He won't have fed you. He doesn't understand breakfast. Cup of coffee and he can run all day.'

Raisa falls on the rolls. They are sweet and fragrant. She is shameless. Outdoors hungry.

'Coffee?'

She shakes her head, mouth full of currants and cinnamon.

'I think it's modern nonsense, but it's your baby,' Torfey says.

'Where was I?' Raisa asks.

'Papeyshellir,' Tryggvi says.

'The Cave of the Papars,' Torfey says.

Raisa mimes her confusion.

'Before we came—the Icelanders—there were others,' Torfey says. 'The Papars. Monks.'

'They lived in caves,' Tryggvi says. 'On rocks.'

'What do you call people who live out in the wild alone?' Torfey asks.

Raisa tries several words before finding the right one. 'Hermits?'

Tryggvi and Torfey nod.

'They came from Ireland,' Torfey says. 'They were men who found their god at the edges. Small islands, high cliffs. They sailed up to the Scottish Hebrides, Orkney and Shetland and the Faroes, setting up monasteries.'

'In boats made of leather,' Tryggvi adds. 'Small boats. Six, seven, eight men rowing. They built turf huts, fished, collected birds' eggs. Simple, hard lives.'

'The *Landnámabók* tells us that Irish monks were the first settlers in Iceland. Historians and archaeologists say there is no evidence but of course, with men such as these, evidence will be subtle. They were frugal men who found God not in churches or buildings, but in the living world. They lived light on the earth. They left their names behind. Names are stronger than any building. Pabay, Papa Westray, the Holm of Papay. In the Faroes, Paparokur, Papurshilsur. There are Gaelic tombstones in Skugvoy, and Vestmanna. Our own Vestmannaeyjar means port of the Westman— the Gaels. The *Landnámabók* mentions Papey island as one of the Papars' settlements.'

'Torfey has written a guide,' Tryggvi Oskar says. 'She is a great expert. Not coffee, not tea then?'

'Hot water with lemon in it, please.'

While Tryggvi does that, Torfey fetches a pamphlet and pushes it across the table to Raisa. It is three-folded, home printed, Icelandic.

'The cave has been in Tryggvi's family for five hundred years,' she says. 'It has always been called the Papeyshellir. It has always been the legend that it was the holy place of the hermits in Iceland. In 1980 we called the archaeologists and they spent three months in our back field and at the end they said no no no, this is Norse, clearly Norse. The symbolism, the style. Influenced by the Irish, but eleventh century. The trefoil knot, clearly, is a Hrungnir's Heart! The trees are Yggdrasill, the tree of life. No, they were so busy trying to find meaning they didn't see what was to be seen. It is not a tree symbol; it is the tree itself! And not a tree, but trees. A forest!'

Tryggvi sets down a mug of hot water and lemon. It tastes like wonder-wine to Raisa. The light dims, sudden rain rattles from the roof.

'The Norse found an island of forests,' Torfey says. 'Birch and willow covered the land.' She indicates the grass, now sunlit again and green as riches. 'Us Norse, we cut it down, for building, for fuel, for grazing. Our sheep ate the rest down to the rock and made sure the forest of Iceland would never grow back again. Sheep! Woolly weapons of ecological mass destruction.'

'Torfey hates sheep,' Tryggvi says. 'We are cow people.'

Torfey and Tryggvi Oskar offer Raisa a ride but she limps past the cattle barn to the road to wait for the bus to Vonland. Time enough for Raisa to coax cold humiliation—the runaway who got as far as the next farm—to a small flame of satisfaction. She roved out in the spirit of the wanderer, without destination or intent. Wonder met her. She sits back in the bus seat and is thirteen hundred years away, stepping from a seal-sleek currach onto the black sand, sea-birds rising up before her in a squall of voices. As she hobbles up the track her imagination plants pale trunks and shivering leaves of birches so dense she can see no end to them. She stops at the overlook above Vonland and aches at the kilometres of close-cropped turf. Sheep look up, chewing, ignorant of their guilt.

'You killed it!' Raisa shouts. 'You ate it flat!'

The sheep swivel their relentless jaws.

The Tantes of Vonland take different approaches to the prodigal. Tante Jebet smothers with affection: making food, serving cake, stoking the stove, tending to Raisa's foot, which she catches on the cusp of infection. Kindness and sugar will draw explanation, then contrition.

Tante Hulda keeps a hurt silence that deepens and hardens when fed apologies. She rejects Raisa's offer to help find the polytunnel roof. From the house Raisa watches Hulda and the neighbours from over the ridge set off up country and return three hours later towing polythene sheeting like a captured cloud. She watches them manoeuvre it over the naked ribs and lighting gantries and haul it the length of the growing beds. And she watches the Land Cruiser with LÖGREGLAN on the side lumber over the ridge and draw up in front of the polytunnel-raising. A police officer steps out and tips her cap to the workers. Tante Jebet ventures out through the door like a caravel under full sail. Raisa follows two steps behind. Heel be fucked.

The officer shakes hands.

'Congratulations,' she says to Raisa in English. 'Your first?'

Raisa nods. No Hopeland is ever comfortable in the presence of police. The officer reverts to Icelandic. Tante Jebet interprets.

'This is an official visit. We have to dispose of the crop.'

'The skunk?' Raisa says.

'The crop. Reykjavík knows.'

After the storm the National Energy Authority sent up drones to scout for felled power lines. The operator of a drone circling over Vonland noted the roofless polytunnel and took hi-res pictures. They might be useful for an insurance claim. Then someone spotted what had been growing under that storm-wracked roof. The police at Vík, who have turned a blind eye until now, slowed the passage of the photographs through the investigatory machinery. But the system was in motion.

'We will have to make an official investigation,' the police officer says. 'Make sure we don't find anything.'

She shakes hands again and bids everyone a good day.

Tante Hulda passes Raisa a pair of gardening gloves.

'Wear them. The stems are tough.'

The gloves are Hulda's forgiveness.

That night Raisa stands before the greatest bonfire of her life. Tante Jebet shouts at her to come away that stuff is bad for baby. Raisa thrusts her hands deep in the pouch of her hoodie. Wreathes of wonder blow across her. A vision comes to her. She stands on a high place under a high sun, looking up a valley so dense with trees she cannot see the ground. Steam rises from the leaf canopy. This is not a vision of the past but of the future. Beneath those branches, amid the steam vents, stand the turf roofs and polytunnels of Vonland. A greater Vonland than this, home to hundreds. And the forest is not the birch and willow of the Papars: here are beech and poplar, rowan and alder in the damp places, pine on the slopes. In her vision she follows the tiers of trees up to the heights. The ice: she sees no ice.

To grow a forest around a child as they learn to walk, to name, to see and learn: that is deep faith in a future. A long project. A different Music. The great fire has burned down to the finest, wind-whipped ash. Tante Jebet and Tante Hulda wait, hands folded.

'Right,' says Raisa Peri Antares Hopeland. 'Let's get on with this pregnancy then.'

33

Sunlit days dwindle fast to almighty nights. Weeks are measured in wind and rain. Days reel out in beats: morning nausea, sore joints. Tante Jebet and Tante Hulda set Raisa's breakfast place with supplements and fish oil. She illuminates her skin under the grow lights. Weeding, feeding. Pest control. Toilet calls. Hot water and lemon. Fuck hot water and lemon. Hour ticks of tedium. The same faces, the same words. Three faces staring at each other in the firelight.

The police come back. Two this time, from regional headquarters at Selfoss. They look into each of the polytunnels.

What are you growing here? they ask.

'Salads, chillies, tomatoes,' Tante Hulda says. 'Herbs. Sage, thyme. Parsley. Basil. Tarragon, rosemary. We're pretty self-sufficient here.'

And this one?

Empty raised beds. The plastic roof restretched, patched and lashed hurricane-tight with cable ties.

'I'm going to grow trees here,' Raisa says. 'I want a forest.'

They move to the chapel. The air smells of dust, cold wood and old trapped light. An officer taps a mirror and sets it turning. Subtle harmonics and air currents draw the other mirrors into motion.

'What is this place?'

'We have our own religion,' Tante Jebet says. Planes of pale light drift across her face.

The economy of Vonland has taken a critical hit. Raisa, conscious that she has added two new variables to the economic equations, pores over notebooks at the kitchen table through the long hours of darkness, drawing and planning and scratching out little sums.

'I've an idea,' she announces. She turns the notebook around. The two Tantes pore over it in the firelight.

'If you want to,' Tante Hulda says. Her smile is like a season turning.

'When?' says Tante Jebet. Her smile is like a morning arriving.

'Tomorrow.'

In the morning Raisa takes The Vehicle down to Route 1. She arranges her painstakingly lettered signs for five kilometres each side of the turn and parks up. Vitamin D! Green sunlight! Fresh salad! Peas! She tucks the blanket around her, saving battery power for the radio. The first day the cars, trucks and buses go by from dawn to dusk. The second is filthy rain. Raisa throws polythene sheeting over the vegetables in the truck bed but they are still sopping and stale by the time she makes it back to Vonland. The third morning she rises before light, cutting a fresh crop.

The third day, a car stops.

'Is that radicchio?' the woman asks in English.

'It's radicchio,' Raisa says. 'Try some.' She pares an outer curl of crimson leaf with her harvesting knife. The woman tastes, nods. 'Good and bitter, ain't it?'

'I'm having friends for dinner,' she says. 'Two please.'

'Grill them, then into the oven with Taleggio on the top until it melts,' Raisa says. 'Phenomenal.'

'How much?'

Raisa adds a friends-for-dinner premium.

'That is for nothing.'

'Shop local,' Raisa says. 'Everything is from just over the hill. Picked this morning. Please tell your friends.'

The woman drives away with a box of radicchio, frisée, butterhead lettuce soft and sweet and robust herbs. She tells her friends and next day they make a special trip from Selfoss.

'We liked your radicchio,' he says.

'It's so expensive this time of year,' other he says. They buy four heads and take two cavolo nero.

'This is clean eating,' he says. 'So low carbon.'

'Powered by volcanoes,' Raisa says.

'Do you have any puntarelle?' other he asks.

'I don't. If you want to order, I can grow it and email you when it's ready.'

'If you were on Twitter, then you could let everyone know what's fresh,' he says.

That night Raisa researches puntarelle and finds seeds from an Italian grow-your-own company.

'Gotta spend money to make money,' she says to Tante Jebet, who manages Vonland's finances. 'Gimme the card.' She completes the order and sets up a Twitter account. The next day, under her blanket in the car, she tells the three people who stop for salad veg that she is taking orders. Word passes up and down Route 1. Cars stop. Twitterers follow. Direct messages arrive. Can you get scarola, Hamburg parsley, mizuna? While the puntarelle grows fast and full under the pink lighting, Raisa clears and plants beds in the former skunk tunnel.

Her forest will rise. Not yet. Not this winter.

'Do you know what would be good?' Raisa says on the shortest day of the year. 'Something so I don't have to sit freezing in the car all day.'

Tante Hulda looks up from the fireside with a wild smile. At the dinner table she presents a screenful of designs.

'You take the payments online,' she says. 'They get an unlock code. Simple.' She builds it single-handed in two short days. Raisa tweets to Vonland Veg's followers. The store huddles under a steep-pitched roof and beetle-brow eaves; an elf-house for vegetables. The Vonlanders gather around the laptop to watch Raisa collect the payments through PayPal and send out the code to the lockbox.

'I can automate that,' says Tante Hulda. 'And I'll put in a chiller. You'll need it in the summer.' She buys two kilometres of cable and runs it over the ridge and down the valley to the veg-house where she has already installed two repurposed chiller cabinets from a bankrupt shop.

'We'd get a lot more if we went hydroponic,' Raisa says. Tante Hulda's eyes light again.

Von Veg takes another hefty capital hit to buy racks and cells and piping for the Nutrient Film system but water and power are free and Tante Hulda ships in animal waste from the farm down the valley. In return they ask for a hookup to Vonland's geothermal power plant. Tante Hulda and folk from the farm are out on the hillside every available February day installing cable and phase converters.

Raisa converts polytunnels to hydroponics. Bed by bed she frees growing space in the former skunk-house. Now is the season. Raisa fills the newly vacant beds with tree seedlings. She swallows her cod-liver oil tablet, dials the lighting to full spectrum and slips out of her quilt coat and lies down naked in the future forest of Vonland.

———

While the radicchio and puntarelle, the arugula and Castelfranco, the mizuna and the agretti and the Naga chillies grow in nutrient-rich water, a human grows in the waters of Raisa.

She becomes alien to herself. This constant hunger: What? These swellings and aches: Why? She bickers with her Tantes at a dropped word or a stray look. The dark mask of freckles around her eyes looks permanent. Her mind is decomposing. Long hours in the car watching for potential buyers, hand-fertilising courgette flowers with a paintbrush, she finds herself making up names and futures for her baby.

Malady Malarkey, acrobat and prophet.

The Jug Child. Condemned to a life in a solitary cell, because . . .

Futurismo, Market-Gardener of Mars!

Peabody, Politician, Priest, Profiterole Queen.

Petit Lemo, whose superpower is to turn into a flight of oystercatchers.

She welcomes the appointments at the clinic at Vík like festivals. The Vehicle is needed for the veg trade so she rides the bus. The feeling of escape as it pulls away from the stop calls joyful tears. The ride is never long enough. Passengers try not to stare at the crying pregnant brown woman.

'Do you want to know the sex?' Dr. Rósný asks her after the second scan.

'Why? It's a kid,' Raisa answers. Dr. Rósný introduces Raisa to the Mýrdalshreppur Prenatal Group. They meet on Thursdays in the Community Centre, eighteen women from Hvolsvöllur to Kirkjubæjarklaustur. Midwives and doulas give talks, saleswomen deliver pitches. The women share stories and plans, complain, compete, laugh a lot. There is prenatal yoga in pairs, swimming and much mindful oiling of bellies (sandalwood, coriander, dilute myrrh). In a visioning session Raisa finds herself peeking at the same time as a chubby, red-cheeked young woman. Eyes connect. Smiles of shared mischief become giggles. The young woman glances outside. They barely make it through the door before collapsing in aching laughter.

'Do you know what I'd like?' the red-cheeked young woman says. She has the palest blue eyes Raisa has ever seen. 'Coffee.'

'Coffee,' Raisa coos. They find a table in the café and order a solitary coffee. The young women lean over it and inhale. Char and wood, a lift of spice and the offer of bitterness. Nothing could smell less natural or more human.

'If only it tasted like that,' Raisa says.

'My name is Signy,' the young woman says.

The next time Raisa rides the bus into Vík she sits up bright and happy at the prospect of seeing Signy. They are the bad girls of Mýrdalshreppur Prenatal Group. Signy makes Raisa lunch in her guest-house on the eastern side of the village, then drops her back at Vonland in the 4x4. Her husband, Óðinn, is away constructing a new ferry terminal at Seyðisfjörður.

The car rounds the ridge and Signy stops as Vonland arrives in view.

'It's bigger than I thought,' she says. 'And smaller.'

Tante Jebet and Tante Hulda wait, hands folded in their sleeves. They make hot water and lemon and take Signy on the tour. She delights in the heat of the polytunnels. Stands silent in the Yata-chapel and asks no questions.

'How much is your geo?' she asks as they stand inside the infidel anthem of the steam pipes.

Raisa sees again the creation-light in Tante Hulda's eye.

Signy leaves with an armful of veg and Tante Hulda's email address. The next Thursday Raisa rides to Vík beside a bulging net of fresh salad which she distributes to the prenatal group.

'Free sample!' she announces. Eileif the enabler watches with tight irritation. 'You can order on Twitter or Facebook. We take PayPal and we can arrange deliveries.'

Eileif takes Raisa aside afterwards to dress her down for using the group to sell salad subscriptions.

'But it's okay for Nestlé or whoever to flog their weird shit,' Raisa says. 'I am organic, non-exploiting, good for you and local.' She throws a line back from the door. 'Hyper-local.'

Every Thursday after that Hulda takes Raisa and a truckload of salad boxes up to the community centre and drinks coffee while The Vehicle recharges. PayPal ticks up hourly, seeds flow into Vonland and Tante Hulda assembles grow-racks and connects piping long into the dark hours.

'Charging The Vehicle is a major constraint on our expansion,' Tante Hulda says. 'It is an interesting problem.'

Every day Raisa lies down among her tree-lings. She does not need the light now—the days stretch towards June at the same speed at which they shrank. She loves imagining she is a giant, a Gulliver, prone in a nano-forest. She inhales the phytoncides and plans her rewilding by child-stages. When the baby takes its first steps, she will be ready to plant out. By the time it talks the valley floor will be forested. Age nine it will run through the saplings. At age twenty the branches will reach its head. Forty and she and the kid will lie as Lilliputians in the world of leaves and steam of her vision. The world will warm, the climate will change and when she is gone the trees will range unbroken from the lava fields to the black basalt sands, as she saw in the Cave of the Papars.

Gone. Hell of a thought.

Before that there's the business of giving birth. Raisa grows heavy and slow and racked with a new pain every day. She imagines she sloshes as she walks. Tante Jebet massages her feet and applies soothing oils and poultices. Raisa wants it over. The date—June 5th—is set, Dr. Rósný's last scans completed, the bed in the hospital in Selfoss booked, the midwife and birth-doula prepped. Two weeks before the due date, Raisa has a muscular spasm that can't be mistaken for anything other than a contraction. Her waters break in polytunnel 3, between the arugula and the mizuna. She yells and yells and yells, suddenly alone and insignificant in the monstrous isolation of the Mýrdalsjökull littoral.

Tante Jebet, dozing in the Yata-chapel, wakes and comes to help.

'It's too early it's too early!' she cries.

'Well it's coming!' Raisa yells.

'The Vehicle!' Tante Jebet commands.

'Give me the phone!'

Tante Jebet surrenders her mobile. Raisa makes a call. Fifteen minutes later Signy slides to a crunching stop in front of the chapel.

'You shouldn't be driving,' Tante Jebet chides. Signy is two months behind Raisa.

'Let her fucking drive!' Raisa yells as she is helped into the rear. 'Oh my fucking God your leather seats!' Signy covers the hundred kilometres to Selfoss in forty minutes.

At two thirty A.M. on Tuesday, May 22, 2012, after a four-hour labour, Raisa Peri Antares Hopeland gives birth.

'What is it?' Signy asks.

'A kid,' Raisa says. 'Just a kid.'

34

N 63°29'13.80" W 19°10'57.78" 16:00 June 21, 2012
Icelandair 1602 YYZ–KEF. Landed.
Icelandair 1689 SEA–KEF. Landed.
Icelandair 1627 DUB–KEF. On approach.
Air France 889/Icelandair 547: FIH–CDG–KEF. Landed.
Kenya Airways 128/Icelandair 565 NBO–GVA–KEF. En route.
Avis car hire, Keflavík: four-wheel drive, 112-hour rental, CDW and sat-ellite navigation + child booster seat.
Ferry arrival 03:00 Seyðisfjörður. MS Norröna. *Minivan and one camper-van en route westward on Route 1. Total of 16 passengers.*
Bus: 07:45 departure Reykjavík Harpa Concert Hall–Vík í Mýrdal. En route.
Route 1: two kilometres east of Skógar, eastbound. Three touring bikes: panniers, handlebar bags, 1 child trailer.
Suðurland N 63°29'9.79" W 19°12'3.87". Backpacks, hiking poles, tent. Two walkers. Third day from Hella. Arriving Vonland.

'Stars!' Tante Jebet's preaching voice sings from the staging at the centre of the clutch of polytunnels. 'Hail and well-met!' The gathered applaud as best they can with hands full of bilberry spritz, placenta dopiaza, hot dogs and salad. The brass section of the South Iceland Youth Jazz Band raise their instruments to fanfare. Tante Jebet wags a finger. Not yet. Tante Jebet commands the small stage like the bridge of a storm-weathering trawler. She welcomes family and guests from the wind's twelve quarters on this day of highest and greatest light. You must have been magnificent when you spoke for Jesus, Raisa thinks. Make a stone believe. The baby grimaces and gurgles in the sling. Raisa rocks and shooshes.

'Last Starring I was at, I never thought mine'd be next,' Raisa says.

'I've never been to one at all,' Signy says. 'Here, put them next to your heart.'

Raisa lifts the baby and rests them against her breasts. Their head moves in time to her breathing. Signy found it hard to learn the Hopeland way with pronouns and still makes mistakes but she has been a better post-natal nurse than the one from the clinic and best of friends.

Tante Jebet throws her arms high and wide.

'Make light!'

'Get that?' Raisa shimmies a hip at Signy; the pocket, the pocket, there is something in the pocket she needs. Signy passes her the yata. Raisa catches light in her tiny mirror and sends it to join the swarm of sun-motes playing over kynnd and witness, band, catering tables from the hotel over the ridge, bar, hot-dog stand flamboyant in fairy-lights and neon, polytunnels, and Tante Jebet, holding high her own yata, eyes wide as if she sees the worlds beyond the flickering light. Tante Hulda throws open the doors of the chapel. Sun rays beam from within across the gathered nation.

'A star is born!'

Now the horns play their fanfare. Raisa mounts the steps to the stage. She lifts the child high and presents them to the people of the east, of the south, the west and the north. Voices cheer, brass blares.

'Star Vega, constellation of Tenemos the Hair-Strung Harp ascending!' Tante Jebet proclaims. 'Curious, kind, brave. Force of creation, force of destruction. Vega faces the future and shouts out into Big Time. Name this child.'

'Atli Raisasbur Vega Hopeland!' Raisa shouts. Fuck, the kid is heavy.

'Stormtalker!' Captain Jónþór Saiph calls from the witnesses. Raisa nods.

'Atli Raisasbur Vega Stormtalker Hopeland!' Tante Jebet declares. The crowd cheers. The youth brass unleash a new, funkier fanfare. Raisa basks in the affection and admiration under the long light of midsummer. Then she slides Atli Vega Stormtalker back into the sling and takes them to meet their nation.

35

Placenta Dopiaza
Serves 18–20

10 tbs vegetable oil

8 green cardamom pods
3 cinnamon sticks or two tsp ground cinnamon
12 cloves
1 tbs black peppercorns

10 large onions. 5 sliced, 5 finely chopped
12 large garlic cloves
150 g fresh root ginger, peeled, grated

1 tbs turmeric
4 tbs ground cumin
1 tbs chili powder (or more. No less.)
1 tbs salt
1 500 g pot skyr
500 g human placenta
Other veg. Potatoes are good. As much as you need to feed.

Gold or silver edible foil
Lemon wedges to serve

Method:
Dry roast the whole spices until aromatic. Remove from the heat and re-serve.

Heat the oil and cook the chopped onions until deep gold—the deeper the colour, the deeper the flavour.

Grate ginger and garlic. Yes, grate. Don't bother fannying around with crushing and peeling garlic. Take the whole unpeeled clove and just grate it straight in using a microplane grater. The skin stays on one side, the precious garlic goes through to the other. Mind your fingers and thank me. Same for ginger. Mix with the skyr and stir in the dry spices.

Trim the placenta and cut into centimetre cubes. Add to the pan with the chopped onions and brown. Add the skyr-garlic-spice paste and bring to a slow boil.

Peel and cube spuds about 2cm on a side. Add, stir.

Simmer slow for 40–50 minutes, adding the sliced onions 30 mins before the end of the cooking period. The onions are the heart of a dopiaza and must be allowed to shine.

Serve on a generous dish of honour decorated with the edible foil. Lemon wedges cut the sweetness of the onions and the richness of the oil.

Under no circumstances be tempted to add tomato or coriander. They are of darkness.

Serve with roti, chapatti, naan, or paratha.

36

The solstice sun is low now and still Raisa presents a bone-weary Atli Stormtalker to the nation. Her feet ache. Atli feels like a lead cannonball.

Atli, meet the Mýrdalshreppur Prenatal Group sisters. Dr. Rósný. Enabler Eileif. Their husbands, wives, partners. Their children, chasing around the polytunnels, kicking balls, spilling drinks, eating hot dogs.

Meet Óðinn Hálfursson, Signy's husband. A mountain of a man, he moves like geology, his laugh erupts in hot geysers. Óðinn has auditioned for *Game of Thrones*. A Wildling, maybe a featured role. He should hear soon. Filming starts in October.

Atli meet your nation: Hopelands from the north, from the islands, ocean-divided Hopelands. From Vale in Oregon where Hulda lived in a geothermal-power-themed polyamory twenty-five years ago. From the University of Guelph in Ontario where Hulda first learned to use the power of water and hot rock to change the world. From Kenya's Rift Valley where the veins of the planet run close to the skin. Danes and North Germans, Swedes and a knot of Faroese, come by car and motor home and ferry.

Atli: Meet your fellow Stormtalkers. Dave Oliver, Coil of the North, in metal heaven in the land of volcanoes, geysers, elves and Norse gods. Rev. Hope Oyedepu, Coil of the East, in Episcopalian collar with her yata over her cross. Tante Margolis, on a stick. She had a fall at the house. It's too big for her, the steps too many and too steep. After Atli has been passed around and cooed over Raisa asks about the Christ Church coil.

'Fucked,' Dave Oliver says.

'The damage went deep,' Hope Oyedepu says. 'Parts of the coil are fused with the organ pipes.'

'It's building again,' Tante Margolis says.

'Christ does not give us a spirit of despair,' Hope Oyedepu says, 'but the east is darkening.'

'If we install the Soho coil, we can reorder the lines of force,' Dave Oliver says. He cradles Atli in his tattooed, weight-trained arms. Rocks the child like a song.

'Trap the malign energies,' Tante Margolis says.

'Heal the people,' Rev. Hope says. 'We need your permission. You are the coil's guardian.'

'I need to talk to someone first,' Raisa says.

Atli: Meet Lisi, with a paper plate of salad, bread and curry in one hand and a wooden fork in the other. She wears a Biba graphic print dress and white patent boots. Lorien, still dressed like a budget hiker, hair tied back, squints at the lowering sun.

'Show me,' Lisi insists. Raisa offers her Atli and she jumps back as if presented with a snake. 'I don't want to hold them, just look at them.' She peers at the baby. 'Igh,' Lisi pronounces.

'We've enrolled her at a local school,' Lorien says. Raisa notices a glitter in the open neck of her supermarket fleece. A yata.

'I'm not going,' Lisi says. 'They're weird. They think bad thoughts.'

Raisa hooks Lisi's arm and steers her towards the geothermal plant. Lisi watches steam plume into the evening sky.

'Does it make this noise all the time?' Lisi yells, hair dewed with condensation.

'Day and night,' Raisa says. 'So.' This can be avoided no longer. 'Brightbourne . . .'

Over a wet winter Morwenna withdrew from the porte cochère room by room through the house to her bedroom and the library where she spends days online, taking tea and swearing at Brightbourne's slow and temperamental broadband. She dresses for dinner and drinks a bottle of wine a night, plays cards. She no longer cooks or washes clothes. Lorien wears the keys of Brightbourne on her belt and with spreadsheet and a clear eye takes on a survey of what can, what can't and what must be saved. Uncle Auberon has rediscovered his dance music which he booms in the ballroom at architecture-threatening volume. It carries him back to Beirut, Istanbul, Rhodes in the late 1980s, early 1990s, when he still held some beauty and the world some passion and colour. The Music works through its computations and iterations and ringing changes and variations. Most weekends at least one devotee will pull into the stable-yard and ring the special bell and Lisi will take them to the hydro-house, unlock the door and let the Music flood down the valley.

'And you?' Raisa asks.

'I do the cooking now,' Lisi says. 'Lorien is terrible. I'm good. Won't do bacon, but. Auberon loves bacon.'

'I meant, Lorien's yata?'

'That was Auberon. He was interested in our way. Like he always had the same thoughts. The things in the wood. The orgone engine. He gave me sherry and asked me about Hopeland. One night he turned the mirrors in the ballroom to face each other and lit a candle between them. I didn't see nothing. Neither did he. Lorien did. She asked about joining and I said, well, it's not a joining thing. You are. You do. Kynnd Nelson Cassiopeia came over from Wandsworth and we had it on the terrace and Lorien turned into a Brightbourne-Hopeland. Then Auberon opened the French windows and I felt them come into the house. Creeping like cats.

'But, listen! Jacob and Demetrios from Dorling are coming over. They're going to see what they can do with the stables and the walled garden.'

'And Amon,' Raisa asks. 'What about him?'

'Gone, Raisa.' Lisi fixes Raisa with her heavy stare. 'The day after you left. He spent the whole day looking for you. Texting you. I had to tell him. I shouldn't'a had to do that.'

'Is he all right?'

'He'll always be all right,' Lisi says. Raisa's breath catches. Did Morwenna tell her the secret of the Grace? An embittered woman imprisoned in a crumbling house may indulge her darknesses. 'You broke his heart, Raisa.'

Raisa hugs Atli tight to her, talisman against guilt. The kid squeals.

'It's complicated,' she says and hates the weakness of those words.

'He loved you, Raisa,' Lisi says. She is relentless. 'He went west. He's following the family connections. He was at the Brooklyn Hearth. He's moved on. Still west.'

'Tell him,' Raisa starts. 'No, don't tell him.'

Lisi fixes Raisa with her bottomless eyes.

'Okay,' she says after long judgement, then sees that Raisa's attention is not on her.

'Hold Atli,' Raisa says. 'If they get heavy, give them to Signy.'

'They're heavy,' Lisi says, holding Atli with the stiff discomfort of humans unused to babies but Raisa is running now. It's time for the most difficult words.

———

A wicker effigy, many lives high, stands arms outstretched on a parched plain under evening light. The left hand holds an upright tree branch, the right an inverted wicker bird. The sun drops beneath the horizon, lightning jumps to the hands and the effigy bursts into flame to wild cheering and dance music.

At most gigs the drum kit holds upstage centre but with this band that place is owned by a substantial pipe organ. Three manuals, pedal bass. A white woman with long blonde hair builds a wall of stained-glass arpeggios as the band comes in, instrument by instrument. A thunderous ensemble chord and chain lightning leaps from organ pipe to organ pipe.

Purple curtains open and a mobile stage moves forward. On it are a tall glass tank full of water, chains and theatrical padlocks and a man in high Victoriana. With a cane. Upstage right and left two giant Tesla coils cast an arch of lightning over his head. He points his cane, the lightning jumps to its ferrule and then to the tank.

'Pity we never got past previews,' Finn says. 'The musical of *The Prestige* could have rocked.'

He swipes the video off his phone. He and Raisa stand among ankle-high trees. Wooden hands grasping for a sun. They are Emanations tens of kilometres high in the miniature world of Raisa's forest. Breathe in pine and broad-leaf musks, humidity and polyphenols.

'Looks good, Finn.'

'I'm busy, Rai. Never out of work.'

'Finn, about . . .'

'I'll try and be involved as much as I can.'

'Finn . . .'

'I want to be there. Not only Stardays and holidays.'

'Finn, Atli's not yours.'

'Oh,' he says, and then oh again. Raisa has seen anger on his face, loss, failure, resentment, spite. Never this disappointment. He's thought about this. More than thought. Hoped.

'So, they're . . .' he says after a time.

'They are,' Raisa says. She doesn't want to say that name, either. Names and a thousand wasp-bright betrayals.

'You go off to Ireland. You don't come back. Lisi doesn't come back. I don't know where you are. Tante Margolis says you're expecting and I'm thinking, are they mine? Every day and night. Months, ticking away. Then I hear there's a Starring, in Iceland, at some Hearth called Vonland. So I come.'

She takes his face between her hands. Oh man. Man face. Stubble and cheekbones you could sculpt ice with. He is as beautiful and perilous as a young god.

'I could move here,' he says.

'Don't do that,' Raisa says.

'I don't see him here.'

'Don't get patriarchal on me, Finn.'

'I'm not but don't you want . . .'

'What are you saying, kynnd?'

'It's not only the kid.'

She feels a little glow, like the last heat of a low sun on a long evening. He would be a warm body in her sleigh-bed. He would be morning beauty. He would be laughing and language she could speak and sheer fucking magnificence. And he would be the backwards turn. The step away from what she has here in Vonland. Salad veg and secrets in stones and this bonsai forest at her feet. And Atli. Only forward, on through the shining solar systems of her infinite family. Like Amon, out there somewhere, falling from star to star.

At the heart of her micro-forest she kisses Finn with ferocity.

'I got a life here now. And you got a name.'

The youth jazz band plays a final-set brass chord. She and the heavy little kid will be needed for the goodbyes.

'Listen Finnevar Mikael Hamal. The coil. I'm giving it to you. It always was yours. I didn't win it clean, Finn.'

'It's . . . It's not right. Like you say, not clean.'

'Will you fucking take something from me, Finnevar Hamal?'

'Thank you,' he says, and again, because he did not hear in his first thanks what he meant, 'thank you Rai.'

At his old name for her she softens and melts a little and thinks in the rush and torrent of the moment, oh fuck it, she's got another ten minutes to play with before Signy comes looking.

'Been a long time,' she says. 'Gonna be a long time again.'

She steps close and goes down on her knees among the nano-pines and then down on him and his laugh goes into a gasp, into *whoosh*, into the pink glow of polytunnel number 4.

37

The quad bikes take them to the head of the lake and there the ice waits. Raisa's lived at the foot of the ice cap for ten months now, felt it shape and cast the weather, felt its constant pressure on the land and the volcano mumbling in its sleep, but until today she has never seen it. She imagined blue, sparkling purity, smooth as a rink. Sólheimajökull is dirty shades of grey, spiked and smeared with black debris, a mountain of smaller mountains.

'Looks like the cover of *Kid A*,' Raisa says. In the back-frame, Atli already feels a weight. Briet the glacier guide claps a hard hat on Raisa's head, hands her an ice axe and checks the baby-frame.

'If you go down, go down on your face.'

She checks Raisa's boots are tight and that there is no give in the crampons.

'You're good.'

This expedition is thanks returned to Tante Hulda for running a power line five kilometres up the valley to the glacier-hike centre. Two guides will take Raisa and Atli up onto the ice, together with Óðinn Hálfursson. Ten days ago Signy gave birth to Tekla Signysdóttir. Óðinn rushed back from the port job, claimed all his paternity leave and within a week Signy was ordering him out of the house. Go with Raisa, she said. Be my representative. Like the Pope.

The path climbs the side of the valley, skirting the fractures and crevasses where the ice fissures under its own weight. Oðinn takes her hand to make the crossing from track to the glacier itself.

'I can take Atli,' he says.

'I want them with me,' Raisa says.

The ice is gritty, slushy, grey and unreliable—the summer was the warmest on record and the glacier is pocked with fresh rots and potholes and deceptions. Raisa extends the hiking pole from her ice axe to pick a way between the ridges and berms of ash-coloured slush. She moves with careful, premeditated steps over the icy grit but time and again her pole stabs through the fragile crust into a melt-hole. These have a name, Raisa recalls. Glaciers have words. Kames. Bergschrunds. Kettles and suncups.

Briet and Pálína lead the expedition down into a sinuous channel between two sun-sculpted ice-crests. Raisa sets her face against the hard
wind blowing down from the high ice. Sólheimajökull is an eight-kilometre
tongue lapping from the main ice cap. Another glacier word: katabatic
wind. The flow of air under gravity from a higher country. Always blows
from the same quarter. Never stops. Summon katabatic wind!

Vibrations travel through Raisa's pole to her gloved hands, the thrum of
water running fast and deep beneath. Raisa pokes her shades up her nose,
the high sun glares hard. The trail rises towards the body of the glacier.
Beneath her helmet her scalp prickles with sweat. The kid is heavy as a
moon. She should have taken Oðinn's offer.

Two kilometres up-glacier, Raisa sees how this ice rivulet connects to
the great ice of the Mýrdalsjökull. She stands, gritty water trickling around
her feet, taken by wonder. Ice and earth exist in mutuality: The mountains,
the valley give shape to the glacier as the ice slow-sculpts the terrain. Cliffs
rounded to nubs. Steep-sided mountain streams gouged into troughs. Every
boulder and stone, every piece of grit rolled and graded and carried by water down to the littoral. In this part of Suðurland the coastal plain is seven
kilometres deep. Water and ice work with centuries. Millennia. The land
can change in an instant. Deep under the ice Katla waits. Every few decades
she turns in her sleep. Twice in the previous century eruptions breached the
ice cap. A year almost to the day before Raisa's expedition, Katla erupted
and sent a torrent of ash and water surging down its south-eastern flank.
The bridge at the Múlakvísl was blasted to splinters in an instant. Vegetation is slowly colonising the outwash plain. This will happen again. Geology protects Vík from the volcano-flood, but Vonland's valley runs directly
from the ice and the fire to the ocean. The 1755 eruption lifted the entire
ice cap three metres and sent a wall of water, ice, rock twenty metres high,
screaming south at two hundred metres per second. It struck the South
Iceland plain like the fist of Oðinn and scoured it clean.

Jökulhlaup. That's the glacier-word that made the biggest impression
on Raisa.

Katla is overdue for a Big One.

'Look at this, Atli,' Raisa says. She turns to allow the kid to take in the
world of ice and light and stone. Her heart is luminous. Every breath sings.
In the sun glare a gleam burns brighter, halfway to the high ice where
Tante Hulda and her devices wait. Raisa settles Atli on her back, leans into
her pole and walks.

Tante Hulda trekked up before dawn towing her arcane tools on a sledge. It is no quick or easy matter to bore a hole through a thousand years of ice. Hulda crouches to pump it clear of meltwater, face manic behind her ice-goggles. One by one the expedition peers into the hole. Óðinn shoulders in too close to the beam and Hulda slaps him away with a torrent of Icelandic. A simple clockwork heliocentric mechanism focuses Hulda's array of concave mirrors and burning lenses on the hole but ice is adamant and northern sun is weak and she needs hours of daylight to melt down to a depth that will bind the talisman for a lifetime.

Lisi had the idea, bouncing around Vonland the hangover morning after the Starring.

'You got too much of the Music in your ears,' Raisa said, filthy-tempered thanks to Atli puncturing her sleep every forty minutes. The idea clung: a Long idea, a project as Big Time as a forest and more intimate.

'I will need two clear days,' Tante Hulda said. 'One to test, one to bore.' That afternoon the weather closed into a month of steady drizzle interspersed with pummelling easterlies. One by one the kynnd returned by the paths they had followed to Vonland. Finn stayed two days in the hope of repeat sex, before leaving disappointed but reconciled. Then a lens of high pressure slid over southern Iceland; Tante Hulda looked up into an endless sky and declared tomorrow would be the day.

Hulda slips her measuring rod into the hole.

'That's about a millennium,' she declares and turns a key in the clockwork. 'Give or take a few decades.' Mirrors slide away from the sun and everyone stares into a twenty-centimetre-wide, metre-deep funnel melted into the Sólheimajökull. 'Move fast, it's refreezing.' Raisa slips Atli from her back and settles them on the ice. She strips off a glove and wriggles the talisman from a pocket. She holds it up, a mirror in the sun; a ten-centimetre stainless-steel coin that Hulda laser-cut with runes in her workshop.

'Atli,' Raisa says. The congregation repeats the name. Raisa squats and holds the talisman up in front of the frowning, squinting baby.

'May 22nd, 2012, constellation of Enitharmon ascending,' Raisa says. 'Long travels.'

She drops the disc into the hole. It wedges sideways nine hundred years down.

'We are stars,' Tante Hulda whispers. The assembly wait for the runwater to freeze around the talisman, then Raisa shoulders Atli. Óðinn tightens the straps and adjusts the seat.

'I'll follow you down,' Hulda says, dismounting her reflectors and con-
densers and lenses and wrapping them in love-soft chamois.

For eighty years the talisman will travel buried in the glacier at the speed
of ice, slow but certain. In 2092, Atli Raisasbur Vega Stormtalker Hopeland, whoever they, she, he or pronoun may be, can stand at the foot of
Sólheimajökull and watch a spangle of sun-washed steel tumble from the
breaking ice into the outwash lake.

I'll be long gone by then, Raisa thinks. Ashes under Vonland. Vonland
under ashes, perhaps. Or swept by Katla into the sea. Whatever built time,
built big.

On the trek down, she asks Óðinn to carry Atli. Briet and Pálína find
it adorable.

38

Don't fall in love with my family, Raisa warns as the days shorten and Signy proposes regular light-dates for Tekla with Atli at Vonland. The kids roll in the full-spectrum lights and scowl at the vitamin D supplements, however well disguised they are in smoothies. The women loll in bikinis in the sustaining lights of the forest tunnel. Raisa and Signy talk. The season at Signy's house has not been happy. Óðinn didn't get the part he wanted in *Game of Thrones;* not Mountain, not Chief Wilding. Minor Wilding and occasional White Walker. He rattles, he growls. The summer season was bleak. Visitors want more than clean sheets, deep beds, a wholesome breakfast. Óðinn dreams of outdoorsiness, a wilderness lodge, a spa. Trekking and trailing. Wildland adventures. Signy has a proposal. Build a new guest-house at Vonland. Let the wild creep in around it.

Raisa hears the proposal inside the proposal. Open your valley, invite us to your Hearth, your nation.

Signy was warned.

On winter solstice Signy, Óðinn and Tekla are welcomed into Hopeland in a low-key, intimate Starring. Easy to join, hard to leave. Their stars are Miram, Chertan and Pleione. Tante Jebet spent gleeful weeks calculating the ascendant constellations. Signy Miram, Óðinn Chertan and Tekla Pleione will sell the old guest-house and while the new one is being built live in the end building of the Vonland Great House. It will be crowded, noisy, smelly, loud. Like Icelandic houses of old.

Spring equinox, when the Emanations of the Third Host evict those of the Second Host and squat in their sky, Raisa kneels on a plastic bag, poking saplings into holes in a forty-five-kilometre-per-hour wind and thirty-degree slanting rain. She feels like a woman from a near-future religious dystopia. Atli bounces in a weatherproof cradle, rocked by the wind, cooing.

Fucking forest.

Tante Hulda watches, amused. Tante Jebet gave up half an hour earlier when her knees grew sore.

'Enough!' Raisa declares, stands painfully up and swings Atli onto her back. Ten square metres planted. Ten thousand to plant. In the end house are coffee, kids and Signy and Óðinn filling out a planning application for their new guest-house.

Eight days before their second birthday Atli Raisasbur Vega Stormtalker learns to run. They run from the high gables of the old house to the new guest-house. Run from Tante Jebet, big and booming and scary in the way that old people can be, to Óðinn, big and booming and scary in the way that weather can be. Run from Raisa, run to other-mother Signy. Run to Tekla Signysdóttir, who too is learning running, and together they run through the now-nine polytunnels of Vonland. They run in and out of the spa bothies by the thermal pool. They run around the pipes and trusses of the expanded geo-plant. They run between the slim, fragrant saplings of Raisa's forest. Sometimes they snap those stems and Raisa looks up from her planting and swears in English.

On autumn equinox, the night when the First Host enters the Starry Skies with gifts and lights in their hands and the Hopelandic year begins, Raisa plants her final tree. By first snow, seventy percent of Raisa's trees are dead.

39

From Raisa's Wilding Book

Post-polytunnel dead trees:
  Birch, hazel, willow: 40%
  Scots pine and Norway spruce: 70%
  Broad-leaf: 100%

Sheep are cunts. Fucking woolly side-eyeing cunts. They can smell a tree from ten kilometres. Then eat it.

8 wrongs:
  Wrong place. Birch, hazel and willow are waterside and wetland trees. DO NOT STICK THEM ON A BARE MOUNTAIN!!
  Wrong exposure. This side of the hill has wind two hundred days a year. That side has direct sunlight for a week either side of summer solstice. The wind scratches that trunk against that rock like brain-itch.
  Wrong drainage. Rapid runoff and fast-flowing streams suck good stuff out of the soil. Too little drainage is bad too. Pines get bad foot-rot.
  Wrong soil. Too thin, too sour, too weak, too heavy, too light.
  Wrong water. See *Wrong soil*.
  Wrong light. Trees grown under 24/7 grow lights get blinded by these things called day and night. Too much light in summer, too little in winter. Trees have diurnal, seasonal and annual clocks. Good word, diurnal. First time I saw it, I thought it was to do with owls. Sounds like owls.
  Wrong country.
  Wrong wrong wrong wrong wrong.

That winter Raisa growls through the house in Uggs and Minion pyjamas, light-starved and cabin-crazy. Every room smells of kid shit kid drool kid clothes kid food. Pink light glows through snow frosting the polytunnels where Mediterranean salads flourish, feet washed in warm, nutrient-rich water. Outside, under snow, rain, wind, her forest dies.

That winter Raisa learns.

She learns about succession. Eruption, rock, moss, grass, dwarf birchwood, flood/eruption/quake. Reset.

She learns about lichen. The first-comer, the survivor, the union of algae and fungus that is more than the union of those two realms of life.

She learns about the mycorrhizal network. That there is a vast realm of life twined into every other form of life on the planet, a web of reaching, fibres so fine and dense that it would, laid end to end, stretch halfway to the centre of the galaxy. Mind, as they say, blown.

She learns about symbiosis. That the dualism of competition versus collaboration is binary ape-thinking. Life is complexity. Life sends its roots and shoots and fibres around human definitions.

She learns that forests make their own climate. That a forest is an organism. She understands what she felt living under her oak in Epping Forest, what the oak felt, what called her name.

From Raisa's Wilding Book

A forest is much much more than trees. A forest is bugs and fungus
and bacteria. Birds and beasts and chemicals. Movement and flow.
Time and energy.
It thinks in seasons, speaks in decades, acts in centuries.
I know what I been doing wrong.
I need to let a little wild in.
I'm not a Papar monk. I'm a Stormtalker.

Spring equinox blows four seasons in an hour and Raisa is up the valley scattering fistfuls of spores from plastic buckets. The mycorrhizal network can be bought by the kilo online and delivered by Amazon Prime.

She gives the hyphae time to infest, inveigle and infiltrate (up to thirty-four sexes, she read, eyes wide) while she starts a new forest. Fresh seedlings raise their leaves to the pink grow lights. Little darlings. Raisa peels back the polytunnel sheeting and exposes them to the short, sharp shock of Icelandic spring. Tough love. On the summer solstice she gathers the survivors and parcels them out to family, neighbours, visitors, veg buyers.

'Throw them anywhere,' she instructs in her mixture of Icelandic and English. 'Far as you like, hard as you like. Don't pick, don't choose. Close your eyes if you like. Throw 'em and move on. Don't look back.'

All that day they move up and down the valley, lobbing, throwing, dropping, kicking little bundles of root and shoot and soil. Tante Jebet shuffles on her stiffening Achilles tendons, giggling as she sends seedlings spinning from her fingers. Óðinn has a catapult that he uses to launch tumbling trees far up onto the high slopes. This thrills Atli and Tekla but they don't have the strength to draw the bands so they content themselves with chasing up and down the slopes in that solid job toddlers can do all day without tiring, making glorious mess with trees.

They lope, limp, stagger back to the Hearth leaving five thousand seedlings scattered at random across the valley of Vonland. Some will root, a few will grow, fewer will thrive. What's important to Raisa is that it's a forest, not a plantation. She let a little unpredictability, a little wild in. A thing abandoned on the cold hillside, left to fend for itself.

The following morning she starts looking around for the next thing.

40

At the end of that summer a car comes around the hill and drops down into Vonland. A Land Cruiser, shiny new. Signy and Óðinn step out to give welcome. It drives past their fresh-painted, wood-scented, soft-bedded, new guest-house. It drives past the veg shop and hydroponics farms. Its driver is not a community nurse; not the principal of the preschool in Vík come to see if Atli and Tekla would like to come see what they're missing; not a plainclothes cop checking whether the Hopelands have slunk back to skunk.

The car's driver is Sindri Ólafursson and he comes with a proposal.

He brings eight copies of a spiral-bound presentation, a laptop and a palm-sized projector. The only place big enough to accommodate his show is the guest-house lounge. Sindri is short, bearded, chubby, informal in the way that costs. He wears ugly-expensive glasses. Óðinn makes coffee. Tante Jebet, bored already, takes Atli and Tekla out into the light and everyone else settles around the projector on whatever furniture has been assembled.

Slide one: a radicchio.

'This is your past,' Sindri Ólafursson says. 'Tastes are moving away from leaf and chicory-based salads to root vegetable macédoines. Trend-hunters predict mooli and other radish variants will be fashionable. Root vegetables are not amenable to your growing regime here. There is another crop that will flourish here and will make a lot more money.'

He clicks up a slide of a long row of racked computers.

'Data. You have the perfect set-up for a server farm.'

Clicky. Hydroponics racks beside the computer racks.

'Data centres are like polytunnel farms. They have the same requirements. Power and water. Except they need them in different ways. They need electricity, not light, and they need coolant. You have both. Your own geothermal power supply and glacial meltwater.' Light gleams from his glasses. 'It's even possible to sink server farms into the ice and let the glacier cool them directly.'

Tante Hulda sits forward and rests her chin on her folded hands.

'What do you propose?' she asks.

'I propose building a data centre here at Vonland.'

'What kind of data?' Signy asks.

'Social media. It's the killer app. Twitter. This year, one hundred million users made three hundred and forty million posts. Each day. Within five years, that will be a quarter of a billion users and a billion daily posts.' A click, a chart, a curve climbing like a rocket launch. 'Instagram. It went to Android over a year ago. Upload photos and videos of your life and share them with your friends and followers. The perfect lifestyle-envy app. Ten million members in its first year on iOS. Within ten years, there will be over a billion. If Facebook paid a billion dollars for it in April, you can be sure it isn't going away. This is the future.'

'We have supply deals with hotels,' Raisa says.

'I have calculated this,' Sindri says with another graph. 'Even with the projected expansion of tourism in Mýrdalshreppur, you would still use only a fraction of your potential geothermal power. You could add greater value crunching data. And data is scalable. Vegetables aren't.'

'You've kept a close eye on us,' Tante Hulda says.

'You might kind of say "stalking",' Raisa says.

'You say stalking, I say due diligence,' Sindri says. 'Am I wasting my time here?'

'I'm interested,' Tante Hulda says. 'Let us do our due diligence.'

'Of course,' Sindri says. 'Here's my card. I'll be at the Hotel Dyrhólaey.'

'We supply their veg,' Raisa says.

Sindri turns in the doorway. 'I want to call it D-Centric. That's a name, isn't it?'

They watch him pack his show into the Land Cruiser and drive back around the hill.

'He's a cunt,' Signy says in English.

'A right cunt,' Raisa says.

'But is he our cunt?' Óðinn says.

'Cunt!' chorus Atli and Tekla, brightly, coming up the steps.

In a long twilight Raisa takes Atli to the beach. They stand on the edge of the black sand and play Dolly's Swimming Lesson. Atli sets Dolly in the surf and lets the backwash carry her into the sea. Dolly floats on her back, staring up into the sky, arms upraised. Raisa and Atli watch her drift further and further out until Atli cries 'Dolly!' and Raisa steps into the foam-lap to rescue Dolly.

Sindri left an echo, a stain on Vonland. Raisa had been looking for change to her cocooned hidden place. Sindri's plan thrills her, calls the lightning inside her, but Atli makes her conservative. She must keep her baby safe from harm, of will and of happenstance. Things to do and undo. Like the word 'cunt'.

'Dolly want another swim?'

Atli nods and sets Dolly in the foam-run and waves their arms as the wash carries her out towards the dark weather-front enfiladed across the horizon. They are small, so immediate on this huge beach, minute as shells.

'Dolly! Dolly!'

Caught by the turning wind Dolly sails out beyond the tide-run into deep water. Little plastic hands wave. Raisa wades knee deep, thigh deep. Deeper. Breast deep. This is how stupid mothers drown. The ebb tide holds Dolly greedily. Raisa reaches, snags Dolly by a foot. Holds her tight in her fist as she sloshes back to shore and plods dripping up the black sand.

'Dolly's done swimming,' Raisa says. She plonks Atli in front of her on the quad bike and zips Dolly tight inside their parka. The ocean cold bites the bone. She shivers, wind-whipped and frosty. She guns the quad back across the beach to the main road and the track to Vonland.

'Ask Signy for cookies,' Raisa orders. She has seen lights moving behind the church's small windows. Jebet speaks with the Emanations. 'And for Dolly too.'

Shivering, she opens the church door. Aged wood, old dust, captured summer-light. Jebet stands at the focus of the mirror-mobile. Bright rectangles turn, an aurora flows across her body. Sun in her mouth. She wanders among reflections of reflections. Raisa sits dripping on a pew at the back.

'You're wet, lovely.' The mirrors turn in momentary unison and come to rest. More than wind moved them.

'Dolly went for a swim. What did you see?'

'No answers.'

'Are there ever?'

'Of course not, lovely. All the Emanations say is, "It's not up to us".'

'Great help.'

'I think so too. And they say it so beautifully. Pagan poetry.'

'I was thinking, down at the beach. We should go in with Sindri. For Atli and Tekla. The ones to come. Invest in them. Like an heirloom.'

Tante Jebet sits beside Raisa on the high-backed pew.

'We need to protect this place and ourselves,' she says.

'I've an idea about that,' Raisa says. It came to her on the cold, wet ride back from the sea. 'We form a company and like hire out space and power to D-Centric. We always control power and space. So we can tell him to fuck off, if. When . . .'

Tante Jebet nods.

'Talk to Hulda. She's of the same mind. Signy too. Óðinn, lovely boy, hasn't a clue. The Reykjavík kynnd have legal connections. They could make it straight.'

'I'll do that.' Raisa opens the church door. Light pours in. Dust hangs in the air.

'Clean socks,' Tante Jebet says. 'Look after your feet. You have a name for this company?'

'I do,' Raisa says, one hand on the door lintel. 'PBV. Powered By Volcanoes.'

Tante Jebet claps her hands in delight.

41

For Atli's fifth Starday Vonland hums with insects, small birds and cooling fans. Where mizuna, radicchio, watercress unfolded roots in rich water, server racks stand, rank on rank. The nine polytunnels hold data farms and the heat-exchange system. Soon that sound will change to wheels on dirt, power tools, cranes, construction workers. If one October storm can dump a polytunnel halfway up Katla, then polyethene is no secure roofing for computers. D-Centric and PBV will convert the polytunnels to stout sheds, low-profile, aluminium-clad, grass-roofed to meet Vonland's environmental remit. Where D-Centric is client-oriented and wears suits with no ties, PBV is informal, friendly and dresses in outdoor wear but is no less a business. Hulda is the engineer, Raisa is the pitch. She always had the charisma for the sell.

Tante Hulda has drilled a second geothermal borehole to serve the data centre and planned a new geo-plant to be built outside Vík to supply the health and community centre, the school and a project dear to Raisa after years of waiting for The Vehicle to recharge: an EV fast-charge point at the gas station.

'There are no electric cars in South Iceland,' Óðinn says.

'Install a charger and they will come,' Raisa says.

The day before the construction crews arrive Raisa finds Tante Jebet among the server racks.

'What's this one?' Jebet asks.

'This is Twitter. That one is Instagram and the one over there is *Eve Online*.'

'Oh yes, that game.' Jebet looks up. Unlike plants, the racks require no light beyond that which glows through the translucent plastic. The new sheds will be completely dark. 'Why doesn't it smell? It should smell.'

'It does.' Plastic and power; the musk of computation.

'No no. Twitter is words, isn't it? It should smell of bread and hair and honey. And colours. This should shine gold.' She cocks her head. 'Why don't I hear anything?'

The sound of fans and coolant pumps envelopes them.

'Chatter and violence,' Tante Jebet says. Raisa does not mention the CG effects for the third Mazerunner film, rendering over in polytunnel four. 'Chatter and violence and darkness.'

Nor does Raisa mention that Sindri has been pressuring her to host big porn sites; Xtube, Pornhub, Aebn. The money rolls in like weather, Sindri says. Money to enlarge the guest-house with a hot-pool spa. Money to expand PBV's empire of lava. Money to replace The Vehicle with a PBV fleet, to add extensions to the house for Svafa and Otti in from the Akureyri Hearth, to set up educational trust funds for Atli and Tekla. To negotiate land for forest; carbon sequestration is more profitable than sheep. Because Raisa knows that Sindri is a little scared by her, she has won every dispute with D-Centric, but as the money expands the agreement between PBV and D-Centric tightens. She could be trapped by Sindri's money. Capital has come to Vonland. The hidden place is exposed.

42

Some days cold air slips down from Mýrdalsjökull to overlie warmth held in the valley and a fog-film slides in to cover the canopy of Raisa's knee-high forest. Then Tekla and Atli play a special game. They lie on their bellies and wriggle between the trees. They might be giants or forest wurms. They laugh a lot. The thirty-centimetre fog-bank soaks their shoulders, their asses as they hump along (for the way of the game is to keep your arms strictly—strictly!—at your sides) hunting each other wump wump wump through the fog-forest. They hoot, they growl, they roll, laughing laughing laughing.

'Omma omma omma!' goes Tekla out there amongst the foggy trees.

'Yeeeee!' yells Atli.

'Ommmmmmmaaa!'

'Yeeeeeeeee, tyuuuuuu!'

'Nyawwwwwwwww?' Tekla and Atli stop their burrowing at the new, rising cadence. 'Nyaaawwww?' They stand up, heads above the clouds. Look at each other. Again the new voice calls; then a head, shoulders, arms and body rise out of the fog.

'Okay kids, time to go in,' Raisa says. 'Kinder tomorrow.'

Atli opens their mouth to make the cry again and keep the game going, the world away.

'Atli, let's go. Tekla, you too.'

The kids disappear under the cloud layer and pop up at her feet. Atli emerges last. Raisa takes their hand. She held off sending Atli to kinder—a full year after Tekla. She didn't like the teacher—teachers never leave the classroom—and couldn't trust the school to get the Hopeland way and the pronoun right. Over the summer she saw Tekla outgrow Atli in confidence, sociability, curiosity. So Berglind Oddsdóttir was invited to Vonland so Raisa could explain about boys and girls and kids, about names and forms of address, about toilets and changing. Then off to Vík they went, in a new PBV pickup, with a new backpack (Minions), and Berglind Oddsdóttir introduced Atli to the class and explained that they were a kid and how to talk about them when they weren't there and everyone asked, *What's a Stormtalker?*

Tante Jebet waits at the house door, rolling her eyes as she always does at the grass stains and the prospect of dirty paws tracking muck over her floors. Atli pulls back at Raisa's hand. Frowns. Pouts. Storm is coming.

'No!' Atli says. They pull their hand away from Raisa's.

'You need a shower, kid.'

Atli scowls at Tante Jebet and tries to kick her.

'Okay. Time out. Church?'

Atli loves the church, the darkness and the sudden light, the patterns that never repeat. Raisa suspects they can see what she can't. She sits Atli on the steps of the little wooden pulpit.

'Is it kinder?'

A nod.

'I thought you liked it.'

Atli shakes their head.

'Tekla likes it,' Raisa says. 'All your friends are there.'

Atli shakes their head fiercely.

'They're not friends. They don't like me.'

'Why do you think that, Atli?'

A fierce, hawk stare.

'They like her, they don't like me.'

'Atli, you called Tekla "her". Is this about her being a girl and you being a kid?'

'They won't talk to me.'

'Maybe they don't want to call you the wrong thing.'

'They talk to Tekla.'

'Tekla was born before Signy and Óðinn came into the nation. She was always a girl. In Hopeland, you can be whatever you want to be, as long as you want.'

'I don't want to be a kid anymore,' Atli says.

Raisa's breath catches. The day has come. She had hoped it would be in a vague, sunny future when she'd had time to prepare and rehearse. Here it is: a foggy afternoon in early September.

'I think I'd like to be a boy,' Atli says.

Here among the mirrors Atli-the-kid dies. Atli-the-boy-she-doesn't-know-yet steps from the reflections.

'Are you sure?' Can anyone ever be sure in affairs of the self? 'You can change if you don't like it.'

'I'd like to try it,' Atli says. 'I'd be a good boy.'

'You'll be a beautiful boy,' Raisa says, voice breaking. She looks at Atli, kid-fat growing into boy-lithe, skin the colour of this old church pulpit, freckled like a hunting cat, a lightning-cloud of hair. Look at them. Look at him. A boy. For as long as he likes. Maybe forever. Not a death, Raisa realises, not an ending. An adventure beginning.

'I'll help you,' Raisa says.

'Are you all right?' Atli asks. His eyes are fearful. What has he done to his mother?

'Oh I am, I am,' Raisa sobs. She falls on her knees in front of Atli and hugs him to her. Cries wet joyful tears down his grass-stained back.

'I'll give it a go then,' Atli says. 'Can I still wear what I want?'

'You wear whatever you like, son.'

43

FINN AND THE GREAT SPIDER OF THE TWELFTH ARRONDISSEMENT

The giant spider climbed the clock tower of the Gare de Lyon. A leg stretched up in a hiss of hydraulics. Vapour sprayed from the joints. Another leg unfolded like a multi-tool. The spider lurched higher. The crew clung to the railing of their howdah. The crowd oohed. Theatrical peril is the blood of any show.

Finn Hamal Hopeland checked his safety harness and armed the primary coils.

'We want it to shoot lightning bolts,' the creative director said to Jean-Jacques Polaris, Coil of the South.

'For bolts you want Finn Hopeland,' Jean-Jacques Polaris said.

'You're our Tesla engineer.'

'He's the true Arcmage.'

The creature designers asked Finn Hopeland, 'We're going to have our mechanical spider climb the Gare de Lyon. Can you make it shoot lightning bolts up the tower?'

'I can wrap the entire station in lightning,' Finn said.

So he spent ten days high over the twelfth arrondissement in climbing harness with cherry-pickers and high lifters and climbing riggers brought over from the open ribcage of Notre Dame, cabling and installing and wiring and fixing high-frequency alternators and resonating transformers.

A million people watched the great spider tippy-toe down Boulevard Richard-Lenoir, across the Place de la Bastille, along the Rue de Lyon. Police had closed the Place Louis-Armand two hours before the show but still had to clear a path to the station for the creature and its pilots.

A heavy tractor bore the body of the Great Spider of Paris. Levers were thrown. Hydraulic cylinders moved. Pipes quivered. Cables swung. The jib lifted the spider high above the Place Louis-Armand. A leg trembled, reached up. The onlookers held their breath. Another leg. And the spider began to climb.

'Tesla standing by,' Finn said into the walkie-talkie. Spider Control directed operations from a cherry-picker across the plaza. The Great Spider was an illusion, relays and servos and actuators inside a light fibreglass carapace built onto an extending jib and wired back to the massive six-wheeled tractor. *If the spider is climbing the Gare de Lyon, no one looks at the tractor. Or the men in the howdah, pulling levers.* That was all the trick of it.

'Cues 156, 157 in three, two, one,' Spider Control said.

The pilot shifted the control sticks. Finn knocked off the safety and fired up the coils. The Great Spider of Paris unfolded palps from under its head, lifted them and lightning arced between them.

Finn heard the crowd roar. He grinned.

'Cue 158 in three, two, one.'

In her position behind the parapet the technician threw the relays. And the Gare de Lyon burned! Electric fire ran the length of the roof of the concourse. Teardrops of blue plasma dripped down the façade and bounced from the glass awning. A torrent of arcing and re-arcing electricity poured from the top of the clock tower. The spider raised its forelegs: Did it battle the arc-storm, or had it thrown an electric web around the station?

Whatever, Paris roared.

'This beats the shit out of Jean-Michel Jarre!' the co-pilot yelled over the seething hiss of electromancy.

Team Spider met up in a Marais jazz bar. The band was trying to finish sound checks, the spider-techs were loud on cocktails and adrenaline. They rose and toasted and sang at Finn Hamal, the magician, as he came swinging. The band complained to management.

One million people, the spider-folk chanted at the band. *We played to one million people!*

'Do you want a job!' Jean-Jacques Polaris shouted to Finn. *Arcmages attract each other by mutual electromagnetic charges. And champagne.* 'With the Machines!'

'What do you mean?'

'I've done enough! I'm tired!'

'Your job!'

'I've had enough lightning in my life!'

Lulls in the celebration and sound check coincided. In the silence the whole bar heard Finn say, 'Thank you, but I have to go back to London.'

'London.'

'I broke things there and left them lying.'

44

FINN AND THE COIL OF SOHO

That same night as footage of the Great Spider played on all French news channels Finn Mikael Hamal Hopeland took the Eurostar back to London.

He knew better than to expect anything of Soho, his old home. But he went anyway, feeling for a prickle of power among the green tea bars and Filipino eateries and day spas. Numb, inoffensive, burnished to a pleasing façade. So to South London. Wandsworth was evaporating house by house; whole streets bought up and embalmed for investment. Brutal rent rises had closed every Australian bar and Jamaican restaurant on St John's Hill. He crossed Wandsworth Common to Dorling Avenue to the gate at the back of everything. He remembered the code. He remembered with a flash-burn of shame what he had done the last time he was here. Blackening leaves littered the great garden. Tattered flags and banners snapped wetly in the after-storm gusts. Buddleia grew in the cracks between walls and roofs. He saw chipped paint, missing tiles. Rotted decking on the stage. Where were Jacob and Demetrios? Where were the children?

He turned his face eastward. The City had advanced to Spitalfields Market but its money infected every part of the old east. For five hundred years waves of arrivals pulsed through Spitalfields, one community aspiring up and out, another flowing in behind it. The latest wave was displacing the Somalis: money from the Gulf, from Russia, West Africa, the vanguard of wealth fleeing climate change. Money never quits. He walked past the shuttered shops, the dead pubs and collapsed Bangladeshi restaurants, the parked Teslas filling half the street, the scaffolding and rubble chutes of gentrification.

Christ Church was a dark, brooding, umbrageous bird. He felt ill claws sink into his shoulder.

Old Fournier Street was dead. The pandemic had only hastened the city-cancer. Spitalfields' houses stood empty and eyeless, idly accumulating value like fat.

He rang the bell of Arcmage House. Even it seemed diminished, cowed, its power stymied. Waited. Distant voices, the smash of bottles. Expected footsteps; their lightness, their uncertainty unexpected. The great door slowly opened. Tante Margolis's face was bright with delight, but the years since the Vonland Starring had diminished her, drained her energy. Finn saw an old Cypriot woman, hair black, lightning in her eyes but her body rusting with arthritis. She leant on her stick.

'Finn Mikael Hamal.'

'Melora Cassiopeia Margolis. I'm here to help.'

He found the old way in and climbed the path through the hollow bones of Christ Church. The masonry hummed, the organ pipes breathed bass plaints. In the cupola he opened the shuttering around the Soho coil.

The prize beyond price.

He had not seen it since the duel of lightnings. Barely then. It had been his, once. It was his again.

Not beyond price. There was a price, a high one. He had paid it.

The coil was unpowered, yet furtive streamers of electricity scampered across the dome of the secondary, swift and bright as lizards. He felt unwelcome fingers stroke his hair, his skin. He closed his eyes, his ears and turned his senses inward, to the blood radio, the music induced in the salts and ions of his body fluids. He attuned to the great chord; the primal electromagnetic drone shivered with glittering harmonics as the coil resonated with the transmissions of taxi radios, pirate music stations, 5G. He winced to a needle of discord. Almost-voices hissed inside the primal static.

Resonances were awry. The coil still guarded the East, still contained the malignities beneath the church inside its cage of electromantic meridians but it was out of tune, had slipped a little further from harmony each year he had been away from it. Or was it that the ill was growing, feeding on the energy that had carved up old Spitalfields, served warm and bleeding to the City?

Years to drift of alignment, years more to retune it.

He shuttered the Soho coil.

By the time he got out of Christ Church's 4G dead zone there were three new job offers on his phone.

45

On the third pass, Lorien is at the gate and the way opens.

'But,' Atli stammers. And, 'What?' And, 'We went past here. Twice.'

'You need someone to show you,' Raisa says.

Lorien waves from the stone stile. A track curves into the trees. She swings into the back seat of the hire car with a familiarity that erases the years.

'I'm Lorien Nekka Hopeland,' she says. Face thinner, angles harder, a grand grey streak in her hair. Still dressed in budget outdoor-wear. 'Chatelaine of Brightbourne. Welcome to my home.'

'I am Atli Raisasbur Vega Stormtalker Hopeland,' Atli says with gravitas. 'I am pleased to meet you.' Raisa turns into the drive as Atli shakes Lorien's hand. His eyes widen. 'Where did the gate go?'

The forecasters predict that this will be the warmest summer in history. Brightbourne's woods agree. The leaf canopy grows so dense that Raisa must drive with headlights to avoid steering into the ditch. The openings that once allowed vistas of Broighter Wood, the valley, the lawns have filled with shrubby growth. Was the drive this long? A fork—now she remembers. Raisa glimpses whitewashed stonework at the end of the right-leading track past the rhododendrons.

'Is he here?'

'He came home yesterday,' Lorien says and there is the house. Brightbourne's face is clear, fresh-painted. No blistered plaster, no flaking render, no stain of mould. The roof shines with new slate; windows fit flush and clean. Glass gleams, no moss greens the seals. The drive is level and un-holed, crunchy with new gravel. Raisa parks under the porte cochère. Standing at the open door—her, oh her.

When Raisa saw Lisi at Atli's Starring she saw a girl—a child, an ungainly dress-up chest urchin. Here stands a dark-skinned, dark-eyed young woman, grown into her bones; a hand taller than Raisa, solid, packed muscle. A Space Marine. She has outgrown Brightbourne's clothes-closets and stands impressive in a tank and baggy jeans rolled up above the ankle, held up by braces. She ties her hair back with a skulls-and-roses scarf. Tattooed bar lines and notes spiral up her right arm, wrist to shoulder. She intimidates as she welcomes. If Lorien is chatelaine of Brightbourne, Lisi is its sentinel.

Atli presents himself and proudly repeats his great name.

'Welcome to Brightbourne, star,' Lisi says. The kynnd, waiting in the dim, portrait-haunted hall, pour from the house. Hands, hugs, smiles, names. Some Raisa remembers from Dorling Avenue—Jacob and Demetrios, builders, movers, Tesla-coil roadies—some from Starrings or Fastenings, or Speedforths, like this.

'So many people!' Raisa says, then squeals in joy as Griffith-George pushes through the scrum.

'I retired,' he says. 'So, I'm here. I don't like what's going on with London.'

Some Raisa does not recognise. Quieter people, shyer people; people less forward. Lorien has opened house and family to people with nowhere to go; those dispossessed by war, famine, persecution, the changing climate. They're not yet kynnd—Raisa understands their reluctance to lose themselves in the vastnesses of Hopeland. Don't fall in love with my family. The warning, the promise.

One Raisa can't see. She knows where to find her. While old kynnd and new fuss over Atli—dizzy and show-offy with so many admirers—she steps into the old coaching room and finds the hidden door by the stove.

Morwenna turns off her radio and waves a reluctant hand from her camp chair.

'Sorry I didn't come down. So many people. Such fuss.'

Raisa sits on the parapet. Between indigo-edged clouds, the sun glows warm on her back. Her flight landed in rain, she drove through showers. The Golden Place keeps its Graced climate.

'You're hiding from me, aren't you?' Raisa says.

'Of course I am,' Morwenna snaps. Ten years have broadened her. She is a ship-of-the-line in her loose floral print dresses, in her summer aspect as figurehead of Brightbourne atop the porte cochère.

'I was angry,' Raisa says. 'So so angry. So so long. You put a curse on me and then told me to keep it secret.'

'I was saving you, sweetie,' Morwenna says. 'Anyway, quid pro quo.' She sees Raisa's frown at her Latin. 'You did the same to us.'

'I see kynnd,' Raisa says.

'So do I,' Morwenna says. 'He—it is a he, isn't it? He is . . .'

'He is.'

'I hate that you saved the house,' Morwenna says. 'Filled it with people and saved it. None of us could ever have done that.'

I've seen it a scorched shell, Raisa thinks.

'Christianity is such weak tea,' Morwenna continues. 'All that neediness. It's so much more satisfying to hate your saviour, don't you think? He's in the Pilgrim Bedroom. Jet-lagged to hell. Don't blame him. Can I trust you to keep the Grace?'

'You can,' Raisa says. Early summer breeze carries a tocsin of bells from the valley. The Music still plays at Brightbourne.

Raisa knocks. No answer. Knocks again, whispers a name. No sound. Opens the bedroom door. A pillar of sunlight between the not-quite-meeting curtains of the dark room dazzles her. The air smells of sleep, dust, honey, shoe-leather, tweed. Ten years collapse in a breath.

The quilt is thrown back, hastily exited. Raisa searches from room to room. In its lean years of the previous century Brightbourne converted a number of third-floor rooms to self-contained apartments to let. Now that the house's incomers outstrip Jacob and Demetrios's conversion work on the stables, they are tenanted again. Wide seventeenth-century floorboards creak to new feet. The walls seem to expand outward like lungs filled with the pressure of fresh voices.

An unfamiliar, light-filled passage turns out to be the gallery between the kitchen and the outbuildings. Raisa remembers it decaying, leaking, skeletal. Now it smells of fresh paint, just-set concrete, plaster. Cement dust scuffs under her soles. Music washes over her. Beat-driven, sequenced. Amon music. She follows it to a new place, a barn loft converted into a work-space. Original beams, fresh white walls, skylights and plenty of power sockets. Amon Brightbourne works at a folding table that holds a MacBook, a tiny keyboard and an Ableton pad. Bluetooth speakers stand in the corners. Music surrounds Raisa: a beat track to which Amon adds new elements, subtracts, edits sounds that do not please him.

Eyes, mouth, muscles, bones have set deeper, bedded in. Still the country-boy brogues. Is that the same suit? He has not gained a pick of weight. His freckles are deep and many-layered. He's lived in the sun. He wears his hair long. Red as the fox. It falls around his face as he bends over his instruments. He flicks it back behind his ear, it falls back again. His hands are so beautiful as they compose a bass line, send it to the beat-pad, bring it in, take it out again, bend and shape it. Weaving sound and time.

Amon is the sole colour in the stark room. His music is warm and insistent, like a dog. Excited and enthusiastic. Raisa hates to break his rapture but she must.

'Amon,' she says.

He jolts back on his kitchen chair. The music dies. She sees fear and joy and anticipation and dread.

'Oh,' he says. 'Um.'

He stands.

'Um, I'd offer you a seat but there's only one chair and you might feel a bit uncomfortable if you were sitting and I was standing. Sort of interrogatory.'

She's forgotten his accent. It melts her.

'Let's go to the library,' he suggests and scoops his MacBook into the soft leather satchel she remembers from the Tesla days. She touches it as he passes. The leather has grown softer, thinner, tougher. Real skin. Amon leads Raisa a way she has never gone before, opens a door she never knew existed beside the fireplace in the morning room and they step out of a mystic bookcase into the library. Low chairs sit on either side of the window; pleasant for light and outlook when reading bores.

'Amon, I . . .'

'I know about him, Raisa,' Amon says.

'Amon, you are . . .'

'I know that too.'

'How?' Raisa asks, put out that her rehearsed reveal has been spoilt.

'Lisi told me.'

'Little tout,' Raisa says.

'Not so little. She can bench-press one hundred kilos dead.'

'Easy. It's not much, one hundred kilos. You know jack-shit about weights, Amon Brightbourne.' He looks terrified. Joke, tweed-boy.

'Where is he?'

'Lorien's giving him the grand tour and then Lisi will take him to the Music.'

'And he knows? About?'

Raisa leans forward in her low eighteenth-century chair to lay a hand on Amon's knee. Bony. All joints and angles.

'You'll like him. He's ten. So he's still adorable. He's as scared about meeting you as you are about meeting him.' As she was, on the drive down from the airport, on the flight south across the ocean, every day since the word came from Lisi that Auberon Brightbourne had died. 'Where you been, Amon Brightbourne?'

Travelling from star to star, across the constellation of Hopeland. A night in Mexico City, a month in Helsinki, a minute in Bilbao, a year in Tel Aviv, sheltering from the pandemic. Steered by the music: gigs and residencies and commissions. A residency in the San Juan Islands writing music for a game about family and loss. Every week he ferried to the next island to spend the afternoon in the music room of an elderly and respected composer. They took tea and grew excited about ideas. Business-class to Necker Island to play forty minutes of bespoke composition into the ears of a billionaire socialite. The condition: that he lock it with an NFT crypto-key available only to her. He sat breath-close with his client, set the buds in her ears and watched the carnival of ecstasies and small, sweet hurtings play across her face by the light of a Caribbean fore-dawn. Raisa remembers a night of perfect intimacy in the Wandsworth tree-house. How can she be jealous, eleven years after?

'It's not the same,' Amon says. 'The music. The mega-clubs; they're fading. London's the city of the dead. The pandemic laid waste to everything. It'll be years before people remember how to dance.'

'Do you still make them cry and feel cosmic?'

'I do. So, you, Raisa Peri Antares Hopeland?'

'Raisa Peri Antares Stormtalker Hopeland,' she says and tells the story of the name, and from that to how she became Salad Queen of South Iceland, then the Forest Maiden, and now Mistress of Volcanoes, with twelve data centres feeding from PBV geothermal power and hydro.

'And I'm opening a network of EV charging stations around Route 1 so you're never more than an hour from a charge point. All supplied by local geothermal.' She passes a card to Amon. An erupting volcano, flowing lava, clouds of steam, forking lightning: her name, her position: *Talker*. Amon tucks it into the waistcoat pocket where you put things you will never look at again. 'I talk, Amon. Always could. We're energy rich, resource poor; use what you got, not what you not. We should be all-electric. Cars first, then trucks. Buses! I got so many ideas! Am I talking fast?'

A different section of library opens and Lisi and Atli walk out. The boy's eyes are wide.

'I met the Music,' he says. 'It goes round and round and round but never the same.' He blinks at the clock on the fireplace. 'Is that the time?' Then he sees Amon. 'Oh. You're . . .'

'I am,' Amon says. He gets up from the low chair to offer a hand to Atli. The boy shakes it solemnly.

'Call me Amon,' Amon Brightbourne says. 'I am pleased to meet you, Atli Vega.'

'Stormtalker,' Atli says.

'Atli Vega Stormtalker. Welcome to Brightbourne. Mi casa es tu casa.'

'I speak Spanish,' Atli says. 'And Icelandic, English and some Swahili.'

'Maybe I should leave you two,' Raisa says. She sees panic in Amon's eyes.

'Dinner in an hour,' Lisi says from the secret door.

'So, you met the Music,' Amon says as if talking to a police officer. His hands are deep in his pockets, his shoulders slumped. His hair falls around his face. 'I make music too. Brightbourne is a house of music. Would you like to see that?'

'I would, Amon,' says Atli.

Raisa closes the secret door to the morning room.

46

Dinner runs late and loud. Voices and stories around the long table, bottles passed and glasses drunk. Lamps are lit as summer twilight deepens beyond the window. Lisi cooks a Hopeland mix of cuisines—Jamaican curry, jollof rice, focaccia, salades composées, ramen served on venerable china. The ritual of dressing for special dinners is still observed at Brightbourne. The dining room resembles a pantomime evacuated from a burning theatre to a country hotel. Whatever Morwenna chooses she always looks like a hippy cloud. Lorien relaxes in 1940s Land Girl chic, rocking back in her chair. Lisi wears a man's tux and formal pants. She has pulled her hair back and mascaraed a pencil-line moustache on her upper lip. Jacob and Demetrios have come down to the big house as gentleman spy and riverboat gambler. Griffith-George brings his London City Airport hi-viz out of retirement and that is costume enough. Raisa wears a wrap-over blouse and wide-legged lounging pants: 1920s vamp. Atli dresses in a Fair Isle over a shirt with a bow tie and plus fours. He sits beside Amon, who is never not dressed up. Twin tweed-boys.

Hands tell truths and Raisa watches Amon's. Long-fingered, thin to skeletal. Skin loose, pale, freckled down to the final finger-joint. Flexible, animated but tired. Hands that never know rest, can never fold and be still. Always something for them to explore, to draw out. It must be exhausting to be always lucky, to land right, to be Graced. He smiles in the candlelight, listens with bright attention, shares moments with Atli. He catches Raisa looking at him. He doesn't look away immediately. When everyone rises from the table and takes the dishes to the kitchen to help with the washing up because the old patterns won't stand the dishwasher, Raisa waits behind, opens the windows and steps over the low sill into the garden. The breeze that carried the morning's little fluffy clouds has ebbed into a colossal indigo stillness. House, grounds, river and woods are a painted cell across which she moves like an animated spook. Spangle-stars fade in one by one over the shoulder of the backdrop mountain. Tree trunks are pencil strokes that move aside as she approaches them. Paper bats fistle. Ferns jostle out spores. Dwarves with lanterns should part the undergrowth; around the next tree she ought to meet a caterpillar on a toadstool or a gnome riding a snail. She gets high on chlorophyll. Iceland's growing season is short and fierce: a shout. Ireland danders—in its increasingly paltry winters, last leaf meeting first bud—until every cell is swollen and gravid. Life bursts from every pore.

Raisa emerges from the small wood by the bench above the old turbine house. The Music sounds clear tonight. She cuts around the far side of the feeder pond. She doesn't want to lose time to the Music. But some eddy touches her, for when she comes to the side gate from the stable-yard, under the arch of black ivy berries there is an unfamiliar car outside the porte cochère. She didn't see its lights. She didn't hear the engine, the tyres on the gravel, the slam of doors.

The French windows of the ballroom stand open to the night. Music pours out. Raisa draws closer. Piano and organ, gifting each other themes, improvising and varying, transforming them, passing them back by the light of six candelabras. Closer. Raisa waits in the darkness beyond the glass, a silver moth. She fears breaking the enchantment. Amon sits at a full-size keyboard. Facing him at the ballroom grand piano, a man of late middle age plays with matching intensity. Tanned to the edge of weathered, long wizard's hair tied back in a silver ring. Neat, silvered beard. Lean-faced, Rigel-blue eyes. He wears loose linen in greys and earths, and is crowned by a round hat of the type Raisa used to sell to East London middle-aged men when she helped on a market stall in the late 2000s. He looks up—no, Raisa understands: he has no need to look at the keys—he looks out, away from the music into the world music comes from. Amon catches the look, smiles and, seemingly without effort or thought, matches the transition to a new theme and mode.

Raisa comes to the open window. Amon is soul and old church, with occasional samples and loops where he finds a sequence that sets the pianist nodding. The piano man is jazz modes and meandering improvisations that wander long from their home but always within sight of its chimneys, like an adventuring child. Nothing about this music should work but it is joyful and glorious and spiked with shards of eternity. A breath of wind flickers the candles. A spray of notes eddies in from the river and Raisa understands. The musicians improvise around stray phrases of the Music. Raisa must tune her senses to concert pitch to distinguish the themes they hear, to appreciate how closely they are in harmony with their source. Every change, every new measure or mode, they come back from wherever they have been in their explorations and land on the new theme, though no one has ever heard the water-music-computer wheel it out before.

They glance at each other, nod, smile. Raisa knows who the pianist is now.

Hadley has returned to Brightbourne.

47

THE PILGRIM, THE DERVISH, AND THE BEAR

In the final decade of the twentieth century, Auberon took his satchel and a much-weathered grip and went out from the gates of Brightbourne to seek the mystic. In his seventh decade he had become enamoured of the contemplative religions and after years of filling up the library with books, concluded that the finest was Sufism. He went to Istanbul, which he insisted on calling Constantinople, and spent five giddy nights immersed in the folded histories of the Queen of Cities, then crossed the Bosporus to find what survived of the old Sufi orders in their heartland, Anatolia. He climbed foot-worn paths and precipitous stone stairways to contemplation cells carved into the soft tufa spires of Cappadocia. He stood from morning to night encountering the many silences of the wooden mesjit of Hacıbektaş. He shuffled with the pilgrims past Rumi's tomb, bowed his head and folded his hands as the grandfather beside him held up a tiny girl to wave to the Mevlana. He wandered the old dervish house of Konya trying to capture the simplicity, the unity, the mystery in the kitchens, the reading room, the austere cells, the dancing-hall. Oneness eluded him. The world was irretrievably broken, many, scattered.

He came down to Antalya, took the bus along the Turquoise Coast, heartsick and disillusioned. The Sufi way was dead in Turkey. Yet Dalyan's rock-cut tombs intrigued him. He found a small hotel near the river and sat at a tin table under a parasol sipping raki and watching the tour boats swing into the wharf. The boat boys were pretty. He had determined to get very drunk when he noticed a brochure in a plastic caddy on the bar. Dervish Show! He took a leaflet to his table. The glossy paper, the posed photographs, the over-lit spectator shots warned him what to expect. The hotel booked him a ticket. Half-drunk he followed the audience along a path of lights hung from tree branches into the dome of a former hammam. The central göbektaşı had been removed and two circles of folding seats set up around the walls. Auberon found a seat in the front row. The musicians took their places and tuned up. The dervishes entered in their white robes and tall hats. The dede bowed to the dervishes, then to the musicians. They struck up their instruments. The dede folded his hands. The dervishes nodded, took a step here, dared a turn there, feeling the flow of the divine. One by one, like planets forming, they started to whirl. And wonder spun from them.

The musicians played, the long white skirts of the Mevlevis flared out, the dede walked among the spinning dancers and Auberon understood. The old orders, abolished by Atatürk seventy years before, had not gone away. They hid in plain sight. The audience saw a Dervish Show. The dervishes saw the true sema. If the divine is not one with the mundane, it is not One.

After the audience had shuffled back to late dinners and drinks, Auberon Brightbourne went down onto the dancing floor to speak with the dede. The leader was a short man of late middle age with a neat moustache, bad dentistry and crow's-feet around his eyes. He spoke no English. A young dancer, a newly qualified lawyer, translated, but the dede needed no translation. He spoke louder and more clearly than language. Spirituality radiated from him. An aura of the divine cloaked him and it was natural, unaffected, humble. He shone. Through his years and travels Auberon had met a few people—a former missionary in Shanghai, a teaching nun in Mullingar, a perpetual pilgrim in Roncesvalles—who had shone with this particular holiness, but none burned as bright as the dede.

The dede spoke of the unity of God, of simplicity and service, of the training and untraining, the seeing and unseeing. Auberon heard only the crackle of his blazing god-light.

'Your dede is a most special man,' Auberon said to his translator when the dervish master excused himself to get changed and have a smoke. 'A true holy man.'

'He is a car mechanic,' the translator said with pride.

That night in his hotel room Auberon sat by his open window looking out at the fairy-lights of the moored riverboats. He imagined himself a dervish. By day he would guide tourists to the Lycian tombs or the turtle beach. By night he would turn his right hand up to the power of God, his left to earth and let divinity arc through him. He would step into the whirl that is the heart of reality. No division. One thing. He imagined never leaving this town.

'No,' he said and smiled and was at last content for he had found in a bifold hotel leaflet, under tourist cameras, the thing he had sought. It lived in plain sight. That was enough.

The next morning he checked out of the hotel and went among the boats until he found a gulet that would take him to Rhodes. Turquoise deepened to ultramarine as the coast fell into the horizon. The sky was clear and the sun stood brilliant. Already the dede's divine light was fading. The wisdoms were decaying into platitudes. The gulet rattled over a brisk chop. Auberon clutched his satchel, pulled the brim of his hat low and tried to squeeze the high sun out of his eyes.

His room was cheap and clean and looked onto water and in the evening he went to the bar he had researched. The clientele there was too young, too handsome, too self-absorbed to have any interest in him so he sat outside on the sloping street with a bottle of retsina and slowly smoked an entire packet of Marlboro Lights. A cat shared the street with him. Towards midnight the music started in the back room, an unvarying machine beat that erased comfort or conversation. Auberon got up to leave. The cat had already fled. The wind shifted and bowled litter up the street. It turned Auberon Brightbourne so that instead of going to another bar or his hotel he went to the club room. The music was chemical: Most of the men were bare-chested, some down to jocks and socks. Lights gleamed from sweating skin, shaved pectorals, hairless heads. The floor was rammed but Auberon saw that each man danced only for himself. Enclosed, inward. Pained ecstasy. Desperate yearning. Joyous escape. The DJ was bent in a trance over her decks. The beat was dislocating. Every sensation here was designed to whirl men out of the mundane world into another.

'Watch this please, it's precious.' He handed his satchel to the barkeep for safe minding. He took off his hat. His jacket. Set them on a table. Opened three buttons on his shirt, rolled up his sleeves. Auberon Brightbourne strode onto the dance-floor. No hesitant, testing steps here. He must throw himself in. He swallowed the four-on-the-floor and the heat, the spinning lights, the intimidation of other skin in his personal space. He danced as late-sixties Irish nano-gentry must: flailing and awkward but without self-consciousness or irony. Irony is the murderer of honesty. Those men who could see him nodded, smiled and gave him space to spin on. The bearded face of a chubby, middle-aged bear in a leather chest-harness leaned in to Auberon and bellowed in a South African accent, 'Come with me!' Auberon's heart leapt. He had glimpsed the darkroom behind the speakers. He followed the South African back to the edge of the bar. The man backed him up against the door-arch, hemmed him in with arms. Auberon was breathless with fear and excitement.

'You're a brave man,' the South African said. His body hair was sworled with sweat. The whirl is in all things. A click of his fingers and a lozenge-shaped pill was between his fingers. He held it up before Auberon's wide eyes. It was stamped with an image of a bulldozer. 'You deserve this.'

'What does it do?' Auberon said.

'First is free,' the South African said and popped the pill onto his out-stretched tongue. He leaned in breath-close to Auberon.

'"All loves are a bridge to Divine Love",' Auberon said and closed his eyes and opened his mouth to the kiss of ecstasy.

The pill was as bitter as age.

The South African stepped away, swiped a bottle of water from the bar and passed it to Auberon.

'Stay hydrated,' he ordered and headed back to the floor. Auberon followed; they found a point of gravitational stability at the centre of the floor, where the lights and the speakers focused. The DJ cross-faded into a piano intro. Time hung. Then the bass kicked in, the dance-floor lifted, the world caught fire and Auberon Brightbourne understood.

'This!' he shouted, 'this is the greatest thing I have ever heard!'

48

The sun sets in East Tyrone on June 25, 2022, at 22:10. At 22:15 the first firework explodes over Broighter Wood. Cheers on the UFO Terrace, glasses raised and as the pyro fades, a spoonful of Auberon Brightbourne's ashes sifts down upon the summer trees. At the decks, Hadley Brightbourne spins up the first tune: Robert Miles, *Children*. Feet tap, a drumroll builds, breaks and five more rockets rip up the darkening western sky. Hadley has curated the playlist; Amon has set up the clever show-control relay to the launchers in the woods. Oohs and coos as star-stuff snows down. Dario G, *Sunchyme* now.

'I used to dance around to this when I was a kid!' Raisa shouts.

'He said it was the only music he could feel,' Lorien shouts back. 'He'd drive up to Sugar Sweet or Harmony and come back off his tits. Until the peelers caught him.'

Auberon Brightbourne's memorial instructions were brief. Fireworks. Decent champagne. That boom boom music.

Brightbourne turns out for the Speedforth, as have sundry dog-walkers, runners, bird-watchers and ramblers who encountered Auberon on his danders around the demesne. Also family lawyers, car-fixers, accountants, librarians, the priest and the rector (never the pastor, who was of an evangelical bent Auberon found crass). His tailor and wine merchant. Auberon outlived most of his cohort but brothers and sisters from his rebirth as mystic raver are here: promoters, old club DJs, nuns, New Age gurus and Lagan Valley Wiccans. Old elegant men who may have once been lovers, faded minor Irish aristocracy, middle-aged men who may have been members of electronic bands.

'I love this!' Raisa says as Hadley spins up *Chime* and Amon's software sends a fresh launch up in a stream of red sparks. 'Soundtrack to my kidhood!'

'Accensione, salire, detonazione,' Lorien says.

Lisi found Auberon in a folding camp chair on the UFO Terrace. The family religion that the new lives brought to the house intrigued him. It dowsed his deep current of mysticism. In the great lockdown he tried to rebuild his orgone accumulator to catch and concentrate the energies of the Emanations. They were too subtle for his spirit plumbing and orgasm trombones. He hung mirrors and lights but never saw the reflection inside the reflection. That final summer he spent evenings that rolled into nights on the UFO Terrace listening to the wind in the wood, the water and the Music wheeling through time and tried to catch the song of the Emanations. When Lisi found him in the morning, his face shone with rapture.

In the end ninety years of Auberon Brightbourne was reduced down to two kilos of powdered bone-ash. Brightbournes and Hopelands spent three days spooning him into the warheads of ninety rockets. 'He shall not go out on a whiff and poof,' Morwenna declared. Great-Uncle Auberon would explode in sparkling sun-showers.

Hadley's set plays *I Heard Wonders* by David Holmes. Amon taps the keys and by flights and hosts the ninety rockets of Auberon Brightbourne's life burn as brief constellations over Brightbourne.

49

And she's awake, starfished on her back across the bed. No breath in her lungs. No word in her throat. All neural electricity potentials set to zero. She's paralysed and something stands by the side of the bed, looking down at her.

'Raisa?' Atli's voice.

'Fuck!' she whispers and the night terror breaks and she can move again.

'Raisa, something's trying to get into my room.'

She sits up, blazingly awake.

'Like . . . brightness? But it's too early and this is the wrong side of the house. And it's the wrong bright.'

Raisa pulls on a tank top and pants. Potential weapons: a shotgun on the wall, a Masai spear propped in the corner, snowshoes above the washstand, a rank of trout-fishing poles. She lifts a poker from the old cast-iron fireplace that hasn't been lit in three generations.

'Get into my bed. Whatever you hear, whatever you see, do not get out. I will deal with this.'

The poker is a fearsome thing, the length of Raisa's forearm, heavy as a mace, sharp-pointed and armed with a claw for hauling glowing logs into proper fireplace order. Wrought iron: a weapon to smash the wasp-paper skulls of faery folk. Raisa knows what she faces.

She closes her bedroom door, advances down the corridor to Atli's room, bludgeon hefted. Brightbournes gaze from their portrait frames. She opens the door. Atli chose the room for its four-poster bed and its drapes are pulled. His phone glows on the bedside table, recharging. Jacob and Demetrios finished rewiring and resocketing the house the day before Auberon died.

The stale air smells of ten-year-old boy.

Raisa opens the window curtains and looks out. A gibbous moon frosts the lawn. She rattles the lock of the sash window in secular defiance. Sits on the edge of the bed. Waits for it to return. The bed is high, she swings her legs. Looks under the bed, rattles the poker around. It bangs off suitcases, hatboxes, cartons of dusty hardback books. She's tempted to lie down. Just for a moment. Keep the poker beside her. Within easy reach. She might fall asleep; it might cast its dread paralysis on her and sneak past when she can't move, only roll her eyes and mouth stifled warnings.

She sits up, grasps her poker. Good cold iron.

The glow brightens so slowly there is no point at which Raisa can say, that was dark, this is light, but once noticed, it draws her, a bar of deepening gold in the gap between the curtains. The glow brightens to molten metal. Raisa waits. She feels calm, contained, certain. She is not afraid; this is not a ghost, a thing made out of fear: This is an apparition. Uncanny but not unholy.

The heavy curtains bulge. Gold leaks across the carpet casting long shadows from chair legs, side tables, Atli's abandoned dinner clothes and capsized shoes. The curtains part, a face peeps out, looks around the room: the face of a pre-pubescent boy, with the biggest, roundest eyes Raisa has ever seen. Cat-eye pupils. A shining face. Glowing hands part the curtains. The apparition steps into the room.

The Brilliant Boy of Brightbourne takes in the room. Bed, tables, wardrobes, dressing tables, and the paraphernalia on the walls are lit bright as day.

The Brilliant Boy takes a step towards the bed.

'He's not here.' Raisa lifts the iron poker. 'I took him away from you.'

The apparition halts, raises his hands. His palms blaze with otherworldly stigmata.

'I am Raisa Peri Antares Stormtalker,' Raisa says. She brings the poker up to eye-level. 'I boss lightning. And I got words for you.'

The Brilliant Boy tilts his head, frowns. Dazzled by his own light.

'Who asked you here? Who said you could come into this room? This house? My boy's life?' The light shines hot on Raisa's face. 'And why boys? Never girls? I tell you, no girl would want your Grace. No one in their right mind would. So go away. Out of this house. Out of Atli's life.' The Brilliant Boy looks into her eyes, face shimmering with light, long hair dripping fire. 'Be off with you,' Raisa says. The Brilliant Boy stands before her, burning. 'Go!' She lunges with the poker, stabs the Brilliant Boy through the heart. For the first time he recognises her, recognises anything outside his continuum. His mouth opens in surprise? Disappointment? He reaches out to grasp the poker and detonates in a flashbulb pop that blinds Raisa through closed eyelids.

The room is dark, the room is empty. The air smells of sunlight and dodgems. Atli's phone blinks on its table, charged now, and the light beyond the slit in the curtains is the indigo at the edge of dawn.

And she's awake. Starfished on her back across the bed. She can't move. Paralysed by waking shock. Another sunrise, still alive. Where is she? Her bed, her room and light hot through the window. Brightbourne.

'Atli?'

Crunch of gravel, voices. One Amon, one older. Raisa pulls on pants and a tank top and opens the curtains. Blinks in the hard light. Hadley's hire car stands on the gravel. Hadley leans on the open door, Amon stands hands in pockets. The two men embrace briefly, the car turns and drives off. Raisa watches Amon watch it turn onto the drive and disappear into the tunnel of trees.

She finds him in the porte cochère room on the small chair by the secret door.

'Oh hey,' she says. She sits in the other chair. 'I saw you out the window.'

'I'd kind of like . . .' Amon starts.

'I saw him go,' Raisa says.

'I thought he'd stay,' Amon says. 'Even a day or two.'

'Too much Grace,' Raisa says.

Amon looks up, sharply.

'I've known for a long time. Morwenna told me.'

'She shouldn't have. It's our thing.'

'It's not though. It's my thing now. The firstborn, she said. Always boys. Atli's a boy now.'

He hadn't realised. He'd never thought. Always land on their feet. A charmed life. She leans forward.

'I killed the Brilliant Boy. Last night. He came to Atli's room. I was waiting for him. I stabbed the shit out of him. With a poker.'

'You can't kill him. He's an apparition.'

'Well he went up in a big spark-ball. Like a firework.'

'He'll be back.'

'Don't think so. I'm still an Arcmage. Queen of Lightning. Atli won't be there. He won't catch it. The Grace. I can't have that, Amon. I can't let that into my family. It would destroy Hopeland. Morwenna told me another thing, back then. A thing she didn't tell you. Your dad neither. She told me about the Price. She told me not to tell you.'

'My dad?'

'The Grace has a price.'

'I know; the house . . .'

'Not the house Amon, everything.' She should stop. This is cruel. Crueller than cruel. Once when she was a kid she played up and down the River Lea with Kynnd Sofia Acrux. She caught a lamprey and delighted in showing Raisa its horror mouth, ring upon ring of teeth. Teeth all the way down. She is cruel like a lamprey's mouth. 'Everything, everyone, Amon.'

'What are you saying?'

'They should'a told you, Amon. Morwenna and Hadley. Your charmed life? It means shit life for everyone else. You're like . . . what do you call it? Zero-sum game. You, Hadley, all of you all the way back.'

Amon jumps to his feet, paces sharp with agitation. The little antechamber is three steps by three steps.

'This is fucked up. Fucked up.'

'They thought they were being kind.'

Amon collapses into the chair across the fireplace. He looks older. She sees his father. She sees Auberon. She feels the time-wind on her face. She feels fragile, flaking like old plaster.

'And you?'

'It's the reason I went to Iceland. She told me not to tell you and I couldn't be part of it. So I ran away.'

'Not a word. Nothing. You broke my heart, Raisa.'

'Not one day has gone by that I haven't thought about it. Should I have stayed? Should I have told you then and there? Should I tell you ever? Not one day, Amon Brightbourne.'

'And now you have. And you're all right. All happy in your head. You and your boy. Well fuck you, Raisa Hopeland. Fuck your family, fuck this house and fuck everyone in it.'

Amon slams the porch room door behind him. Every piece of glass shatters. The house shakes. The portraits on the Infanta Staircase open their eyes. Raisa steps barefoot over broken glass to follow Amon outside.

'Amon!'

White reversing lights change to red. Harsh gravel under her soft soles. 'Amon!'

The car turns around the rhododendrons. Raisa tries a few pursuing steps and limps to a halt. Lights between the trees. He's driving fast. Hard.

'Shit,' she says. 'Fuck.' And a parting shot. 'And when did you learn to drive, tweed-boy?'

The house, roused, waits for her in the hall. Morwenna looks down from the landing. By accident or unconscious intent she stands beneath the portrait of the Brilliant Boy. Raisa fixes her with a glare.

'I told him,' Raisa says. 'The Price.'

Morwenna's mouth twitches. It might be a smile. She turns and goes back to her room.

50

The house is small and neat, a steep-pitched turf roof between stout stone side walls, windows framed to the sun. It is a short, mindful walk through small trees from the Great House and its kidhood kitchen, bed, smell. A thoughtful wooden bench rests beneath the south-looking window. Here Raisa sits in October sun listening to Atli explore his house. It's filled with boy-pleasing details—cabin beds tucked under the eaves at the apex of the roof, hidden cupboards and secret doors, the other staircase. His big feet clatter against sanded floorboards, wooden steps, landings.

A call from above. Atli's big face grins down at Raisa. His hair falls forward, a slipped crown. Don't ever cut it, Raisa whispers. Boys too often do that when they move out; change everything, make themselves new and strange. She glances up, fearing she speaks aloud. Atli leans on the window discovering his new outlook.

Vonland Boys' House stands on the valley's north-western side below the chest-high tree-line of Raisa's forest. Tree growth compounds every year now as the northlands warm and the growing season stretches and the mycorrhizal network connects connects connects. The Great House and its extensions form a circle of roof-triangles above the trees, a crown lost in a wild wood. Vapour jets from five locations in the valley now. Tante Jebet insisted that the data centre sheds be painted a harmonious green but their right-angled geometry always clashed with Vonland's psychogeography. Now they are coming down, the information they processed shuttling to new centres at Vík, Hvolsvöllur, any farm or settlement that wants to make money stabling data. In their place a ring rises: the new PBV headquarters, the Eldfjallahús, modelled on the annular tulous of Fujian. Wood, stone and turf and glass will stand four floors high: an elven fort, stumbled upon. In the spirit of the old Chinese ring-houses, there will be one external door, and every room will look onto every other across the central court. Open, democratic, panoptic. Unlike Sindri's glass-and-steel box in the new corporate village at Borgartún.

'This is for me,' Atli says.

'For you,' Raisa says. 'Provided . . .'

'I clean, cook; look neat, smell sweet; no stinky feet. Yeah yeah yeah.'

'Or another boy moves in.'

Atli closes the window. Raisa finds him sitting on the bottom stair, arms wrapped around his knees.

'About that,' Atli says. 'Does it have to be boys?'

'It's the Boys' House,' Raisa says. She sits on the doorstep, as unable to enter uninvited as a vampire.

'But does it have to be?'

Raisa knows she does not need to answer. She and Atli sit side by side, companionable, unassertive on the step. The new House smells of gloss paint, fresh wood, recent electrics.

'Could it be a house for someone who's . . . sometimes . . . a boy, and then sometimes, something more?'

'It's a house,' Raisa says carefully. Picking Atli-kid and Atli-boy up from the school bus, they sat side by side like this in The Vehicle, then a PBV car. And he would talk. About his day, his dreamtime, his futures (this afternoon, this summer, when he was big), his fantasies and his small fascinations that over the years would crystallise into character. Just as Lisi talked to Raisa and she to Lisi, when she rattled them up around East London in the Arcmagical Volvo. Hopes and delights and infuriations. Tiny amounts of all the spices that make up a life. Not looked at, not scrutinised, not under the oppression of eyes, the words come. Eye contact is grossly overrated.

'There's another me,' Atli says and dares a glance from under his hair. 'He's not a boy, or a man. He's not even he. He's an hé. Hé is male, kind of.'

'Will I know him?'

'Hé's sitting right beside you.'

'Are you hé right now?' Raisa asks.

'Not right now. You'll know when I am. But I'll still be Atli Stormtalker.'

'I'll make mistakes. My Icelandic, it ain't great. Endings and that.'

They speak in English. Raisa's Icelandic is still weak and idiosyncratic but she can hear the difference. An accent, a keystroke, a shift of placement of the tongue, and a whole new person appears.

'That's all right. I can't even see who hé is quite yet.' He glances at her again and beneath his hair she glimpses someone new and different and a little wild. Someone she doesn't know yet. Someone Atli doesn't know. Beyond tags and identity labels. 'What I'm asking is: Is there a house for hé?'

'You're sitting outside it,' Raisa says. 'The kynnd need to agree to it. I will support you but . . .'

'I have to make my case. Our case.'
'You make the case. Deal?'
'Deal. And we love this house.'

N 63°29'13.80" W 19°10'57.78" 12:00 October 23, 2025
From Akureyri.
From Reykjavík.
From Vík í Mýrdal.
From Vestmannaeyjabær
From Vonland: the kynnd arrive.

The kynnd gather in the church on a day of squalls driven before a deepening south-easterly. Such a wind blew a cloud of painted lady butterflies and Raisa here thirteen years ago. For the past three summers the painted ladies have returned: alive, feeding, breeding. The warming climate has made southern Iceland an important habitat for *Vanessa cardui*.

The yatas have been taken down to make room for the visitors but still the kynnd press against the walls. Raisa sits at the end of the pew nearest the door. Nothing more off-putting to a performer than Mum bright-eyed in the front row. Birch branches beat beyond the stained-glass window. Wind rattles the roof. A draught sets the sanctuary candles guttering. For a moment the church breathes in unison.

Atli is here. Raisa turns her head to see who has come. Hé stands in the porch, trading careful hugs with hés young kynnd. Eight of them now, the youngest three years old. Hé will always be the forerunner. The explorer. Hé is dressed for adventure. New rock boots, rust red. Sheer capri pants; over them, a short yukata, sleeves wide enough to hide fantastical beasts and wondrous stories. Open-chested—hé's going to get cold, Raisa thinks. Amy Winehouse eye make-up, a line of white crosses hés lips and descends hés throat, hés chest to vanish in the meeting of the yukata. Against hés skin it looks like a line of light shining out of hé. But the hair, the hair! Hé's dyed it red and added massive extensions to turn hés do into a cumulus of rust and air. Driftwood antlers have been worked in. The construction is almost as big as hé is. The kids work hés look; forking up hés hair, adjusting the sit of the driftwood tiara, touching up nails, eyes. A nod, a deep breath. Hé processes up the aisle. Raisa's heart could burst.

Where did hé *get* all this stuff?

Atli's hair brushes the door posts as hé passes through the wooden screen to take hés place at the table where the candles burn. Tante Jebet rises on her sticks. She has faded, grown frail, but her preacher's voice never fails. She welcomes the kynnd. She bows to Atli. Hé takes out hés phone. Now Raisa knows what hé keeps in hés sleeves.

'Stars! I am Atli Raisasbur Vega Stormtalker Hopeland,' hé says in hés clear, fresh-broken voice that Raisa still cannot identify as her child's. Hé glances at hés phone screen. 'Thank you for coming. Long ways some ways. I want to talk to you about my name.' A murmur crosses the congregation. 'Not Atli, that's an approved name. Not Vega, because everyone is a star.' As below, so above, the voices murmur. 'Or Hopeland because that's being a citizen. Or Stormtalker, though that's the best name. I want to talk to you about Raisasbur.

'Raisasbur. Raisa's-kid. Not Raisa's-son or Raisa's-dóttir. Raisa's-kid. Now everyone can use that name if they want, but I was the first. For a long time, I was the only one. In school everyone asked me what to call me and I said Atli. Or Stormtalker. So they did. Then they asked me, okay, if you're not a son or dóttir, how do we know what you are? And I said, I'm me and they said, yes, but boy or girl? And I said, I'm still a kid. And when I said, okay, I'm going to be a boy, I was still Atli Raisasbur. And now I'm a boy, and someone else, who's talking to you today. I don't know much about Christians, but when this was their church, they used to give a talk every Sunday. A sermon. A teaching lesson. This is what I want to teach you today. It's a new word. A short one. Hé. Can you say that?'

The gathered kynnd repeat in unison.

'Hé, hé, hé, hés.'

Hé, hé, hé, hés, the nation answers.

'When I got my names, bur wasn't proper legal. It was a big change, a big challenge. Weird. I made everyone uncomfortable with my weird name. But they moved towards us because they could see it was right.

'What I'm saying is, like, names were once a big thing; now they're not. Pronouns were once a big thing, now they're not. Sometimes Atli Vega will be he, sometimes hé. You'll know when. And maybe, houses don't need to be a big thing. Some people aren't completely boys or girls—where's the house for them? Not either. Both, neither. Other. Sons-house, dóttirs-house, burs-house.

'Karl-Maria Lindner had these ideas like ahead of his time, but what worked then doesn't always work now. Karl-Maria knew that things have to change. We can change names. We can change our selves. We can change houses. I propose that the Hopeland community here has a Burs' House as well as a Girls' House and a Boys' House. For kids like me, or not like me at all. For anyone. That is what I'm asking you. Thank you for listening to me. I'm done now.'

Applause, cheers, whistles in the House of Emanations. Raisa gulps back tears and finds herself on her feet, clapping, grinning. She daren't look at Atli as hé returns down the aisle. Hés bur-kynnd hug and kiss hé in the porch and the church falls silent to vote.

The vote is carried. Not unanimously.

The kynnd return to Akureyri and Reykjavík, to Vík í Mýrdal and Vestmannaeyjabær, to Vonland. The next day Atli moves into what is now the Burs' House. By tradition hé prepares a meal for those hé leaves. Tekla helps hé. Hé is a terrible cook and hés tolerance of dust and disorder is beyond even Raisa's but the two aspects of Atli live in that house alone for three years until Embla Cassiopeia moves out of the Great House into the edge-of-adulthood and wants something other than just girls. The Burs' House is yellow, the Girls' House blue, the Boys' House green and when it is built, the House for those who aren't any of those will be white. And the climate warms and the summers stretch and the trees of the forest of Vonland grow taller and reach their branches up around Atli's house.

51

The weather forecasts snow but Raisa takes the PBV car up to Reykjavík anyway. She does not like the city but Sindri has proposals and she must hear them from him face-to-face. She does not like the clothes business expects her to wear. She does not like the offices—a lewd jut above Reykjavík's demure skyline. She does not like to see D-Centric's logo nuzzling much too close to PBV's. Like an abusive date. She does not like the boardroom, steel and glass and wood forced into unnatural shapes and positions. Branded water and terrible terrible coffee. She does not like Sindri Ólafursson. As Signy, Tekla and Atli chorused, he is a cunt. That truth hasn't faded over ten years. But Raisa's no longer sure he is her cunt.

Sindri and his team occupy one end of a long, impressive and overdesigned table. Raisa can see her face in the polish. She takes the window end, a silhouette against big sea and bigger sky and the mountains behind Grundarhverfi. She's bigged-up her hair to enhance her presence and mystery. She hates playing such petty corporate games.

She sets down the proposal document half read.

'So, your idea.'

A project manager lifts a hand. A mist-curtain unfolds from the middle of the table and lights with an animation of D-Centric and PBV's logos.

'No PowerPoint,' Raisa says. 'Pitch it to me. If you can't sell it with words, it's too complex.'

Looks, protests on lips. Sindri nods. The illusion vanishes.

'Blockchain,' Sindri says. Raisa has studied it, enough to know what she doesn't know. 'It's the future. Cryptocurrency and NFTs are the start of it. We jump to second-generation applications: smart contracts, automated escrow, distributed ledgers, proof-of-work. We have the hardware; you have the power. Electricity supply is the key to shifting the world to a blockchain economy. Global cryptocurrency mining consumes fifty terawatt-hours. PBV's current output across all modes of generation is twenty-five terawatt-hours. We anticipate using one hundred percent of that output for blockchain operations and in addition, all PBV's planned offshore operations. Wind farms, offshore geo. All of it. By its nature blockchain requires increasing amounts of energy so the project has in-built potential for expansion. It creates its own demand. We have the perfect partnership for the global blockchain revolution. It's beautiful.'

The far end of the table turns its attention on Raisa.

'Sindri, I understand your proposal. Post your presentation on the secure server and I'll put it to the board.'

Raisa's habit on her rare visits to Reykjavík is always to change out of her business attire before leaving the building. She pulls on loose comfortable pants, rural boots, knitwear in the executive bathroom. It's a release, a little wilding. She kicks the death-dust of the pitch-meeting off her boots. She finger-combs it out of her hair. Her PBV car pulls into the front of the building and her heart lifts a semi-tone higher at every eastward turn. At the head of the valley where the road loops down like a dropped sash to Hveragerði she sees a wall of darkness taller than the world. The promised storm.

Above her desk in her wood-and-glass office in the Eldfjallahús at Vonland Raisa keeps a framed photograph of Elon Musk. Underneath, on a piece of A4 in 120-point Arial Black are these words:

Don't be like Elon

The air swirls, curdles, hangs and snow is there. Conjured. The world beyond Raisa's windscreen whirls into a frenzy of wind-whipped flakes. The car drops into automatic winter driving mode. Raisa has learned it's safer letting the car drive. In any weather. In moments the highway dwindles to two sets of tyre tracks, to a railroad. Red taillights. Headlights scatter from surging snow crystals. White-outs are not white but infinite grey. The screen shines with notifications: weather reports, updates. The snowstorm steepens to full blizzard. An alert flashes: Safety and Rescue are closing the roads. Get off the highway, seek shelter. This storm could last a day or two. The car identifies a guest-house five minutes away and makes a booking. The access road is outside the car's self-drive parameters, so Raisa takes the wheel and crawls over the bridge and along the track, guided by golden window-light. She beats through whipping snow to the porch.

'Well, this wasn't expected,' the guest-house owner says. 'Takes you back to when we had proper winters.'

She eats with the family, who are are related to Signy's people in Vík. Everyone is related. Swipe up on the dating apps for degrees of incest. Her room is warm and generous with windows. She lies on the bed to watch the storm until darkness shrinks the universe to a snow-cloak draped around the house. Sleep will not come. Sindri's idea blows in her head like eddying snowflakes. She reads the proposal; the paper is slick, the ink glossy and heady. Smiling people pointing and lots of charts. The economics are sound—Sindri is fastidious with money. PBV will grow, Vonland will thrive, the deal will secure her vision of the Hopelands' future to the edge of deep time.

Raisa lies back and links her fingers behind her head. She's never grown out of snow. Its magic never tarnishes. Water changed to spun crystals, soft flakes: this is deep mystery. She imagines the guest-house caught up in a whirlwind of flakes. Dorothy of Kansas in a snow-globe. Snow dropping on South Iceland, on Vonland, covering the tall roofs of the Great House, the circle of the PBV building. On Atli's yellow house, the high gable window thrown open and Atli leaning on elbows looking out. On the dark sea, dissolving into it, each unique flake annihilated. Her imagination crosses that sea to Brightbourne wreathed in whirling flakes, its many windows shining. Snow piling in the window frames, blowing into the porte cochère to gather in the corners. The Music ringing through the snow. Seven years since she heard it; by its own life span, not one heartbeat closer to its conclusion. It is not snowing at Brightbourne. It has not snowed there for a decade. It never will until the Early Anthropocene, when humans undo the world, ends and the Middle Anthropocene, when humans restore the world, begins.

Raisa shivers. Wind gusts outside her windows. She opens a screen and calls the kynnd.

In her eighth decade Tante Hulda is a whetted hatchet of a woman, face deep-lined, eyes and mouth narrow. Her deep kindness, her gentleness, remain in-folded until she is with Tante Jebet. Then the creases open like the blades of a clever knife into useful tools: smiles, glances, patiences. Tante Jebet never fully recovered from the pandemic, has been fading since the day Raisa met her. She suspects that what makes her endure is the truth that Vonland needs two hearts—hers and Hulda's—to keep it alive. Like a Time Lord.

'I read Sindri's material. I've done a few figures.' Hulda holds up a scrawled-over envelope. 'The energy usage is . . . extreme.'

'I done a few figures too.' Raisa ran hers on a spreadsheet. She doesn't trust her hand-numbering. 'The money is extreme.'

'It's a consideration,' Tante Hulda says.

'Not the only consideration.'

Now Tante Hulda opens the edge of a smile.

'Call up the board,' Raisa says.

It's after midnight when Raisa's machine lets her know the Zoom guests are in. Her screen fills with faces from a dozen time zones. An engineer from the Toronto house. A journalist from Copenhagen. Two coders formerly from the Tel Aviv house who had moved out and on and into new relationships. A professor from UNAM in Mexico City. Icelanders, PBV kynnd. An economist from Rabat.

They say:

In less than five years the energy consumption of Sindri's blockchain venture will outstrip PBV's projected renewable energy expansion. The computations necessary to maintain the distributed ledger consume electricity on a geometrical scale, let alone chip cooling, new server farms, cabling. Technology creep will drive Internet of Things–connected devices to blockchain security. An IoT fridge will need to process blockchain calculations to order milk securely. Ubiquitous blockchain contracts and ledgers offer privacy and security but threaten to commodify human activity. All life could become financialized. Everything is tradable. The concept of proof-of-work—that a record of performed calculations guarantees the validity and value of a blockchain calculation—is valueless. The work is useless work.

Effortism. Prisoners on a treadmill, turning a crank that does nothing. The entropy of the system is colossal.

At three thirteen Raisa thanks the kynnd for their contributions and dismisses them. She calls up Tante Hulda. The screen fills with PBV board members. Some of them are faces she's already talked to.

At five twenty-two the board comes to a vote.

With morning a warm front moves in and by noon Safety and Rescue reopens the roads. Raisa turns the car to Reykjavík, orders up *Graceland* and sings all the way back to Sindri's head office, where she sets herself at the end of his obviously designed table to tell him that the partnership between D-Centric and PBV is dissolved.

52

He comes on a day of grey. Grey port by a grey sea. Grey stone moles, grey frown of a ferry terminal. Lazy lick of can't-be-arsed grey water up the black sand. The drearily flat land is a greyscale print of sea-grass and outflow grit. To the north rises the edge of Eyjafjallajökull's lava shield, to the south the peaks of Bjarnarey and Heimaey break the horizon.

Raisa waits in the car at the Landeyjahöfn ferry terminal.

'Shite then, shite now,' she mutters.

Three pieces of colour in the entire universe and she put them there: the hydrogen fuelling dock, the PBV car, Raisa.

Twenty-two years since she crossed that gangway from the ferry to the terminal. Buying the ticket with the money the *Los Ascending* crew gave her. Waiting for the bus on the hard metal bench. Watching loaded refrigerator trucks roll off, empty ones roll on. Watching the ferry turn and head back to the islands. They ran on bunker fuel then: ferries, fisher fleet.

Cars, trucks, buses were easy. The new challenge is uncarboning the planet's marine transport.

She sees the masts and stern gallows over the seaward wall and steps out of the car. *Los Ascending II* rounds the breakwater. She is a tight, trim ship, sea-wise and pugnacious like her forebear. A yata still turns in the bridge window. Captain Lind waves from the bridge. Her father, Jónþór, only ever saw *Los Ascending II* from his living room window. A heart attack ended his command before the ship was out of the slips; then circulation problems, gangrene, a double amputation. Sepsis ended it. Sepsis and the despondency of the fisherman fallen from grace with the sea. The yata catches the afternoon's sole spark of sunshine.

There he is. Oh God, there he is. On the deck.

And she's terrified. Paralysed. Can't speak, can't move. Only her heart. Stupid gallumphing heart.

He looks terrific, smiling up at her. Geological. Deepenings and openings. His hair long, grey streaked, tied back with a silver ring. He wears the New Edwardian style as if he inspired it. You should always be in a coat like that, Raisa thinks.

Lightning in his eyes. She feels old old old.

'Embrace' is too formal a word. 'Hug' is too childish. On the quay she wraps, enfolds, crushes, drinks in the heat and solidity. And he her. Tectonic plates merging.

'Raisa Peri Antares,' he declares, then remembers. 'Stormtalker.'

'Finnevar Mikael Hamal.'

'Finnevar Mikael Hamal Grand Primary,' Finn says.

Then she notices that his face, his hands, his exposed skin are covered in a net of faint silvery scars.

Yellow snow-poles mark the soft edges of the single-track road across the gravel plain. The approaching truck convoy is at least two kilometres away. Raisa already feels apprehensive. She wouldn't intend to steer straight into the path of the lead truck, but she might do it by accident, or while distracted. Or just.

'This car is on auto?' Finn asks.

'You don't trust my driving?'

'You do?'

Raisa hits the self-drive tab and the car turns in to a pull-out while the trucks pass by to the port.

'You said Grand Primary,' Raisa says. The car moves off again.

'I did,' Finn says. 'I am.' These are the days of diminishing light among the Electromancers. The Coil of the North has worn a tube up each nostril and pushed around a little oxygen gurney for the last five years but still wheezes with breathless delight every time he sees a metal show lit by Tesla-light. The Coil of the West never recovered from the end of her network weather career. From the lantern of her West Galway house she challenges each storm-season Atlantic front and tries to draw its power into her coil, and from the coil into her, to push her life forward, storm by storm. They come more often, the storms, with the changing of the weather and the world. The Coil of the East cares full-time for fading Tante Margolis and between Arcmage House and the ministry of her strange, lightning-crowned Christ she has no time anymore for electromancy. She has an apprentice, a junior imam at the Brick Lane Mosque who has the spark in the back of his eye. The Coil of the South is in the final stage of bladder cancer and spends his terminal days wandering with his childhood self beneath the trees of haunted Brocéliande, mind luminous with cosmo-logical strength painkillers. The true forest, the matter world's Brocéliande, dries out season by season, racked by terrible fires.

And Finn, by the acclaim of Tante Margolis and the Order of Electro-mancers, is Grand Primary.

'I rebuilt the Christ Church coil,' Finn says. 'Twenty-three years, on and off. You can't imagine it.'

'I haven't exactly been slacking, either,' Raisa says.

'I know; Atli . . .'

'Yes, Atli. And a nice geothermal power company which will launch its biggest venture yet in five days. International partners across the north. And a foundation. I got a foundation now, Finn. Nýttnorður. New North. New ideas, new technologies, new politics, new ways of living, new life. So, I can imagine it.'

'You got me beat there,' Finn says.

'Actually, when I say "got", I mean, "I'm in." The kynnd got the founda-tion. I mean, what you going to do with all that money?'

'So you moved on from PBV,' Finn says.

'I'm a stýra of the ráðh. Really, stýrimaður. Some people have trouble with Icelandic words.'

'Arcmage, Stormtalker, stýra,' Finn says. 'That's some collection of ti-tles.'

Raisa play punches him.

'It means Steerer. Kind of like a Tante. What we do is identify areas where PBV money can help people change the world—big or small. I've got this big event, PBV's biggest launch coming up.'

'You told me.'

'And I'm telling you again 'cause I get this message that Finn is on the seas and will I drop everything and pick him up from the boat?'

'Sorry. Thank you.'

'From Landeyjahöfn.'

'Electromancy business.'

'Okay,' Raisa says. It is an article of electromantic dogma that an Arc-mage on business should not share the stratosphere with their element, save in direst urgency. Too much of a temptation to the Emanations. Raisa holds her curiosity until the high turn around the ridge into Vonland. 'What electromancy business?'

Finn leans forward, gazing wonder-struck at what lies before him. Raisa stops the car. All is green, all is covered and blessed by leaf and needle. The pointed roofs of the Great House, the church hiding like a bird under the leaf canopy: these he knows. The steam plumes from the geopower plants he can infer but the guest-house, the spa, the ring of the old PBV Eldfjallahús—now outgrown—the Houses of Growing up at the edge of the tree-line, the community hall—new, wonderful. She sees with his eyes; his delight makes it new and wonderful to her.

'Twenty-two years, Finnevar Hamal,' Raisa says and starts the car and it takes them over the hill down to Vonland.

After dinner with Signy and Óðinn at the guest-house Raisa takes Finn into the forest of Vonland. They pass through the shoulder-high scrub and under the green eaves into branches so dense and intertwined a squirrel might cross from one side to the other without touching ground. If squirrels lived in Iceland. The umbra beneath the leaves sounds with a hundred high songs: flutings and whoopings, whistles and burbles. Blackbird and robin; wren, chaffinch and blackcap. The warm grey air presses sound to the earth; every wing-burst, call and response, crack and creak and wind rustle is skin-close. High-summer insects catch the dappled light; butterfly wings glow. Raisa bats away midges. She remembers the butterflies; always forgets the midges. The scents of growth and decay, life and rot intoxicate. Only in the past four years have the trees matured into forest. All grown up. It has its own life now. She senses a little wild among the trunks. This may be the year she camps out listening for the footsteps of Lightning Woman.

Steam wraiths haunt the trees. Ghost birches encircle the curving wall of Eldfjallahús, a clearing inside a clearing.

'Pity PBV got too big for it,' Raisa says. 'I love this place.'

They pass through the one entrance into the circular courtyard. A few slipped roof-shingles gather moss on the stone flags. The glass window-walls are dusty, bug-spackled, sap-smeared; the wooden galleries silvered with age, opening dark cracks.

'Is anyone using this?'

'I thought maybe the Foundation but the ráðh's thinking is we're best distributed. Scattered but connected.'

'A constellation,' Finn says.

They leave the Eldfjallahús and navigate by footpaths and birdsong to the Great House. Its turf roofs form a ring of green triangles rising above the leaf-line, a crown lost in a forest. Ferns and mosses grow over the twenty years of rural detritus—polytunnel hoops, sacks of hardened concrete, the stripped corpse of The Vehicle—but feet have worn desire lines between the trees; and cars, bikes and quads fill the open space before the house.

'It'll be hard to leave this,' Raisa says.

'You're leaving?'

'After the launch. Busy girl, Finnevar Hamal.' She smells his disappointment like leaf-mould. 'Nýttnorður is sending a fleet to Greenland. We're working with the Naalakkersuisut on a big project. Like a hundred-year project. Thousand, maybe. When the ice goes, when the people come—and they'll come—when the world changes, what next?'

'This?'

'Maybe. Maybe different. The North's changing. Life finds a way.'

The church, the old wall and lych-gate appear through the ash trunks. Everything that Vonland does is in a circle. Close by the churchyard wall on the east side stands Tante Hulda's stone. Unimaginable that she would die before Tante Jebet. Jebet was the sick one, the decrepit one, the one fading from life. At first she asked every day where Hulda was. The time it took her to remember that Hulda was dead grew longer. This past year she no longer asks. She sits in her chair in the sun, feeding from it, watching the children and listening to the alien birds. Raisa rests a hand on the stone pillar. Moss blurs the inscription: HULDA CELAENO HILDURSDÓTTIR. ENITHARMON DESCENDING.

Raisa opens the lych-gate and leads Finn by the hand to the church.

'PBV stopped being fun. It got to be business. Good business, but business. Business is a terrible way to do business. You ever been to Brightbourne? Suppose not. They have this thing. The Music.'

'I've heard of it.'

'Fifty years in and it's still tuning up. What I worked out about it: what'll keep it going to the end is people. Same with Nýttnorður; people knowing when something needs to be oiled or repaired or tightened and people knowing when to step out and let it run itself.'

The church interior is cave-dark under the praying hands of the ash leaves. Dark planes brighten into ambient grey then fade again: the great yatas turning. Once a high wind blew in from the east, set the forest's top tossing, cast coins of light through the leaves and the high windows onto the yatas. Raisa sat in a constellation of dancing spotlights; mirror to mirror to mirror, reflection to reflection to reflection. Today the church smells of stale air, cold tile, wood infiltrated by slow fungus and leaf-rot and she still has no idea what moves the mirrors.

'The joke is I never finish anything and Atli never starts anything. Atli floats. Bit of helping out at the guest-house here, bit of modelling there, bit of professional socialising, bit of off-road tour-guiding someplace else.'

'You offered him a job?'

'I offered him and hé a job. Didn't want it.'

'Hé?'

'Atli has hés own gender. Which hé is sometimes. Like we have our own religion.'

'But we don't have to believe it.'

'Neither does hé. Praxy, not doxy.'

'The modelling makes sense.'

"Oh. He's gorgeous. In demand, every social event. Hé spends more time up at the Reykjavík Hearth than here. Thing is, Atli-he doesn't want what Atli-hé wants. Reykjavík, Vonland. Truth? He and hé have no idea what they want. Did you ever meet Tekla? Signy and Óðinn's bur. She and Atli were the only kids in Vonland for a long time. Like one life two bodies. But they grew apart. She went to uni, travelled. Went into the world. She's with PBV. Very good. So sharp. Atli? Turned me down.'

Old wood from another climate creaks in new warmth.

'I'd like Atli to be a stýra after me, Finn. He and hé's got the heart for it. A great heart.'

Two mirrors brighten, turning to catch each other's light. Dust sparkles. She thinks it's dust.

'So: What electromancy business?'

53

FINN BATTLES THE DEMON OF SPITALFIELDS

He arrived in a great equinoctial storm. By the Hammersmith & City line he came to Aldgate East. If the Central Line smells like dust and rosined strings and the deep tunnels of the Northern line blood and old water, the Hammersmith & City is ghosts all the way.

Rain punished Commercial Street. He was the only soul abroad. He turned his collar up, set his hat against the storm. At the foot of Christ Church the wave of ill radiating from the stones almost shoved him into the splashing traffic.

Fournier Street cowered.

A bell sounded deep inside Arcmage House. Kynnd Rev. Hope was slow to answer the door.

'How is she?'

'Failing. She knows it.' He hung hat, coat dripping on the Victorian coatstand. 'You may find her disturbing.'

Tante Margolis sat by the old fireplace in the kitchen. He saw a twist of waxed paper, a puzzle of knotted threads, bones in a silk bag.

In only three months, she had crumpled and faded.

'What are the doctors doing?' he asked.

'Nothing,' she said from her chair. Her hands were vellum origami. Draughts and earth-currents blew around her feet. 'Nothing they can do, nothing I want them to do. It's Tesla's price. The electromantic fields twist everything, in the end.'

He embraced her as if she were spun sugar. Her apprentice Arcmage, Xaaji, a slight young man uncomfortable between worlds of mosque and electromancy, stood at her shoulder.

'How's the tour?'

'Money in the bank. They weren't happy me leaving before Red Rocks.'

'Xaaji,' Tante Margolis said. Xaaji took a long leather case stamped with gold-leaf arcana from the Welsh dresser and laid it on the kitchen table. Tante Margolis rose from her chair, painfully unwrapped two tall staffs, each headed with a fist-sized brass orb.

'I offer you the paraphernalia and office of Grand Primary of the Order of Electromancers.'

She could barely lift the staffs.

He took one in each hand, set their heels on the floor and heads level with his shoulders.

'I accept.'

Tante Margolis clapped her wasp-paper hands, Rev. Hope and Xaaji bowed and that was all the magic and ritual of it.

'What is it you need me to do?' he asked.

'You were out there,' Rev. Hope said. 'You felt what it's like.'

'I've been up there,' Xaaji said. 'It's not holding it.'

'I need you to finish it,' Tante Margolis said.

'I know what I have to do,' he said.

He tooled up in the old laboratory. He opened deep wooden drawers filled with glowing amber rods. He dismantled a theremin and swaddled it in bubble wrap. He packed a knapsack of gold-leaf electroscopes. Museum pieces, beyond obsolete yet charged with old magic. He searched the house from lightning lab to basement for boxes of brass drawing pins. No tin, no aluminium; only brass. Last of all he brought the 1970s beanbag from the guest room, leatherette cracked and flaking, unzipped it and poured the tiny polystyrene beads into four mason jars.

'Kynnd Hope, Xaaji, I'll need you.'

They slipped back into Christ Church. He showed Xaaji the electromantic use of the foil electroscope and the three of them worked Hawksmoor's sternly classical nave. Where the gold-foil leaves trembled they crouched and scanned the electroscope patiently over the floor. A strong kick, a finger went up. The others nodded. Mark it with an upturned drawing pin. Where the signals were multiple or ambiguous he came with the theremin to pass hands and antennae over floor and pillars, listening intently to the music until he found a true note. Mark it. Noises haunted the Baroque interior. Rattles and clicks, rhythms in the traffic rumble. The church stirred, uneasy on its foundations. The Arcmages worked on.

Long after midnight the last electroscope fluttered and the last pin was laid. On the floor the cardinal points of an unseen pattern were marked out by brass drawing pins.

'Okay,' he said. Each took a jar of polystyrene beads and an amber rod. Rev. Hope had already marked the best positions on the gallery. They charged their rods and touched them to the metal lids of the mason jars. Then, on his command, they removed the lids and swiftly hurled the beads out into the air of the nave.

Electromancy!

The breath-light charged beads floated on electrostatic winds, drifted, flocked like murmurations. Electric fields grabbed them, drew them down into flux-lines. The last beads rolled and settled. Marked out in soft white snow was a pattern: a shield and a crown, an inverted cross, crenellations, six small circles.

He took pictures on his phone.

'Well, that couldn't be much clearer,' Rev. Hope said.

'It's the seal of a demon from the *Goetia*,' he said. 'You pick up stuff touring with metal bands.'

'Count Royne,' Xaaji said. 'Sixth King of Hell. Creates towers and buildings, breaks down walls, makes the seas rise and reveals riches. You pick up stuff at the seminary.'

'Okay, let's clean this up,' Finn said. 'We've work to do.'

Rev. Hope fetched the Henry from the store.

Two days later the film crew rolled in. The ruse still worked. Do Not Cross tape went up; kynnd in hi-viz kept back the rubberneckers. A crane lifted the Soho coil from the tower. Finn helped bear the coil on a wooden pallet to the centre of the nave.

A scent of lily of the valley filled the church.

He cabled up the coil. He ran it up and down the power spectrum. Twenty years since it had summoned the blue lightning. He set the pillars ringing and called harmonics from the organ pipes. He retraced the seal of Royne on the church floor and marked its cardinal points with drawing pins, spike up, precisely placed. He edged the Tesla coil into alignment with the pattern of forces. The day was half-lit pewter overcast, tombstone-still but the church creaked and boomed. It did not need the voice of the coil now. It spoke to him in stone and clay and blood. The tension, the rolling nausea sent him four times to the vestry toilet. He set up the secondary electrodes and tested the safety set-up.

The church almost pushed him out of the door. Two dawdling police officers tried to guess which movie star he was.

'Timothée Chalamet,' he said. The storm of malice blew him up Fournier

Street. That night when he set out back to the church it had steepened into a full-force gale. There was no reason for him to wait until dark, except that no one ever battled demons by daylight. It took the authority of Grand Primary to tell Rev. Hope she could not come with him. There must be a Coil in the East: in case. He asked Xaaji to be his second and squire. They ducked under the yellow warning tape.

He armoured up in the vestry. Greaves and hauberk, chain-mail boots and gauntlets. He slid anti-UV lenses into his eyes.

'Ya Rabb protect your heart.'

He took Xaaji's head between his mailed hands and kissed him on the forehead.

'I want you to leave. Don't argue. Whatever happens, whatever you hear or see, do not enter the church. I will come to you.'

He pulled on the casque. Xaaji handed him the high staffs of office.

Alone in the nave, the church turned all its hostility onto him. Malice so strong the air hummed. He was armoured and he was armed. He stood facing the coil across the map of drawing pins. He stamped the foot-switch. Primaries and secondaries powered up. The top coil dripped fat blue licks of electric fire. From communion table to font the church flinched. Pillars throbbed. Kitten-arcs pounced between the organ pipes.

He laid the Arcmage staffs in a saltire on the floor before him.

'My name is Finnevar Mikael Hamal Hopeland, Arcmage and Grand Primary of the Order of Electromancers!' he shouted. 'And I say: no pasarás!'

Thumbs out, first two fingers upright, last two fingers pointing forward. Left-hand and right-hand rules. Law of generator, law of motor. He threw his arms open and lightning leapt to his fingertips. He brought his hands together, pushing the hissing lightning in until it was a blazing rod. He thrust out his hands and threw the rod of plasma to the floor. Electricity flashed around the pattern of drawing pins. They lifted into the air, each pin-tip star-bright.

'With lightning I bind you!'

Theatrics: more stuff you pick up from metal bands.

The church shook to its poisoned roots. The fillings in his teeth ached; the metal fixings where he had broken his ankle slipping from a ladder rigging the Sultan's Elephant puppet for Royale de Luxe burned in the bone. Beneath the pins the floor darkened. Vile ichor osmosed from the plague pits buried under Christ Church into a pattern: the seal of Royne.

He took up the electromancers' staffs, one in each hand, and stepped through the web of lightning. The lines of force flowed over his armour in a momentary blue aura, then snapped back to mirror the dark seal below. Inside the electromantic circle the malevolence was rust in his heart. He thrust out his twin staffs and the Tesla coil answered with a crackling ribbon of plasma. He gritted his teeth, caught the stream on the two brass orbs and held it, held it until he was half-blind with the nova-light and could smell his own singeing skin. Slowly he separated the staffs. One stream became three, an Arcmage's triangle of power. Sweat streamed stinging into his eyes. At the centre of the triangle the air glowed; ions tied in the knot of field lines.

Every Arcmage knows they work with more than lightning.

'Royne!'

It came to its name. It could not refuse. The fields of force hooked into it, drew it into the orb at the centre of the triangle. Faces writhed and shape-shifted, faces of blue plasma, faces of avarice and contempt and intolerance. Faces of greed and want and envy. Finn gripped the twin staffs. The rods shook with power. Energies he had not summoned pushed at the limits of his craft. Ferocious electrical forces were eating away at the pins that shaped his containment pattern, brass evaporating into plasma. He had only moments to bind the demon and discharge it to earth. And it was fighting, tearing at its lightning cage. The brass globes atop his Arcmage staffs glowed red, redder, began to soften and melt. He dropped them with a cry of pain.

The faces came together and he beheld his adversary. It wore his face. It lunged; the containment ruptured. The boom rattled every piece of stained glass in its leading. Brilliant white flashed over Spitalfields from every window. He was blown backwards. Movie bodies fight-fly through the air to bounce up on their feet, ready to rumble again. Real bodies hit hard, even armoured in chain-mail. Have the breath mashed from them. Crack ribs. Are stunned. Concussed. Agonised.

Field lines writhed and shaped the arcs into the form of a man. The Grand Primary staffs flew to its hands. The lightning man raised them like spears. The spears stabbed for his lungs. He rolled, reached, ripped a shoulder. Hit the emergency shut-off. The coil scrammed. The demon evaporated. The levitating drawing pins dropped to the floor.

'Fuck,' he whispered. 'Oh fuck.'

He crawled to the porch. Burned, agonised, cracked and bruised. The air smelled scorched. The Tesla coil smoked. He dragged himself upright and staggered to the door. The Hopeland crew saw the armoured figure lurch from the door. They helped him down the steps, laid him flat.

'Get an ambulance!'

'Too slow. Get him in a car.'

'Get him out of that armour!'

Xaaji's face bent over his.

'I told you to leave.'

'I did.'

The chain-mail was still warm to the touch. His compression-wear base layer was scorched and holed.

'What happened to you?' the triage nurse asked at A&E.

'Special effects accident,' Xaaji said. The doctors diagnosed a cracked rib, a sprained ankle, a pulled muscle in the right shoulder, mild concussion and bruising. Trivial. Non-trivial were the first-degree burns over Finn's exposed skin. Annular burns the size of chain-mail armour links. He spent two nights in the burns unit and was discharged back onto the demon-haunted streets.

'Had worse on *Bat Out of Hell: The Musical*,' he said in the cab back from the hospital, high on painkillers. But he had been badly beaten.

'You browned-out everything east of Liverpool Street,' Xaaji said. They both read the implication: and that wasn't enough.

'Tell the clean-up crew: only go in in daylight,' he said.

The cab took the long way round, down Brick Lane, out of the shadow of Christ Church.

He went into deep sleep. He had always had the gift of sleeping anywhere, any time. Sleep and heal. In the clockless hours he woke from elemental sleep to feel a body slip in beside him. Xaaji. He was small, dog-skinny but warm and wonderful. He rolled to him, draped an arm over his flank and fell back into the sleep at the bottom of the universe. Finn Mikael Hamal Hopeland's truth was this: in victory he was hot, brave, magnificent but in defeat no heart on earth could resist him.

Burn scars would mark his face, neck, hands for all his days. Silver rings, like scales.

54

'I see a new North,' Finn says. The musky dim of the church has grown dank and stifling. Raisa closes the door on the subtly shifting yatas. 'People, cities, forests and animals. All guarded by four coils. One here, one in Greenland, one in Siberia, one maybe Svalbard. Four coils channelling the planet's electric field. Defending the North.'

Insects haunt the evening, clouds of tiny Emanations.

'You want the Eldfjallahús,' Raisa says.

'I need to start again. We're getting old, Rai. We need new Arcmages. A new Order. You said Atli doesn't know what he—hé—wants. I could make Atli paduan.'

They cross from clearing to shade and the shift of light illuminates the glossy marks of old burns on his hands, his neck. She lifts a hand to touch them, he stays her.

'It burned me, Rai. With my own lightning.'

'Come with me.'

'I couldn't beat it.'

'Come with me. There's a thing I want you to see.'

From darkness through high-summer light into a small clearing among the shivering birches.

'Do you know where we are?' She doesn't let him answer. 'Look.' She draws a shape on the moss and undergrowth with her finger and it appears; a ghost in the soil: a long rectangle vanishing back among the trees. Old greened-over foundations.

'This is the tunnel?'

'All grew out'a here.'

'Where you . . .'

'On Atli's Starring. Yes.'

He looks around him, putting a roof on the world, changing the light, shrinking the trees back to ankle-high saplings.

'We could reprise,' Raisa says.

The katabatic wind sets the leaves trembling and all the birds of Von-land sing.

'We could.'

Raisa still sleeps in the same room, the same sleigh-bed she was given when she blew through the door of Vonland on an autumn storm. The shuttered bed is cosy, warm, intimate, perfect for every bedroom activity except sex.

The groan of Finn heaving himself out of the sex-nest he built from quilts and yoga mats on the floor wakens her. He opens the shutters and peers out at the trees. Light streams around his body and turns his scars to fish-scales. Raisa sneaks from her night-sleigh to kiss the small of his back. He starts.

'Sorry.'

'Sorry.'

'It's only five o'clock,' Raisa says.

'I can't get used to the light,' he says.

She makes coffee and they sit together in the kitchen over the cafetière. She glances at him when she thinks he can't see her. He was the swagger-ing boy, easy on the eye, with a charm that made you smile. Never lacking people to sleep with. The battle with the Spitalfields demon burned away his old arrogance. Beneath is a brave vulnerability, a seriousness of intent and purpose. His art, his craft has scarred him but it's all he owns. Brave, burned soldier. Raisa pours more coffee.

'About the coil.'

He sips coffee from a Nýttnorður Foundation mug.

'What about it?'

'I think we can accommodate you. But it'll take time and time I ain't got. I got to go up to Reykjavík.'

'Your big event.'

'Þor.'

'Þor.' He stumbles over the Icelandic Þ.

'Óðinn'll help you get the Eldfjallahús into some kind of shape. He's good at construction. Meet me here, this day.' She flicks a hotel booking from her phone to his. 'If you want, come up a day early and buy yourself something for a big launch party. I've a room booked for five days.'

'I need a day for clothes shopping?'

'We got an aesthetic.' She flicks cash to his phone. 'About Atli. You got an idea for him, I got an idea for him. I'm thinking . . .'

'What's his idea for . . . him?'

'I'll arrange dinner. Before I go to Þor.'

They both look up at the whir of an engine, the crunch of gravel. The slam of car doors, the great door of the Vonland house creaking open. And by high electromancy, Atli and Óðinn are in the kitchen. They are both layered and booted in hike-wear. Wilderness boys. Atli wears cute triple stripes of blue sunblock on each cheekbone.

'We were taking an early walk up Sólheimajökull,' Óðinn says.

'It's our glacier,' Raisa explains to Finn.

'We found something,' Atli says.

He takes a metal disc engraved with runes from the pocket of his hiking leggings and sets it on the kitchen table.

55

All the long light hours sun licks the ice. Every lick turns a molecule-thick layer of ice to water. It sweats from the face of the glacier. This is known, this is measured. Unmeasured, unknown, is the warmth that increases every year, pushing autumn further into winter, pressing winter back to its dark redoubt. Over many warming summers a shadow appears in the ice, a dark pebble indistinguishable from the general muck and detritus swept up by the glacier. Summers more and the dark shape gains shape and definition, lick by lick. An edge emerges from the ice. Once that edge is exposed to direct sun, the rest happens quickly. The dark shape absorbs heat, melts free within days. Years to hours.

The object is a metal disc engraved with runes. It lies angled in a small suncup but as the ice melts around it, it settles until it presents its maximum surface area to the sun. The process accelerates. The suncup widens into a bowl, then early-summer rain flushes the medallion free. Its journey begins. It slides into one of the many rivulets that score the surface of the glacier, the sudden flood pushing it down the channel to join a wider stream to another wider still until it plunges down a moulin into a roaring underworld, rushed along ice tunnels, dashed through meltwater-sculpted cathedrals, bowled down blue crevasses. A torrent flicks it into an ice-pot where it circles for three weeks until another late-summer storm sends a deluge down through the glacier's undercroft and scoops it free to chase it down through caverns and chutes, channels and culverts to gush from the foot of the glacier in a meltwater torrent and settle to the bottom of the outwash channel. Where it remains, half-silted in gravel like the One Ring, until a glint draws the eye of a trekker on a dawn ascent. Who kneels, picks up the disc so that it catches the sun, frowns at the runes engraved on the surfaces. She passes it to her guides. Óðinn angles it to the sun. He passes it to Atli.

'What does it say?'

ATLI. MAY 22ND, 2012, CONSTELLATION OF ENITHARMON ASCENDING. LONG TRAVELS.

56

They take a corner table in the hotel restaurant, quiet, away from the tour parties but three people of colour still draw looks in Mýrdalshreppur even into the 2030s. Or maybe just Atli. High-waist lounging pants, bolero jacket, white filigrees coiling down the left side of hés face, hair sculpted back into a point. Reverse unicorn, Raisa thinks. And: Where does hé get the money from? And: How does he do it so quickly? Yesterday he came rolling down from the ice in full great-outdoors-wear, rune disc in his hand. Today hé wears it in a leather harness on the back of hés left hand.

'So what do you want?' Raisa asks.

Atli twirls the stem of hés wine glass between hés fingers. Second bottle. Hé's had most of the wine. Hé's getting to the stage where the car won't work for him. Hé'll find a bed here. Atli has people to sleep with all across Iceland.

'What I want.' Hé releases the glacier talisman from its leatherwork and sets it on the table. 'This was supposed to take my whole life to work down through Sólheimajökull.'

'Eighty years,' Raisa says.

'Whatever, that's a long time frozen in ice.'

Even twenty-two years is long. Raisa sees back along the trail of Atlis. Baffled and bereft as Tekla drove up the valley road and around the corner of the mountain to university and the lifeline between them stretched and snapped. Throwing open the gable window of the yellow Burs' House every morning to look at the world. Bold in the shadows and Emanations in the church when hé spoke to the kynnd. Fearful when Dolly sailed out to sea. New and strange when she held them up to the sun and the Emanations. Before ever their name and time and stars went into the glacier.

Twenty-two years is long and twenty-two years is twenty-two breaths.

'What I want is I don't want stuff given to me.'

Raisa throws her hands up. Stars, she'd love another glass of wine, but tomorrow is the Þor launch and an emotional hangover is bad enough.

'I've got my name back,' Atli says. 'It's like, there are two parts of me. One part was up in that glacier. The other is in Brightbourne. It's mine, isn't it?'

Finn pours Raisa a glass unprompted.

'I . . . suppose,' Raisa says.

'I want to go there. I want to see everyone again. And I want to go and see him.'

'Amon?' People look over again, this time at the raised voices. Raisa glances at Finn. His mouth twitches.

'After . . .' Raisa says.

'Twelve years.'

'And suddenly—what? He pings you on social media?'

Finn rests his hand on hers and she resents it.

'No, I pinged him.'

'You got in contact with him.'

She defies the wine. Defies it.

'And what did you say? Hi, remember me? Your son? Can I come and see you?'

Finn lays his hand over hers. Raisa snatches hers free. Her anger surprises her. Another old memory released from the ice.

'He replied. He'd love it.'

'Where is he anyway?' She tries to sound unconcerned. Even she can hear her failure.

'Ava'u.' For a few moments Raisa can't place the name. Then it arrives, drops from the Emanations into the ocean in a splash of green and gold: the islands where Karl-Maria Lindner derived the idea of Hopeland. Of course Amon Brightbourne would end up at the heart of the legend. They will always be lucky. They will always fall on their feet.

You can't kill him, Amon said, the last morning she saw him, the morning she drove him away from Brightbourne. Atli too has always been lucky, loved, privileged. A charmed life.

'You're set on this,' Raisa says.

'I am. I have to. I need all parts of me, Raisa.'

'And after?' Raisa says. 'Him?'

Atli shrugs. Hé weaves the talisman back into its nest.

'The Order of Electromancers could always use a Stormtalker,' Finn says.

'The Foundation can use a stýra,' Raisa says quickly.

'And that's you all telling me what you want for me again,' Atli says. 'You know what I want from you?'

'What?'

'Some money.'

Raisa kicks Finn under the corner table before he can laugh.

57

The electric plane flies south of south-west across white-crowned waves, cresting and breaking, train upon train, endlessly running. It is as small, streamlined, elegant and wind-worthy as a tern. Like a bird, it is autonomous, but Reykjavík Civil Aviation requires a pilot and the passengers like the reassurance of a human at the control pad.

'Ten minutes,' the pilot announces.

Raisa presses her face to the window. Sea sea sea. Endlessly running. The plane slips into descent. Raisa shivers at the shift in her inner ear. The shiver becomes elemental memory: staggering onto the deck of *Los Ascending* to shout back at this same sea, to whisper the lightning and turn a storm. These waves have run without let or change since then. The sea swallows time; swallows everything. Then she sees white plumes rising from the horizon. Smoke from the waters. Not smoke. Steam.

The rig comes into view. So small. So isolated. One hundred thousand tons of concrete and steel, bobbing like a cork. The tilt-fan comes in fast around the rig, pivoting about the axis of the landing pad.

'Can you take us around again?' Raisa asks. Tekla Pleione Signysdóttir Hopeland from PBV has her phone out. The pilot lifts the joy-pad, takes control from the AI and banks out in a long, wide loop to let them view the platform. Þor 1 Reykjanes. Steam jets from vent pipes. Cranes blink warning lights; crew modules defy the sea and sky with brilliant orange. The hydrogen tanks stand ten by ten, each the size of two cargo containers. The plane circles again and she sees the Neo-Panamax ship standing a kilometre off, awaiting a pilot. The aircraft swivels its fans, unfolds wheels and settles onto the H at the centre of the landing pad. The deck crew run out a refuelling line. The door opens, steps unfold. Raisa tries to make herself impressive in her weather gear. Offshore installation manager, operations team leader and offshore operations engineer step forward to welcome the guests. Behind them the rest of the PBV team wait, windswept and seasick.

'Hard hats,' the pilot calls. Raisa claps the helmet on her head, adjusts mic and headphones and leads the funders down onto the platform. Camera drones cover the handshakes and relay them back to Reykjavík, to Oslo, Copenhagen, Calgary.

Raisa breathes deep. Sulphur and steam. Electricity. The rig hums with power. She is two hundred kilometres from land on a geothermal rig anchored over the Reykjanes Ridge. The rig crew is here. The PBV team is here. The Foundation is here, in the frame of Raisa Peri Antares Stormtalker. Media and investors on both sides of the Mid-Atlantic Ridge are watching. Þor 1 is ready to go onstream.

Throughout the ceremony the wind steepens. Camera drones dip and veer trying to hold position until a gust sweeps one to perdition in the running waves far below and the media director grounds them. The wind summons moans and howls from the rig's rails and gantries, trusses and decks like a Penderecki threnody. Rig crew turn up their collars and hunch their shoulders to the wind, camera angles be fucked. Some old hands have been out here since the drill ship sank the exploratory boreholes. They're wise to the Reykjanes Ridge.

Tekla has spoken. The co-funders have spoken. Now Raisa takes her turn. She tucks fly-away hair back into her helmet while holding down a lectern keen to follow the camera drone into the North Atlantic.

'It's been a long road!' she says. Wind rattles over her microphone. 'Literally! From the Route 1 EV ring to here.' Raisa skims down her speech. She has flown out here to talk to a flock of drones. Publicity theatre. 'And this only the start.' Cycling advocacy officer to geothermal power company executive to futurological Foundation steers-kynnd. 'Þor 2 off Jan Mayen and Þor 3 at the Azores will also come online when we press the button. Carbon-free transatlantic and transpolar shipping is real now. And tomorrow, up where the continents divide, we'll show you one amazing future!' Don't forget the product placement. 'The Nýttnorður Foundation and PBV: one vision. Now I'm going to ask Tekla Signysdóttir and Margit Solberg from the Norges Statens Pensjonsfond Utland back up here.'

Raisa pulls off her mittens for the ceremony of the Big Red Button. Hands numb, heart hot with excitement. The long road reaches from Vonland to the first recharging station in Vík, then around the island. Then off the island to its fishers and ferries to fleets of ocean-going tugs towing three decommissioned oil platforms to new bores into the Mid-Atlantic Ridge. The three partners place their hands on the switch.

'Þor stage one is now operational,' Tekla Signysdóttir says and three hands come down on the button. It isn't connected to anything, but crane booms swing fuelling hoses out over the sea and the steam vents blow five well-stage-managed calliope puffs. Applause, whoops from the rig crew. Raisa hugs her project partners. Ragna Sivertsen, Þor 1's offshore operations engineer, clears the deck.

'High wind warning,' Ragna says. 'Civilians inside.'

'I hope Maersk *Freja* makes it in,' Raisa says. 'We need to show that ship fuelling up.'

'We can fuel in up to storm force eight,' Ragna says. She is a short, self-possessed Faroese; a twenty-year veteran of oil and gas rigs from the Barents Sea to the Jeanne d'Arc Basin. She shines with competence. She is the woman who will come out of the wreckage, get you into the immersion suit, into the lifeboat, safe to shore. Raisa notes a yata hanging in one of the control room's panoptic windows. 'You'll get the shot.'

Raisa's pilot buzzes her.

'Weather update. We have a half-hour window to take off or we're here until this clears.'

The plan had been for a live-relay press conference and the flight back to Reykjavík the next morning, but the easterlies can storm for days on end and the Þor 1 launch is only the overture to a grander opus. The big container ship has moored at the spar. In the control room Ragna swings the fuelling booms into position. It's going to be okay. More than okay. The world changes direction here and her hand helped turn it. The wind smears sudden tears across her face. Tears come readily these days.

'This will be entertaining,' the pilot says. The plane lifts, a gust catches it and slings it across the pad and over the edge. The aircraft bucks in the wind, then the grey-faced passengers are three hundred metres high. Raisa's stomach is still on the pad. She presses her face to the window. The sea is a running wave-train, spray smearing from the crests, but the fuelling booms steadily pump hydrogen from the rig's storage tanks to the Maersk *Freja*'s. It will be the first transatlantic-transpolar powered by electricity alone.

'We did this,' Raisa says as the plane climbs away from the rig. Her partners echo her words. Under the engine hum, the aerodynamic rush and the confinement of the cabin, she whispers: 'I did this!' The plane enters the cloud layer and the buffeting wipes away Raisa's jubilation. Save it for tomorrow, for the big show. The plane bucks, Raisa grabs her armrests, shivers wide-eyed through the jolting, but only for moments. Then the plane breaks out above racing clouds into blue.

58

Just as she knows knows knows she will never get out of this hell-cloud, will die in this bouncing, rain-lashed composite shell trapped flying forever between worlds, the hell-cloud opens and drops the plane out above the lights of Reykjavík so much faster and so much closer than it surely should be. Then she is down and her phone pings with notifications like a fruit machine. In the short drive to the hotel she's swiped away most of them and the world has stopped lurching. The car hurries Tekla and Margit Solberg to their hotel. Rain hard and flat. Raisa dashes to the lobby.

Please be nice for tomorrow. Emanations, for once hear me. You've already fucked up the big switch-on. Please don't rain on my launch.

'Has Finn Hopeland checked in?'

The receptionist checks and Raisa watches the Skúlagata street-lights thrum. Rain angles down the window, car lights smear to streaks of red motion. Out across the whale-road she pictures the rig. Steam jets into the driving rain. Up in the control room, screen-lit, Ragna watches over Þor. A yata turns slowly above her. Maersk *Freja* feeding hydrogen to its fuel cells, driving north north-east towards the polar seaway. Powered by volcanoes.

Raisa thinks she may have a little crush on Ragna.

'Yes, Finn Hopeland checked in this morning. Shall I call the room?'

'No, I'll surprise him.'

Thinking (she waits for the elevator): cocktails. Heroic cocktails from room service. And the hot tub on the balcony. She always gets the room with the hot tub. It's sexy in a storm. Thinking (the elevator doors close): maybe cocktails and hot tub, then food. Thinking (the doors open): maybe cocktails and hot tub, no food. Thinking (she thumbs open the suite door): hottubcocktailssex.

Sees a bottle of wine in the chiller on the desk, two glasses. Sees Finn open the window from the balcony hut tub and pad in. Ass naked. Scar-scaled. He pours two glasses of wine.

Raisa turns to stone.

'I've wine,' he calls. A second naked figure on the balcony. Big-bellied, red-bearded, man-mountain Óðinn. He takes the offered glass. Rims clink.

Quietly, Raisa closes the door. Quietly she walks to the elevator. Quietly she tries to breathe.

What is keeping the lift? She needs to get away clean, unseen, quick. No attention. No looks. Professional professional be professional. Kynnd is kynnd. Finn is Finn. It doesn't mean anything. It's the Hopeland way. Fuck the Hopeland way. The Hopeland way feels like molten lead running through the ventricles of her heart.

The elevator's here.

'My fucking day, Finn!' she shouts to the closing doors.

She hooks in a car and has it book a smaller hotel on the other side of the peninsula. She studies the minibar. Dignity won't let her raid it.

What is wrong here? Neither of them has a claim on the other.

What is wrong is that she saw Finn and Óðinn but who she thinks about is Amon Brightbourne.

'Fuck it all,' she says and goes instead to wash her hair. Shake it out. Wash it clean.

59

What here reminds her of the day she became an Arcmage? Not the location. That was a paradise garden, walled in red London brick. This is Þingvellir, the rift where hemispheres separate and Iceland is born. The Ginnungagap. PBV has booked the visitor centre and bussed staff, guests, funders and media up from Reykjavík in a fleet of autonomous minibuses. From the viewing gallery she sees fifty kilometres in every direction.

Not the food: no weed, no placenta three ways. Vintage English seck and mostly vegetable-based canapés. Raisa lifts a glass of fizz from a passing tray. She's earned it.

Not the music, which is shit. The Starring was towers of dub, car-crash guitar chords. Stars! And she was lifted up in the branches of a tree by music made just for her.

She has it. Her dress. It's the same blue she wore that day. Tights the same red. Better fabric, better cut, better shoes. The Foundation and its PBV parent reject corporate business costume. For the launch three new local designers have been commissioned to produce a range of clothing, from the presentation team to the waiting staff. Raisa compares her people to the funders and reporters in heels and ties. Never trust anyone in a tie.

Amon Brightbourne wore a tie. Gloriously, whimsically, unselfconsciously.

She sees Finn, at the centre of a clutch of guests, charming and interesting and looking like he's smelted from the very stuff of Þingvellir. He catches her look, frowns a *where were you?* He has no idea. At least he didn't try to smuggle in Óðinn. Raisa slips away before Finn can lose his entourage and come to her. She catches sight of Atli. Hé came. Hé glories in loose greys, left cheek a net of tumbling white hexagrams, hair gelled up into a corona. Every eye turns to hé, everybody is drawn to hé but hé cuts a steadfast course through the party to Tekla, funky and glorious in Milla Snorrason. They hug hard and deep and long.

But it's showtime. The waitstaff choreograph attention to the speaking platform in front of the panoramic window. Panes polarise to screens, a PBV introductory video runs. Tekla takes the lectern, poised and confident. She welcomes the guests, explains the significance of Þingvellir—the site of the old Icelandic parliament, the most venerable in the world; the place where continental plates meet and also divide, the source of PBV's energies—and lets them feel the continental rift beneath their feet for a few moments.

The presentation begins. Together with its partner the Norwegian sovereign wealth fund—Margit nods—and the Nýttnorður Foundation—Raisa lifts her glass—PBV announces its global offshore geothermal power network.

'The shipping industry is responsible for three percent of global CO_2 emissions,' Tekla says. 'It's also one of the slowest to decarbonise. Hydrogen fuel cells are the future of shipping but the problem has always been access to fuel. Hydrogen ships simply need to refuel more often than hydrocarbon ships. Within five years the Northeast Passage will be open for six months of the year.' Clever animations play out on either side of her. 'The polar route from East Asia to the North Atlantic offers significant savings in time and fuel cost. This is where PBV leads the hydrogen revolution. Our three deep-sea refuelling rigs have opened the North Atlantic to carbon-free shipping. Over five years PBVs will open the entire Northeast and Northwest Passage lanes to hydrogen-fuelled shipping, connecting Pacific and Atlantic over the pole using geothermal and offshore wind power.'

The viewing window map-zooms to the top of the world, swoops in on the waters between south Greenland and north-east Canada. Animation: peaceable wind turbines spin in a high-running grey sea.

'PBV is proud to announce a new venture with the Naalakkersuisut—the government of Greenland—to develop a refuelling hub in the Davis Strait.'

The animation soars out into that corporate presentation favourite, the world map. Lights in the ocean, a constellation of power rigs.

'The global expansion of the Þor offshore network,' Tekla continues. 'A grid of forty PBV geothermal, wind-and hydro-power rigs will revolutionise international sea-freight. The ocean is electric.'

Bombastic music, heart-stopping animation, cheering and as much applause as hands holding flutes of seck can summon.

Raisa works back to the door. Partners and funders have been summoned up onstage: The applause covers her departure. Someone cuts in between her and the exit.

'Good show,' Sindri Ólafursson says.

'We always give good show.'

'Yes you do. Though I foresee problems with territorial licenses. The Russians won't like you drilling for hot rock in what they see—rightly or wrongly—as their waters.'

'You always head straight to the problems.'

'Life is problems.'

'How's D-Centric, Sindri?'

'Less showy but no less successful.'

'What are you doing now?' Raisa asks though she knows and Sindri knows she knows.

'Data capture and mining. Now, *that* is the future. We have partnerships with major analytics companies on six continents.'

'Congratulations.'

'Your rigs—when you get them established, we must talk again. I'm interested in offshore data havens. It's good to keep things out of the hands of governments, don't you think?'

'I'm not the one to talk to.'

'I'd like to make you an offer. Not PBV. Not the Foundation. You. I've always respected you, always liked you.'

Behind me, Satan.

Sindri holds out his right palm and an image appears in it.

'That the new Huawei V30 glove?' Raisa asks.

'It is.'

'I like how it matches the skin to your, well, skin.'

Sindri looks pleased. His palm displays a short animation: an ocean-going rig piled with what looks to Raisa like apartment blocks, solar panels and wind turbines. The rig transforms, blossoms: twenty-storey apartment petals unfold around a calyx of green space, swimming pools, plazas, sports grounds—an ocean lotus. Between the petals pleasure boats ride at mooring. The mandatory blimp manoeuvres to a mooring mast. This flower is part of an archipelago of floating cities: fast hydrofoils streak between them. The animation pulls out to show pontoon after pontoon of wind turbines to the horizon.

'*Oceanea* Seastead,' Sindri says and closes his fist on the vision. 'An ocean-going, free-living, independent micro-nation.'

'I've heard about this,' Raisa says. 'Some uber-libertarian tech-baron tax haven.'

'It's an extra-territorial alternative polity.'

'I'm sure it is.'

'The *Oceanea* culture cluster is a political, social and technological creative hothouse for alternative polities. Other ways of being human. Floating culture laboratories. We need new ways to live if we're to survive this century. You don't have the monopoly on micro-nations, Raisa Hopeland.'

'Raisa Peri Antares Stormtalker Hopeland,' Raisa corrects. 'As below, so above. What do you want to offer me, Sindri Ólafursson?'

'A place on board. I'm offering you a chance to buy in early.'

'You're selling me a time-share on the USS *Apocalypse*?'

'That's clever, Raisa. Clever. This is a genuine offer.'

'So I can weather the Perfect Storm with Elon and the billionaires' club.'

'You have valuable talents and abilities.'

'And a network of deep-sea hydrogen rigs.'

'The analytics companies spotted it years ago. There is something ahead of us. A great filter. Environmental, certainly. Climate change. Topsoil depletion. Maybe another, bigger pandemic. Mass automation. The collapse of the global middle class. Water wars. All of these.'

'So ride it out on your privileged Noah's Ark?'

'And your family is . . . what, Raisa Hopeland?'

The knife goes low and organs-deep.

'Anyone can join my family. Takes no money, no privilege, no status. And you know, Sindri? I'll stick with family. We've a ten-thousand-year future ahead of us. I've seen it.'

She's also seen Brightbourne in ruins, the Music silenced.

'The offer is always open, Raisa. I feel I owe you. If it's not for you, at least think of your son.'

'You know, I used to think you were a cunt, Sindri,' Raisa says. 'I was wrong. You're an archcunt.'

She pushes past him into the lobby and gift shop and the grey, white and blue world.

'If you ever change your mind,' Sindri calls. Up on the platform Tekla answers questions.

She raps on the door of the first bus in the parking lot. The driver looks up from her knitting and opens the door.

'Can you take me back to Reykjavík?'

The driver is about to tell her wait, then recognises the face of the Hydrogen Queen. Raisa goes to the back. She always was the kid in the back seat. The bus moves off then stops abruptly. A banging on the door. The driver opens the door and Finn jumps on.

'What's going on, Rai?'

'I got back a day early, Finn,' Raisa says. 'Did Óðinn like the wine?'

'Okay,' Finn says. The driver engages the parking brake. 'Look, it doesn't . . . We don't . . .'

'I know that. And we don't, either.'

'I'm sorry.'

'I was . . . well. Timing, Finn. Your timing was always sweet. Or shit.'

'He is hot,' Finn says. 'I haven't wrecked things have I?'

'You made some things clear in my head. It's not you, Finn. Don't fancy yourself.'

'Kynnd is kynnd. As below . . .'

'So above. I'd kind of like to get back to Reykjavík before everyone turns up with their freebie bags.'

'Are we all right, Rai?'

'We will be.'

The driver swings out of the car park. Raisa looks back at Finn standing outside the visitor centre, hand raised in farewell. On this cold, wind-scoured highland the Icelanders came and stepped down into the rifts and chasms to settle feuds, make peace, shape law. Raisa sprawls out across the rear seat and takes out her phone. In outer Reykjavík the hire car wakes that will carry her onward again.

60

Raisa breathes deep. Sea and stone. Sulphur and sodium chloride. Eld-fell growls again. Growling volcanoes are good business. The old business. This is new business. Raisa came to Landeyjahöfn in darkness and took the ferry to the islands as the sun rose. The light is long and innocent. Clouds mantled in gold and imperial purple pile high as basilicas. A gusting easterly, strong enough to kick up a chop in the narrow harbour, sets the smaller boats nodding to each other. Raisa ties her hair back, turns up her collar. Twenty-three years ago she stood on this quay. The islands have been her horizon, sometimes stark in dawn light against a dark sea, sometimes hidden for weeks in mist and winter-grey, sometimes leaking smoke across the sky when Eldfell stirred, but she has never been back until this morning. The wind holds *Los Ascending II* snug against the quay. Captain Lind is fuelling. Raisa stays behind the chequered tape. The Hydrogen Queen should observe the safety warnings for her own element. The hoses disconnect, and booms swing back with flashing lights and petulant bleepings.

'Hello the ship!' Raisa bellows. 'Permission to come aboard!'

'Permission granted!' Captain Lind yells from an open window. 'Welcome aboard Stormtalker. Stow your gear and come up for coffee.'

In two passageways Raisa is lost. Raisa realises she follows memories one ship and two decades old. On this boat she has her own cabin, not a berth with the crew. A crew-member directs her to the bridge, where Captain Lind waits with the promised coffee. The radio fires updates. The crew prepares for departure. Raisa keeps back: not her space, not her element. She has brought nothing green with her.

Lind orders power from the fuel cells. *Los Ascending II* shivers, angles out from the dock, spins in Vestmannaeyjabær's narrow harbour. She handles her ship with precision and authority. Past the tip of the mole, through the narrow strait beneath the breath of Eldfell, north of the island to bear west-south-west on a long-running sea. Raisa watches the islands fall into the ocean until only the plume of Eldfell breaks the horizon and her coffee is cold in its insulating mug. At last the volcano is lost and she thinks of the lives back there on the island.

The Nýttnorður fleet waits forty kilometres south-west of Reykjavík over the Skerjadjúp. *Los Ascending II* sights them shortly before noon. Three ships: one former Arctic surveyor, one light transport, one repurposed Canadian Coast Guard cutter. Captain Lind asks permission from Fleet Commander Captain Yuka aboard the cutter *Aiviq* to join the squadron. Yuka welcomes Raisa and asks for a few words for the mission. Raisa thanks the Greenland Inatsisartut for the welcome it has extended to her family, and the people of Kujalleq and Qaqortoq Municipality for allowing the Foundation to develop new ideas for the New North.

'Green Greenland,' Raisa says, then apologises because that sounds shit. She's lost the words. The charisma has flowed to Tekla.

Captain Lind brings *Los Ascending II* into fleet order. Captain Yuka gives a command. Launchers lob bundled packages high into the air, bridle cables snap taut and clever memory plastic unfurls into star-sails. The wind catches the fabric. Kites unfold across the golden sky. Twenty parasails fill with the easterly, billow and dip and hold the wind. Engines throttle back. The wind swells the sheets. Carried by a cloud of wings, the fleet sets sail for the open ocean and the coast of Greenland.

Raisa blinks up a music file and sends it to Captain Lind's control windows.

'Permission to play, Captain?'

'My grandfather liked this,' Captain Lind says. The opening wheezing stomp of *The Boy in the Bubble* fills the bridge. The sails dip and swell and carry *Los Ascending II* into miracles and wonder.

TWO
PRINCESSES

61

The plane banks hard left. Its shadow falls across Amon Brightbourne. He shades his eyes, follows it out across the lagoon to the place where turquoise drops into ultramarine. Watches until it is lost in the convoys of cumulus running full-sailed before the easterly.

The boy is gone and nothing can be good again.

Mua International Airport is as far from the capital as geography allows; nowhere on the island is more than ten kilometres from anywhere else. The wind keeps the heat a breath short of insufferable. He could walk. He should walk. Walk it out. Saturday is walking day; people out and about will ask him if the boy got off all right. Tell him how fine he was, how kind and handsome, how proud he should be. Five steps beyond the airport turn-off a Nissan Elgrand pulls up beside him. A cry of 'Malo Eimoni!' comes from the window. A face beams. Laea the Uber. 'He get off okay?'

'He got off.'

'Want a ride?

'No, I'm fine walking thanks.'

Five more cars stop on the road across Ava'utapu to offer him a lift. He turns them down. *That palangi who plays the organ. Is he crazed? He'll burn up in the sun.*

The road brings Amon out on the lagoon shore by the Royal Tombs. The paint on the wall that shields the mausoleums of the Tu'is from the common gaze is blistered and mould-stained but the three crosses atop King Siaosi Tu'i II's replica Calvary can be seen from every part of the island. The sheep safely graze. You can't have a Calvary without sheep, King Siaosi decreed, and shipped four ewes and a ram in from New Zealand. There isn't enough grass to sustain them, so their eighth-generation descendants are fed imported sheep-nuts by the hereditary Royal Shepherdess.

Amon might program Cecil Frances Alexander's *There Is a Green Hill Far Away* for morning service.

The Tu'i Calvary is the island's highest point only when there isn't a cruise ship in. A sea-monster lies pressed against the pilings of the Pulotu

Wharf. Carnival *Mardi Gras*. It loomed on the edge of the horizon for a day, now it's a wall of steel across the lagoon. The cruise business was slow to recover from the pandemic but since Amon washed up on Ava'u the number and size of ships has crept up. There's talk of recommissioning the two liners mothballed up at Niua, ostensibly waiting conversion to hydrogen. A fleet of buses passes Amon, swings into the dock and pulls up beside the ship. Piglets to the sow. Royal Palace, Royal Tombs, the blow-holes at Pangai, pre-booked wellness sessions at the spa resorts on the north-western horn of the atoll followed by traditional dance and umu or back to the boat for the Taste of the Islands buffet. The tourist shops along Pulotu Road roll up their shutters and set out their tables and racks in anticipation of the pre-cocktail Sundown Stroll. The harbour officer on the barrier greets Amon.

'Six and a half thousand!' he shouts. 'Biggest this year!'

More Chinese and Taiwanese fishers at Wharf 39. Like the cruise ships, the boats are getting bigger. More Chinese on the signs outside the karaoke bars. Toyota pickups and minibuses draw up at the King Siaosi IV inter-island ferry terminal in coughs of black diesel. Ava'u remains in the Late Oil-Age.

Amon stops to wipe sweat from his face. The street to the left will take him past First Mua Church to Queen 'Anaseini College and his campus bungalow. Ahead, where the road curves towards the island's western horn, is the Royal Ava'u Hotel. The bungalow will be empty, quiet, still smelling of him. The Royal Ava'u has green lawns, white loungers, a blue pool. Air-conditioned bar. People who know his name. Lovely, lovely gin.

The guard on the palace gate hails him.

'He got off all right?'

'He did.' Amon squints at the sky. 'He'll be landing in Nadi by now.'

'Be safe now, Eimoni.'

The bar staff have the first one lined up for him.

'Welcome back, Eimoni.'

He takes his high-backed stool at the left corner of the Dateline Bar and the space falls into the old alignments. The long perspective of the bar, the grand piano. Tables, only one occupied at this hour. Beyond French windows the lawns run down to the private beach, strewn with plastic. Pulotu Road curves around to the glorious mess of wharves and ships, containers and portacabins. Carnival *Mardi Gras* fills half the horizon. The buses head out on their prescribed circuits. There stands sheep-shriven Calvary. The gods are in their heaven, all's okay with the world. Amon Brightbourne observes the condensation droplets form and merge on the underside of his martini glass, achieve critical mass and slide down the stem. The bar staff, smart in monogrammed white shirts and dark tupenus, wait for him to take the first sip.

Lift it and look it in the eye. Observe the haze and coil of the oils in the clear gin.

First the touch of lips.

Inhale. There is no taste without smell.

Then the tilt, the flow. Let it curl over the tongue so cold it paralyses the taste buds. Texture: between silk and oil. The sting, then the numbness, then the slow glow, the mouth filled with incense. The gin first, then the high musk of homeopathic vermouth. No olive. It took the staff a long time to understand that a good martini needs no fruit. A good martini comforts, whispers, beguiles, mystifies.

The swallow is nothing. The handing over of alcohol to the peristaltic system. Down-the-hatching.

'Good, Eimoni?'

'Magnificent, Susitino. Four Pillars?'

'No fooling you. Another?'

He already feels the flush, the uplifting pressure at the base of his brain.

'Surprise me.'

While Susitino chills, rinses the glass with vermouth, selects, stirs, Amon taps the flight-tracking app on. Fiji Airways 02 Nadi-Auckland has switched on its transponder.

'What do you think this is?'

Amon sniffs the offered martini, takes a sip. High junipers and London refinements over a lower phenolic, gluey base. Salt.

'I'm getting America. Iodine.'

'Hawaiian,' Susitino says. 'New in.' He shows Amon the bottle. Amon looks out at the blinding lagoon and drinks Hawaiian gin martinis until Fiji Airways 02 rolls out from the terminal, takes off and climbs to cruising altitude.

'Again?'

Amon taps his glass. The little yellow plane icon turns south-east over the blue pixel ocean.

'We wondered if there would be anyone to drink it.'

Amon drinks Hawaiian gin until the flight starts its descent into

Auckland, though he doesn't rate it for martinis, or anything other than an unsubtle fruit-based cocktail.

He's gone.

The Saturday-evening people take their places, the rest of the tables fill with tourists wandered up from the boat. Amon pushes his empty glass away from him, gets down from his high stool, creases the aches out of his back and hips and steers a careful course between chairs and stools and tiki lampshades along the treacherous length of the bar to the piano. The staff smile. On the stool, the lid open, he feels certain, rooted. Everything in its right place. The regulars turn their stools. He usually starts with *Lady Be Good*. Dead white boy lounge music. Today he leads with *Love Is a Losing Game* and segues into *There Is No Greater Love*. Dead Jewish girl lounge music. His fingers drift to Tom Jobim. *Águas de Março. One Note Samba*. The cruise boat people call Susitino to their tables to buy a drink for the piano player; he refuses and explains. With full dark the tourist band arrives and sets up. Amon finishes on *Back to Black*, shakes hands and claps shoulders with the musicians and walks onto the bat-haunted lawn. Carnival *Mardi Gras* is a wall of lights, a floating arcology. BPM from the pool party strides over the water. He's breathless in the dark heat, the heavy humidity.

'God go with you, Eimoni,' the new palace guard calls. Amon lifts finger to brow in salute. Electric scooters swerve past him on Pulotu Road. Voices, hip-hop, V-pop from the bars. The street-lights end a hundred metres inland from the coast road. Amon thumbs up his phone torch and weaves across the school playing fields. His feet know the way but there is always the possibility of a stray dog or a piece of abandoned domestic junk.

Hours since he thought of Atli. Amon turns on the flight tracker and stops to squint at the blurred icons. There he is, eleven thousand metres above the ocean. Now the regret and self-loathing swell. And subside. On the porch of his bungalow a little light flashes.

A stumble closer and he sees a figure in the darker darkness. A movement and screen light illuminates a young woman's face.

'Um,' says Amon Brightbourne. The young woman looks up from her screen. The little light, head height, keeps flashing.

'At last!' Ava'u vowels with an Aotearoa lilt. 'Amon Brightbourne?' She can say his name.

'You? Are?' he asks.

'Kimmie Pangaimotu. Could you open the door? I've been holding this thing up for fucking hours.'

The flashing light moves and he sees what it is: catching the phone-shine, a spinning yata.

With Kimmie comes a kit bag, half her size. And Kimmie comes island tall, island broad. She drags the bag into Amon's lounge and fills the room.

'So where do you want me to put it, 'ofa'anga?'

'Um, come in,' Amon says. His living room tilts around him. This takes more coping than he is equipped to deliver.

'Maybe I'll leave this here,' Kimmie says. She drops the bag with a soft solid thump and collapses heavily onto Amon's sagging sofa.

'Who are you again?' Amon asks.

'The fabulous Kimmie Pangaimotu.' She tilts a flirtatious head, flutters eyelashes, ta-dahs hands. She wears a lot of rings. *'EnZee GeeTee? Drag Race NZ?* Oh come on.' She flips her phone open. 'What's your Wi-Fi, 'ofa'anga?'

'Pangaimotu . . .'

'Is an island. No man is an island.'

'Kimmie Pangaimotu . . .'

'Is no man. Applause, 'ofa'anga. Anything to drink? You will not believe my day.'

No man, no woman. Fakaleitis, fa'afafines, mahus: many words across Polynesia for third-gendered persons. Assigned male at birth, raised female, becoming both and neither, as they wish to express themselves. Complexities and subtleties outside the Western taxonomies of gender. By custom the keepers of the aiga—the extended family—they are true and wise advisers, spiritual counsellors, carers, negotiators. Their place in the societies of Hawaii, Samoa, Tonga and Ava'u is well-established and respected, though missionaries brought suspicion and hostility with their Jesus. The fakaleitis were tougher than Western Bibles and cultural theories. A tall, broad faka-leiti in formal government tupenu stamped Amon Brightbourne's passport and biocontrol certificate at Mua Airport and welcomed him to the king-dom. Stoutly Presbyterian Queen 'Anaseini College's welfare officer was an elderly, ever-smiling leiti who oversaw her kids with a care equal parts community nurse and Mother Superior. The fakaleitis were Ava'u's infor-mal civil-and-social service. None were under forty. Amon wondered if the culture was fading under the pressure of Western gender norms. Welfare

Officer Salote corrected him firmly. Young leitis quit the islands for societies with horizons wider than caring and public service. As Kimmie Pangaimotu left three years earlier for Aotearoa and the dream of showbiz.

Amon hauls a bottle from the toilet cistern. He tried to forget the places
he hid gin when Atli was with him. Only computers forget to order. By the
time he returns with glasses Kimmie has found his password, switched on
his screen and connected her phone.

'Be amazed, palangi. Be very amazed.'

Amon flinches at the assault of noise and colour. He downs a shot.
Swinging lights, shiny floor, tinsel and chrome. Quick cuts of a roaring
audience, God-voiced narrators. It's a TV talent show, Amon decides.
Here's Kimmie in leggings and a red tank top, nervous, hands fluttering,
OMGing into the host's microphone. *What you going to do for us? I'm going to
sing.* Silence in the cheap seats. Then a strutting, pouting, finger-wagging,
twerking, roof-raising, seat-wetting, heart-bursting *Rehab.* Audience on
their feet. Judges on their feet. Kimmie tear-stained, panting in the spotlights. *You're through!* lights across the judge's desks.

Tears in Kimmie Pangaimotu's eyes as she watches the Steadicam
circle her screen self. The Jimmy Jib picks up the shot and swings across
the standing, applauding celebrity judges to the ovation of the ecstatic
crowd.

'I killed it, Amon,' she shouts. 'Slaughtered it!'

Swipe, next clip. Same show, same judges, same stage. Better make-up,
higher heels, glorious frock. Sequins and flash. Winner's swagger to the
backstage banter. She works the camera with confidence and sass. *How
Far I'll Go.* Judges with their fingers over their mouths. Audience in pieces.

Amon pours.

Clip three. Semi-finals. Please welcome Kimmie! Pangaimotu! Another
song from *Moana: We Know The Way.* Perfect for a two-minute talent show.
These are the semis so she has dancers. Even Amon can see that the chore-
ography patronises and stereotypes. The audience goes wild: it loves loves
loves Kimmie Pangaimotu.

'I told them, I said I want to do *Back to Black,* but they said no Kimmie
Pangaimotu, you sing fucking *We Know The* fucking *Way.*'

'You'd have slaughtered it, Kimmie Pangaimotu.'

'I would, Amon Brightbourne. I so would.' She freezes the image. 'Out
in the talent-off to an urban dance group. Diverse! My leiti ass. Fucking St
Mary's Bay Māori and stage-school white kids. *I'm* diverse.'

Ava'u an fakaleiti runner-up in the semi-finals of *New Zealand's Got Talent* was enough to build minor celebrity but not a career. The breakfast shows and early-evening magazine shows dried after a few weeks. The personal appearances at hotels and beauty pageants and dance competitions, at small-town carnivals and Pacific Island diaspora feasts, eked out for a year. A *Whatever Happened to Kimmie Pangaimotu?* article on the *New Zealand Herald* site led to invitations to reality shows. *Celebrity Come Dine with Me*. *Celebrity Lip-Sync Battle*.

'Lip-sync? Kimmie Pangaimotu don't lip-sync! Kimmie Pangaimotu sings! They wanted me to be a judge on *Drag Race EnZee*. That one; I went to meet them. They had me announced. I went to auditions. Oh, Amon, those lost Pasifikan kids. I saw how they wanted them to look. How they wanted them to play it. And I said, no no no. This isn't drag. These aren't drag queens. They're fakaleitis and fa'afafines. This isn't something you put on or take off in the dressing room. It's a different gender. I'm a leiti.

'The palangis didn't want to hear. Slap-ass and pout. That was all they wanted. Guh-url. They had their Western ideas and they weren't interested in anyone else's. So I turned my heel and I walked, Amon Brightbourne. Kimmie Pangaimotu quits *Drag Race*! All over social media. Pick of the day. Shock! OMG! INZ.'

'INZ?'

'Immigration New Zealand, 'ofa'anga. Kimmie overstayed her visa.'

'You were . . .'

'Deported. Got back this morning.'

The inbound leg of the same flight that took Atli away. They might have crossed in the tiny lounge.

'The yata . . .' Amon begins.

'I'm kynnd, 'ofa'anga. Kimmie Mimosa Pangaimotu Hopeland. The Auckland Hearth said you'd be here. Oh yes; "As below . . ."'

'So above.' The response comes without thought.

Don't fall in love with my family. Easy to join, hard to leave. He never joined. He travelled star to star, a wanderer, 'Oumuamua. Drawn to the warmth of the lives and relationships, looping out of their gravity as soon as the first rooftile fell, the first plumbing failure, the first vehicle or IT malfunction. The Grace endures. In these days of drawing dark, when he feels old, when he seems irrelevant, when his music is far from anyone's taste, when his fingers and toes ache, when gin calls his name: the Grace is all he has. The sole constant of Amon Brightbourne. He's been fourteen months in Ava'u, longer than anywhere since Brightbourne. The collapse hasn't arrived yet. But there was Atli, and now Kimmie. Dare he allow himself to hope?

'Kimmie, why are you on my sofa?' Amon asks.

'Because Fahu Kalasiah turned Mormon.'

Amon has noticed the aggressive expansion of the Church of Jesus Christ of Latter-day Saints across the archipelago. Missionaries—likeable young men warmly welcomed into Ava'uan family culture, fed, politely listened to. A school, then a church. Now a hospital. Converts: enough of a threat for Presbyterians, Catholics and Wesleyans to agree to an ecumenical Sunday of sermons denouncing Mormonism as gross heresy. Influence: in last year's elections the new Family First Party took two seats from the Progressive Party in the Fale Alea: the political world turned upside down, in Ava'u's small demos. Siotami Faleta'u (Kolovai: FFP) had manoeuvred into the Ministry for Training and Education and was proposing new LDS-funded schools. With them, curriculum changes in history, biology, gender and society.

'Wouldn't let me across the door, Amon. And if your mehekitanga converts, the whole aiga converts with her.'

Amon learnt quickly that Karl-Maria Lindner had taken from Ava'uan culture only those elements that sat with his philosophy. Island life is more complicated, conservative, coercive. He has yet to work out the full hierarchy of the aiga, who has rank and who has authority and who gains both in certain rituals and traditions and how these change with migration and exposure to other cultures and, yes, proselytising religions.

'Your parents, what do they say?' Parenthood baffled him; who could share space with whom, the dating apps that told you your degree of relatedness, how children could be adopted, loaned out like library books or given to people the aiga thought needed some.

'Over the horizon, Amon.'

Amon admires the Ava'uan death-euphemism. Gone west, over the horizon, beyond sight, into other oceans.

'The Princess,' Kimmie adds.

'I'm sorry.' There is a reef, Amon has discovered, beneath Ava'u. Its name is *Princess 'Akusita*. On a March night in 2023, the inter-island ferry sailed from King Siaosi IV Wharf and never reached its destination. He knows it sank with one hundred and twenty-one lives; that the tragedy touched every family on the three islands, that questions were asked that never received full answers, that it reverberates still, as he's felt the coral spine of Ava'utapu tremble in the greatest storms. No one has ever spoken to him openly of it, everyone knows he knows and that when he needs to hear, then voices will speak. The trauma of the *Princess 'Akusita* rises time and again from low tides; threatening wreckage, to be navigated around.

'Well,' Amon says, 'Since you're here; last room on the left. You might need to change the sheets.'

The sound of Kimmie's bag dragging down the hall is like a murder victim being shifted.

'It'll do,' Kimmie declares. 'I'm classy but I'm not fussy. God sail you safe to morning, Amon Brightbourne.'

'And you, Kimmie Pangaimotu.'

Orphans and the storm-blown. Atli departs, Kimmie arrives. You never pull free from the family. He's a Hopeland whether he wants or not. Amon pulls up his flight app. Atli is five hours out from Los Angeles. Auckland to Los Angeles. Los Angeles to Reykjavík. Reykjavík to Nuuk. Into a new life. Amon regards the quarter left in the bottle on his sheet-music-strewn coffee table. It is clean and pure and welcoming and he gets up and leaves it there.

62

He only makes it through the processional because it's unaccompanied and he can hide shivering behind the organ console. He's brutally hungover. The choir knows it. The congregation knows it. The Minister and Assistant Minister and Kirk Session know it. The choir gets him through the psalms. He gives them a note for the anthem and stands to conduct. Ava'uan harmonies lift him. Not angel-high. Nose-off-the-ground high. He nods off twice during the sermon but after the closing hymn ditches his intended recessional for the *Finale of Widor 6* and gives it all the rafter-shaking prog a Viscount 400 can muster. He catches Assistant Minister Akalesi's disapproving eye: she suspects that Amon's church music shows a want of true belief. She has not forgiven him for reprogramming the organ to full cathedral voice. To her the whooshes and slurrings of the big Hammond sound are the chorus of salvation.

After Widor Amon chats to the congregation on the bright green lawn under the bright blue sky. *Did Atli get back safely? That was a lovely anthem. It's good you've given that Kimmie a place to stay. What came over them? Such a good family. Can you convert back from Mormonism? We'll hold a prayer vigil. Will we see you at Family Service?*

No. Amon doesn't hold with guitars and drum-kits.

He disentangles himself from the churchgoers and walks up Pulotu Road past the palace, past the Royal Ava'u, past the resort hotels to a small private jetty signed for the Apia Island Resort. The boat knows to wait for him. By tradition, Apia, a cedilla on the C of Ava'utapu, is exempt from the strict Sunday observance traditions of the main island. There is his regular table under the shade by the fishing jetty. Amon settles onto the lounger. His regular waiter arrives with his regular martini.

'Good afternoon, Eimoni.'

'Good afternoon, Stivi.'

The dew clings heavy on the glass, the moiling boundary layer between vermouth and gin is a portal to magic realms and it scents the air with cool abandonment.

Amon picks up the glass and in one move pours the martini out onto the sandy grass. Gin and hot dust. His stomach clenches.

He's sick of himself. Sick.

He lies back on the lounger in his Sunday tweeds and brogues hating away his hangover. It lingers, the party guest who won't go home.

A private-hire ocean-fishing charter arrives at his jetty. Big voices banter and brag past to the Island Bar. The loungers and tables fill. On another Amon Brightbourne Sunday he would be two martinis up, trying not to think of Monday.

Atli has changed everything.

Stivi sets the empty glass on his tray.

'Another, Eimoni?'

'I'm all right. I might sit awhile.'

Stivi was in the choir in Amon's first term at Queen 'Ana. Decent tenor but his real interest was rugby rugby rugby. He trialled for a Romanian team, flew out to Bucharest. It never came to anything.

A ship's horn sounds across the lagoon, a walls-of-Jericho blast: I am leaving harbour. Carnival *Mardi Gras* departs Pulotu Wharf like a moon separating from a planet. Amon watches it with the deep fascination of small repetitive things. It's a long, slow vanishing over the horizon. Loud voices, people glancing over at his lounger. He's occupying paying infrastructure. It's New School Year tomorrow. He has music to plan. And Kimmie Pangaimotu to accommodate.

Laea the Uber waits at the jetty. She's dropped off a bundle of Chinese tourists.

'Malo Eimoni. Want a ride?'

'Yes please.'

'I have another pickup,' she shouts.

Kimmie waits under the palm-thatched porch of the Blue Horizon Resort and Spa. She wears leiti civvies—tank top and leggings, flat pumps, hair pulled up into a stark bun. Big handbag. She bangs down heavily beside Amon.

'So, ask me.'

'Ask you what?'

'So, Kimmie Pangaimotu, what takes you to the Blue Horizon this Sunday afternoon? Looking for a job, that's what. What job, you ask? Spa queen, 'ofa'anga. Kimmie has skills. I've done nails.'

The car sways around one of the many potholes.

'I can pay you,' Kimmie bellows in Amon's ear. 'Rent and that.' Laea the Uber pulls up outside Amon's bungalow. He opens the door to the sound of Family Service. Four-to-the-floor, ying-ching praise guitars. And a thing much worse.

'Fuckers! They've reprogrammed my organ!'

63

Kimmie Pangaimotu is a shower-singer. Disney favourites, old karaoke hits. Her strong alto storms the high lines like a military beach landing.

She can sell a song, Amon thinks as he puts together his material for School Opening.

Kimmie's *Hakuna Matata* explodes into a roar of rage. She storms from the bathroom in a too-small robe.

'Water?'

'Water?'

'Where is it?' She points to her hair, covered in white reefs of collapsing shampoo bubbles. 'I go to rinse and nothing.'

'Oh,' says Amon. 'I forgot to tell the water people there's two now. The tanker won't be round until tomorrow. I could call them, they might give me an advance.'

'The tanker?'

'The water tanker.'

'We have a water tanker?'

'Everyone has a water tanker. Except the hotels. And the bottling plant.'

'Since when do we get our water from a tanker and not from a pipe like God intended?'

'Well technically . . .'

'Do not fuck me off, Amon Brightbourne. Kimmie Pangaimotu has her first client at nine thirty and it is of cosmological importance that she look divine. What's wrong with the water?'

'Well, they expanded the bottling plant . . .'

'Royal Ava'u Water? The Pure Heart of the Pacific?'

'Filtered through pristine coral sands. Drop by crystal drop. It's boomed in China and Indonesia. They increased output.'

'So we ship our water to Jakarta for someone to carry around in a Gucci water-holster while we wait on a tanker.'

'And the price went up again last week.'

'Fuck the tanker. I have a head full of soap.'

Amon finds a two-litre bottle of Evian in the fridge.

'I'm going to wash my hair with Evian?'

'It's half the price of Royal Ava'u.' Amon offers the bottle. Kimmie snatches it away. 'Though you might want to keep it for coffee.'

Kimmie thinks a moment, then thrusts the Evian back at Amon.

'Make coffee. Make very good coffee.' She returns, hair rinsed, glossed with coconut oil and tied back. Amon smells gin.

'I know your hidey-holes 'ofa'anga.' Kimmie snatches up her bag. 'There'd better be water by the time I get home.' The door swings shut behind her.

'Do you want this coffee?' Amon asks.

Queen 'Anaseini College assembly hall is a cavernous, cantilevered barn, wood and white, crammed with young people. New School Year is sacred in Queen 'Ana. Pupils in starched white shirts, shoes shining, hair gleaming with coconut oil, sit cross-legged on the floor on their best behaviour; feral summer a day behind them and a million years ago. The hall surges with five hundred voices. Amon apologises his way up the row of teachers and sports stars in the corridor behind the stage.

'Sorry, water problem.'

The hall falls silent. Amon Brightbourne takes the stage. Faces look up at him, youngest at the front, boys to the right, girls to the left. He lifts his hands and the hall shakes to the wall of sound. Archipelago voices instinctively move to part singing. Queen 'Ana's school song is shaped for Ava'uan voices: strongly modal and easy to harmonise. It has the hymnal majesty of *Nkosi Sikelel'iAfrika* and the swinging heft of *You've Got a Friend in Me,* tunes Amon Brightbourne never expected to see share bar lines. Amon holds the final note but before the school can break into cheering he points to the basses at the back, on their feet now and swaying to the wimoweh chant from *The Lion Sleeps Tonight.* The sopranos pick up the ooh-ah-ooh-wah, then dancing boys burst onto the stage and the assembly erupts. Their sipi tau is full of dancing hands and stomping feet and flicking heads. The new kids scream, clap their hands. Now Amon lifts his hands and the singers shift without dropping a beat to *Swing Low, Sweet Chariot* as the Queen 'Ana Rugby First XV marches onto the stage in ironed shorts and clean shirts and properly pulled-up socks. The team takes positions on either side of the stage and Amon segues into *When the Saints Come Marching In* for the academic procession. The kitchen staff and cleaners lead, then the corps of janitors and the school engineer. Next the office staff, the school welfare officer and rugby pitch groundskeeper. Now the teaching staff enters. Amon is low on material so he circles a finger for a repeat of *When the Saints.* Heads of departments. Deputy head. School chaplain. Rugby coach and sports physiotherapist. Last, principal Rev. Dr. Sifa Sikahema. The song breaks up into apocalyptic cheering. Amon steps back into his ordained position next to the First XV coach. Rugby, music and religion: the three pillars of Queen 'Anaseini College School.

Amon's Ava'uan is too weak to follow Rev. Dr. Sifa's commencement speech but he hears his Ava'uan name and steps forward to bow and receive the cheering. And he is lifted.

Rev. Dr. Sifa calls the horn. A trumpeter from the marching band comes forward with a conch horn. He lifts it high, then blows three great blasts. At each Rev. Dr. Sifa calls welcome and the school responds. Rev. Dr. Sifa nods, Amon lifts a finger, the drums begin, basses and altos take the introduction and then the voices burst into the recessional: *Let the River Run.* The new kids are in hysterics. The boys kick in underneath the sopranos and there is not a dry eye on the platform.

'Thank you, Eimoni,' Rev. Dr. Sifa says, sniffing back tears.

On New Year Day school closes early. Amon calls the water company. Yes, Kimmie Pangaimotu is staying with him. Is it that family thing? Yes it is that family thing and can he get an immediate top-up, oh we're tight today, here's a hundred pang'a, maybe tomorrow, okay here's a hundred and fifty. The tanker crew reels in the hose as Kimmie Pangaimotu sweeps up in the Uber. She holds up a palm in Amon's face.

'Uh uh.' She doesn't break stride. Straight to the shower. Songs and waterfalls. Kimmie returns in a Blue Horizon bathrobe, hair up in a stolen towel, to land hard on the creaking sofa. 'Feet, Amon. Old women's feet. Hands I know. Hands I like. Hands have jewellery and give fat tips which Kimmie likes.' She describes in nature-documentary extreme close-up their corns. Their bunions. Their gnarled toe joints. Their sandpaper heels. Their brown fungal nails that shatter like antique vases when clipped and send shards ricocheting around the foot room. Their peeling soles, their toes squeezed so tight by fashionable shoes that no cleansing light has ever shone there. 'Kimmie is traumatised, 'ofa'anga. Buy her dinner. Is the Blue-fin still good?'

'Chinese fishermen.'

'Good food then.'

'Chinese private security.'

Kimmie names six alternatives.

'Tourist bar, shut, sports bar, shut, karaoke, someone got knifed.'

'Royal Ava'u then.'

'Royal Ava'u prices.'

'Kimmie's gotta eat, 'ofa'anga.'

They walk to the Royal Ava'u. The kilometre takes an hour: every family, every store-owner, every sundown walker stops to congratulate Amon on his New Year concert. The kids came home throwing off arcs. And good evening, Kimmie, lovely to see you back.

Susitino finds them a table away from the tour groups. The prices are as Amon feared. Kimmie orders the ahi. Amon swallows hard. Ocean-fish has risen in price as it vanishes from the stalls and shops.

'I'll have an omelette,' Amon says.

'I'll shout you next time 'ofa'anga.' Kimmie raises her water glass. 'Pedicures and podiums. First days.'

Amon clinks glasses.

'So,' Kimmie Pangaimotu says, 'since I'm picking their pubes out of my bed: Who is Atli Hopeland?'

64

When Atli came the sun shone brighter, colours were clearer, the air was more transparent and filled with perfume. Time did not drag and limp: time had shapes and edges.

He had tried not drinking the week before the flight arrived but each night the apprehension came to his door and settled on his sofa and he drank with it; gin, too warm, too neat, too much. Atli might loathe him. Despise him. Blame him. Feel nothing for him.

Amon waited at the airport behind dark glasses, quiveringly hungover, apprehension deepening like a cyclone into dread.

Atli came out of Customs. Twelve years ago, Amon met an alien, big-eyed and blinking, in the library of Brightbourne. Amon met another alien. Taller, bigger. Wrapped in some kind of black kimono/toga/chiton. Hair scraped back in tightly planted cornrows, bleached blonde and fixed with a small silver skull. A white line the width of two fingers ran from the exposed chest up the neck to the lower lip. Amon followed the line of the line to eyes he knew. Big eyes blinking at the light, the heat, the colour after a Northern winter.

'Atli Vega Stormtalker,' Amon Brightbourne said. 'Welcome to Avaʻu.'

Atli embraced like a rugby maul.

'You're Atli,' Laea the Uber said. It was a name an Avaʻuan could say.

'You're Atli,' said Mrs. Sinipata at the supermarket.

'You're Atli,' said the school night-watch and the chatty palace guard and Susitino at the Royal Avaʻu, where they ate that night, after Atli stowed hés gear, and slept a bit, and explained hés two genders and selves and pronouns.

'I'm being looked at,' Atli whispered over gin at the long bar.

'There's only twenty-one thousand of us,' Amon said. 'And you are a bit of a novelty.'

'No, not that,' Atli said and lowered hés head and flicked hés eyes (silver sunrise make-up around each for formal dining) and Amon followed the glance to a table of young North Americans (he thought, by the accents, the poise, the loud entitlement), in particular one young black woman who held his gaze.

'Buy her a drink then,' Amon said, and Atli did and Susitino sent it over and pointed back to the bar and that was the cue for Atli to join them and spend the rest of the evening with them which was not how Amon had seen this developing so he moved down to the piano and played as much Bill Evans as his skill could manage.

'My name is Tiwa.' She was a post-grad at Berkeley, researching the role of gossip in Polynesian women's culture.

'Atli Raisasbur Vega Stormtalker,' Atli said.

'Stormtalker,' she said with mild mockery.

'Well, I do come from Iceland,' hé said and that was the start of it.

As Amon had prophesied, Atli was an overnight celebrity. At Sunday umus, aristocratic receptions, kava parties, spa visits, sightseeing at the blow-holes; Atli baffled, outraged and wowed in equal measures, with Amon by day, Tiwa by night. Those nights Amon drank at home, alone, chafing.

'I'm going off to the islands,' Atli announced one gin-sad night. 'Tiwa's going to show me.'

'Atli,' Amon said to the closed bedroom door. 'I need time with you. I have all these questions.'

Amon came to see him off on the inter-island ferry. Atli had left all hés things in his room.

'Make sure you go to Sunset Fales on Niua,' he called from King Siaosi IV Wharf. 'Mention my name.' The ramp was hauled back, the engines started. 'Call me any time!'

Atli had his back to him and his arm around Tiwa. Amon thought her more stiff and uncomfortable than her usual educated languor. It wasn't Sunday but he went up to Apia and his usual lounger and had Stivi bring him his usual gin martini and watched the ferry sail out through the gap in the reef and over the horizon.

65

AVA'UAN INTER-ISLAND FERRY: NIUA-OFU-MUA. TWO
HOURS OUT FROM NIUA EN ROUTE TO OFU. TIWA AND
ATLI STAND AT THE RAIL. THE NIGHT IS WARM, THE
WIND GENTLE, THE SEA PHOSPHORESCENT.

ATLI: I wondered where you were.

TIWA: Well I'm here.

(BEAT)

Just looking. At the sea.

ATLI : The sea. It glows. I suppose that's worth looking at.

TIWA: There's a tone in that sentence.

ATLI: Tone?

TIWA: A tone. Peeved.

ATLI: Peeved?

TIWA: Are you just going to say everything I say back at me?
People usually grow out . . .

ATLI: Well you had a tone when you said, 'Just looking.' And
'At the sea.'

TIWA: Oh for God's sake . . .

ATLI: Okay. Okay. What it is . . . is like. Well, have I done something?

TIWA: What do you mean? Done what?

ATLI: Maybe this is just me . . .

TIWA: Don't do that.

ATLI: But it seems to me like you don't want to be round me so much. Back in Mua . . .

TIWA: Mua was Mua. This is . . . No, it's not. How can I say this without sounding vile?

(BEAT)

So, you said, 'Maybe this is just me.'

ATLI: Wait. You mean, just *this* me.

(BEAT)

You don't like this Atli as much as. . . .

TIWA: I just don't see how you can be both.

ATLI: I am both.

TIWA: Okay. Okay. You need to hear how that sounds to me. That just sounds like sitting on the fence. Middle of the road. Afraid to commit.

ATLI: Excuse me? What?

TIWA: Okay. Not wanting to commit to an identity because you're afraid you might lose out on something. It doesn't seem real. True.

ATLI: You think that?

TIWA: I want you to be real. I need you to be real.

ATLI: I'm very real. All of me. If this is the only way it makes sense to you, both of me.

TIWA: I think we have a problem here Atli.

ATLI: I think you do. I'm fine. Here I am. Fine. This is me walking away. Fine. In the lounge door. Fine. Opening the door, Tiwa. All fine. And this is fine too. Me saying this: I do not need you to validate me.

66

Amon shuffled stiffly, one eye gummed shut, from bed to bathroom to the kitchen to find Atli surveying the fridge.

'You know you have no food?'

Amon knew better than to answer.

'I flew,' Atli said. 'From Niua. That's why I'm early.' He headed out to Pulotu Road for breakfast. He returned just before the mid-day heat.

'Want to go to the Calvary?' Amon asked.

'Okay,' Atli said. They'd been before but it was a thing to do. They walked down to the square green hill and considered sheep.

'I'm thinking I might go back,' Atli said.

'Okay,' Amon said.

'To Greenland.'

Amon had not been surprised that Raisa had blown on from Iceland and PBV to Greenland and a reforesting carbon-capture project.

'Okay.'

'She wanted hé but not him,' Atli said. The sheep chewed blissfully along the contours of the mound.

'Thought so,' Amon said. 'Want a drink?'

'You drink far too much Amon.'

'I know. I fucked it Atli. I do that.'

'I know about the Grace.'

'Atli . . . have you ever . . . been lucky?'

'I don't have the Grace, Amon.'

'You are lucky. One more question, then that drink. Does she have any-one?'

'Raisa? She never has anyone for long.'

'Damn. I presume you don't want to go to the Royal Ava'u.'

'They'll be there.'

Amon knew a Filipino fisher bar back of Wharf 39. Atli drank Royal Tonga Beer, Amon drank dreadful home-stilled gin and asked Those Questions.

Did Brightbourne still stand? Did the Music still play? How was Lorien; how was his mother?

Before he came to Ava'u Atli had spent time at Brightbourne. It was a community of noisy, chaotic, evolving Hopeland kynnd. Morwenna had retired to the top floor. On fine days she still sat on the porte cochère with her coffee and her radio surveying the demesne. Lorien and Lisi were partners now, a Hopelandic Fastening, with a four-year-old, Nanerl Sirius.

'And my dad?' Amon asked. 'Your grandfather?'

Atli had met Hadley Brightbourne only once, at Auberon's Speedforth. He could hardly remember him, but he had heard Lorien say to Morwenna that Hadley wasn't well. That he might need to come out of the sun, back to Brightbourne.

'You know why I'm asking this?' Amon said.

Pulotu Road welled to the tumult of ferry arrival. Cars, pickups, East End and West End buses, the island's three taxis and Laea the Uber.

'It's your home,' Atli said, twirling a beer bottle between his fingers, rolling the knurled base across the table.

'And it's your home,' Amon said. 'Atli Raisasbur Vega Stormtalker Hopeland, you are the heir to Brightbourne.'

Sudden shadows fell into the bar. The ferry pulled in to King Siaosi IV Wharf. Dock hands shouted, engines roared, ramps clanged and banged and drowned all conversation.

The next day they went to the airport. Amon carried Atli's bag. Always easier to move on than stay. Always a place to go. Travelling star to star.

'Give Raisa my love.'

'I will.'

Then he flew away.

67

The spa manager sets two elasticated plastic bags on the countertop.

'No-shoes or blue shoes in the Cloud Grotto.'

'Blue shoes,' Amon says and pulls them over his brogues. The effect is inelegant but less so than bare feet. Kimmie would scorn his pterodactyl toes, his trilobite toenails.

'You will be hot in that,' the spa manager warns. She opens the door to gusts of menthol-scented steam.

'Tweed is suitable for every occasion,' Amon declares and enters the Cloud Grotto. He peers into the dim, steamy light. It is indeed a grotto, with sculpted rocks and ledges. A bonsai waterfall splashes over tiled boulders. Water drips from fake stalactites, scented steam puffs from stalagmites. All tiled in white tesserae, the rocks rounded into seats, benches, loungers. Bamboo and copra, the hiss of steam vents. Ocean sounds. Then he hears the music. 'Ah. I understand.'

He shuffles back into the Wellness Hub and peels off his blue shoes. It's early, the only others in the Blue Horizon are the cleaning teams and the lap swimmers in the Waters of Kele infinity pool.

'It's shite,' Kimmie says. She's picked up the word from Amon and uses it enthusiastically and knowledgeably. 'Come with.' Kimmie beckons Amon through a mother-of-pearl door into the Footsteps of Nafanua treatment suite.

'Panpipes,' Amon says.

'Panpipes and feet,' Kimmie says. 'Eight to six.'

Outdoors in Atalapa's Garden of the Sun, terrible New Age music plays from speakers disguised as tikis.

'Where did you get it?' Amon asks. He sips Sacred Chai in the hotel's Cleanse Bar. Even here soft pianos chime and swell.

'It came with the package,' the manager says. 'The license goes up every year.'

'We have to listen to it, Eimoni,' the chai-barista chirps. 'On a loop.'

'What do you want me to do?' Amon asks.

'I've heard your stuff,' Kimmie says. She sucks noisily at a thick green smoothie.

'I don't make it public,' Amon says.

'Your keychain is only as good as its master password, 'ofa'anga.'

'Can you make us new music?' the spa manager asks.

'I don't know . . .' Notes already flock around him in sky-filling mur-murations. Modes and keys with signature emotional resonances. Some-thing that can be heard every day and not rub the edges of the soul raw. Perhaps procedural: music not so much composed as generated. Varia-tions. Like the Music. Amon's eyes widen. 'I could put some ideas down. See if you like it. It won't be free. I don't do things for exposure.'

'I can pay you,' the manager says. 'Not a lot.'

'I don't need a lot. But I do need some.'

'Please help us, Eimoni,' the chai-barista pleads.

The notes flock all day, flickering past the windows of his classroom, roost-ing in the branches of the acacias like bats, rising up in a cloud and taking shapes in the sky: battleships, whales, armies of women warriors. The Em-anations stand tall as storm-clouds as Amon crosses the rugby pitch to his bungalow. As below, so above.

Ableton needs an update. He needs more cloud storage. The headphones connection is laggy and someone has spilt something into the MIDI key-board and the middle C sticks. The update does basic things differently. He is still learning the new asset management system when Kimmie comes home and starts the theatrical hushed creeping around that is more disrup-tive than any banging and shouting.

Amon sighs in exasperation and pushes back his headphone.

'Can I hear it?'

'I've just set up the session files.'

'When it's set up can I hear it?'

'Kimmie, can I make a wee rule here? When I am here, with this, I am in my studio. I'd ask you to respect my studio. Please.' Amon pulls on the headphones again. Even with full noise-cancelling the presence of Kimmie in his peripheral vision—kicking off her shoes, eating snacks by the fistful on the sofa, flicking through the television channels, laughing and spitting in turn as she scrolls her phone—breaks his concentration. He slams shut the lid of the MacBook.

'Was that me?' Kimmie says. 'Sorry.'

Amon scoops up his instruments.

'Well, if you're done, where shall we go for dinner?' Kimmie says.

'I'm not done,' Amon says. 'And you're a grown woman; feed yourself. Grown leiti, I mean.' He goes to his bedroom. No door has a lock in Mua so he pushes the bed against his and waits, nerves jangling, until he hears the front and the screen doors close. He works through the swift evening-fall into the night, through Kimmie's noisy return, through her discovery that he is, indeed, still in his room, through her tippy-tap at the door, right into her appliance-rattling snoring which to Amon is the most beautiful sound in the world because it is the seal of solitude and peace.

The screen flickers—the electricity supply has never been sturdy but the government promises weekly to solve both that and the water issues. Twelve twenty-seven. Amon's lower back stabs at the slightest movement. A curl of ocean-tang creeps through his window-louvres and calls him into the clear, deep night. He walks to the rugby pitch's halfway line and listens. Trees rustle. Wind in the scabby grass. The groundskeeper has not been able to water the pitch this summer. The footsteps of the night-watch on patrol. Occasional wheels along Fangaloa Road. Snatches of music from the karaoke bars. The perpetual throb of Mua's power plant; the plaint of a sacred sheep on Calvary's green hill. Aircraft overhead. One of the new hydrogen-powered ones. They have lean, urgent engines. He tracks it by sound from west to east across the island. He finds Ava'utapu's sounds, isolates them, pushes his hearing beyond them. He pushes it beyond the horizon, to the throb of marine engines out on the deep water. Another cruise ship coming. Last he pushes down between the coarse grass blades into the bones of the island. He feels the sub-bass rumble of coral resisting endless ocean. The *tsk* of a bat calls him back to the surface world and he collapses the planes of sound down into one polyphony. This. All this. Immerse them in the sounds of the island like fish in water. There is no wellness without music.

Footsteps. Light in his eyes. The security guard stands before him, torch in hand.

'Eimoni, are you all right?'

'I am now.'

'Can I help you?'

'I've found what I need. Good night.'

———

'Who wants to meet me?' Amon asks.

'I'm not telling you,' Kimmie says. 'You need spontaneity in your life, 'ofa-'anga.' She puts on maximum leiti and insists Amon don the full tweed. Shave. Polish shoes. Moisturise moisturise moisturise. She looks stunning: tall, poised, features regal, shining hair pinned with mother-of-pearl combs. Amon feels like a puppet about to be written out of the show.

'The last time I did spontaneity I ended up with Atli,' Amon says.

Kimmie taps Laea with her palm-frond fan and instructs her to take them to the Blue Horizon's VIP entrance. The manager welcomes them on the red carpet with clear delight.

'Thank you, Eimoni, thank you!'

She guides them through the spa from zone to zone, music to music. It doesn't sound awful to Amon.

In the Deep Blue Dreaming studio a class of women beats through a Zumba class. The women are young, tall and broad. Some wear skirts over leggings, for modest dress matters in Ava'u. A young woman in galaxy-print leggings and a crop top with the word ZUMBA printed in white leads the class. She shouts moves into a headset. Amon nods to her music. Most Zumba playlists are salsa for people who know nothing about Cuban music. This navigates the east coast of funk on a following wind of jazz chords. Amon knows her. Everyone in the archipelago knows Princess Elisiva Ta-'ahine Pilolevu. Middle of the three children of King Siaosi Tu'ipulotu Tu'i.

The Princess finishes her routine and dismisses class with a personal goodbye to every woman in the group. She flings her towel over her shoulder, drinks deep from a bottle of Royal Ava'u and beckons Amon and Kimmie to her.

'Highness.' Amon remembers the Bow to Be Made When Faced with Aristocracy but Unsure of Protocol that Auberon taught him. Princess Elisiva Ta'ahine Pilolevu bids them sit with her on the floor. Amon folds his long limbs like a stiff mantis.

'Ta, please.'

Elisiva Ta'ahine Pilolevu: Ta. She will not wear the pandanus-leaf crown, so she works to improve the health and well-being of the people of Ava'u. Princess Ta'ahine community health centres, diet clubs, children's exercise groups, men's health schemes have sprung up across the islands. The Ava'uan diet has been driven towards cheap carbs and fatty imported meat and their attendant Western morbidities: chronic obesity, diabetes, hypertension, coronary disease, arthritis. Anger grows by the day—the slicing away at the fisheries, the creeping privatisation, the water, outsiders buying influence on the islands. Princess Ta, in her cloak of royal inviolability, channels the anger into community action.

'I like your music, Amon Brightbourne,' Princess Ta says. She can speak his name.

'Thank you,' Amon says. 'Your own is pretty good too.'

'I'm throwing a party,' Princess Ta says. 'For my big sister's thirtieth birthday. It's a landmark.' Princess Halaevalu has Williams syndrome, adores music, and is adored. 'I hear you play big clubs.'

'The mega-clubs were a long time ago,' Amon says.

'You also make small music,' Ta says. 'For five or six people. Sometimes one or two. I want to commission you to make a private set for my sister. About forty minutes. Big beats. You will be paid.' Amon has run into many instances of the House of Tu'i expecting goods and services for nothing but the honour of patronage. 'My own money.'

'Half up front, half on delivery?'

Kimmie twitters at the effrontery. Princess Ta beams.

'If you start today, my office will pay you by midnight.'

'I'll need to know what your sister likes.'

'You'll do it.'

'We have a deal, ma'am. When is the party?'

Princess Ta names a date five days hence. For a forty-minute, custom set? Challenging.

'Thank you,' Ta says. 'Now, if you please, I need a shower.'

Amon struggles to his feet a moment ahead of Princess Ta. She sweeps from the studio to the changing room. Kimmie is at Amon's shoulder.

'Know this, palangi,' she whispers. 'I set this up. I will fucking be at this party. Okay? Okay.'

68

Kimmie briefs Amon on the short walk across the rugby pitch and along Pulotu Road to the palace.

'That bow you did at the spa, do that. The introduction will be long. Flatter them. They expect it. Even Halae. Speak when you're spoken to. Do not turn your back. Do not show the soles of your feet. Try and keep your head lower. And no touching under any circumstances. Major Fia is a dear sweet man but he will shoot you. This is an informal occasion, and it's about a family function, so the order of status will be King's Mum, King's Aunts if they're there, King's Grandmum, then any Princesses. They'll make allowances for you being a palangi but try not to fuck it up. Direct everything to Queen Mum Elenoa. You probably won't meet the King. Not on a first date. His mum will tell him everything that is going on.'

'Good morning, Eimoni,' the marine on the palace gate says. 'And to you, Kimmie Pangaimotu. Please go to reception.'

The Leiti Fetuu—Fakaleiti Attendant of the Royal Household—meets them on the far side of security. The palace is a wide, rambling colonial pile of red roofs, white porches, dormers and windows shuttered against the blasting sun. It is nothing like Brightbourne and yet Amon can think of nowhere else. Princess Ta and Princess Halae receive Amon and Kimmie in the Coral Room, a large, fusty-smelling salon furnished in retirement home. With them are Queen Lavinia and the Dowager Elenoa. The House of Tu'i stands tall and dignified.

'You play, Mr. Brightbourne,' the Queen Mother says, indicating the baby Bechstein. She likes old jazz, Kimmie whispers as Amon opens the lid. Tolerably in tune. Amon rolls out a medley of American songbook favourites. The Dowager Elenoa looks to her granddaughter. Tears track down Princess Halae's cheeks. 'Delightful, Mr. Brightbourne.' She nods and the room empties but for Amon and Princess Halae.

'You ask me about what music I like,' Princess Halae says.

'Sit with me please,' Amon says and Princess Halae places herself on the edge of his piano stool and plays tune after tune after tune on her phone, telling Amon why she loves it, what's so great about this singer, how this beat moves her. She sings, she moves her hands in the very beautiful dance—the po—of her islands. Amon picks out themes and improvises; some make her frown, some make her clap her hands with delight, some spark her own improvisations, sung in an unsteady but confident falsetto. Then Fetuu comes to tell Princess Halae that it's time.

Amon meets three times with Princess Halae. The third session he comes just for her garrulous, sunny, welcoming personality.

The composition is straightforward; the skill lies in giving her something familiar yet fresh and expansive.

'Can I hear it?' Kimmie asks.

'Certainly not,' Amon says and again pushes his bed against his door and password-protects his files.

69

A thalassocracy is a sea-state, an empire of ships. Of port cities connected by sea-lanes. Of trade winds and dream archipelagos. Of navigators and horizons. The first great thalassocracy was that of the Austronesians. Two and a half thousand years ago they sailed from their peninsulas and islands to the Resplendent Isle, to the Karai Mandalam coast of south-east India, the islands of the Indian Ocean and to great Madagascar. Carthage, Dál Riata, the Chola Empire, the Hanseatic League, the Republic of Pirates, the Empire of Japan: all thalassocracies. And between 950 and 1500 CE, the Tu'i Tonga Empire.

Or:

First there was the sea. Above it Pulotu, the spirit-world, and between them the rock Touia'o Futuna. On this rock lived three sets of twins: Biki and Maimoa'o, Fonuavai and Fonua'uta and Hemoana and Lupe. And yes they had sex with their twins and yes they had twins and those twins had children by their twins so it's pretty stinky on that rock Touia'o Futuna between heaven and the deep blue sea. Think of it like a 1970s Roger Dean album cover. Or concept art from *Avatar*.

Two minutes in and your head is already turned with names and whose daughter is she, whose son is he, but the ones you need are Tangaloa Tufunga and Maui. Yes, him. He gets everywhere in Polynesian mythology.

Tangaloa Tufunga and Maui set the islands in the blue sea. Tangaloa Tufunga threw down chips from a piece of wood he was carving and the islands of 'Eua, Kao and Tofua appeared. Not to be outdone, Maui cast his fish-hook into the ocean, felt a bite and hauled Tongatapu, the rest of the Tongan islands, and Fiji, Samoa and Ava'u from the depths into the light. Jealous, Tangaloa Tufunga (in the shape of a plover) took flight over the islands and, onto a submerged reef, dropped a seed which sprouted, grew, and drew the reef out of the sea. It became 'Ata and the seed germinated. It grew into a creeper which the plover pecked in two for no reason other than that's what deities in creation myths do. The creeper rotted, a maggot fed upon the rot. Now Tangaloa Tufunga pecked the maggot in two. From it humanity was born. From the head was born a man: Kohai. From the tail was born another man: Koau. From a morsel that fell from the beak of Tangaloa Tufunga was born a third man: Momo.

Maui, recognising the clear shortcomings of this as a creation myth, brought wives from Pulotu the spirit-world and with the maggot men they became the ancestors of the Tongan and Ava'uan people.

Yes, I will get to the feuds and fighting, 'ofa'anga. Know this: from maggots came men. Kings are different.

Some say it was Tangaloa, some say 'Eitumatupu'a: whatever. Some god had sex with a mortal woman 'Ilaheva Va'epopua and she birthed a son 'Aho'eitu: born not of maggots but of gods and humans: first of the line of Tu'i. In the inevitable sibling rivalry, 'Aho'eitu was killed, cut into parts, those parts stirred in a healing cauldron and resurrected—the standard résumé for a semi-divine monarch.

From his royal fale of Popua 'Aho'eitu Tu'i sent canoes to Eua, to Ha'apai, to Vava'u. Further: to Fiji and Samoa. On their way they swept through the insignificant archipelago of Ava'u. The incumbent House of Tuita knew better than to fight but 'Aho'eitu's Tongan marines massacred them anyway. 'Aho'eitu installed a cousin by marriage, Lord Tu'ilakepa, as viceroy and sailed on to the divine islands of Samoa. Tu'ilakepa changed the name of his house to Tu'i to show his kingly chops but Ava'u was a sleepy province of the Tongan thalassocracy, a supply-depot on the sea-road between Tonga and Samoa.

The great Tongan thalassocracy unravelled, as all must, and Fakatoufif-ita Tu'i, twelfth viceroy of Ava'u, saw a chance to seize history. He declared himself Tu'i of Tu'is; King from horizon to horizon, sunrise to sunset. He had made for him the 'Akau Ta, the war-club of the Tu'is, upon which each monarch carves their days and deeds. Over the centuries the original war-club has been extended until it's more wizard's staff than war weapon.

The passing of Fakatoufifita Tu'i sparked a bloody succession war between his three sons of murder, dismemberment, and cannibalism, sharks gorging on the entrails of the defeated, castration and the eventual victor launching his royal canoe over the bodies of his brothers and their captured soldiers.

After the wars the brothers of Tu'i Ava'u, sickened by blood, lived peaceful, exemplary lives through many monarchies. Surplus males could be fed
to the endless wars, exiled to the other islands as diplomat-hostages, encouraged to become fakaleitis or quietly disposed of if they found none of
the offered careers acceptable.

That was the last colourful incident in Ava'u's history. The Tu'is intended it to stay that way.

When Aleamotu'a Tu'i (first of his name) welcomed Captain Cook he
directed him to the richer societies of Samoa and Tonga.

Aleamotu'a II ensured that Ava'u was too small to attract the attentions
of the European empires while his son, the first Tu'ipulotu, understanding that a national acceptance of Christianity would forestall one of the
great excuses of colonialism—the missionary—presided over a denomina-
tional dance-off. Catholics vs Methodists vs Presbyterians. The Catholics
had the authority and theatre, the Methodists had the reforming zeal and
social conscience, but the Presbyterian minister, from a covenanting tradition, had the Scottish Metrical Psalter. Those psalms, moving in great a
capella chordal blocks, chimed with the musical traditions of Ava'u. King
Tu'ipulotu I embraced Presbyterianism with the zeal of man born not from
maggots but from half-deities. The kingdom had moved a long way from
dragging a war canoe over the crushed bodies of princelings.

Siaosi Tu'ipulotu II Tu'i negotiated the rapprochement between Ava'u,
its island neighbours and the British Empire through accords of friendship
that maintained Ava'u's royal independence.

Siaosi Tu'ipulotu III—much-loved, still-mourned—turned the House
of Tu'i into a constitutional monarchy and gave over executive power to
parliament, the Fale Alea. He renegotiated relationships with his Pacific
neighbours, protested French nuclear testing at Moruroa and signed Ava'u
to the Nauru Agreement protecting the Pacific tuna fisheries. He swore,
hand on the haft of the 'Akau Ta, that the House of Tu'i would forever
serve and defend the people, islands and spirit of Ava'u.

King Tu'ipulotu IV was short lived, little regarded, and is remembered
only in the name of the inter-island ferry terminal. He was pious and a
rugby fan.

Tu'ipulotu Tu'i V oversaw his own personal enrichment from horizon
to horizon, sunrise to sunset, through the systematic privatisation, looting
and exposure of Ava'u to international and corporate politics. He manip-
ulated the Fale Alea into pulling out of the Nauru Agreement to license

the tuna fisheries to Chinese, Taiwanese and Filipino fishing fleets. When the Ava'uan economy faltered, he invited Nestlé to set up the Royal Ava'u Water-bottling plant. Before it became the must-see accessory in Shanghai and Kuala Lumpur, Royal Ava'u Water became the brand of stars and West Coast influencers. The company's marketing of purity, tranquillity and authenticity steered Ava'u into the woo economy. Ava'u has more spas, wellness centres, mindfulness retreats, self-discovery oases, chakra-realignment garages, angel-summoning platforms, and coral therapy grottos per capita than anywhere on the planet. Tu'ipulotu's Maundy Islands Development Corporation licenses new hotels. There is talk of casinos. King Siaosi Tu'ipulotu Tu'i V has a palace in Toorak in Melbourne, where the real money goes. Marble and glass, an infinity pool, Bentleys and not one Karmic Pyramid, Ava'uan sea-salt chamber or Meridian Tune-up bath. If his father was a nonentity except at rugby matches, his son is actively detested. His money never flows to the islands. The stench of corruption hangs in the air. Nothing is as good as it should be, everything much worse than it used to be. Ancestors fume, smoke shrouds the future. Male youth unemployment is seventy percent. Workers in Aotearoa, Australia, Alaska send airfares to their younger siblings. Get out. Those young men who can't whittle away lives in aimless fighting and crystal meth.

Protests in the street, disquiet in the houses but none may touch the king. None but the fakaleitis.

Tu'ipulotu Tu'i V has three children. Eldest is Princess Salote 'Ofefine Halaevalu. Born with Williams syndrome, she is bright, cheerful, outgoing, loved by all and quite unable to inherit the 'Akau Ta.

Second child is Princess Elisiva Ta'ahine Pilolevu: Ta.

Youngest is Prince Siaosi Vaka'uta 'oPulotu, golden boy and heir apparent, post-graduate student at Brigham Young University–Hawaii and constitutional crisis in waiting. His conversion to the LDS Church (the better to secure development deals) may prevent him from laying claim to the 'Akau Ta. Primogeniture versus Kirk Session.

And halfway between ocean and heaven, the small gods cling to their bobbing rock, so many now there is no space between their bodies, and look down at the islands afloat in time and salt water and say, yes, better never to have left Touia'o Futuna.

70

What a swell party this is. The king in informal short-sleeved shirt and tupenu (dress-code: court casual), Queen Lavinia and the Dowager Elenoa as dress-down as their status will permit. All twenty-three members of the Fale Alea, all twelve Lords of the Isles. Ministers of religion and education, prominent figures in law, medicine and sport. The entire national rugby team. The reigning Miss Teuila. Civil servants. Business people, including the CEO of Royal Ava'u Water (King Siaosi's brother-in-law) and the King's Chinese investor-allies. A handful of consuls. Tourism luminaries. The captain of the Norwegian *Diamond* cruise ship, moored at Pulotu Wharf. Chief of police, head of the Defence Force, Royal Shepherdess. The palace lawns are watered and groomed and set with oil lanterns on bamboo poles. A generous bar and a small discreet jazz combo from the Norwegian *Diamond* dispense their cheer. Staff dragooned in from the island's hotels serve proper champagne and skewer-food.

In the white pavilion with the view over the harbour Amon Brightbourne and Princess Halaevalu stand face-to-face, almost breath-close.

'Can you hear me?' Amon says. Princess Halae nods.

He taps Play.

Princess Halae's eyes unfocus. Her mouth opens. Her brow creases. Bliss dawns across her face. She smiles. Her eyes crease. She closes them, the better to dwell in the music. She nods, her hands dance. She sings; la and mm and brief scats into beatbox puffs and hisses. Major Fia, commander of the Royal Guard, glances over. He looks away when he sees the rapture on her face.

How Amon misses this, the sacramental intimacy of music made for you, only you. Music no one else need ever hear: only the maker and the listener. Intense and close as sex. More vulnerable, more potent. None of the DJs and producers who worked the mega-clubs understood when Amon stepped out of the dawn to lead the dancers out from their clubs hand in hand in hand through the streets to the beach, why they stared into the sunrise and returned salt-streaked with tears. Ecstasy is a small place, ephemeral and private.

He remembers the luminous joy on Raisa's face up in the tree-house at Dorling Avenue. And again, in the gloaming woods of old Brightbourne. A different music, a different bliss: of mystery, mortality, the briefness of things. She heard the horns of Elfland, the chords of the numen.

And here, under this matelot moon, Princess Halae is a soul in rapture. It's a rare grace, seeing his art work immediately, directly, physically in the body of his listener. Amon feels her breath on his skin. Her eyes roll under her closed lids and he knows to a beat which clip of which track is playing. In the long migrations through the constellation of the Hopeland, in the teaching, the playing, in the drinking, he lost this wonder.

Her eyes open.

'Again, again!'

He poises his finger over the loop command. Princess Halae's hands fly to her mouth.

'No, Mr. Valaiti'voni! I can't! It is like chocolate. I eat too much I get shits. But some time.'

'It's yours, Your Highness.' Amon waves his hand over his phone and sends the file to the Royal dropbox.

'Thank you, Mr. Valaiti'voni,' Princess Halae says. Amon loves the sound of his surname in Ava'uan. 'That was the best present ever.'

'It was your sister's idea,' Amon says.

'How did you do . . . No. I don't want to know. It's magic . . .' Her Ava'uan moves beyond the horizon of Amon's comprehension.

'Thank you, Highness,' Amon says. He's worn flat. It's always this way after a set. Kimmie steers across the lawn with a glass in each hand and behind her Princess Ta, big face beaming. Behind her, a shadow; a broad man in a formally informal jacket and tupenu: Prime Minister Sionatani Vuna Pohiva.

Kimmie thrusts a flute into Amon's hand.

'You deserve champagne,' she insists.

'I want water.'

Kimmie sniffs in disdain, downs Amon's glass in one and goes to find him water.

'Thank you with all my heart,' Ta says, grasping Amon's hands in hers. Heads turn, eyebrows rise at the breach of protocol. What can you expect from someone who exercises in public, with commoners, wearing a belly top bearing the word ZUMBA? 'You have made her year. I think everyone is a bit jealous of my present.' She presses her hands tight around Amon's.

Her hands are strong. She sees the twitch of discomfort in Amon's eyes and releases her grip. 'Composer fingers!' she cries. Fetuu the Royal Fakaleiti steps in to whisper in Ava'uan to the princess. 'The Lords of Niua expect me,' she says to Amon. 'They come over four times a year; Christmas, Easter, harvest, rugby internationals. And events where they can be seen. Small islands, big people, they say about Niua.'

Now Prime Minister Pohiva steps forward to shake Amon's hand.

'I must congratulate you, Mr. Brightbourne, though I don't understand what you did.' Pohiva's English is ivy-clad and sun-warmed. He is a practising lawyer and professor of international jurisprudence at the University of the South Pacific. 'It seems a private, intimate music. So different from our musical culture. Choirs, big bands. Ensembles.' Pohiva steers Amon towards a server holding a tray of food.

'I love what I do with the choirs at Queen 'Ana and First Mua, but what I love most is looking my audience in the eyes and seeing what they are feeling.'

'Like law, Mr. Brightbourne.' The prime minister lifts a skewer of flash-grilled tuna. 'Do try one. Every island boasts it has the best tuna in the ocean but I sincerely believe ours is the finest. Of course, an Ava'uan tuna starts as a Tongan tuna and ends as a Samoan tuna. I remember when we ate like kings. Now lamb flaps, turkey tails and corned beef. Everyone else's offal is a feast for Ava'u. Enjoy this while you can, Mr. Brightbourne. Soon not even the Royal Family will be able to afford it.'

'I don't understand.'

'We are about to sell off another slice of our fishing grounds to foreigners. Soon you will be able to skip a stone from Wharf 39 to the edge of Ava'uan territorial waters.'

'You're the prime minister . . .'

'In music you play the notes, you conduct and you have music every time; complete, perfect. In politics, less so. His Majesty has solved our water crisis. We are to have a splendid new water purification plant, thanks to the government of China. In return for which their trawler fleet can fish our ocean down to the last shrimp. And it's nuclear powered—a new design called a small modular reactor—so it will require Chinese staff and a Chinese security presence. Her Highness's next birthday we will celebrate with lamb flaps and radioactive seawater.'

'Why are you telling me this, Mr. Pohiva?'

'No Ava'uan man or woman may touch the king. Our royal staff have always been fakaleitis. Outsiders.' Prime Minister Pohiva glances to a huddle of his political colleagues. 'Good evening, Mr. Brightbourne. A true pleasure.'

Kimmie bounces back with a flute of sparkling water.

'What did Old Turtle want with you?' Before Amon can answer that he feels recruited to something he never joined, Kimmie says, 'Never mind! Kimmie has news, 'ofa'anga! Who do you think is Princess Ta's newest leiti-in-waiting?' She throws back a fresh flute of champagne. 'Kimmie Pangaimotu is working for the firm. Leiti, personal assistant, secretary, adviser, stylist, confidante. Kimmie is hot! Say "Kimmie, you are a star", you miserable skinny palangi!'

Amon congratulates her but notices Prime Minister Pohiva and Fetuu talking, glancing, talking again. And the prevailing winds that blew him to this island shift to a new and permanent quarter.

71

A comment. Sinipata Stores, 07:00. Amon Brightbourne buys a six-pack of Evian. Noting that the price has gone up again, he remarks that everyone will be a lot happier when the new water supply comes online.

A question: What new water supply?

An answer: the new Chinese desalination plant. You hadn't heard about it? It's atomic.

A conversation: Mrs. Sinipata tells Mrs. Meletoni tells Mrs. Ha'amoko and within the hour the story has gone from one end of the island to the other, from shore to polluted shore.

A post: The first appears at 09:30. By 11:00 it has been shared in three media and jumped to the outer islands.

A page: 12:00. Matangi Ava'u, the kingdom's main news site, runs the story and asks the palace if it is true that the king has signed away the island's fishing grounds in return for a Chinese nuclear-powered desalination plant? The palace declines to confirm or deny the rumour.

A denunciation: 16:00. Lady Tuita, Minister for Energy, Information, Disaster Management, Environment, Climate Change and Communication, tweets on the official government account decrying fake news and gross insult to the Crown, whose only, eternal thought is the well-being of its people. By now the story has spread to the Ava'uan diaspora communities in Aotearoa, Australia, the Philippines, China, the US and Canada.

A phone call: 16:30. Matangi Ava'u, long a fly in the eye of the Ava'uan government, makes a call to the Chinese consulate in Fiji, which refuses to take the call and fails to respond to any subsequent emails.

A hit: A tweet by @niuapiraterebel06 (five hundred and eight followers) is picked up by K-pop band SKGT and posted on their Instagram feed to twelve million followers. Most of whom don't care about anything that isn't in a smart suit with a precision haircut, but there are enough other celebrity followers to send @niuapiraterebel06 viral.

A global news story: 24:00. Reuters, Associated Press, AFP and NANAP notice a ripple in the mediasphere. It's a good David and Goliath story; tiny Polynesian island kingdom versus the planet's most powerful nation. With added nukes. Copy goes out to the main subscribers. Seventeen hours after Amon Brightbourne's casual comment to Mrs. Sinipata the world is talking about Ava'u's deal with China. Phones ring off the hook at the government press office; the servers go down. Which only stokes the crucible where the rumours are smelted higher, hotter.

A thousand flowers. By next dawn the rumours are dashing between the houses like small children. The plant has already set sail from Shanghai. Or Guangdong. Or Shenzhen. It's the size of a suitcase, it's the size of a cruise liner. It's in the South China Sea, it's in the western Pacific. It will be here tomorrow. It's not Chinese, it's Russian. Or American, pretending to be Chinese. False flags. There's a navy ship with it, maybe a frigate, maybe an aircraft carrier. Maybe a secret submarine will pop up in the lagoon and soldiers pour from it. No no, the reactor workers are Special Forces in disguise. A thousand of them, or ten thousand. Niua will be concreted over and turned into an airbase. Ava'u's Defence Force will be placed under the command of Beijing: I heard this from my son who is a palace guard and, well, he should know. All those Chinese tourists at the spas: spies. They know secret martial arts that can kill you without touching you.

The islands resound with voices. All-Ava'u Radio booms with the phone-in opinionati. People take to the streets. Two hundred women sit down and block Pulotu Road, singing and clapping their hands. A crowd gathers outside the Fale Alea. Voices turn loud and ugly. A second chanting crowd shakes the gates of the Royal Palace. A large mob of young unemployed men storms Wharf 39, attacking any fishing boat with ideograms on the hull with dock debris. Under a barrage of concrete chunks and fishing crates the crews cast off and withdraw to the lagoon.

Ava'u riots. The police are outnumbered, out-nimbled by fit young men grown up on under-employment and rugby. The Defence Force pulls back to protect the Crown.

11:00. The government issues a social media release condemning the violence, promising severe consequences for further disobedience and ordering the protesters to return to their homes, businesses, schools. The Moderator of the General Assembly, the Co-Adjutor of the Sub-Diocese of Ava'u, the Methodist President and the presiding Bishop of the Latter-day Saints unite in rare ecumenism to urge a joint call to prayer, sobriety and repentance. The spirit of Christ is not a spirit of rebellion.

11:30. All-Ava'u Radio announces that Princess Elisiva will speak to the kingdom at 12:00, which will also live-stream on Matangi Ava'u's site.

12:00. Princess Elisiva Ta'ahine Pilolevu goes live. She regrets the violence and anger on the streets. She recognises grievances and hurts. The world is changing, Ava'u is small but proud. She notes the influence of social media, gossip, rumour and the international press. Lies have wide wings. What is truth in these times? Truth is that her family will always strive for what is best for the people of Ava'u. Your family is my family. We are all one family. Difficult times confront our beloved islands. We must work together to build a future for all our people. Please: return to your homes; let calm and peace reign. My family will listen, and we will act. God bless Ava'utapu, Ofu and Niua, our bright islands in the ocean. God bless you. Everyone hears the choke in her voice, sees the tears on her face.

My family, everyone notes. Not *the King. Ava'utapu, Ofu and Niua.* Not *the kingdom.*

Amon Brightbourne hides in his bungalow listening to the surge of voices, sirens, bangs and booms from the street. Outside is not a wise place for a palangi. Kimmie messages: she's holed up in the palace. Exciting, isn't it? Rattle of firecrackers, the revving of moped engines. Shrieking tyres, cheers and jeers and the splintering of glass. He smells burning petrol, burning plastic. At one point he starts upright at what sounds like shots. He remembers how he strayed an innocent into the 2011 London riots, escaped the consequences of his folly by Grace alone. *Good things happen to you because bad things happen to everyone around you,* Raisa said the night of Auberon's Speedforth. Grace was fleet and light; the Price was slow, lumbering up over the horizon, inevitable.

The noises and voices ebb towards midnight. He falls asleep in his armchair and is woken by the morning birds. He has a monstrous thirst. He ventures out to Sinipata's store. Broken glass litters Fangaloa Road. A burned-out HiAce still smokes: he feels the heat from the ash-white steel skeleton. The air reeks of burned plastic and petrol. Chunks of concrete, ripped-out metal fencing, placards and plaited banana-leaf plates. A surprising number of single shoes. Amon exchanges greetings with the people he meets. A *whoosh*, a bang, everyone cringes. A puff of smoke. Some kid has set off a rocket.

A comment. Mrs. Sinipata in her store. Crooks and liars, the lot of them. Prime Minister Pohiva, the Fale Alea, the Twelve Lords. Even the royals—God grace them. That Princess Ta is the only one I trust.

An invitation: Kimmie returns that evening, in her civilian dress, hair a mess, face bare. Frazzled. With a bottle from a gin cache Amon had forgotten about.

' 'Ofaʻanga, Kimmie has to sleep for a thousand years. Before I do, Ta wants to know, this Sunday after church, would you come with her to visit the blow-holes?'

72

Amon visited the blow-holes on his third day on the island. He visited them last with Atli. Between the two excursions he has been to the blow-holes five times, in all their moods and explosiveness. Apart from the blow-holes and the Tuʻi Calvary, there is fuck-all else to see on Avaʻutapu. Eighty percent of its land surface is built up. The reef is a bleached skull-yard and what's left of the beaches is carpeted in plastic. But a princess has invited him, on a boat. So Amon waits on the Royal Wharf, shoes shined, hair combed, attire curated and supervised by Kimmie Pangaimotu for a Sunday afternoon jaunt.

He's greeted on the jetty by Prime Minister Pohiva, with security. In polo shirts and shades.

'Her Highness regrets she will not be able to come with you to see the blow-holes. She has asked me to host you in her place.'

Security steps back from the gangplank to the royal boat, a trimly retro lozenge of burnished wood, white nautical gloss and fingerprinty brass. They step behind Amon, closing any return to the jetty.

'Mr. Brightbourne?'

Prime Minister Pohiva sits with Amon on the cream leather banquette at the rear of the boat. His men take the helm and the boat burbles away from the jetty, across the glowing lagoon towards the gap in the reef. The Avaʻu archipelago lies on the western lip of the Tonga trench, Amon recalls. Ten thousand metres down to the subduction zone where continental plates go to die. The drivers open the throttles and the boat lifts its chin and powers out into the deep blue.

'You have loose lips, Mr. Brightbourne.'

'I'm sorry . . . I mean . . . I shouldn't,' Amon stammers. The prime minister's directness takes him aback. Island ways of indirection and context are easy for an Irish lad. Mr. Pohiva wears vintage tortoiseshell Wayfarers and Amon sees himself all too clearly reflected in the dark lenses.

'Months of negotiation, Mr. Brightbourne. All my team's painstaking work: undone by careless words. How can China trust us now? With nuclear material?'

Amon stammers again.

'The King is furious. He wanted you charged with treason. I coun-
selled him against that. The Crown has enough adverse publicity. You
would be on the next flight to Fiji had Their Highnesses not interceded
for you.'

'Ta and Halae?'

'Their Highnesses. And the Queen Mother. She liked your jazz. The
King has turned his attention to hunting the . . . the word is mole?'

. 'Mole.'

Prime Minister Pohiva frowns.

'An odd word. I have only an intellectual understanding of what a mole
is. We have no moles on these islands.'

'We have no moles on my island, either,' Amon says.

'Really? So far His Majesty's investigations have returned only rumours.'

'You told me.' Amon says. 'If anyone's the mole, it's you.'

Prime Minister Pohiva grins beneath his Ray-Bans.

'Yes I did. And you went straight out and spread the story. You have no
discretion, Mr. Brightbourne. And I could not be more delighted.'

The boat bounces hard. The security men stand firm as masts.

'You wanted me to spread the story?'

Prime Minister Pohiva nods and his crew turn the boat to the shore,
towards the shelf of old coral limestone at the western hook of the island:
the blow-holes.

'Our king is not a good king. He has consistently failed to rule for the
benefit of his people. He is not a good man. He has enriched himself at the
expense of his subjects. Many of whom still adore him. A growing number
do not. There are people—citizens—in all levels of society who believe
that the kingdom would be better served by another monarch. A queen,
not a king.'

'Ta?' This traitor-talk makes Amon's head swim. It sounds as unreal as
James Bond dialogue.

'Her Highness is popular, dedicated, immensely capable, selfless and
intelligent. Everything His Majesty is not.'

Every seagull has a microphone taped to its leg, every fish skimming
silver just below the surface has cameras for eyes. The sky is full of drones;
satellites spin in low orbit to train their lenses on him, bobbing in a 1950s-
retro wooden speedboat on the ocean.

'Does Ta know?'

'Of course.'

The pilots nudge closer to shore. Ink-blue water breaks in a ruff of foam around shallow-lying rocks. The boat lifts on the swell, the surf-line surges white on grey. A boom, a geyser of spray. Stone and sea tremble.

'You used me,' Amon says.

'I did. I'm sorry, Mr. Brightbourne.'

'I was your useful idiot.'

'I wouldn't choose those words, Mr. Brightbourne.'

'Yet I was.'

'Let's say there are privileges and freedoms palangis enjoy that we do not.'

'Why am I here, Mr. Pohiva?'

The prime minister sighs. The surf-line thunders, pillars of spray launch skyward. The boat rolls heavily, broadside onto a rising swell. Amon grips the butter-soft leather armrests.

'Public passions are aroused. The king's popularity has never been lower. After her broadcast, Her Highness's has never been higher. If we move now, we can achieve a peaceful transfer of power.'

'With the greatest respect, you didn't answer my question, Mr. Pohiva.'

'I need another indiscretion from you, Mr. Brightbourne.'

The security men turn to look at Amon. Flow-tide drifts the boat towards the break-line. The blow-holes boom and the geysers plume and their spray mists Amon's skin.

'Why should I do anything for you? You used me.'

'I did. I apologise. There's a Latin expression: Pro tanto quid retribuamus.'

'"For so much given, what shall we repay?"' Amon grew up in a house haunted by classical whispers: Latin, Greek, Hebrew and Sanskrit, incantations on the staircases, conspiracies up and down the galleries.

'We need your help, Mr. Brightbourne.'

The voice from the roof, Raisa clinging to the gutter with fingers and toes like a superhero as London spasmed, fires burned and helicopters scoured the night. *I need your phone.* The decision of an instant, a rushing in his head, a stab of desire set his foot on the fire escape that led him across the rooftops, across the constellations, across the archipelagos of the heart.

'What do you want me to do?'

'You will receive information that will encourage the King to abdicate in favour of his daughter. Your mission is to make it public. Very public.'

'The useful idiot gets a fool's pardon.'

'Again, I wouldn't choose those words. And there is risk. There is risk in everything. We will try to keep you safe.' Prime Minister Pohiva's security—monoliths of men, slab-faced, stone-handed—nod. 'The worst that will happen is you get moved on to another part of your constellation family. We may not be so fortunate. But we believe it must be attempted, and attempted soon.' The security men tilt their heads again. 'Will you help us, Mr. Brightbourne?'

Amon remembers the bright faces, the massed voices of thunder shaking the assembly hall's girders with the commencement song. He sees the women in their go-to-church tupenus fanning themselves in the pews in First Mua; he sees them on Monday spreading their mats in the shade of the arcades of Fou Market, laying out the memory cards, unlocked phones, knock-off sportswear, shades, make-up, pharma, unfolding their parasols. He sees the bobbing screen-lights of the spa workers walking home from the hotels at bat-flight. The dogs, the taxi drivers, the old men who fish from the King Siaosi IV Wharf. The proud, handsome young men with nothing to do but walk up one side of Pulotu Road in the morning and down the other in the evening. The bus drivers, the tour-tat shop owners, the bartenders, the food servers. The Royal Marines who greet him as he passes the palace, the shopkeepers who know his name and his grocery list. The crabs that haunt the scrub of grass outside his front door, the giant millipedes that want to make it past that door into his house, the spiders vast as battle-kites that know the trick. The gulls slipping from wind to wind.

So much given.

'Yes,' he says. 'I will. Yes.'

The security men smile like sun behind a clearing squall. Prime Minister Pohiva removes his dark glasses.

'Thank you, Mr. Brightbourne.'

'What happens?'

'You will be contacted by my agent.'

'Your agent?'

'This is your world now, Mr. Brightbourne.'

'That commission. For Princess Halae, it wasn't a lucky break was it?'

'Very little that has happened to you since arriving in the kingdom has been a lucky break.'

'So no coincidence that Kimmie Pangaimotu turned up on my doorstep needing a bed?'

'Oh, Mr. Brightbourne. No one our age believes in coincidence.'

Mr. Pohiva turns to survey the shore. 'I think we've spent a convincing amount of time seeing the blow-holes. You should take some photographs.'

'I have photographs,' Amon says.

'For the time stamp, Mr. Brightbourne.' The prime minister nods and his security up-throttle engines and turn the boat seawards across the roll. 'As I said, this is your world now.'

The crew synchronises the throttles, the boat lifts its head and powers of twin tails of white boil across the indigo sea.

'Kimmie?' Amon's shout turns heads across the campus, from caretaker's fale to rugby pavilion. Eimoni has raised his voice. Eimoni never raises his voice. Street dogs, drawn by his tone, follow him across the desire lines that lace the green space in front of the staff bungalows. 'Kimmie!'

No word from the house. He turns on the veranda to bellow at the diarrhoea-coloured dogs. They cower, ears back, tails tucked. Amon shouts Kimmie's name through the house. By now a small crowd has gathered on Fangaloa Road. What is Eimoni so angry about? Who knows? Palangis are always angry about something.

No Kimmie Pangaimotu but a memory stick in Amon's MacBook. He clicks it. The stick opens a trove of documents. Reports, transcripts, spreadsheets, emails. Photographs, video clips. Affidavits and logbooks. Gigabytes of information.

This is how you kill a king.

Amon cuts everything from the stick. Shut the lid on his MacBook and it will be lost in whatever un-space exists between the cut and the paste. There is a price to the Grace, Raisa said. Amon creates a new folder. *Princess 'Akusita*. Pastes in and locks it behind his strongest passwords. He reformats the memory stick, ejects it and slips it into a pocket. The casual burglary that spirited it into his MacBook could as easily spirit it away again. He stares at the screen, long enough for the afternoon to steepen and diminish into the fleet twilight of the tropics.

A knock at the door. Amon cries out and kicks over table and laptop. He is still shaking when he opens the door to Rev. Akalesi. She stops on the veranda. It is not seemly for a woman and a man unrelated to her to be alone indoors together.

'Eimoni, we would be greatly honoured if you could play for the Family Service.'

'I thought the praise band . . .'

'They do, they do. They would like to play with you. In the spirit of Christian harmony.'

'I don't know any of the music . . .'

'It's easy to pick up.'

Amon recognises the Ava'uan ask that is not an ask and may not be refused.

'I'll improvise.'

A MacBook is as easy to spirit away as a memory stick. It goes in Amon's old satchel, after he sets up two separate cloud storage accounts and uploads *Princess 'Akusita* to each. The evening congregation greets him with delight. Will he be playing with the praise band every Family Service? He opens the console of the Viscount 400 and a terrible doubt lands: Are two cloud accounts enough? Are any enough?

This is your world now.

After the service Rev. Akalesi indicates she would like a word with Amon. He switches off the organ, clutches his satchel tight under his arm.

'That was mighty praise.'

He had hated every minim and quaver of the service. The lyrics were trite, the music banal and the true dedication of the band's—four lower-sixth formers—was clearly to metal. Amon obliged with power chords from the Viscount and the bass player nodded in appreciation when Amon came in on the back of his Alabama 3 walking line with the organ's bass pedals. The last band member packs up his guitar.

'Such a friendly church, Eimoni.'

Amon Brightbourne imagines police going room to room, drawer to drawer.

'It is.'

'We care for each other,' Rev. Akalesi says. 'As Jesus commanded. We try to be. The church is the body of Christ. Every part works with every other. If one part sickens, the whole body suffers. If one part weakens, the whole body weakens.'

'St Paul's First Epistle to the Corinthians.'

'Sometimes the part is so weak, so diseased, that it threatens the health of the whole body. The teaching of Jesus is clear here: it must be cut away, for the good of the whole.'

'I thought the teaching of Jesus was if thy right eye offend thee, pluck it out?'

'"All Scripture is breathed out by God and profitable for teaching, for reproof, for correction and for training in righteousness",' the Assistant Minister says.

'It is, Rev. Akalesi. I'll see you next Sunday, Rev. Akalesi. Morning service.'

The shakes hit on the veranda. Amon manages to open the house door and tumbles to the sofa. He can't breathe. His head roars to a bass pedal of dread. Gin. Dear gin. The only God who asked nothing of you. Kimmie can't have found all his stashes. That would mean going out, being exposed, feeling eyes on him that see him now as a different creature. A spy. A traitor.

Fuck them. The shudders ebb, the fear subsides. He looks at his room and sees what is there. Everything is how he left it when he went to Family Service. There have been no searchers. His enemies obviously thought a warning from the Assistant Minister would suffice. Amon opens the MacBook. Password and thumbprint unlock *Princess 'Akusita*. He deletes it, double deletes it, erases it from all memory. He opens one of his secure cloud storage locations. There's safety in cyberspace. Documents fill the screen. Amon picks the Tu'ivakano Inquiry report and starts reading.

Fuck them all.

On March 18, 2023, the RAFC *Princess ʻAkusita* sailed from King Siaosi IV Wharf, Mua, Kingdom of Avaʻu.

It was the ferry's maiden voyage on the Avaʻutapu-Ofu-Niua route.

One hundred and ninety-one people were aboard.

Princess ʻAkusita was a ro-ro ferry built by Imabari Shipbuilding's Marugame yard in Shikoku in 1994.

Princess ʻAkusita was forty metres long, with a central car deck with bow and stern doors. A two-deck superstructure was erected over the car deck. The ship was rated for two hundred and fifty passengers and twenty vehicles.

Princess ʻAkusita served on the Seto Inland Sea between Yawatahama and Usuki under the name of *Miyajima-maru*.

In 2007 *Miyajima-maru* was sold to M. J. Singh of the Coral Sea Shipping Company based in Vanuatu, renamed MV *Leinani* after the owner's favourite granddaughter, then resold in 2008 to Polynesia Shipping in Fiji.

MV *Leinani* worked for fifteen years between the islands of Fiji.

In 2022 the Fale Alea of Avaʻu voted to replace the ageing inter-island ferry *Queen ʻAnaseini*.

Avaʻu's high commissioner to New Zealand, Prince ʻAhoʻeitu, negotiated an NZ$40 million grant to purchase and refit a new ferry.

A special-purpose royal corporation, the Royal Avaʻu Ferry Company, was established to manage the purchase, refitting and running of the ferry service. This company replaced the existing Royal Avaʻu Steamship Company.

The RAFC inspected the *Leinani* in Suva, obtained seaworthiness certificates and purchased the ship for NZ$38 million.

Hon. Samueli Havea, Member for Kolovai, observed that he considered the ship overpriced.

In December 2022 the *Leinani* sailed from Suva to Mua's Royal Shipyard to undergo a refit budgeted at NZ$2 million.

Samueli Havea, in a statement to the Fale Alea, observed that the refit budget seemed inflated and that repairs and refit would have been better carried out in Suva, which had more advanced shipyards.

On February 22, 2023, the *Leinani* was renamed *Princess 'Akusita* by His Majesty Siaosi V Tu'i in a naming ceremony attended by the entire royal family, the nobility and church leaders.

February 25, 2023, the *Princess 'Akusita* commenced sea-trials under the command of Captain Maka Mataele Tei.

On March 18, 2023, at 20:00, *Princess 'Akusita* sailed from King Siaosi IV Wharf, Mua, Kingdom of Ava'u.

The weather forecast for that night was for ocean swell of up to four metres dropping to one and a half metres as Tropical Depression TD09F cleared to the west. Wind speeds were fifty kilometres per hour decreasing to thirty. Visibility good.

At 23:00 the decaying core of TC Nisha ran into TD09F three hundred kilometres north-east of Fiji, transferring heat energy and momentum and upscaling the merged weather systems into a cyclone. The evolving tropical cyclone veered west.

At 00:30 the Fiji Meteorological Service forecast wind speeds by dawn of eighty kilometres per hour, gusting to one hundred and twenty, with wave-heights up to eight metres. The cyclone was deepening and would arrive in the Ava'u/Samoa sea-region as a tropical cyclone by 09:30 that day.

Princess 'Akusita was scheduled to dock at Poloa in Ofu at 06:30, where Captain Maka planned to shelter from the cyclone.

At 01:00 *Princess 'Akusita* put out a Mayday call. Coastguard logs and logbook entries from ships that diverted to assist reported water on the car deck. At 01:05 Captain Hara of the Auriga *Imperator,* a car carrier bound from Yokohama for Santiago in Chile, reported a distress beacon.

Captain Hara remained in radio contact with *Princess 'Akusita* until 01:12 when communications broke up and ceased one minute and thirty-five seconds later. Captain Maka's words from that minute and thirty-five seconds are garbled but subsequent sound enhancement extracted these phrases: Bow door. Vehicles shifting.

All contact with *Princess 'Akusita* was lost at 01:20.

All ships in the area entered search-and-rescue mode. Fijian, Samoan, Tongan and Ava'uan Defence Force vessels were dispatched. Three drones were launched from Fiji. Deteriorating weather and extreme range meant they could only spend a few minutes over the target.

Princess 'Akusita carried two lifeboats and ten life rafts. The drone survey showed a flotsam zone, three life rafts and a number of bodies. The weather was deteriorating, it was night and sea conditions made infrared cameras unreliable.

Flotsam included life jackets, flotations, loose deck cargo, foam upholstery and women's tapa mats.

The drones relayed the GPS co-ordinates to the rescue ships. The first to arrive was Auriga *Imperator* at 02:30, followed by MV *Star Electra,* a bulk carrier, at 04:00 and Norwegian *Ovation,* a cruise liner, at 04:50. Faced with darkness, poor weather and the sheer size of his ship, Captain Hara declined to start searching immediately, out of safety concerns for survivors.

The water temperature of the south Pacific Ocean between Samoa and Ava'u in March averages 28°C.

The rated capacity of each of *Princess 'Akusita*'s lifeboats was twenty.

Dawn on March 19, 2023, was 06:40. All three first-response ships commenced search-and-rescue procedures. The Fijian drones refuelled and returned to the search area. They were joined by a Royal New Zealand Air Force Boeing P-8 maritime patrol aircraft which assumed command of the operation.

All naval vessels were on station by 12:00. The area was experiencing storm force 9 winds, sea state 7. Spray hindered visibility.

A crowd began gathering at King Siaosi IV Wharf before dawn. Despite the weather, by noon it numbered two thousand.

Sunset on March 19, 2023, was 19:00. At this time the search was abandoned for the night. Seventy people were rescued from three life rafts, one raft by Norwegian *Ovation,* one by the RFNS hydrographic survey ship *Kacau,* one by the frigate HMNZS *Te Kaha.*

No live bodies were recovered from the sea. There were no lifeboats found.

The seventy survivors of the *Princess 'Akusita* comprised: fifty-two men, sixteen women, two children. Among them were the entire crew of eight.

One hundred and twenty people drowned on the *Princess 'Akusita*.

News was slow to arrive in Ava'u. The enormity of the loss became clear only at 22:00. By then half of Ava'utapu's population was on King Siaosi IV Wharf. Similar congregations formed at the ferry terminals on Ofu and Niua.

At 23:00 the king spoke to the nation and declared three days of mourning.

Not one family on Ava'utapu was untouched by the *Princess 'Akusita* disaster.

Some women, following tradition, wore the mats of mourning for a year and a day.

Over the following ten days the survivors were repatriated to Ava'u. For his own safety Captain Maka was held in Apia on Samoa and interviewed by Ava'uan police under legal counsel.

March 22: a Royal Court of Inquiry into the sinking was established, Lord Tu'ivakano chairing.

The first session of the *Princess 'Akusita* Inquiry opened on March 25, 2023, in Queen 'Anaseini College Hall and immediately adjourned for the purposes of gathering evidence, statements and depositions.

On March 25, a group of eight women in mourning mats sat down in the road outside the Fale Alea and sang songs and hymns. They resisted police attempts to move them. When the police threatened to charge them with obstruction of the king's highway, they moved to the grass verge opposite the parliament gate and insisted on exercising their right to peaceful protest.

March 25: the RFNS *Kacau* arrived at the site of the sinking and sent down a ROV.

Princess 'Akusita lay on its port side in ninety metres of water. The vehicles lay along the port bulkhead of the vehicle deck, corroborating witness reports that the load had shifted and the ship had capsized.

The ROV's camera showed that the bow door was missing. The submersible located the door three hundred metres astern of the wreck, indicating that the door had sheared off before the ship sank.

The ROV's cameras inspected the vehicle deck. Scuppers were blocked. There were extensive patches of rust on the hull and vehicle deck.

The ROV moved to the passenger decks. Here most of the victims were found. Many were still wrapped up in the tapa mats in which they had slept, overwhelmed by the speed of the disaster.

The next day the ROV returned to the bow door. Close inspection revealed the locking bolts were sheared through. The lock mechanisms of the visor and the inner doors were badly corroded.

The ROV evidence presented to the Court of Inquiry suggested strongly that the locks had failed under hydraulic pressure from waves. They proposed that the visor had separated and wrenched the loading ramp free, causing the failure of the inner doors and allowing water onto the vehicle deck. Free surface effect made *Princess 'Akusita* critically unstable.

After the vehicles on the car deck shifted to port, the ship was doomed.

Princess 'Akusita capsized and sank in under two minutes.

The Court of Inquiry began taking evidence from witnesses.

Survivors, crew, staff of the Royal Ava'u Ferry Company and international expert witnesses were summoned.

The singing women appeared outside Queen 'Ana College Hall. They can be clearly heard on the recordings of the inquiry. They returned every day that the inquiry sat.

On questioning, marine engineers from the University of the South Pacific, salvage company South Sea Towage and Imabari Shipbuilding deposed that *Seto*-class ferries were rated for storm forces up to 11 and the *Princess 'Akusita* should have survived the sea conditions of that night.

On May 28 First Mua, St Peter Chanel, Centenary Chapel and the Mua Temple held memorial services. Memorials were also observed on Ofu and Niua.

The wreck of the *Princess 'Akusita* was designated a maritime grave.

The Court of Inquiry took evidence from workers at the Royal Shipyard on the quality of the repair and refits to make *Princess 'Akusita* seaworthy. Several confirmed the images from the ROV that showed corrosion, painted-over drainage, jammed and rusted machinery.

The Court of Inquiry now turned its attention to the competence of the crew on the night of the tragedy.

Lord Tu'ivakano focused on three critical competencies: the competence of the vehicle deck crew in securing the doors, the general competence of the ship's company in operating a vessel quite different from its predecessor, and the competence of Captain Maka's command in heavy weather.

The vehicle deck crew were asked whether their unfamiliarity with the new locking mechanisms might have caused them to overlook safety procedures or warnings. *Princess 'Akusita's* bow and stern loading doors operated differently from those of *Queen 'Anaseini.*

The crew were asked if they could have saved more lives. It was noted that the entire crew survived.

Captain Maka was brought to Mua to testify. The inquiry centred on whether his command decisions had exposed his ship to structural pressures outside its design parameters.

Hon. Samueli Havea, who had questioned if the *Princess 'Akusita* had been overpriced, now questioned why the inquiry had moved so quickly from the seaworthiness of the *Princess 'Akusita* to the actions of the crew.

18 June 2023. Mua Coroner's court passed verdicts of unlawful killing in the case of the 121 victims of the *Princess 'Akusita* sinking.

20 June 2023. The Court of Inquiry charged Captain Maka Mataele Tei, First Mate Taniela Ta'ufa and Chief Engineer Viliami Taufatofua with manslaughter.

3 July 2023. The Court of Inquiry produced a 200-page report. Blame was clearly laid on the command of the *Princess 'Akusita.*

The report went out to the islands. All-Ava'u Radio streamed a full reading on its website. Families read it to each other. Its shortcomings were apparent. The state of the ship, the responsibility of the RAFC, the questions raised over the purchase of the *Princess 'Akusita* were glossed over in favour of blaming the crew.

Samueli Havea spoke on AAR questioning the conclusions of the Tu'ivakano Inquiry.

Nevertheless, Captain Maka, First Mate Taniela and Chief Engineer Viliami were charged with manslaughter and a trial date set.

Samueli Havea crowd-funded his own private investigation into the *Princess 'Akusita* disaster. Its areas of inquiry were the financial arrangements of the RAFC and any potential cover-up by the Tu'ivakano Inquiry. Funding came largely from the Ava'uan diaspora.

Immediately the Havea investigation came under attack from Lord Tu'ivakano, who protested that his reputation had been offended.

The trial of the 'Akusita Three began on September 3, 2023. The trial lasted six weeks, under a panel of three judges.

The three trial judges, Justice 'Opeti Fanguo, Justice Sau Faupula and Justice Valamotu Palu, tightly circumscribed the defence. No evidence on the seaworthiness certificates of the *Princess 'Akusita* was permitted. The prosecution called no witnesses from the RAFC, denying the defence the opportunity to cross-examine under oath.

The judges reached a verdict. Captain Maka and First Mate Taniela were found guilty of manslaughter and sentenced to ten and eight years respectively. First Mate Viliami was acquitted. Ava'u does not have a prison so the convicts were sent to Samoa.

The defence lawyers announced an immediate appeal on the steps of the courthouse. Samueli Havea denounced the verdict of what he called a show-trial and called on the people of Ava'u to protest a gross miscarriage of justice.

Demonstrations in Mua, Poloa and on Niua were immediate and widespread. Crowds gathered outside the Fale Alea and the palace. Concerned for his safety, King Siaosi moved the royal household to his Australia home and remained there for four months.

Matangi Ava'u and AAR condemned the trial. The news site published twelve questions unanswered by the trial and Tu'ivakano Inquiry. It led with a picture of King Siaosi washing the feet of his ministers and senior clergy at the Maundy Thursday service under the headline, *You wash their feet; what about your hands?*

The next day Matangi Ava'u was banned, its sites taken down. AAR was taken off air. Matangi Ava'u's editor, Siale Saulala, and Samueli Havea were charged with the offence of disrespect to the Crown.

The Hon. Havea, having been tipped off about an imminent arrest, was taken to Samoa by family boat and from there fled to New Zealand, then Malaysia which did not have an extradition treaty with Ava'u.

In return for an apology, and a written guarantee not to pursue any further investigation into the *Princess 'Akusita* tragedy, the charges against Siale Saulala were dropped.

Samueli Havea's assets in Ava'u were frozen and he was found guilty in absentia. His aiga remained on Ava'u.

This was the deal. Mr. Havea would remain silent on the *Princess 'Akusita* and conduct no further investigations. In return his extended family would enjoy the protection of the king.

Effectively hostages.

The Hon. Samueli Havea's findings were these:

Princess 'Akusita's seaworthiness certificates had been falsified. Officials were bribed in the Fijian Ministry of Commerce, Trade and Tourism.

Documents leaked from inside the Polynesia Shipping Company confirmed that the price of the ferry had been inflated by NZ$2.5 million. Likewise, the repair and refit budget had been inflated.

Payments for the ferry from the RAFC showed a complex chain of financial transactions through multiple holding companies registered in the Cook Islands.

RAFC's auditors, ILC, were also registered in the Cook Islands, a notorious tax haven.

The stolen money had likewise been moved through shell companies that paid into the account of Tu'i Holdings, King Siaosi Tu'i's investment company.

The refit crew had been encouraged to change their reports on the state of the *Princess 'Akusita*'s seaworthiness to the Tu'ivakano Inquiry.

The findings of the Tu'ivakano Inquiry had been perverted.

Captain Maka and Chief Engineer Taniela had been scape-goated.

The Havea Report concluded that the RAFC had knowingly permitted an unsafe and unseaworthy ship to set sail on the night of March 18, 2023.

That the king milked NZ$3 million from the New Zealand government grant.

That the king had interfered in the investigation into the sinking of the *Princess 'Akusita.*

That the king had actively obstructed justice.

That the king was complicit in the deaths of 121 of his subjects.

Samueli Havea died in 2030 in George Town in Penang, Malaysia, from metastasizing cancer of the thyroid. A request from his lawyers for his body to be returned to Ava'u for burial was refused.

The data contained in the Havea report was returned to his family. The king sequestered the report but not before grandson Sake Havea digitised the entire report and stored it in a data haven in Iceland.

Knowledge of the findings of the Havea report was widespread in Ava'uan political circles.

In 2032 Prime Minister Pohiva approached Sake Havea to negotiate access to the Havea report.

The Havea report contained a solid paper trail of payments, names, accounts and corporate ledgers connecting the Crown to the overinflated tenders. It contained sufficient evidence of criminal activities by King Siaosi Tu'i to make his continued role as monarch untenable.

Prime Minister Pohiva gathered a cabal of politicians, intellectuals, business-folk, clergy and concerned citizens to effect a transfer of the monarchy to Princess Elisiva Ta'ahine Pilolevu.

In 2033 Prime Minister Pohiva, through his agent, passed the contents of the Havea report to Amon Brightbourne.

And Amon Brightbourne is afraid.

74

'Flourish!' Kimmie Pangaimotu commands. In the gallery Amon hits a button on his pad. Disco horns flare, moving lights swivel and scatter brilliants from Kimmie's glitter-foil boa as she strikes a pose. 'Flounce!' Another glowing button on the play-pad. 'And flourish flourish flourish.' Amon's horn section funks hard and Kimmie seems to explode into a million shining lights as she skips downstage for the climax of her dance. Amon takes out the light show and segues into the traditional dance sequence. Kimmie slings the boa to her rivals down in the body of the ballroom, playing with their phones, watching with shark eyes. She steps out of the diamante heels and by a slick transformation that Amon still cannot fathom though he has seen it twelve times, in two moves changes into traditional costume.

'Kill it. Kill it!' Amon kills the show. When Kimmie learnt that he could do full show control, not just curate her music, her imagination effervesced. 'You were a beat off in the pickup there.'

Amon knows he wasn't.

After Christmas and New Year, after the summer holidays end and the schools return, amidst the work work work, one star shines. The Mz Starshine Contest. If the Ava'uan Holy Trinity is rugby, music and church, its apostles are pageants. The greatest of these is the Miss Teuila Contest in November, when the kingdom chooses its queen of grace, talent and beauty. The islands come to standstill for three weeks of heats and finals. At the year's antipode is the Mz Starshine Contest; St John the Divine to Miss Teuila's St Peter. Mz Starshine is the fakaleiti community's pageant of grace, talent and beauty. Irony, camp, performative queerness have no place here. Mz Starshine is deadly serious.

'From the "Queen B, learn from me" bit,' Kimmie says, slipping on her shoes. Someone hands up her boa. Amon resets the cues. The metronome clicks her in. Horns, lights. Sashay into the tau'olunga. Amon notices the noddings, the whisperings at the tables. He brings the sound and light show to its finale. Kimmie pants under the moving spotlights. Her face is jubilant. And blackout. And back to working lights.

'Okay.' The next tech crew waits tetchily by the dimmer racks. 'One more time.' Amon resets the cues. And in.

75

Amon hears the back door open. He lost himself tweaking the Mz Starshine cues. One o'clock. Late for Ava'u. The back door. Amon sits up. Intruders. Agents. Ninjas.

'Kimmie?'

The kitchen door, footsteps, a bedroom door. He knows the creaks; he knows the weight and timing of the footfalls.

'Kimmie?'

Amon cracks open her bedroom door. Against the glow of the school's security lighting through drawn curtains a silhouette sits on the bed. He reaches for the light-switch.

'Leave the light, Amon.'

What speaks in the dark room is shards and shreds of a voice. Amon hits the switch. Kimmie cringes from the light. Ripped clothes; blood running from her nose, her ear; her right eye crimson and black. Lacerations on her hands, her forearms where she tried to defend herself. Bouquets of bruises: flowers of assault.

'Leave me alone, Amon.'

'I can't.'

She looks at him now.

'It hurts, Amon.'

He fetches a basin of warm water, a sponge, paper towels.

'I'm sorry, there's not enough for a bath,' he says. Kimmie dabs her skin. Pink dissolves into the water.

'What happened?' Amon asks.

'Ta asked me to work late. I was walking back. And.' She flutters fingers over her right hip. 'Help me with this.' Amon eases off her shoes, peels down the black work leggings. Her right thigh is bruised knee to hip. The fingers of her right hand are swollen black.

'You need to get those rings off.' A few squirts of washing-up liquid helps them twist off. 'Did you recognise any of them?

' 'Ofa'anga, how long have you lived here? Everyone knows everyone.'

Amon finds a tube of just-expired Savlon and applies it in slow, kind smears to Kimmie's leg. 'One of them was my cousin Salesi. Nothing fucks you like family.'

Kimmie strips down to her pants. You are not looking at a man, Amon tells himself. A leiti is always a leiti.

'Why?' Amon says with simple wonder.

'Oh, Amon,' Kimmie says. 'A message. It's always a message. In my closet. Fifth from the right. Pass me that T-shirt.'

'The hibiscus flowers?'

'They're heilalas.'

Amon moves to help her pull the big soft shirt over her head. She holds up a hand.

'I don't know how to ask this,' Amon says. 'But, um . . .'

'Say it, Amon Brightbourne.'

'Mz Starshine?'

'Amon, look at me. Look at me!'

Amon lowers himself clumsily onto the bed beside her. He would offer an arm, a comfort, but he still doesn't understand Ava'uan rules on social touch. Especially with fakaleitis. Fuck it. He shuffles closer, puts an uncomfortable arm around her. Kimmie stiffens. *Done the wrong thing again, Amon Brightbourne.* Not done the wrong thing. He is the wrong thing. Chaos bringer. Darling of entropy. He doesn't pull away. In time, Kimmie relaxes against him.

'What are you going to do?' Amon asks.

'What can I do? It's over.'

'Then they win.'

She stiffens at his uncivil abruptness.

'There's some co-codamol in my room,' Amon says.

When he returns with pills and water Kimmie has pulled on fresh leggings, cleaned her lacerations. She has found a bottle of gin, presumably hidden in a parallel universe. Amon takes it and sets it on the chest of drawers.

'You need to be sharp.'

She smiles weakly and swallows two co-codamol.

'It's like a rape,' she says. 'Yes. It's a violation. Bodies doing what they want to another body.' She can't look at Amon. '*My* body.'

Amon feels like another violator. After a long, necessary silence, he says, 'Kimmie, when you came here. That first night. You told me your parents had gone over the horizon. On the *Princess 'Akusita*. Tell me about them.'

Kimmie hesitates. She can't understand why this question, why now.

'Please,' Amon says.

'I will then, kynnd,' Kimmie Pangaimotu says.

KIMMIE AND THE *PRINCESS*

When we met, I told you my name. You said Pangaimotu, that's an island. Yes Pangaimotu is an island. A small island. Rocks and a niu tree. 'Motu' in Ava'uan means little rock. But it's our little rock. It's a joke out in Niua. We were given it by Lord Vaea five hundred years ago. I think we helped him win some war. No one's ever lived there. Once a year, someone has to go and visit it. Actually set foot on it.

It's quite a job. You get to Niua, then you have to arrange a boat to Pangaimotu. There aren't any of us left on Niua but there're people, the 'Akau'olas, we stay with. You can only land on Pangaimotu if the weather is exactly right so you could be waiting on Niua for days. And you do not want to get stuck on Pangaimotu.

No one likes going so we make it a lottery. We used to play games to decide it but it didn't seem like a prize if you won. So we draw shells from a bag. Black shell and you book your tickets and message the 'Akau'olas.

In 2023 we were few. Mafile was au-pairing in Singapore, Pangi was in Oz, Peni was in Eritrea with the peacekeeping force and Fa was coaching at an Aotearoa school. The season was turning so we had to get it done. So, we drew the shells. Fa'e pulled black. We went down to the ferry wharf. We made all the old jokes. Count the rocks three times. Say hello to the tree. Chase away the Chinese. They got on the boat and we waved them off and Fa'e texted us until she was out of cell range.

By the time we got home the wind was rattling the roof. We joked: poor 'Akau'olas, they'll have Mum and Dad for a week. At least. I messaged Fa'e to text us when she got into Poloa. We knew the time, we added Ava'utapu time to it, then Ofu time to that and texted again. No answer. I called. We all called. Then we heard that the Defence Force had been called out and that the *Nafanua* was setting sail. In weather like that. AAR said the *Princess* was overdue at Poloa. Then it was like a storm breaking, only that storm was social media. The *Princess* was running back to Mua. The *Princess* had lost power. The *Princess* was taking on water. The *Princess* had gone down. Everyone was safe. There were no survivors. All they rescued was a pig. I wanted to shout shut up shut up shut up! Everyone stop! None of you know anything.

I went down to the pier. Why? These were the people I wanted to shut up, stop talking, stop giving your stupid opinions. When you are with other people, right next to them, you start seeing the people, not hearing the voices. You start listening. You start talking.

So it came out. Bit by bit. The *Princess* had gone down. Some people had been rescued. Not all the people. Not enough people. Who was rescued? We didn't know. Numbers started coming through the radio. Seventy-two rescued. Phones started to ring. Screens lit up. Those who got the calls, the messages, drifted away. They were the families of the survivors. We got angry then. Why would no one tell us anything? Where was the Minister for Transport? Why had the king not spoken? When there were no more calls, no more people to drift away, we knew no one else would be rescued. Still we waited. We had to be told. At last the king came on the radio. The *Princess 'Akusita* had sunk. There were seventy confirmed survivors. No more were expected. The search was being wound down. Numbers were hard because there are always last-minute walk-ups and stowaways but one hundred and twenty were unaccounted for. We must count the missing as dead.

We were silent for a moment. Then the shouting started. A few voices, then a few more, then everyone on the wharf. Shouting at the radio. Shouting at the king. We shouted because we couldn't ask questions. Wasn't the ship the best money could buy? Hadn't it passed all its safety checks? Wasn't Captain Maka the veteran of thousands of crossings? Had he not seen the ocean in its every mood? Weren't we sea people, the children of navigators? But you can't ask the radio questions.

So we went back to our homes, because whether we stayed or went nothing would change what had happened out in the storm. There's a kind of helplessness that's like peace—nothing to be done, nothing can be done. Real and unreal too. How can a day that starts with Fa'e checking the grand-kids' school uniforms were clean and smart and Tamai shouting at the reports from the Rugby World Cup end with them sucked down into the ocean? Unreal. Real.

I tried to imagine. I imagined them on a deck full of panicking people. I could not think of them that way so I pictured Tamai trying to help Fa'e, them being together at the end, as the water came in. Then more details of the disaster arrived and my imaginings changed. The *Princess* sank so quickly. I saw them barely awake, shocked! I saw them hold hands. I saw water burst in, the boat go down fast into the dark. I saw their faces, seeing me, Amon.

Every family on Ava'utapu was touched by the *Princess 'Akusita*. We listened to the reports from the inquiry. We watched the trial. We knew the lies and the cover-ups. We saw the hounding of Samueli Havea and how the Royal Family closed ranks. We saw the rewards for loyalty. We knew what the king had done. We did nothing. It's not the Ava'uan way. The Ava'uan way is to keep your head low and not look and get on with your happy life. But how can you when there is something back there, a great dark disease, a cancer in our history?

Not all of us kept our heads down, Amon Brightbourne. Some of us looked up.

'Thank you,' Amon says. 'I'm honoured.'

'Fuck honoured, 'ofa'anga. Will you do it?'

'Kimmie, I did it twenty-five minutes ago.'

76

At six A.M. Laea the Uber takes Kimmie Pangaimotu to the Blue Horizon where the staff brings her by the VIP entrance and takes her through their enchanted grottos. They bathe her. Massage her. Scrub and oil her skin. Paint her nails. Zhoosh her hair. Glow shine buff and burnish. Fade the bruises into her skin tone. Body-paint over lacerations. Eyes, lashes. Lips. Teeth. Dress and jewellery. Accessorise, moisturise. Ten hours later Laea delivers her to the Royal Ava'u Hotel.

Amon Brightbourne, fidgety in the lobby, throws up his hands in wonder.

'You are stunning.'

'Anything?' Kimmie whispers. They process into the grand ballroom.

'Nothing,' Amon answers. He has been at the venue since noon. Stealthy paranoia drove him from the bungalow: It was altogether too easy a place for an arrest. An abduction. An assassination. The island's foremost hotel seems altogether safer. State violence abhors an audience. And it's been good to be busy. Busyness diminishes the three Conspiratorial Fears:

First fear: That he didn't do it right.

Second fear: That he didn't do it at all.

Third and greatest fear: That he did it perfectly and no one cares.

The Ocean Ballroom is a mosh pit of voices. Whole families have encamped, staking claim to floor space with mats, food containers, bottled water and make-up kits. Techs chase children from the stage, again and again. The PA booms with sound checks. Impromptu singing breaks out. The Mz Starshine Contest starts at 19:00. At 20:00 Front of House is still trying to clear the ballroom and set up the tables. Still family and guests pour in. At 21:00 the ballroom doors burst open and Kimmie's girlfriends from Blue Horizon stampede in. 21:25 and the hotel gets the contestants backstage. At 22:15 the houselights dim and Fetuu, Your Glamorous Host, steps into the spot and picks up the mic.

At thirty minutes her opening speech is concise. It involves a lot of thanking, name-checking and crying from the sheer *awesomeness* of what's happening in this ballroom.

The hotel has assigned a suite of rooms for the contestants but between leitis, assistants, costumes, make-up trolleys and shoe racks, Amon ends up perched on the edge of the wash-hand basin.

'Fabulous news,' Fetuu announces. 'We have a super special guest to present our awards! Please welcome to the Mz Starshine Contest, Her Royal Highness Princess Elisiva Ta'ahine Pilolevu!'

Ballroom and backstage erupt. Amon and Kimmie stare at each other.

'This isn't in the script,' Kimmie shouts through the din.

The first notification chimes on Amon's phone. Then another. Then another. His phone lights with icons.

In the Nanaimo Hearth between the woods and the water lives a woman—prominent in the CP press agency—who commissioned Amon to compose a suite of lullabies for a baby who would not sleep. The music—susurrating, mysterious, oceanic—charmed the child but the mother more. He had been paid with a note of quid pro quo. In those two minutes Amon was absent before Kimmie told her *Princess 'Akusita* story, he sent the entire archive to her.

Spread like the stars across the sky.

Fetuu announces the first round, Mz Professional. Music rejoices, voices cheer, Popi 'Ofanoa dashes past the dressing-room door to the stage in pencil skirt and perilous heels. Under the ruckus, Amon mouths *It's starting*. He opens news sites. The story is low down the algorithm—it's only a handful of Pacific islands—but it's everywhere. Everywhere and reaching further.

'Radio,' Kimmie whispers and pulls her stool close to Amon to hear the AAR app while the Mz Starshine aspirants try to convince the jury of their commitment to public service and their vision for the anga faka'ava' u. The Ava'uan way.

'It's reached here,' Amon says. 'They know.'

'Shut up,' Kimmie hisses.

The Aotearoa police have frozen the accounts of a number of Ava'uan companies. The Minister for Overseas Aid has announced an investigation into misappropriation of a grant to the Royal Ava'uan Ferry Company.

'We're on,' Amon says.

'Shut up,' Kimmie hisses again. Police in Suva have opened a criminal investigation into the certification of the *Princess 'Akusita*.

'No, we're on. Now.'

Fetuu fills until Amon arrives in the lighting box and signals the stage manager. Kimmie swings onstage to *Uptown Funk*. Team Blue Horizon leap to their feet clapping and boogying. Amon listens to her vision of an open, free, green Avaʻu. He can't see Ta. Amon gets Kimmie off; backstage they slip out into the gardens to eavesdrop on their conspiracy. Fiji, Tonga and Samoa—Avaʻu's oldest ally—call for a statement from the king. Silence from the palace. Amon and Kimmie freeze. A siren approaches, Dopplers pass.

'Ambulance?' Amon whispers. Conspirators need to whisper.

'Police,' Kimmie says.

Amon checks his news feeds. A surge of beats from the hotel heralds the second round of the contest. Mz Dazzle. The *Washington Post* has sniffed out a trail of stinking money from the RAFC's main offshore company to tatty petty dictatorships from Central America to Central Europe to Central Africa. Avaʻu—rather, the royal companies—are a prim little Pacific island money laundry. Prince ʻAhoʻeitu, high commissioner to Aotearoa, has been hastily recalled to Avaʻu, minutes ahead of being apprehended by the police. *The Guardian* examines Royal Avaʻu Water. Where the money went. What the people drink. Still no word from the palace. The cabinet has demanded a meeting with the king. The Twelve Lords of the Isles, even loyal House Tuʻivakano, have distanced themselves from House Tuʻi. And in twenty minutes Kimmie Pangaimotu must be onstage.

'I want more,' she says. 'I have to hear the king say he did it.'

And the king speaks. All-Avaʻu Radio reads the statement. Kimmie translates. The royal family has suffered a vicious and insolent attack on its integrity. Lies have been peddled by the fake media. The honour and character of the king has been insulted. Traitors, backed by foreign influences and international conspiracies, have tried to remove the king and install their puppet. Some of those traitors hold the highest offices in the kingdom. Prime Minister Pohiva, Lords Vaea, Vahaʻi, Veikune and the Ladies Tupua and Tuita have been arrested and charged with sedition. The Fale Alea is dissolved. Martial law is declared. All citizens are to return to their homes and remain there until further notice.

'Fuck,' Amon says. 'Old Turtle.'

'He's all right,' Kimmie says. 'He just texted me. They're at the palace. Siaosi is bluffing.'

God save the king, God save Avaʻu, the announcer says and the radio goes off air. Amon swipes to a mirror streaming site.

'They'll take the mobile network down next,' he says. More sirens. Only five vehicles in Mua have sirens and they are all on the streets. 'Martial law?' Amon asks. Music thuds from the ballroom. 'Are we safe, Kimmie?'

'No one's safe, 'ofa'anga. Now get in there. A coup is not pissing on my starshine.'

From the lighting box Amon sees phones shine at every table. Ava'u is learning. Can the people believe what their feeds are telling them? He seeks out Ta in her seat at the judge's table. She sits formal and perfect in traditional dress. Does she know what Amon did? Does she fear police bursting through the door to arrest her? She bends to whisper something to her colleague as Contestant 7 winds up her flounce and flourish to tepid, half-handed applause as the audience thumb through social media on their phones.

'She's in place,' the stage manager announces on the cans. Fetuu takes the stage. Outside the coup flutters in an uncertain wind. Inside, ten thousand sequins glitter.

'My dear people, please welcome back, Kimmie Pangaimotu!'

Amon pumps up the walk-down. The moving lights swing, and there is Kimmie, centre stage, a rainbow, a galaxy.

'You star,' Amon says into the wall of sound. 'You absolute shining star.'

The lights go out. The music dies. Voices clamour. Amon hears screams. Hard bright stars awaken: The audience find their phone flashlights. Beams bob around the Ocean Ballroom. Some catch Kimmie, paralysed onstage, and strike glitter-ball reflections from her costume. By his own phone-light Amon navigates from the lighting box to the external balcony. Hotel, harbour-front, streets and buildings are dark. The only lights are the fishing boats at Wharf 39 and vehicles. Is that fire on the slopes of Calvary?

In the ballroom audience and contestants huddle in their shelters of light, uncertain what to do. There are drills for wind, for flood, for cyclone; nothing for coup. Amon works along to the stage and finds Kimmie centre, where the spotlights died.

'Are you all right?'

'I'm all right, 'ofa'anga. I'm all right.'

Blue light pulses through the porthole windows of the ballroom's doors. A hush falls. Voices, the crackle of radios from the lobby. The ballroom doors burst open and figures in military uniform surge into the room, helmet lights weaving from table to table, face to face.

The marines are here. They move through the room with armed authority.

'They're asking, where is Princess Elisiva?' Kimmie whispers to Amon.

A movement on the dark dance-floor, the sound of a chair scraping back.

'Here I am.'

Every helmet light turns on Ta. She turns to face the soldiers. The marines form a semicircle. Major Fia, Malietoa of the Royal Guard, steps forward. Ta does not look away from his light.

'Elisiva Ta'ahine Pilolevu. At zero-thirty-five this morning, your father, His Majesty Siaosi Tu'ipulotu Tu'i the Fifth, abdicated the titles, privileges and responsibilities of the monarchy of Ava'u. The abdication letter names you heir to the 'Akau Ta. Major Fia turns to his lieutenant and takes possession of a tall staff. He offers it in his two hands, head bowed, eyes lowered. 'Do you accept?'

Ta takes the 'Akau Ta, the staff of kings.

'By the war-club of my ancestors, I accept this honour and vow to serve the people and islands of Ava'u with all my heart and all my soul and all my life, God grant me strength. Carve my name with pride and my deeds with compassion.'

She hammers the foot of the 'Akau Ta on the sprung ballroom floor. One, two, three times.

'Long live the queen,' Major Fia proclaims. The marines place hands over hearts and shout with one voice, *Long live the queen! Long live the queen. Long live the queen!* By the third repeat the whole ballroom is on its feet.

Between sea and heaven, the floating rock Touia'o Futuna is now so rammed with twins of twins of twins, gods and demigods and semi-demigods, godlets and godlings that all that can be seen, to the eye that can see, is a quivering globe of noisy flesh. Yet sometimes the world below interrupts their petty bickering and they look down.

The islands are full of noises. Fires and lights. They smell smoke. A ruction in the House of Tu'i. *We always knew those half-maggots would never come to any good. Look, there goes a Learjet. Siaosi has a Lear?* He has a lot of things people don't know about.

The eyes of the gods see far. They watch the Lear fly up over great Ocean. They see it line up on the landing lights of Tullamarine Airport in Melbourne.

So who's . . . Oh, her. She's good. Our islands are in safe hands.

Damage?

One dog run down by a police car. One minor coronary incident when the king shut down the Mua power plant. (Why did he do that? What point is there?) Bruises, sprains. The sheep on the Tuʻi Calvary are missing.

A result. The petty gods of Touiaʻo Futuna cough the smoke from their lungs, shove their hands and faces back into the writhe of bodies. The bickering resumes.

After fifty minutes power is restored and Kimmie Pangaimotu leaves the Royal Avaʻu Hotel with Queen Ta, her Malietoa and her Royal Guard for the palace.

In his bungalow Amon Brightbourne keeps his head low as Avaʻu comes to terms with what happened in the night. The morning finds Mua edgy. Queen ʻAna is closed, as are most shops and businesses. The streets are strangely quiet. The Taists are uncertain in their rejoicing, the old loyalists uncomfortable about how their disapproval might be read. World leaders hail the new queen, even the one-party states, the despotisms and the kakistocracies, which highlights the utter unimportance of Avaʻu. None of the news reports mention the name of the whistle-blower who leaked the dossier that brought down a king. Still Amon feels very thin and very white.

On the third day the invitation arrives from the palace. Would Eimoni Valaitiʻvoni be so kind? He brushes his suit and dyes out the grey in his red hair and there at the gate stands Kimmie Pangaimotu.

'You remembered to shine the shoes, ʻofaʻanga,' she says. She is the Leiti Kimmie now, Royal Fakaleiti. 'I'm so proud of you.'

Queen Elisiva Taʻahine Tuʻi I receives Amon on the bougainvillea walk, in the blossom-heavy pergola.

'Your Majesty.'

'Amon.'

The cloying floral scent does not quite mask the undertones of burning from the Calvary beyond the security fence. The Royal Flock is in cuts and joints baking in fifty umus across Avaʻutapu. And the cascading flowers do not quite conceal the royal bodyguard matching them step for discreet step.

'Congratulations on your accession. The ʻAkau Ta is in safe hands.'

Ta smiles.

'These hands feel shaky. My father throws tantrums and toxic-tweets.

Lawsuits, an alliance of old South Pacific aristocracy, a people's uprising. My dear brother is seriously making a claim. I expect him to convert back to Presbyterianism any day now.'

They emerge from the bower onto the bright lawns. Ta steers for the shade of a stand of palm trees.

'I have another commission for you. I'd like you to compose a piece for my coronation. I want something big with lots of singing. And horns. I like horns.'

'I can do that, ma'am.'

This time she does not reject his use of 'ma'am.'

'I'm glad. This commission, it comes with a post. Master of the Queen's Music. You would be my composer in residence.'

'I'm honoured, ma'am. How would this fit with my work at Queen 'Ana and First Mua?'

'It's a full-time job, Amon.' They step into the jagged shade of the palms. Desiccated fronds rustle dusty under their feet. 'There is also a house with it. You would have to move out of Queen 'Ana. Do you understand the nature of the position?'

'I do, ma'am.'

An employee of a school in the control of a church that had whispered its hostility is vulnerable. An employee of the Firm is fireproof.

'The position comes with a seat on my Privy Council.'

Amon knows enough of the Ava'uan constitution to understand that Privy Council positions are entirely the gift of the monarch.

'Purely advisory,' Queen Ta says. 'Non-voting.'

'I'm honoured,' Amon says again because he doesn't know what else to say.

'Yes you are. Do you accept?'

'I accept. Thank you, ma'am.'

'Welcome, Amon Brightbourne. I want the big music.'

First rule of monarchy is knowing when it's over. Second rule is when to bow, and how much. Already the dip of the head, the 'ma'am' is becoming comfortable.

A charmed life. You will always land on your feet. If this is the Grace, somewhere the Price is accruing.

77

'I'm going on a bike ride!' Elisiva Ta'ahine Tu'i I, queen from horizon to horizon, sunrise to sunset announces. 'Who's coming with me?'

The cyclists whoop.

'Saddle up then!' The queen slings her padded ass onto the spin-class bike. 'Today we're going on a tour of our wonderful island.' Feet clip into cages, heads dip to drop handlebars. Since the Royal Fakaleiti announced that Her Majesty will not give up her drive to improve the nation's health and well-being, her twice-weekly spin sessions at the Blue Horizon are packed out. Women, a few men now. Some old, mostly young. Some fit, mostly overweight. Islanders and visitors. Most last one session and never return. Queen Ta leads an iron spin class. The regulars, diehards and the ones most keen to impress take the front bikes. Major Fia takes the rear.

'Let's roll!' Queen Ta says. Music booms. *Tour d'Ava'u*, by Amon Bright-bourne. No one gets the Kraftwerk jokes woven through it. It's just good, beaty pedalling music. 'Nice and easy out of the palace.' Video appears on every spin-bike screen. 'Wave to the guards!' Everyone turns to wave to Major Fia. It embarrasses him every time. He is proper, proud, handsome, fierce. Malietoa: Great Warrior. 'Pulotu Wharf! Wave to the cruise boats!' Right hand waves. 'Okay, gear up and stand up in three, two, one . . .' The Peloton sprints past the foreign fishing fleet.

Fifty days into her reign, Queen Ta has: been adored. Been loathed. Been crowned. Cancelled education contracts with the LDS Church. Slapped a fat tax on imported meat. Refused further licensing of the islands' fishing grounds. Opened Royal Ava'u Water to ethical investment. Started a women's rugby team. Converted the post of Royal Shepherdess into Minister for National Flora and Fauna. Begun divestment from her father's companies. Hired forensic auditors to expose the full scope of King Siaosi Tu'ipulotu's kleptocracy. Retained a legal team to fight her father's lawsuits to reclaim the throne. Retained another legal team to claim back the wealth he stole. Been hailed by the online news services as the new voice of the Pacific Islands in the age of climate change. Become a social media star through her royal fitness and diet videos.

'Heads down, bums up for the blow-holes!' Queen Ta orders and her class—those that haven't slipped from their saddles sweating and nauseous—leans into the pedals. The music booms and surges—Amon constructed it from field recordings—Ta starts to sing and her class, panting, take it up while their screens explode with geysers of sea water and rainbows. 'Okay! Ease back to Mua!' The pack sits back, hands off handlebars, cruises past the scattered fales of east Ava'utapu under the shade of scabby cassia trees. Calvary Hill stands before them, and the flag atop the palace jackstaff. The 11:00 spin class eases into virtual Mua. Ta praises her riders; they answer with cheers, tears and wild applause. Ta unhooks her microphone and heads to the shower. Major Fia moves quickly to her side. Petitioners surge forward with the problems that only a queen can solve.

The cries of the happily exercised are psalms to the godlets of Touia'o Futuna, their sweat, incense.

How's she doing? the divines at the centre of the flesh-ball call to their kin on the outside. They look down at their islands. They listen. They sniff the air. *The Mormons hate her, the Presbyterians question her commitment to Christ, the Catholics like that she likes rugby. No one cares what the Methodists think.*

The godlets watch, listen, taste, scent and sense and they agree: *She's doing good.* They are about to report *All is well in the islands* when a sub-sub-deity looks upwind and sees something spinning at the edge of the world and says, *Hang on a minute.*

La madre de tormentas. Mother of Storms. Her womb is a patch of the Pacific Ocean 160°E 6°S. Just north of the Solomon Islands. Sea surface temperature 27.5°C. Air temperature at the 500 kPa altitude of -12.2°C. Tropospheric humidity above 75 percent. Minimum distance from the equator: 500 kilometres. Vertical wind shear of less than 10 m/s. Sow seeds of instability—atmospheric waves, a decaying weather-front—and La Madre will germinate cyclones. This mother births gods.

A US president once suggested nuking hurricanes. A nuke wouldn't make La Madre's children blink. The energy released by a South Pacific tropical cyclone is up to 200 trillion joules per day. That's two hundred times global electricity generation, or the equivalent of detonating a ten-megaton bomb every twenty minutes for a year.

In May of the year 2033 in the third month of the reign of Queen Elisiva I of Ava'u, a decaying easterly weather-front runs into a pocket of rising air—no bigger than a city block—twelve hundred kilometres north-west of Samoa and is deflected northward. It's the end of the cyclone season, in a mild year, but La Madre's dance never ceases. On May 10th the US Joint Typhoon Warning Center reports the formation of Tropical Depression 22F/12P. Over the next twelve hours TD 22F/12P encounters a secondary tropical depression and devours it whole. By morning it is a Category 2 tropical cyclone and the Fijian Meteorological Service takes charge. Over twenty-four hours the cyclone deepens at a speed never seen before by the FMS. May 12th dawns on a Category 3 cyclone with one-minute wind speed gusting at 180 kilometres per hour. At 14:00 on May 12th TC 0011M opens its eye. The meteorologists go to their name lists.

Velma. Thou art Velma.

The rule of names is this: a cyclone that kills, that causes widespread destruction, has its name retired.

Fiji sends its drone fleet into the eye of Velma. It returns to Suva battered, barely airworthy, with reports of things never seen before. Cyclone Velma is a gyre five hundred kilometres across. Eight distinct rain-bands. Eye diameter: twelve kilometres. Pressure: 880 kilopascals. Sustained wind speed of the eyewall: 300 kilometres per hour. Increasing as an exceptionally warm ocean fuels the monster. In a morning it ascends from Category 4 to Category 5. There is no Category 6. Fiji's meteorological computers run simulations. Tropical cyclones are skittish, uncanny beasts. They can endure for weeks or wind down into a stiff breeze and a brisk chop overnight. They can veer from their predicted courses; they can loop around themselves; they can track back for a return visit. Petty gods. FMS charts an east-south-east course for Velma over the next three days, threading the eye between Fiji and Samoa. Niua, Ofu and Ava'utapu lie dead in her path. Landfall in Niua is estimated at 11:00 May 15. Five hours later the eye-wall will hit Ava'utapu with peak wind speed of 340 kilometres per hour.

FMS sends out cyclone warnings. Suva calling to the faraway islands. *All you fishers, all you sailors, get out of the water.*

Queen Ta convenes the Cyclone Emergency Committee. All islands go to yellow alert. Neighbourhood safety teams ready their preparedness plans. Cyclone shelters are brought online. All citizens to safeguard water and four days of food supplies. Stockpile fuel for the emergency generators. Solar panels to be removed from roofs. Velma will strike on a Sunday. Stores, bars, resorts, churches and social clubs will close from Saturday midnight. Queen Ta takes personal charge of the preparations, visiting safety teams, touring outlying villages. She swings onto one of the buses evacuating passengers from the Festival *Ocean Adventurer* at Pulotu Wharf and assures them that the Kingdom of Ava'u will guarantee its guests shelter and safety. She jumps down from the back of the royal Ford Lobo to berate a gang of young men drinking on Pulotu Road. 'Go home to your families! Don't waste our time! Look after your siblings and elders.' She sends her marines to arrest an attempted ram-raid on a jewellery and souvenir shop. She visits the Ava'u Meteorological Service for the latest forecast. Velma deepens. Pressure and eyewall gust speeds are off all charts. Velma passes between Fiji and Samoa. Storm-force winds rock Vanua Levu and send flash floods roaring across Savai'i. Contact has been lost with the Hoorn Islands and Wallis and Futuna, a tiny atoll archipelago in the ocean strait. A US storm-hunter flies through Velma's wake and reports the two Hoorn islands obliterated.

Queen Ta takes the mic at All-Ava'u Radio and tells her people to gather their loved ones and prepare for the worst as the first buffets send spray over the seawall at Pulotu Wharf.

'I pray that God will strengthen us and keep us safe,' the Queen says. 'We are a strong and brave people and if we put our trust in each other, we will not fail. God save Ava'u.'

The last flight leaves the airport at 20:00. The plane bucks and jolts on the gusts, climbing heavily against a sky boiling with approaching lightning. The wind sock is horizontal. The airport crew tie down the remaining light aircraft, board up the control tower windows and go home to their families.

78

An hour ago Kimmie left with her queen and Major Fia for the radio station.

'Kimmie will be back soon as she ever can,' she declared before skipping down the steps from the bungalow's veranda to the waiting royal pickup. Low sun from under the hem of Velma's train lit the palace the colour of infection. The storm was a dreadwall of darknesses, from liminal pewter along the horizon to highest, deepest fuligin. 'Stay safe, kynnd.'

'Message me,' Amon said.

Amon had fallen in immediate love with the trim little grace-and-favour bungalow; neat and clean and prim and oh so quiet. He'd enjoyed the peace and privacy for eight perfect hours before there came a banging on the door and there stood Kimmie Pangaimotu with her kit bag and several wheelie suitcases.

'I thought Ta gave you rooms in the palace.'

'Yours are nicer, Amon.'

Now he waits on the soft tan leather sofa, trying not to wait. Distractions won't distract. Music will not enchant. His mind is sodden knitted wool. With every millibar drop in pressure the pain in Amon's sinuses builds until he can bear no more. He throws open the door, lurches onto the veranda and looks upon the face of Cyclone Velma. She is a thing of darkness. She fills the universe, felt as much as seen. Wind lashes his hair across his face, tugs at collar and cuffs, rattles the legs of his trousers like pennants. His skull booms with vertigo. A curtain wall of boiling cloud glows with lightning. Above and outside that curtain wall is another, above that yet another, up and up, level after level until it merges with a world-roof of cloud. Wall upon wall, a citadel of storms. Grey squall-clouds, fast, soft squids of weather spin from the lowest storm-curtain, moiling and turmoiling, dissolving and re-forming. They are stupendous, tens of kilometres across, extreme events in their own right yet dwarfed by Velma in her majesty.

The sea seems to boil.

The heat is intense, the humidity sapping. Amon's ever-inappropriate clothes are soaked through. His skin will not dry. His breath tastes of ozone, ions, deep water.

Atli. Vega. Raisasbur. Stormtalker.

'That's a mighty name,' Amon said one night in the old school bungalow.

'It's a mighty story,' Atli replied and told a saga of the northlands, where black rocks stand guard against the cold sea and the dark nights are long. How Raisa Antares Peri, electromancer and Arcmage, had saved a ship from a terrible storm by learning the name of the storm and speaking it, for right-thinking people know that the only magic is the magic of True Names. Of how Atli had inherited that name, and how that name was buried in a glacier that cast it up before its time and cast him and hé adrift before they had grown into their names and true selves, without certainty or self-knowledge, hoping to hear the thunder in the ventricles of the heart.

Come Atli. Come Raisa. Come you Arcmages and Electromancers, come you Four Coils and Grand Primary. Come mages of rock and sea, forests and deep ocean geopower rigs. Come you Stormtalkers; speak this monster's name and send it whimpering into darkness.

A gust staggers him. The heads of the palms stream leeward like raving demons. Plastic bottles and scrap bound across Pulotu Road and pile up against the palace's metal palings. All is shrieks and whistles, banging and roaring. Cyclone sirens.

He should be recording this. Saving this. The only power Amon has before such forces is to turn them into music.

Rain so sudden and hard it makes him gasp. Inside the rain Velma speaks to him.

Here I am.

'What?'

You called me.

Rain blinds Amon Brightbourne. He scrapes saturated hair from his face.

How could I not come? You summoned me.

A voice: a true voice calling his name.

'Eimoni!' A figure pushes across the lawn through the deafening rain. The leiti Fetuu, tupenu flapping, hair streaming. 'Eimoni! Come to the shelter!'

'I have to wait for Kimmie!' Amon yells.

'Eimoni!'

'I'll be along in a minute!'

Velma steps towards Amon Brightbourne. The wind gusts to storm force. A vanguard squall passes over the island. Rain billows, then clears. Lightning arcs between heaven, Touia'o Futuna and ocean. Seconds later thunder rolls over Mua. Raisa taught him how to tell the distance of a storm by the interval between the stroke and the crack.

'Velma,' he says.

Velma laughs.

That's not my name. She gathers her might in her fist and brings it down on Ava'utapu. *You silly man.*

Major Sosefu Fia parks the royal pickup on the leeward side of the radio station. A tree might come down.

'We're inside the radio station,' Kimmie Pangaimotu says. 'The tree comes down on us.'

'The radio station is stronger than the car,' Major Fia says. 'The president of the United States' cars may be armoured but ours are not.'

The royal umbrella snaps inside out in one gust, flies south to Tonga and points Antarctic the next. The formality of the umbrella is appreciated. Major Fia is old-school.

'You go ahead,' Kimmie says at the station door. Wind-roar deafens. The palms bend like bows. The royal party feels their island tremble to the hammer of storm waves against the reef. 'There's a thing I have to do.'

'Leiti Kimmie, you must stay here,' Major Fia says. 'It's not safe.'

'It's not far and I won't be long.'

'You can't go,' Queen Ta says.

'I'll text, 'ofa'anga,' Kimmie says. Major Fia's lips twitch in disapproval at the familiarity.

'Shall I fetch her, ma'am?'

'No,' Queen Ta says. She props the 'Akau Ta against the desk.

Car horns blare, headlights flash as Kimmie jogs wheezing down the centre of the street, as far from flying roof debris as she can take herself. She shouts back: 'What are you doing out? Go home to your families!'

Where Taufa'ahau Road meets Pulotu Road she stops, fighting for breath, nauseous with exertion. Waves break high over the seawall. A pick-up splashes through the flood. Everything howls. Kimmie looks up. Kimmie beholds Cyclone Velma.

'Fuck,' she whispers in English, for Ava'uan has no equivalent word.

'What are you doing, Kimmie Mimosa?' She answers her own question. 'You go, Mz Starshine.'

She decides roof debris on the landward side of the coast road is a better bet than storm surge. Spray soaks her through less than half-way to Fatafehi Road. Lightning freezes sea-front, harbour, lagoon in an instant of blazing dread. Sea on the sky, sky in the sea, world and air tumbled together. Possessed, dancing.

'As below so above,' she tells herself. Then the thunder arrives, driving the breath from her lungs, the will from her heart. She whispers the names of the Emanations, the white names she learnt in Aotearoa, the Māori names she learnt there, the Ava'uan names the exiles have taken from the old gods and set around them like feather cloaks. Wind redoubled drives her up Fatafehi Road, past the LDS Temple where families unload pickups and transport pallets of bottled water to the cyclone shelter. She calls out her family name. Wet-eyed children look around, afraid. Men look up.

'Are they here?'

'They're home.'

The home stands at the next crossroads. Kimmie braces against the fearful wind that would tumble her with the bottles and the trash paper and the plastic bags. A falling satellite dish hits a parked car in an explosion of window-sugar. The alarm howls, the lights flash.

Every window is lit, every door open. Fa'etangata Fa wrestles a mattress along the veranda.

'Are you safe?' Kimmie yells from the foot of the steps. The palms bend and groan.

'We're going to President Tukuafu's shelter!' Fa shouts.

'Are you all right?'

'We're safe.' He tugs the obstinate mattress to the side steps. 'You? Are you safe?'

'I'm safe.'

Her siblings, cousins, almost-cousins, and all the aiga's many degrees of relativity, carry water, fruit, bags of clothes across the backyard to the temple president's house. The boys wrestle a 4K television unwieldy as a sail and a games console from the Boys' Fale.

'There's space for you,' Fa shouts.

'I have work to do,' Kimmie shouts back. 'I need to know that you're safe.'

'God will keep us safe,' Senior Uncle Fa says.

Looking down Fatafehi Road she sees waves break higher than the rooftops along the wharf. A tide-edge of seaweed and plastic runs towards her on the flood-water.

'Ta,' she mutters and texts that she's going back to the palace. She turns inland and takes the right at the sports stadium. The brightest bolt yet lights an apocalyptic Mua. Kimmie mutters old school-day prayers. Three junctions, each one a wind tunnel. She ducks a whirling shop sign. On Falahola Road an electric scooter comes spinning up the street on its side. Then the storm opens over her.

Queen Elisiva Ta'ahine Tu'i clicks off the microphone. The on-air light goes out. Ta takes off her headphones. Wind booms in the metal roof.

'Thank you,' she says to the AAR producer.

'Ma'am, we should seek shelter immediately,' Major Fia says.

'Not until I hear from Kimmie,' Queen Ta insists. Outside Velma gathers strength and majesty. A distant crashing, audible through sound-tight walls.

'Ma'am,' Major Fia says with urgency. The royal phone plays a dance tune.

'Kimmie is at the palace,' Ta says. 'Now we go.'

'Ma'am, I would advise somewhere closer,' Major Fia says.

'I'm going to St Peter Chanel,' the AAR producer says.

'We will come with you,' Ta says. 'I'll give you a lift.'

'Ma'am.' Major Fia nods at the 'Akau Ta, leaning forgotten against the desk.

Outside the wind rocks the heavy royal pickup. The street-lights bend and howl. Shutters rattle, roofs creak and moan. Plastic waste scooped up from the shore bowls up the roads. Sharp, wind-whipped rain stings Ta's face. The sky opens as she closes the car door. The wipers barely clear the windscreen. Rain beats the vehicle like a hand-drum. Speech is impossible. The headlights reach only a few metres into the downpour. It is like driving in a waterfall. Major Fia slams to a hard stop as something blows across the road, end over end. A plastic shop-front, ripped loose. Every car alarm in Mua shrieks. The gutters are trash torrents. Major Fia takes ten minutes to drive the five hundred metres to the shelter at St Peter Chanel School. The rugby posts have blown down, the roof of the pavilion lies broken like a dead animal against the side of the church.

Major Fia offers two hands to help Ta from the car. In the ten steps to the door of the shelter they are soaked to the bone. The shelter is a windowless concrete bunker, raised up above flood level. Benches down either side. Water, fluorescent tubes, a toilet. Wi-Fi. The benches are packed, body to body, knee to knee. They turn to look, anger in their eyes at more cramming into this tiny safe space.

'May we come in?' Ta asks.

Some try to stand. All lower their heads to the 'Akau Ta.

'Sit sit,' Ta insists. The refugees squeeze up to make space for their queen. She sits on the lintel and indicates that the producer should take the seat. Major Fia stands behind her, back to the door. Water drips from them and pools on the floor. The bunker is hot, humid, stifling but the royal party shivers, wet through. At the far end of the long bench a woman reaches down for the bag between her feet and produces a flask. Without a word it passes up the chain of shelterers to Ta. She uncaps it. Coffee. She pours a capful, takes a sip, passes the cup to the producer, then to Major Fia.

'Thank you.'

Queen and people huddle together and wait for Velma to finish with them.

Half-blinded by rain, Kimmie stabs the keypad to the palace grounds' service gate. She hits the correct code on the third attempt. The Pulotu Road railings are a wall of plastic. The hibiscus walk stands in tatters. The golf cart the dowager Elenoa used as a pretence for exercise lies capsized, canopy shredded. The roof is off the pavilion where Amon played for Princess Halae. Lawn furniture strewn like toys. Wave-water foaming around the security post; flood-water lagoons on the lawn. A light swings and thrashes on the veranda of her bungalow. By its rocking light, she sees a figure in a chair.

'Amon!'

He doesn't hear her, doesn't see her, doesn't know she is there until a lightning bolt freezes the world to the last raindrop in arc-blue. He sees, then unsees her.

'Amon!' She pushes through the waterfall from the overwhelmed veranda gutter. 'Shelter!'

'No,' he says.

'Shelter!'

'Leave me.'

A leiti is taught patience. Patience with those she cares for. Patience with the small catalogue of lives a fakaleiti may live. Patience with the impatient, the hostile, the contemptuous. The stubborn.

'What?'

'I did this. I always do this. I go somewhere, I meet people, bad things come behind me. I came here and I thought maybe it would be all right. No.' The wind lifts another degree. The roof cracks. 'The Grace. And the Price. I called the storm. She's come for me and I have to stay for her and make it complete.'

When did Kimmie Pangaimotu attend to lessons?

'Fuck you, Amon Brightbourne,' she yells. 'Fuck you and your lazy, privileged palangi ass. Fuck you that you think you're so fucking special that the world revolves around you. Fuck you that you sit there and say, poor me, what can I do? Can't fight fate. Well, Amon Brightbourne, fuck your fucking skinny palangi ass off that fucking chair and come the fuck with me to the fucking shelter. And fuck you that I have to say this in English and not my own language.'

Amon Brightbourne blinks. Then he flares his nostrils and gets his skinny palangi ass off his porch chair, clutches his satchel to him and follows Kimmie, no protest, no question.

The palace has battened tight as a ship; windows shuttered and barred; the lobby vases and statues taken down and set safe on the floor. The great lantern swings in an unseen draught. A door behind the grand staircase leads to the cyclone shelter: concrete block–built, white-painted, utilitarian and not at all royal. The palace staff hide here, kitchen to accountancy. Leiti Fetuu and Princess Halae and her people. Ta's staff and security. Queen Lavinia and jazz-loving dowager Elenoa flew out with the deposed king. The shelterers shuffle and shift to accommodate Kimmie and Amon.

Velma strides towards them.

79

And Velma arrives.

The leading edge of the eyewall brushes Ava'utapu. Winds surge from a howl to a scream. The anemometer at the airport weather station reads a gust of 280 kilometres per hour before it is ripped away. Cars flip over, corrugated metal peels from roofs. Velma reaches inside the naked houses and flings what she finds there into the whirling air. Trees topple, one against another against another in a chain reaction that fells entire groves in instants.

In their shelters and bunkers the people of Ava'utapu hear a monster step out of the ocean. Heard, not seen, in crashes and shrieks, howlings and wrenchings; felt in shifting pressure waves, distant concussions, shakes and quakes. Sudden impacts, the bass boom of coral rock shaken to its roots. Families, friends, lovers cower and listen to Godzilla rip their island in two.

Then the lights go out. Cries, some screams, then phone screens bob into light and hands move to start the emergency generators. People try to call separated friends and family, to find out from social media what is happening, but the network went down with the power. Each shelter has a radio. Listeners hunt the airwaves. AAR is silent. Reports from Tonga and Samoa are fragmentary and garbled. Velma's electrical storms wrap Ava'u in a cloak of interference.

Then the water comes. It comes with a sound no one has ever heard before, a drawing-in, pushing-out rumbling hiss; the monster that sucks the marrow from the bones. Dull impacts, rending tears. A tumbling rattle, a torrent rush on an island without flowing rivers. The noise of a billion pieces of plastic detritus grinding as it sweeps in from the sea, a trash tsunami. The refugees know that the island lies so low the storm surge can race shore to shore. Those larger, louder noises must be boats torn loose, pieces of house and shop, vehicles, swept up and carried away. Velma beats down doors, kicks out windows, sweeps everything she finds out into the churn. She lifts whole homes from their foundations, spins them around, smashes them into each other. Trees, power lines, cell towers, every piece of debris added to the storm surge doubles and redoubles its power.

The cyclone shelter designers built their refuges above once-in-a-century floods but Velma is a god. She will not be bound by human projections and engineering. The refugees listen to every impact, every crash and rend, every grinding surge in fear that the next will smash in their strong doors in a wave of debris and water and flood the shelters to the roofs. Water seeps under the sills to become a flow. The refugees scramble up onto the benches. The rising water stinks of sewage, diesel, fish and agrochemicals. Will it stop? Would it be worse to unbolt the door and face Velma than drown in a box of refuse? Some try and are restrained by word, custom or force. Whatever they face they face together.

Then the wind drops. The roar dwindles to silence. Children cry out from the pain in their ears as the pressure plummets to a breathless low. Everything is still. Everything is quiet. In the Bible, Yahweh spoke in the still, small voice after the whirlwind. The people of the Pacific are not such fools. Velma's empty eye passes over the island. People hold their breath, hold their children, hold for the sound of wind picking up again as the outer eyewall arrives.

In six breaths the wind rises from a hum to a roar. Rain returns heavier than before. The sky can't hold that much water. Yet it hurls down, enough to drown a floundering world. The water in the shelters holds steady. Warm foul water laps around knees. They listen for the grinding, sucking crash of the storm surge. Listen again, listen closer. Nothing. They know what that means. The surge has passed. There is nothing left to come down.

It begins differently in each shelter, each strong room and storm refuge. Old women here, a single male bass from a church choir there, mothers calming children, a group of old men who have known each other from another century, a family turned together. The singing starts. Ava'u meets grace and adversity alike with song. Hymns, pop tunes, songs from the shows. Old lullabies, laments, songs of love and battle. The shelters sing with faith and lust, wet feet and hope. Singing through the storm to its other side.

80

Major Fia, a prop forward from the women's rugby team and Queen Ta put their shoulders to the shelter door. Three solid shoves clears the berm of storm wrack.

'Ma'am, let me secure the area,' Major Fia says.

'Stand aside, Major,' Queen Ta says. She hefts the 'Akau Ta and steps blinking into the daylight. It is nine thirty in the morning, the eastern sky is a rack of purple bars across a lilac firmament. To the south-west, Velma's bridal train is grey on black. Pennants of the destroying army. Wind gusts, rain spatters and Ta's first breath is deep and sweet and fresh. On her second she gags on rot, salt, ordure, seaweed, fuel oil, death.

She looks upon her kingdom.

Not a tree stands. Not a house has a roof. AAR's transmission mast lies broken over the smashed radio station. St Peter Chanel is a roofless hulk. The tower of First Mua has toppled into the nave. Cars and boats have changed places. The lagoon bobs with Toyota hatchbacks, noses down like dabbling ducks. A tuna long-liner lies in the middle of Hekoni Road. A Chinese prawn boat is rammed through Sinipata Stores. Groceries are strewn for hundreds of metres across yards and garden plots. Velma wantonly scattered the contents of shattered houses in her wake. Clothes hang from broken palm trunks. Televisions, tablets, screens have been scattered like playing cards. Refrigerators lie on their backs, doors open. Tumbled chairs, stripped sofas. Cushions and soft furnishings bob in flood-water pools. Dead animals are already swelling in the sickly heat. Wood: planks, pallets, beams. And plastic. Everywhere there is plastic. The ocean has regurgitated decades of accumulated toxins in drifts of bottles, styrene chunks, coffee cups, packaging trays, bags and nets and wrap.

The only upright vessel is the cruise ship Festival *Ocean Adventurer* at Pulotu Wharf.

Queen Ta's fingers tighten on the 'Akau Ta. She looks up at the sound of an aircraft. A wink of light in the brightening sun lost behind the thinning northern clouds. Glimpsed, lost. Out of a ripple of bruise-coloured cloud comes a drone. It circles over Ava'utapu, lower with each pass, wings catching the light. It is the only sound, the only moving thing in the wake of Velma. At its closest approach, Queen Ta lifts the 'Akau Ta above her head in her two hands. Holds it high until the drone banks sharply and climbs back into the clouds.

'Major Fia!'

'Ma'am.'

'A report please.'

'Defence Force and police radio is operating. Our naval assets are intact, though damaged. Our air assets have been completely destroyed. We have shortwave communications to Tonga and Samoa.'

'And the Fijians know,' Ta says. 'Major, summon the Disaster Committee.'

81

Amon Brightbourne blinks at the sky above the hall. Bars of indigo cloud whip away on the southward wind. He shouldn't see this. When he was eleven he saw a house burn, an old couple's bungalow on the edge of Cookstown. He walked down from Brightbourne to see it. He had never seen a house burn. Smoke poured from under the eaves; flame licked up from a shattered window, melting the frame and the guttering. He saw fire wild in that house; saw old people's things wreathed in flame. A burning bed. Photos framed in fire. A dressing table ablaze. The fire brigade arrived and his paralysis broke. He ran back through his gates, up his drive to his newly fragile home. He had seen true horror, a wrongness in the weave of the universe. Flames don't come out of homes. It is wrong for bedspreads and hairbrushes and pillows to burn.

He feels the same wrongness looking up at the sky above the roofless palace. Rain-soaked polished wood beneath blue sky. Sunlight at new angles casts improper shadows. The great lantern lies smashed where it fell. Water pools on the marble. Two, maybe three of the statues and vases remain intact. The portraits of the Tuʻis drip, waterlogged. Twigs and leaves and plastic garbage, lifted by an updraught, strew the lobby.

Kimmie calls to him from the porch. By the flukes of tropical cyclones, it has kept its roof. A flotilla of mopeds and motorbikes waits. The queen's staff have already mounted, pillion.

'Full Privy Council meeting.'

'I'm not . . .' Amon stammers.

'The Queen wants you. Get on.'

Amon climbs onto the Honda scrambler, slings his satchel behind him and grips for dear life. The bike burns away. The front of his bungalow has collapsed. The roof slumps over the smashed porch. The scrambler turns out of the palace gates onto Pulotu Road. The bikes are nippy and nimble and can navigate debris-strewn streets where four wheels could not. The devastation stuns Amon Brightbourne. He can't take in the scale, the totality. His mind revolts. This is wrong, so big, so wide, so complete it offends sanity. Tyres crunch broken glass and seaweed. The stench of death, salt and sea-wreck overpowers everything. Amon ducks down in the rider's slipstream. Shame burns him. That he imagined he was responsible for this. Kimmie spoke right. Amon Brightbourne is not the axis of the world. The universe doesn't care about him. His sole relief is that only Kimmie and Cyclone Velma heard him. Velma dies alone on the Southern Ocean and Kimmie is the truest friend he ever had.

Queen 'Ana College rugby pitch is a lake afloat with Styrofoam and dead animals. Muans sweep up glass and seaweed and fish, stretch tarpaulins over exposed roof beams, pile saturated furnishings in the street, clear roads, take chainsaws to fallen trees. So many trees block Fangaloa Road that the convoy heads cross-country.

'Hold tight Eimoni!' the rider shouts. The bikes emerge onto the outer coast road and pull up at the Blue Horizon Resort. The main roof lies in Atalapa's Garden of the Sun but the ground floor is intact. A police officer meets the palace entourage and sweeps them over the squelching lobby carpet past the milling angry tourists to the Ocean Ballroom. A generator drums close by.

Queen Ta helps the staff set up tables and arrange chairs. Amon hangs back by the door. Another convoy-load arrives: Amon recognises Father Isaaki of the sub-diocese, Rev. Dr. Sifa Sikahema of Queen 'Ana College, the directors of the Vaiola and LDS hospitals. The Privy Council, most of the cabinet, prominent citizens and representatives of key services find places around the tables. Walkie-talkies and radios blurt; there is a cheer when a laptop connects to the net. Kimmie takes Amon by the arm.

'Sit next to me so I can translate.'

'I don't think I should be here,' Amon whispers as Kimmie places him at the royal table next to Prime Minister Pohiva.

'It is about what is said, not who says it,' Prime Minister Pohiva says in his formal, considered English.

Queen Ta lays the 'Akau Ta on the table and rises to her feet.

'Let's get started. I open this meeting of the Royal Ava'u Disaster Committee.'

The internet is up. The cable to Samoa is intact.

The satellite ground station is working. Ava'utapu can talk to Ofu and Niua and the rest of the world.

Military and police communications are working and Mr. Fakalava the shortwave radio enthusiast has spoken with Samoa, Tonga and Fiji, and with Aotearoa, where the diaspora community waits with anxiety for word from the islands.

Deaths: fourteen reported. Four from falling trees or other debris, three swept away in a vehicle; an entire family of seven asphyxiated by carbon monoxide from a faulty generator in their home shelter.

(Pause here for cries and tears and prayers.)

Missing: thirty-eight. Twenty-four on ships. Four young men who went to see the Pangai blow-holes in the storm.

Injuries: two hundred and twelve. One hundred and four require medical attention. Vaiola Hospital has been destroyed. Queen Ta asks the LDS president if he will make the church clinic available? He cannot but agree and adds that a mission ship is already en route from Samoa. Rev. Dr. Sifa Sikahema offers Queen ‘Ana's sanitorium and the manager of the Blue Horizon suggests the spa treatment rooms. They're clean and easily sterilisable. Ta is sure the other hotels will follow suit. Captain Ruzza of the Festival *Ocean Adventurer* has offered its sick bay. The ship's azimuth thrusters were damaged in the cyclone. Repairs may take weeks. Ships with medical facilities have sailed from Fiji, the US base on Kwajalein Atoll and Aotearoa.

Engineers are at work to reopen the harbour by nightfall. The island's single mobile crane will be available to clear wreckage by noon. Teams are clearing the airport runway. Mua tower is out. Samoa has assumed ATC over Ava‘u airspace. Repatriation flights for tourists and cruisers stranded by the cyclone are standing by in Auckland and Suva.

The real problem, Chief Medical Officer Dr. Ma‘afu says, is sanitation. Sewage systems have been overwhelmed, the flood pools stagnate and vegetation and flesh rot. Waterborne disease is a real risk. It is likely that sewage has contaminated water supplies.

The prime minister asks if there is a sufficient stockpile of antibiotics.

No. Velma devastated the reserves. Dr. Ma‘afu has contacted Samoa and Tonga. Tonga has a seaplane en route. As Ava‘u gave to Tonga after the tsunami, Tonga gives back. The motorbike network can distribute drugs to local medical teams until the roads are cleared. The Disaster Medical Response teams are intact though the hospital and doctor's offices are gone.

Mr. Taituave, royal engineer, raises concerns that most of the island's fuel-oil supply has been lost and possibly polluted the water table. Without fuel-oil mains, electricity can't be restored. He is not sure how much resilience there is in the emergency generator network. At least eighty percent of the power lines are down.

Can we get the solar panels back up again?

With respect, Mr. Taituave says: Up on what? Not a roof remains on Ava'utapu. Whole districts have been levelled; barely ten percent of Mua's houses stand. Churches, halls, schools, all the places where communities might shelter fared no better. And rain is on the way. FMS is tracking a new tropical depression deepening west of Fiji.

'The *Ocean Adventurer*,' Kimmie Pangaimotu murmurs. 'It's sitting right there.'

'Tell them,' Amon whispers.

'It's not my place.'

'Then I will.'

'No you don't, palangi,' Kimmie says, louder.

Queen Ta notices the muttering.

'My master of music has something to contribute?' she says in English.

'Leiti Kimmie has a suggestion,' Amon says. 'She feels she has no authority to speak on this committee.'

'Leiti Kimmie's suggestions are most welcome,' Queen Ta says.

'The Festival *Ocean Adventurer*,' Kimmie says. 'The palangis are leaving, the ship's not going anywhere until we fix it. It's got power. And food. And water.'

Heads turn to each other around the ballroom tables. Murmurs.

'This is an excellent idea,' Prime Minister Pohiva says.

The debate reverts to Ava'uan.

Queen Ta will go to Pulotu Wharf in person and bring her full majesty to bear on Captain Ruzza.

'And we pay him,' Kimmie translates for Amon. 'Charter his ship. Festival Cruises will be more likely to agree if they can make money out of an inactive ship.' Mutterings of dissent. 'Not the full amount. Enough to make it worth his time.'

Lady Tupua comments that the publicity will be good for the cruise company. She has a proposal for the Lords of Niua: the laid-up cruise ships: What is their state of seaworthiness?

The low words around the tables grow louder and more optimistic.

There is also some capacity at the spa hotels, Blue Horizon's manager says.

'I want damage reports and a plan of action based on this strategy,' Queen Ta says. She stands up, takes the 'Akau Ta.

'Now I will talk with Captain Ruzza.'

'Ma'am, the budget has not been agreed,' the minister of finance says.

'The queen never talks money,' Ta says. 'The queen talks hope. With me, my malietoa, my leiti, my master of music.'

Kimmie prods Amon to his feet, links arms, hurries him out of the hotel.

'Palangis respond better when there's another palangi there,' she says.

Motorbikes pull up in the broken porte cochère.

Queen Ta climbs up behind her rider. Then comes the sound of an aero engine. Amon looks up to see a seaplane roar low over the hotel, coming in from the south, descending fast. He makes out the red-and-white cross of Tonga on its side. It banks sharply on approach to the lagoon.

Passengers and riders saddle up, roll out. Heads down, bums up. Tour d'Ava'u.

82

The godlings of Touia'o Futuna mostly don't feel the weather. Weather is a thing of the world and they are between worlds. But Velma was more than weather, she was of the same divine matter as they and so her rains drenched their bare skins and her winds chilled their flesh so they burrowed deep into themselves, sharing humid, stenchy heat. Velma volleyed Touia'o Futuna like a ball in a squash court. Rolling bowling bouncing howling.

They row their floating rock back to its proper place to find their islands trashed. It's happened many times since they drew Ava'u from the waves. It will happen many times more before the waves finally close over the islands. But there's a smell, from deep inside the rock. It rises up like anti-incense and they chitter and flap like disturbed bats. It is a smell out of place. Something is wrong deep in their islands.

83

Amon tries to refuse the Deck 12 balcony room. Give me one inside. No porthole. Lower decks.

'Fuck no porthole, 'ofa'anga,' Kimmie declares. 'Kimmie Pangaimotu needs a balcony.'

They move into the Deck 12 stateroom, starboard side. Kimmie takes the larger cabin. She has stuff, 'ofa'anga. She hangs her yata over the balcony rail. Protests and guilt aside, it is Amon who spends the most time on that balcony. He arranges his long pale limbs over a deck chair and watches the ships in the lagoon, the aircraft turning and descending into the airport. The first aircraft in are all repatriation flights. So hasty is the evacuation that the cruisers left behind a tideline of personal property: chargers, items of clothing; consumer electronics, tablets, the occasional laptop; some medications or sex toys. Rarely, items of jewellery. A legend appears that a family found a diamond necklace and matching earrings, still in the case, on the bedside cabinet of a Deck 9 aft outside stateroom.

The tourists fly out, the refugees troop aboard. Royal Ava'u Water bottling plant workers. Massagers and hot stone specialists and nail-artists. Water tanker drivers. Staff from the karaoke bars and the restaurants. Aboard.

The van drivers. The bus drivers. The port workers, the ferry workers, the airport workers. The road workers. Aboard.

The men's rugby team. The women's rugby team. First Mua's football team, amateur drama group and choir. Aboard.

The welfare officer at Queen 'Ana's. The rugby pitch groundskeeper. The kid who blew the commencement conch three times. Aboard.

Mrs. Sinipata from the store. The smiley marine who said hello to Amon every day. Susitino from the Royal Ava'u Hotel. Aboard aboard aboard.

Laea the Uber. Miss Teuila 2032. The minister for national flora and fauna. All aboard.

Festival *Ocean Adventurer*'s corridors and companionways ring with strong Ava'uan voices and the feet and shouts of children. There's a school in the Aces High Casino and in the non-denominational devotion space Presbyterians, Catholics, Methodists and other religions hot-pew services.

The Mormons attend their own God-business aboard the LDSS *Hagoth*, docked at the Royal Avaʻu Hotel pier.

Nine thousand three hundred and fifty of Avaʻutapu's twelve thousand nine hundred citizens have found refuge aboard Festival *Ocean Adventurer*. The ship's maximum occupancy is six thousand. Systems and resources strain and creak. Cabins designed for two host families of four; extended families lock open connecting doorways into extended family suites. Children sleep four to a king-size bed, teenage sons roll up in tapa mats on balconies or bathroom floors.

The Disaster Committee tries to allot space justly but people want to be with folk from the old streets and districts. Cabins are traded, pressure put on outsiders to move. Families from higher-deck staterooms find themselves in lower-deck cabins. Clergy, teachers, community leaders mediate. Signs appear on stairwells naming each deck after an old island district or village. Police enforce the meal rota. Groups of community cooks work shifts to prepare huge feasts for entire decks. *Ocean Adventurer* is a happy ship. *Nordic Aurora* arrives, with Niua's three and a half thousand aboard and room for more. Her sister ship *Nordic Polaris* will arrive tomorrow with the population of Ofu. The mothballed cruise liners were slow to wake but they are sea-fast and right. Amon watches *Aurora* rise from the horizon and negotiate the narrow deep-water channel and the relief ships. Bunker-oil smoke belches, thrusters boil green greasy harbour water, a cliff of weather-stained metal slides in behind *Ocean Adventurer* to Pulotu Wharf. The Niuans wave and smile. The ship is a wall of cheering, laughter, loud voices. Amon hears *Ocean Adventurer* answer around him.

In his fascination he misses Kimmie enter. He startles as she taps him on the arm.

'Amon.'

She touched him. She didn't use any endearments. This is important.

'Disaster Committee meeting. Everyone.'

Kimmie finds two seats at a far table in the Showtime Theatre. On the stage Queen Ta, Prime Minister Pohiva, the minister for the environment and climate change and two westerners in Water Aid polo shirts talk with quiet animation. The pheromone of fear is strong in the ballroom. Queen Ta taps a microphone and the committee comes to order. Kimmie leans in to translate for Amon.

'A report from the environment minister.'

Sione Takalula stands. A former rugby professional, he is a big man even by Ava'uan standards. He's a household name, respected, adored, and he stands grey, diminished, fearful on the stage of the Showtime Theatre.

'Usual praising platitudes,' Kimmie whispers. A translator does the same for the two Water Aid representatives. They stand when their names are mentioned. Prime Minister Pohiva had not wanted to involve Western NGOs. Like the Latter-day Saints they are quick to arrive, slow to leave. 'Water Aid has completed its report on the restoration of Ava'utapu's water supply.' Kimmie listens. 'Lots of technical stuff.'

'I'm interested in the technical stuff,' Amon says. He senses concern move from table to table. Minister Takalula mops his forehead with a paper tissue. He speaks. The ground-state rumble of the room drops to silence. Then a roar of voices. Kimmie's hands fly to her mouth.

'What is it, what is it?' Amon shouts over the uproar. Men weep. Women comfort each other. Minister Takalula sits down, sobbing helplessly. Queen Ta's head is bowed. Her shoulders shake.

'The aquifer,' Kimmie says. 'The sea has broken in. Our water. It's dead.'

84

The rain comes, frequent and full in this season. Amon Brightbourne rises from grey listlessness and goes up into the weather. He walks the decks, deserted now that the novelty that had children dancing in the deluge has faded. He prefers it this way. The sounds are clearer, purer.

The women in the doorways, keeping watch over the rain-catchers, see him, soaked bone-deep, red hair straggled, and ask, *What exactly is Eimoni doing?*

Making rain music. The ring of a fresh squall's first drops on a deck rail. The drum of a downpour on the tarpaulins stretched over the lifeboats. The chuckle of water through the sluices. Rain season has a thousand tunes. Amon captures them and brings them back to his stateroom.

The men loading and harvesting ask, *Why is Eimoni doing this?*

For Princess Halae. Each evening Amon comes to the princess's stateroom with headphones and phone. She closes her eyes and he plays music. Sometimes bird music, sometimes praise music, sometimes wind music, or engine music or harbour music. Always ship music. It's all the contribution the Master of the Queen's Music can make in the world after Velma.

Here is a simple equation. On one side are bunker fuel, food and sources of potable water. On the other are three ships, power and electricity and nineteen thousand people from all the islands of Ava'u.

Now the rains are here. Tarpaulins, plastic sheets, shower curtains, anything that can catch and keep water slung from every point of ship and shore that will bear them. Teams of water-bearers fill barrels and carboys, down to the ubiquitous plastic drinks bottles, and ferry them back to the ships. The work is constant, wet, unrelenting, heavy and will add no more than three days' worth of water to the supply.

Kimmie's work keeps her at Queen Ta's side from dawn to dark, so Amon has the stateroom to himself to work on the royal rain music. He opens his MacBook. Uses electricity. Loads his musical assets. Burns fuel. Takes a rehydrating sip. Consumes water. Opens Ableton. Electricity. Works for three blissful hours building beats, then makes coffee. Electricity, water, food. Every sip feels like theft. Every beat is a crime.

By early afternoon the mix is done. Amon opens the balcony door. A thick and humid draught sets the yata turning. He watches the relief boats leave. Why rebuild when the water has turned to salt? Ava'utapu is a dead island. Ofu and Niua are desolate. This is a climate refugee issue now. The plan is to evacuate and relocate. There's talk of Fiji, Tonga, Samoa. The LDS Church has already chartered repatriation flights to American Samoa and the Marshall Islands. The Ava'uan communities in Aotearoa and Australia have opened their doors. Shuttle flights to Suva and Nuku'alofa are stacked over the northern glide-path.

That still leaves three cruise ships filled with islanders with nowhere to go moored at Pulotu Wharf.

And Amon Brightbourne.

The rain music ends. Princess Halae stands, hands cupped right over left. She opens her eyes. She returns the earbuds and thanks Amon a thousand times. Then she announces she will go to the bathroom.

'Amon.' Queen Ta gets up from a club chair.

'Ma'am.'

'Rain music. I'd like to hear that.'

'Of course, ma'am.' Amon hesitates.

She opens the sliding window. Rain falls in a curtain from the balcony above, a plane of sound. 'Close the door, Amon.' Ta opaques the panoramic windows.

'A private audience,' Amon says.

'Privacy is privilege,' Queen Ta says.

'I only have the one set of earbuds,' Amon apologises.

'I have my own.' Ta inserts them, Amon connects.

'Are you ready?'

'I am.'

He presses play. And it's not the same. It can't be the same. She only hears music. It ends; Ta takes out the earbuds.

'Thank you, Amon.'

'This isn't about music,' Amon says.

'No,' Queen Ta says. 'It's about this.'

THE BALCONY OF A SUITE ON THE FESTIVAL *OCEAN ADVENTURER*. NIGHT, RAIN.

TA: I release you from my service, Amon.

AMON: Sorry ma'am, what?

TA: I won't need any more royal music.

AMON: Oh.

(BEAT)
Oh . . .

TA: Please believe me, Amon, this is not personal. I can't afford a master of the queen's music.

AMON: If it's for Halae, I'll do it gratis.

TA: It's not money, Amon. Not just money. How can I have a master of the queen's music when I don't even have a queendom? Salt and wreckage and dead dogs. That's what I rule.

AMON: I understand, ma'am. I'll leave in the morning. I should be able to get a flight.

TA: Where will you go?

AMON: Back to Hopeland.

TA: Your family.

AMON: Not my family.

TA: Kimmie tried to explain it to me. You have your own religion.

AMON: The Emanations and the constellations. As below so

above. Or is it as above so below? You don't have to believe in it as long as it believes in you. I never understood it.

TA: Kimmie showed me her spinning mirror.

AMON: The yata.

TA: I saw something in it, Amon.

AMON: I never have.

TA: Kimmie said she never did, either. But I saw something. Inside the light. Reflections of reflections and at the end of them, so so small. Like the sprout of a seed. I can't say it in English or Ava'uan. I don't think any language has the words. A coil that is inside everything and ties everything together.

(BEAT)
We'll be scattered, Amon.

AMON: I thought Aotearoa had agreed . . .

TA: The decision came through this afternoon. They'll only take one ship. Australia, one ship. Fiji, Tonga, Samoa, one ship between them. No one will take us all. And that's the end of a thousand years of Ava'u. We dissolve like salt. Our stories and songs and ancestries will be rolled up into other people's myths and legends. The old gods sicken and die. The ancestors evaporate. Our names will wear thin and blow away.

AMON: Jesus . . .

TA: Refugee camps and resettlement centres. Communities scattered from Perth to Brisbane. Aigas broken. I don't know what to do, Amon.

AMON: How long, ma'am?

TA: We have five weeks of water left. They'll put us on that fucking island, Amon. Excuse my language. The one for the brown people. It isn't even in Australia.

AMON: Is there anything . . .

TA: No. And I order you to go. You big, long palangi, drinking our water and eating our food! Who do you think you are?

(BEAT)
Joke, Amon.

AMON: I feel like I'm deserting you. All of you.

TA: Well then, make music for us. Your final royal commission! Turn us into music, Amon. All the sounds, all the songs and voices, all the noise and shouting. An Ava'u opera. Music people will play in a thousand years. Yes! Do this for me.

SHE DRAWS HERSELF UP TO HER FULL MAJESTY.
Your queen commands you!

TA LAUGHS UPROARIOUSLY. THE WATER FROM THE BALCONY ABOVE ABATES, WATERFALL TO CURTAIN TO DROPS.
We're losing our privacy screen. All ears on this boat!

SHE OPENS THE STATEROOM DOOR.
AMON: I'll make you proud, ma'am.

TA: You will. Thank you. Fair winds and safe harbours, Amon Brightbourne. God sail you safe.

85

Before dawn he slips the MacBook into Auberon's satchel with the MIDI keyboard and pad. Kimmie snores heroically in her cabin.

A note? No note. All departures should be sudden.

Amon slings the bag over his shoulder. The corridors and staircases are already thronged. Deck 12 is on breakfast shift. Families greet him. None ask what Eimoni is doing at this hour.

The police at the wharf gates nod to him. He bids them good morning. It is a good morning. Pulotu Road still stinks of rot, seaweed, diesel and sewage but the air is clean and the sun rising over the cliff-faces of the refugee ships is warm and kind.

The phone app shows his flight on approach. The flight was expensive. It took him most of the night to make the connections. He couldn't sleep anyway. Ava'utapu to Fiji, Fiji to Sydney, Sydney through Abu Dhabi to Dublin. Lorien or Lisi might pick him up from Dublin Airport and take him the final leg back to Brightbourne. The most expensive leg was the flight from Mua to Suva.

A moped passes: driver, his wife sidesaddle behind him, infant in her arms and a four-year-old perched in front of her father. He still finds the space to buzz the horn in greeting to Amon. Not to wave would be churlish. He has no reason to hide; everyone else on the roads this morning shares a destination. A second moped carries the rest of the family: oldest daughter, siblings. A hefty hoot: a John Deere tractor towing a long flatbed trailer pulls up beside Amon.

Laea the Uber shouts down from the cab.

'Want a ride?' She is the airport bus now. Passengers wave from the trailer: families and generations. No possessions but small backpacks, the clothes they wear and one precious item.

'I'm fine walking, thanks, Laea.'

'As you wish, Eimoni.'

Ava'utapu to Fiji. Fiji to Aotearoa, or Australia, or the US, or Chile or Singapore or Indonesia. The nation scattered and dissolved.

Amon looks up at the first rumble of the incoming flight. There, a speck behind the clouds.

The world stops around Amon Brightbourne. Light, air, sound and motion suspended. Breath ceases. Blood. Electricity. Time itself. And it's there, complete, perfect, every detail exact, connected, shining.

Amon's heart gives a shuddering kick.

So simple.

He turns and walk away from the airport, each step faster and more urgent than the one before. By the Tuʻi Calvary he breaks into a trot. By the Pulotu Road he is in full, silly Amon Brightbourne run, elbows and feet ugly, hair and satchel flapping.

'Forget something, Eimoni?' the police officer at the wharf gate calls.

'Forget? Yes?' he shouts breathlessly. 'Everything everything.'

Wind boom and sun glare. Land and sky whirl, then the camera settles on the face. Afternoon light; in the background water, green and rock. Wooden houses, brightly painted.

'Amon,' Atli says. Wind roars across the microphone again. Atli sits on a plastic garden seat on the balcony of a yellow house, black roofed. Behind him, a massive gas barbecue and four sets of reindeer antlers hooked over the rail. Atli has tied his hair back and the light shines full on his brown face.

'Where are you?' Amon asks.

'In Nuuk,' Atli says. 'The Nýttnorður Foundation House.'

'Are you busy?'

'This, that. Like I do. Why are you asking?'

'I need your help,' Amon says. 'Can you get me a call with Raisa?'

'I could.'

'Soon.'

'How soon?'

'Today?'

Atli nods.

'I'll message you.'

'Thanks. I should go. I don't want to tie up the bandwidth. I shouldn't be here.'

'Sure. Amon, what's that noise?'

It takes Amon a moment to pinpoint the source of Atli's extraneous sound.

'That's Kimmie. Snoring.'

86

In the corridor outside the Showtime Theatre Ta warms up. Lunges. Small tight runs on the spot. Tilts and stretches. She closes her eyes, touches thumbs to little fingers. Breathes with mind and presence. A long moment. Queen Elisiva Taʻahine Tuʻi opens her eyes.

'Royal me up,' she commands. Her leitis-in-waiting wrap the tupenu around her waist and arrange the formal taʻovala over the tupenu. Leiti Fetuu places the three necklaces of the islands around her neck: the cowrie, the shark's tooth, the beads shaped from the wood of the fallen coronation tree. She oils her arms, checks the nail-art. Leiti Kimmie pins the pandanus-leaf diadem to her coiled and oiled hair.

'I'll fix your eyes.'

'I am so nervous,' Queen Ta whispers as Kimmie adjusts her eye shadow.

'You'll slay them in this.'

'Ma'am, I should be with you,' Prime Minister Pohiva says. He too has dressed formally; white shirt, smart tie, formal tupenu, clean and neatly pressed despite the new laundry rationing. 'Your cabinet desires to stand with you. Your foreign minister is highly experienced . . .'

'I have no more devoted ministers than you and Lady Tupua,' Queen Ta says. 'But a queen should speak for her people.' A nervous, mischievous grin crosses her face. 'I haven't got you dressed up in your Sunday suit for nothing. I'll call you when I need you.'

The cinema door opens. A technician bows.

'We're ready, ma'am.'

'I will not beg,' Queen Ta says to her ministers.

The Naalakkersuisut waits in the videowall, five women and five men standing in a neat semicircle before a wooden wall covered with representations of the birds of the High Arctic. The men wear white round-collared smocks and black pants, the women high white boots inlaid with floral patterns in dyed leather and wide collars of intricately worked coloured beads. This is a state visit. A sixth woman with natural hair in a bright blue dress and red tights stands a step behind and apart.

'Brown people,' Queen Ta says. 'We will be all right.'

'The camera is directly in front of you,' the technician says. 'The microphones will pick up everything in the room.'

'So noted,' Queen Ta says. She surveys the meeting room. 'Kimmie, announce me. I shall make an entrance.' She flicks to English, the language in which the summit will be conducted. 'Amon.' Amon Brightbourne has moved back through the politicians, uncomfortable that he has any place here. 'Amon? With me. You're the contact. Three steps behind me and two to my left, please. Speak when you're spoken to.'

'Not a problem, ma'am.'

'Major Fia.' She extends her right hand and her Malietoa is there with the 'Akau Ta. Her hand closes around the staff of kings. Her nails are decorated with traditional tapa-mat symbols of blessing, voyage, contract-making.

'Okay, Kimmie,' she orders in Ava'uan. 'Saddle up and let's roll.'

On the cinema floor Kimmie Pangaimotu draws herself up to her considerable height, flares her nostrils, cups her hands in the po, the gesture of welcome, and bellows, 'Her Majesty Elisiva Ta'ahine Tu'i of Ava'utapu, Ofu, Niua and the lesser islands, queen from horizon to horizon, sunrise to sunset.' Kimmie throws her head back. 'First of her name!'

In her full majesty, Queen Elisiva Ta'ahine Tu'i I goes to meet the Greenlanders.

Queen Elisiva Ta'ahine Tu'i's Speech to the People of Ava'u, June 22, 2033
(Sixty-three minutes in, after the hymns, prayers, praisings, eulogies, compliments and flatteries.)
The Showtime Theatre of the Festival *Ocean Adventurer*

. . . We will work. We will work like never before. The work will be hard and long. We will work to get to the new land and once we are there we will work to build new homes and families. This is not a kind land we are going to. Not like our islands were. We will work to get there; we will work to settle our families there. There will be work for every hand. My ministers have made deals. Good deals. Fair deals. PBV, our sponsors, are working to extend their hydrogen-power network. They mine volcanoes— imagine! They draw up the power of Mafui'e. Where there are no volcanoes they build great reefs of wind turbines. They see a world transformed.

We will build this new future. We will be there at the very start of it, as it rises out of the sea. We will be workers who build, who crew, who administer and supply and maintain. Our hands will build this new world. In this new world, who rules the North rules the world and who rules Greenland rules the North. Greenland needs people. Strong people, sea-wise people, bold people. Jealous eyes watch the North. Russia, America. China and Canada. We are a strong people joining hands with a strong people to become a great nation. It won't be the work of a year, or a generation. None of us on this journey will see the forests clothe the mountains of the northland, or the great ships passing up and down our coasts, refuelling from our stations. None of us will see the great port cities that spend half the year in light, half the year in darkness, or the vast nature parks where creatures of the high north roam wild and free. But our children will.

There is a cost. We must leave our beloved islands. I will not make you. No one takes the voyage to the North who has not chosen it. Who can make an Ava'uan change their mind, once it's set? No one! I swear this on my ancestors: There will be a home for you in the northland. There will be a roof, a hearth; food and the songs we have sung for a thousand years. Our songs, our hymns, our dances. We'll sing new songs. We'll sing of our great voyage, as we sing of our great voyage to these islands a thousand years ago.

We are not refugees. We are not migrants. We are not asylum seekers. We are voyagers.

The night I became your queen I swore a sacred vow on the 'Akau Ta to serve my people and my islands with all my heart and all my soul and all my life. I have served the islands with all my strength but I can no longer do that and fulfil the more important part of the vow: to serve the people. So I pledge to you the love and dedication I gave these islands. For Ava'u is not the blow-holes or the surf on the reef, not the morning light on the lagoon nor the east wind in the trees. Ava'u is you. Is us.

If you grant me your trust, I will lead you. I pledge myself to your service. God give me strength; I will keep the nation together. We kept together through the great pandemic. We were one in the great cyclone that destroyed our islands. We survived, together. This voyage will not be easy. There will be uncertainty, there will be doubt. There will be loss, there will be grief. There will be storms and fear. Our faith will shake. We will ask why we ever set off on this voyage. We will wonder why we ever went to this cold, hard place. But I will not break. *We* will not break. I promise you.

And when I pass over the horizon, I pray whoever takes this staff after me will carve my name with pride and my deeds with compassion.

In the old days, when heaven and earth were closer than they are now, when gods and humans walked together and legends happened every day, we practised the art of ta tatau. We told stories on our skins. They told who we were. They were a commitment. You wore them for life. Over the years we lost this tradition. We should wear our commitment on our bodies. Our skins should tell the world who we are.

(The queen rolls up the left sleeve of her dress. Around her biceps, in good shape from weights and resistance training, is a tattooed band, eight centimetres wide, of chevrons and saw-tooths and triangles capped with curls and semicircles like breaking waves.)

(Loud gasps and exclamations. It's not just the shock of a forgotten way swimming back to the light; there is the deeper implication of old orders and customs overturned. Question of protocol: Who tattoos the Queen?)

I could not be more blessed than to have served you, the people of Ava'u. I leave you with a challenge. A sipi tau. I give these ships new names: *Ava'utapu, Ofu, Niua*. These are our islands now. In twelve days my shipbuilders will complete their repairs. My engineers will start the engines. My navigators will lay in a course due north. My crew will cast off the lines, my helm will take the ships through the passage in the reef into the open ocean. And *Ava'utapu, Ofu* and *Niua* will set sail for a new land. Will you come with me? Will you?

(Roars, applause, voices. Tears. Mostly tears.)

87

Prime Minister Pohiva requests the company of Amon Brightbourne for morning coffee in his stateroom, 11:00 a.m. Dress informal.

Eleven A.M. Amon Brightbourne presses the doorbell. The prime minister opens the door. His cabin lies on port-side. Island-side. The coffee table waits on the balcony: pot, two cups. No milk.

'Instant, I'm afraid,' Prime Minister Pohiva says. 'We must make sacrifices.'

'Why do I feel you want something from me?' Amon asks.

'Because I do, Mr. Brightbourne. Though not so much want something from you as want to offer something to you. You have been a good friend to us. As the leiti Kimmie would say, your guilty palangi ass has served Ava'u well.'

Amon raises his coffee cup in a toast.

'Might it do one more thing for us?'

'And there it is,' Amon says.

'Mr. Brightbourne, by the authority of the Crown and the Fale Alea I offer you the position of Her Majesty's liaison to the Nýttnorður Foundation.'

'Ah,' says Amon Brightbourne.

'It is a great honour.'

'Pro tanto quid retribuamus.'

'I didn't quite hear that, Mr. Brightbourne?'

'It's a great honour.'

'Correct.'

'I should point out that I'm not an Ava'uan citizen.'

'You are now.'

'Can I keep the room?'

'You're entitled to a single room.'

'I'll keep arrangements the way they are,' Amon says.

The prime minister steps into his stateroom and returns with a bottle of whisky and two glasses.

'Something more fitting.' He pours three generous fingers into each glass. The reek of the whisky seduces and nauseates Amon. It would be the nadir of manners to refuse. Amon notes how little remains in the bottle. Pohiva peers at his watch. Amon looks up at the sound of a small, tight jet engine circling close.

'Raise your glass, Mr. Brightbourne.'

A small, fleet business jet descends. The higher port-side staterooms have views across *Ava'utapu* from one side to the other. Amon watches the plane land, turn, taxi to the porta cabin terminal.

'Ava'u is dead, long live Ava'u.' Prime Minister Pohiva throws back his shot. Amon sips. *Old friend,* the alcohol says. *Haven't seen you in a long time. How 'bout ye?*

'You have me at a loss, Mr. Pohiva.'

'The new owners.' Pohiva refills his glass. 'A producer who wanted permission to film on Niua once told me that the three most expensive human endeavours are war, space travel and moviemaking. I can add a fourth. Migrating a nation. Ship chartering. Fuel. Crewing. Insurance. Certifications. Resources. Of expense, there is no end, Mr. Brightbourne.'

'Who's in that plane?' Amon asks.

'His Highness Prince Siaosi Vaka'uta 'oPulotu,' Prime Minister Pohiva says. 'We sold him the islands. He is king now. With his tech-company backers. I've heard they want to turn it into a data haven. Then others say an offshore tax haven for billionaires. I've even heard a spaceport.'

'It's dead rocks.'

'It's still hard to hear that, Mr. Brightbourne. Some of us were slow to convince.'

'Are you convinced?'

'I am now.' Prime Minister Pohiva empties the whisky bottle into his glass. 'A true toast then, Mr. Brightbourne. Her Majesty Queen Elisiva Ta'ahine Tu'i of Ava'u, first of her name.'

'Queen Elisiva. First of her name.'

Prime Minister Pohiva drains his glass. Amon take his polite sip. It smells like sick now.

'Promise me one thing, Mr. Brightbourne.'

'I'll try.'

'Don't get the tattoo.'

The people of Deck 12 starboard must have been waiting for Amon Bright-bourne because no sooner does the elevator close behind him than every door opens on an irate citizen demanding he do something about the noise. Four to the floor. Singing. Weeping. Disney hits. *Back to Black*.

We've rung her bell hammered on her door called her phone, they complain. Make her stop, Eimoni. We have children/key workers/money/status.

Kimmie Pangaimotu, dressed in her Mz Starshine glitter, bellows along to YouTube, phone in hand.

'Sing!' she shouts.

'Could you turn it down?' Amon shouts back. Kimmie launches into a repeat of *Back to Black*. Amon slips the phone out of her grasp and swipes the volume down to sociable levels.

'Fuck you, Amon Brightbourne!' she shouts and launches into a long, loud, luxurious Ava'uan tirade. While she curses, Amon moves around the room removing gin bottles.

'Where did you get these?'

'They're yours, 'ofa'anga. Kimmie found your little hiding holes. Half of what you threw out was water.'

'I'll remedy that now.' Amon has had a brutal, diplomatic day arranging documentation, questions of nationality and rights of settlement with the Greenlanders and the Foundation. He wants a brogues-off, soft-sink-into-furnishing evening. What he has is hell's karaoke. He takes his armful of bottles onto the balcony.

'Wait,' Kimmie cries. She teeters unsteadily onto the decking to watch Amon send the first bottle arcing out over the dark sea. It falls with a profound plop. 'That's a terrible thing to do to good gin.' She does not try to stop Amon as he consigns the gin bottles to the lagoon.

'Give me that,' she says, taking the final bottle. 'You can't throw a damn.' She flings it out into the night with all her considerable strength. She sets herself heavily down on the sofa, hands between her legs.

'I'm an orphan, Amon.'

'Ah,' says Amon Brightbourne.

'They wouldn't stay. No, they'd rather go to some LDS shithole in the Marshall Islands. You know where they're putting them? Rongelap. Atomic Atoll. Scrape away the dirt and it glows down there.

'They went to the *Hagoth* this afternoon. I begged them, Amon Bright-bourne. On the deck, on the gangway. On the wharf. All the way to the

Hagoth before their fucking palangi security stopped me. I wept fat tears and tore my hair. I had no pride, Amon. Look at me! I'm a wet, shiny mess. And do you know what sticks the fucking needle through my heart? They didn't ask me if I wanted to come with them.'

'I'm sorry, Kimmie.'

'Fucking families. Is there any gin left?'

'You threw the last one out.'

'Shit.'

At this hour the wind reverses from blowing onshore to offshore. A subtle turn but enough to stir the ship and set the yata rocking so that it catches the light. Catches Kimmie's eye.

'You have the kid. And the woman.'

'Raisa. Raisa Peri Antares Hopeland.'

'Everyone is a star, Kynnd Amon. No one ever has to leave. They cover you with love and colour and drama and security and community. Why should anyone ever leave?'

'I did. I walked away.' Amon goes to the minibar and returns with a small bottle of Royal Ava'u Water. 'My great-uncle Auberon loved it when the Hopelands came and brought people from across the world. Lost people. Refugees. Noise and chaos. Life.' Amon pours two glasses. 'He hunted for Emanations out in Brightbourne Wood. He could never see them. He never did join the family. The same way, I think he liked the idea of being Catholic. The hierarchy, the mysteries. The sense of old authority. He adored the guilt. He knew the lives of the saints. But he never could accept the faith.' He slides a glass to Kimmie. 'He talked about the twitch on the thread. He'd read it in an old Father Brown book. "I caught him with an unseen hook and an invisible line which is long enough to let him wander to the ends of the world and still to bring him back with a twitch upon the thread".' He raises his glass. 'This is the last of the Royal Ava'u Water.'

'It's still her, isn't it?'

'It's always her.'

'Drink then, Kynnd Amon,' Kimmie says.

'The twitch upon the thread, Kynnd Kimmie,' Amon says. They clink glasses and sip.

'I never could taste the difference,' Kimmie says.

88

The morning dawns clear. The sky stands high blue from horizon to horizon, from sunrising to sunsetting. The three ships of the Avaʻuan migration fleet ring with feet and childish chattering. The voices are elevated—school ends early today—and at the same time subdued. Women come on deck to meet, talk, hang out laundry, walk and be seen. Today their conversations are muted and uncertain. Today the young men don't play touch rugby on the Sky Deck; today the old people shake their heads at shuffleboard.

Today is Sailing Day.

At eleven the big ships warm up. Bunker fuel has the natural viscosity of bitumen. It takes forty minutes to raise it to engine temperature. Stacks billow black smoke.

At noon schools close. The children return to their decks, their corridors, the cabins where their parents dress them in Sunday whites, ironed and pristine. Then they dress themselves in their finest and oil their hair, for this is Sailing Day.

At twelve thirty the smaller ships cast off; three Guardian-class patrol boats, one the Royal Defence Force's, two gifted from Australia, to protect the people on their journey. Seven fisher-craft of the few that survived the storm. Every hull counts.

At twelve forty-five *Niua* sounds three blasts on its horn. I am reversing. Azimuth thrusters churn the oily green water. *Niua* swings into the lagoon. Five minutes later *Ofu* sounds her horn and moves out to join her sistership, station-keeping two kilometres out. Every deck is thronged, every open window filled with voyagers looking their last on Avaʻu.

Thirteen hundred on Sailing Day.

In her royal tupenu and taʻovala, crowned with pandanus, her tattoo gleaming on skin oiled with coconut, ʻAkau Ta in hand, Queen Elisiva Taʻahine Tuʻi enters the bridge of *Avaʻutapu*. In her wake follow her prime minister; the moderator of the Presbyterian church; Father Isaaki, co-adjutor of the sub-diocese of Avaʻu; and her malietoa, her leitis.

'Captain.'

Captain Ruzza sounds the horn. One sustained blast. I am leaving port. Father Isaaki leads the Lord's Prayer over the PA. His words relay to the waiting fleet. Then the Moderator opens the Bible and reads. Ko e fakatupu 'oe langi mo māmani, 'Oe maama, Mo e 'atā, Mo e mavahe 'oe fonua mei he ngaahi vai. *In the beginning God created the heaven and the earth. Now the earth was without form and void, and darkness was upon the face of the deep. And the Spirit of God moved upon the face of the waters.*

He closes the big book.

'Your Majesty?'

Queen Ta steps to the microphone.

'Fair winds and safe harbours, my people.' Her voice cracks. 'God sail us safe to morning.'

She turns from the microphone. Her leitis embrace her. Captain Ruzza gives the order to helm; the thrusters engage. The hull trembles. Water boils against the concrete pilings of Pulotu Wharf. The line of murk between ship and shore widens into a band, into clear water. *Ava'utapu* turns her bow to the open ocean. The last ship sails. On the highest deck the national rugby teams, women and men, run up the flag of the Kingdom of Ava'u; the red field with the white canton bearing the five red stars of the Southern Cross. Someone has found the conch horn of Queen 'Anaseini College and blows three loud blasts. New time begins.

In the chapel, at the organ, Amon Brightbourne lifts his hand and counts in the joint choirs of First Mua, St Peter Chanel and Saioni Wesleyan. An old sea-hymn, a fine sea-hymn: *Eternal Father Strong to Save.* The voices sing strong and united, without falter or break. The harmonies fall in monumental blocks, great ships of sound. All of Ava'u is in them. Amon drops the volume of the organ momentarily: He heard right. Over and above the choir sings a larger chorus: the people on the decks and the corridors and the public spaces, in their cabins and engine rooms and ready rooms. He has no doubt that the other ships sing also; voices rolling across the water. He holds the hymn's final note, then releases the choirs.

'Thank you,' he says in his bad Ava'uan. 'It was a privilege to play with you today.'

He waits until the chapel has emptied, until the corridors are quiet, then resets the manuals, adds voices and pedals, summons music on his screen. Then with what voices and volume a little omnifaith chapel organ can summon, Amon Brightbourne roars out Widor's *Tocatta.*

The patrol boats escort *Ava'utapu* to the head of the fleet. The ships fall into sailing order. The Ava'uan migration fleet lays in a course to the breach in the reef, then north, true north.

Then the boys remember. The lazy boys, the street boys, the Pulotu Road karaoke boys who hadn't time or sympathy for mass tears and grief, who only signed up on the journey because they had nowhere else to go, they remember.

Something almost got left behind.

The gods. The noisy, stinky, squabbling deities of Touia'o Futuna.

How to bring them?

The young men run to the ship's weather station. Sure we have weather balloons. For weather? No. For gods?

Okay.

They run a balloon up three hundred metres on a carbon-fibre tether from the back of the Sun Deck. No eyes see the reaching arms, the clawing fingers, the ropes and cables of divine flesh; the ladders of godmeat along which the godlings climb, clutching for the balloon, the new Touia'o Futuna suspended between heaven and ocean. They crawl, they crab, they slither until the last god squirms into its new slot among the throbbing bodies.

The Ava'uan nation sails out onto the open ocean, towing its gods behind it.

As below so above.

STORMTALKER

89

The tip of the fungal hypha measures five micrometres across and grows through the sandy umbrisol at twenty micrometres per minute. The tip bifurcates, one hypha extends, drawn by molecular cues, the other stultifies and dies back. The hyphae entwine with the fine root fibres of *Taraxacum sect. Arctica,* the Greenland dandelion. Chemicals mingle, carbohydrates from the plant, minerals from the fungi.

A transverse ladybird quests across a dandelion leaf. Red and black, its spots shear into soft chevrons, the signifier of this subspecies. It traverses a fractal world of planes and surfaces, directionless, almost gravityless. It potters on until it meets the thick sole of a Berghaus hiking boot.

The eye of an Iceland gull one hundred metres above Qaqortoq Fjord beholds: rotted icebergs, rocky shores, lichens, grass, dandelions, a transverse ladybird. Scattered shipping containers in primary colours, a jetty and ferry ramp, fuelling tanks diesel and hydrogen. An SUV, a heliport. A woman in Berghaus hiking boots.

Two hundred kilometres higher Chinese environmental monitoring satellite Huangjing 2J passes over south-west Greenland. Environmental monitoring of course means spying, so as well as recording temperature, ice and vegetation cover it also sends back information on the two Royal Canadian Navy AOP ships in the Davis Strait, the Russian submarine they are tracking, the eight Chinese fishing vessels on the edge of the Nanortalik Bank and the USN Zumwalt-class frigate one hundred and eighty kilometres south-west of Cape Farewell. Plus ferries, container ships, bulk carriers, exploration craft, cruise ships, fishers and upwards of forty aircraft civilian and military.

Higher than Earth, lower than the stars, the Emanations tumble. Ahania Leader of the Starry Skies, Enitharmon the Guitar Player, Theotormon the Mercenary, Vala Who Is Several Trees, the great Host of Hopeland, and others yet to know they are Emanations, ones differently divine or entities entirely other. As creatures of more than four dimensions they see outside time; glaciers retreating, advancing, retreating again; currents warming, cooling, reversing, shifting; green expanding, deepening, darkening.

They see from fungal hyphae through the herds of humans stirring, shift-ing, moving as their world changes around them and they realise that they too must change, to the great circle of the aurora. They look around the curve of the world and see stars realign. New gods are coming.

Raisa Peri Antares Stormtalker Hopeland waits at Qaqortoq Heliport. The sun is high and warm. She takes off her Patagonia jacket and slings it into the back of the SUV. She sits on the lip of the open hatch and drinks coffee from a flask. She is nervous. The coffee won't help but it's a thing to do, to not think about being nervous. An ancient Toyota pickup arrives in dust. Two men and a woman with a backpack get out and stand across the heliport from her. She raises a hand. The woman returns the barest of nods. The men ignore her.

The helicopter arrives from the north, turns. Raisa throws the remains of her coffee to the dust. Nervous is anxious now. The Inatsisartut liaison to the Ava'u Project is on that helicopter. Dust, Styrofoam, coffee cups fly as it descends to the pad. Plastic bags plaster the chain-link fence. The blades stop. Raisa jumps down from the back of the Foundation car. A woman steps from the helicopter.

'Raisa Peri Antares Hopeland?' The government liaison is short, brown-skinned, shoulder-length dark hair tied back. Kalaallit Nunaat face. Out-door wear and a Fjallraven backpack. Her left hand carries an all-weather ruggedised laptop case. The other she offers to Raisa. 'I am Nauja Lund.'

The departing helicopter throws up a demon-storm of dust and grit, turns north over the fjord. The two men return to their Toyota.

'I would have sent one of ours,' Raisa says.

'We have a fine air service,' Nauja Lund says. She sets her backpack on the rear seat of the car. The hard case she balances square on her knees. Her English is clear, lightly accented. Primary degree at the University of Copenhagen, post-grad at the University of Guelph, Ontario, Raisa knows. Husband Tuusi, graphic designer. Daughter Siisi, eighteen, son Okak, fourteen. Delegate to the Arctic Council. Adviser to the post-independence diplomatic team. She is a tenacious negotiator, a precise analyst, a cutter-to-the-chase, a diligent servant of the new Greenland. She does not tolerate fools. Which is why Raisa Peri Antares Stormtalker Hopeland is terrified.

'Still fossil, though.'

The Nýttnorður Foundation car moves off with the smug hush of electricity.

'It's five kilometres,' Raisa explains. As etiquette Raisa drives in the town. Autodrive will take it where the concrete ends and the dirt begins.

'I flew over it,' Nauja Lund says.

'Saarloq is only one site. We're developing two more.'

'Nanortalik and Alluitsup Paa,' Nauja says. 'I have been briefed.'

They pass the white block of Gertrud Rasch's Church.

'Ready for tonight?' The Foundation has aggressively advertised its public meeting with Stýra Raisa Hopeland and the new liaison from the parliament.

Nauja Lund pats her computer case.

'I have our presentation. I think for the first few weeks I shall listen more than talk.'

'Okay,' Raisa says. In a few weeks that bay will be full of cruise ships, patrol boats and long-line fishers.

A sudden loud bang low on the driver's side.

'Stone,' Raisa says. 'We're getting more since we announced the meeting. We lost two windshields this week.'

Nauja Lund does not blink. A figure in a hoodie moves with no great haste or furtiveness behind the church.

'I'm sure I will hear the grievances tonight,' Nauja Lund says. The Foundation car makes big dust on the track over the saddle to Saarloq. Raisa imagines it through Nauja Lund's eyes. The site looks small, poor, haphazard. Mobile cranes, earthmovers. Pickups and generators. Piles and pallets of construction materials. Plastic-wrapped bales. Trailers and quad bikes. The big PBV supply ship docked at the new jetty, the smaller Foundation ship *Aiviq* anchored in the fjord. Raisa takes back the car and drives down through the agriculture zone. Frames, roofs, light and aircon. Water. Last, the hydroponic systems.

'We'll run four harvest cycles per year,' Raisa says. 'We discovered in Iceland there's better uses for land than growing food.'

'Where is the housing?'

Raisa pulls up in the open space at the centre of a star of temporary accommodation units.

'This is your apartment here. It's basic but there's everything you need.'

'I mean, for the people.'

'We'll keep them on the ships at first. We extended the charter for another three months. Infrastructure first. Water, sewage, power. Food. Then housing.'

'It will be winter then.' Nauja steps from the car. Raisa notices the scratched dent in the driver's-side door. Bull's-eye on the Foundation sticker. Raisa passes Nauja a green hard hat with the white tree of the Foundation on its prow and an orange hi-viz vest.

'Hard-hat site,' she says, slipping on her own vest and hat, which she hates because she can never get her hair right after it. 'Maybe you'd like to get comfortable?' Power tools whine. Generators thump. Voices in five languages and hip-hop from a radio. 'It's a long way down from Nuuk.'

'I would like to meet your team now,' Nauja says. She shoulders her backpack.

Raisa makes a call from the car radio. A short, square Kalaallit with deep sun-etched furrows around his eyes lopes over from the jetty where he has been supervising the unloading of large pallets from the PBV carrier. His helmet is white with a red Mount Fuji. Foundation green, PBV the white-and-red volcano, Kebec Hydro red and black, Norges Statens Pensjonsfond blue, Nunavut Infra white and black, the Arctic Council white and sky blue, ARCAN orange and pink, which reminds Raisa of her clubbing days.

'Angunnguaq Lyberth, site manager,' she says. She intends this government official to be impressed by the number of Kalaallit working at every level of the Saarloq Project. Nauja Lund speaks with him in Kalaallisut.

'Nive Taunajik, water engineer.' And Vasundhara Barti, head of power and renewables; Mikivsuk Nappaattooq, ecosystems manager; Vigdis Sirius Johannasbur, agriculturalist; Efua Owusu, urban planner; Tan Peng Soon, health and social care; Sara Enoksen, education. Arorá Aldebaran from PBV, Grigory Pantaleyev from the Arctic Council.

The sound arrives a fraction of a second before the aircraft. Two combat jets thunder over Saarloq, climb high above the eastern end of the fjord and turn. Everyone looks up.

'Canadian Air Force F35s,' Raisa shouts as the jets return, lower, louder. They cross Saarloq in a breath then climb sharply into the western stratosphere. Sonic booms shake the fjord. 'Someone overflies most days.'

But Nauja Lund is glancing at her watch. 'I need to prepare for this meeting. Could I see my room now?'

Angunnguaq Lyberth escorts her. Raisa stalks off for a dispirited coffee in the site canteen. Every word she spoke, every answer she gave, every step she took, everyone she introduced, everything about her; her hair her car her private plane her Berghaus boots her polytunnels: wrong wrong. She feels a lumbering idiot.

She looks up from her bamboo coffee cup at the rattle of rain on the window. A cold front has arrived from the west.

90

Raisa dispels the mist screen. Someone turns on the lights. The concerned public of Qaqortoq blink on their hard Lutheran pews. The Foundation has filled Gertrud Rasch's Church fuller than God and his Christ ever did. It smells of furniture polish. The only church Raisa knows that doesn't is the old turf church of Vonland. That church smells of wood and ash and, on occasions, cum.

'I'd like to introduce the Inatsisartut liaison, Nauja Lund,' Raisa says. The interpreter repeats the announcement in Kalaallisut and minority Danish. She also translates Nauja's introduction, which is long and filled with greetings and praisings and thanks to the people of Qaqortoq and is met with much head bobbing and murmured appreciation. After Nauja Lund's speech, which is shorter than her introduction, Raisa opens the meeting to questions from the floor.

Twelve people are on their feet, twenty hands in the air.

'I want to know about the thirty fishing boats they're bringing with them,' shouts the man who has been standing the whole time at the back with folded arms. Murmurs of consternation. Raisa glances at Nauja. She writes intently on her screen.

'It's not thirty fishers,' Raisa says. The interpreter begins.

'We speak English here,' the questioner says.

'It's not thirty ships,' Raisa says again. 'It's seven. Seven fishers. That's all.'

'Seven more taking fish,' the man at the back says. 'And catches are down. Year on year. There's not enough to make a living as it is.'

'And services,' says a woman halfway down the nave on the left. 'Forty thousand people.'

'Nineteen thousand four hundred,' Raisa says.

'Well, we're three thousand people,' the woman says. 'How are services going to cope? The hospital. The schools. The sewage!'

'Like Nauja Lund showed you in the presentation, we're developing three communities,' Raisa says. 'That's six thousand people in each settlement.'

'That's still bigger than any community in Kujalleq,' the woman says. 'We'll be swamped.'

'Each of the new communities will be self-sufficient in services and infra-structure . . .'

'We'll be outvoted on everything!' A young man standing in the aisle shouts over her. She wonders if he was the one who threw the stone at the Foundation car.

'What about jobs?' A middle-aged, heavy-set man is on his feet, finger jabbing.

'There will be jobs,' Raisa says. 'Thousands of jobs.'

'Jobs for who?' shouts the woman in the nave. 'Jobs for us, or jobs for migrants?'

'Jobs for everyone,' Raisa says. She feels a rising irritation in her that could easily become anger. Anger would be disaster. 'Together with your government, we're transforming the economy here in Kujalleq. The future is renewable power and the Northwest Passage. Change is coming. We can either let it roll over us like a wave or we can ride that wave. Greenland has the potential to become a renewables superpower.' She sees the derision in the faces in the pews.

'Did anyone ask us if we want to be a renewables superpower?' says the man who asked about fishing boats. This time the rumble of voices takes longer to die down. She's in danger of losing this. Raisa glances again at Nauja. The government woman is still scribbling on her screen with her stylus. 'Did anyone ask us if we wanted nineteen thousand refugees?'

'They're not refugees,' Raisa says. 'They're employees. Workers.'

'They get the jobs,' says jab-finger-man, who has not sat down.

'Their home is drowning,' Raisa says.

'Our home is melting,' says the young man in the aisle. Now everyone talks. Nauja Lund sets down her stylus and gets to her feet.

'I hear your voices, but I'll tell you what I don't hear. Children. Children shouting, children playing. I look at you and I see five people under thirty. I see a church of old people. Where are your young people? Not in Qaqortoq. Not in Kujalleq. You're dwindling. You're dying here.

'We're building hydro-plants, hydrogen depots, renewable power; but most: a school out at Saarloq. You'll hear children's voices coming over the hill. Children playing in a school yard. Life will come back to Qaqortoq.'

Nauja Lund sits down. In the baffled, shamefaced silence Raisa takes the microphone.

'If we're done here, I'll thank you for your contributions.'

In the car back over the hill to Saarloq she says to Nauja Lund, 'You pulled my ass out of it back there.'

'I did?'

The never-ending lights of Saarloq glow beyond the ridge.

91

Nauja Lund kicks off her heavy outdoor boots with a long sigh. She hangs her hi-viz and hard hat on the peg above the boot rack. A single bedroom study—big enough—shower-room, a small kitchen with a double gas ring and a one-person refrigerator. She slips off her jacket, steps out of outdoor pants, pads sock-soled to the desk by the window, where she opens the laptop. She clicks the tension out of her neck, her shoulders, her wrists, and places a video call.

Tuusi is at his desk, face lit like a Madonna by the glow from his Wacom screen. He won the commission to design in-flight catering material for Air Greenland: from salt sachets to bioplastic coffee cups.

'Still at it?' Nauja Lund.

'They moved the concepts pitch to Tuesday.' A dozen departments and officials have input into the project. 'It's all right. I was expecting something like this. I'll finish the drinks tray tonight.'

'Business or coach?'

'Business. Never mind me. How are you?'

'The woman is an idiot,' Nauja Lund says. 'She comes in throwing money and promises. She has this big idea and everyone has to listen to it.'

'I'm getting that you don't like her.' Tuusi smiles.

'She managed to turn Qaqortoq against her in her first public meeting.'

'Achievement,' Tuusi says. 'What's it like down there?'

'Too early to tell. The work is huge. The clock is ticking. We had the Canadians over today.'

'China has requested an emergency observer session at the Arctic Council.'

'I saw that.'

'Did you see about the claim? The island consortium was bought out by Chinese money. Beijing says this makes the refugees citizens of the People's Republic.'

'Workers, not refugees.'

'What?'

'They're not refugees. They're workers. The Chinese claim is shit. The

Arctic Council will laugh it out of the room. The US and Russia will never allow it. But how are you?'

'I can't turn my head; my shoulders are stone and I feel a thousand years old.'

'How many times have I told you? You sit wrong. You'd sleep at that desk if you could. Go to Kalina in the health centre. She sorted my back. And get some exercise. You haven't, have you?'

'When I get this commission done.'

Now Nauja Lund smiles.

'So how is Siisi?'

'With Paara at Rikke's.'

'And Okak? With his crew?'

'They're getting quite good.'

She smiles again. After eighteen years she still has to ask Tuusi how their children are.

'Give them my love.'

'I will. What's tomorrow?'

'Meetings with the Foundation managers. I'm scheduled to go out to Nanortalik but I want to set up representation from community groups in Qaqortoq. Build slow.'

'You don't have time to build slow.'

'I don't have time not to. Don't stay up late.'

'And you.'

'I have a report to write.'

'I have biodegradable cutlery to conceive.'

Nauja Lund closes her screen. Her rooms are on the seaward side of the site but the floods light up everything and the thin walls are no barrier to the clang of earth-moving machines, the blare of engines, the beeping of reversing warnings. The Foundation provides a sleep mask and earplugs. She hates to feel plugs in her ears. Tomorrow she'll ask the medical centre for sleeping pills. She hears a new night noise. She looks up. Fast aircraft cross the dark over Saarloq.

92

He sees it first from the corner of his eye, a dart of blue, gone before he can focus. Kingfisher blue, like he saw once on the Broighter Burn and never again; all the blue in the universe fused into an instant, an atom of action. Under the desk of his stateroom. He crouches to hunt the blue. Nothing. A few nights later he sees again the flash down along the bottom of the wall, and a scuttle. A wiggle. Again, gone before he can lower his bones to investigate. Three nights later, after an e-conference with Saarloq, he leans back, sighing, in his desk chair and the blue streaks up the wall into the corner with the ceiling. Stops, all motion to no motion in an instant. A lizard, the length of his thumb, splay-toed, opal-eyed, throat pulsing. Jewelled, iridescent blue. He climbs up on the desk, moving in millimetre by millimetre to better appreciate this living sapphire.

'Well, aren't you beautiful?' he breathes.

Kimmie Pangaimotu arrives with a door bang and groan of exhaustion. She sees Amon Brightbourne on the desk, sees the lizard on the wall. Her shoe is in her hand in an instant, heel a hammerhead.

'Filthy reptile!'

'Leave it!' Amon shouts.

Kimmie freezes. The lizard unfreezes and flashes across the ceiling and through a gap between acoustic tiles.

'I'm not sleeping here with that thing up there,' Kimmie says.

'It's just a little lizard.'

'It's vermin.'

'Well I like it,' Amon says. 'It's like a pet. What do they eat anyway?'

'You,' Kimmie says. 'In your sleep. Start with the eyelashes, on to the eyelids.'

The fleet sails north and she accepts the lizard—an azure gecko, she tells Amon. She accepts its mate when Amon finds two tiny slivers of blue clinging, pulsing to his cabin wall. And they don't eat palangis—not enough flavour. Insects and sometimes other smaller geckos. And as Amon discovers when his fly capture-and-contain trap fails, shreds of chicken and pork.

'How would they have got on board?'

'Could have strolled on any time,' Kimmie says. 'People smuggled animals in the luggage. There're chickens on Deck 8. I heard there's whole pigs over on *Niua*.'

The geckos condition quickly to twice-daily feedings on the desk. Amon smuggles scraps out of the Neptune's Table restaurant. He feels guilty feeding limited rations to reptiles. He resists naming them. Reptiles, amphibians, fish, insects, molluscs—with the exception of octopi—don't have names. Phylogeny begets nomenclature. The fleet approaches the refuelling stop at Hawaii and Amon sets himself his next gecko challenge: encourage them to live in his bedroom. His work as plenipotentiary to the Nýttnorður Foundation is not perilous—Foreign Minister Tupua and the Ava'u Project committee chart the difficult political waters—but it is relentless. Little creatures, breathing the same air as he, watching him as he sleeps, are reassuring. His old room at Brightbourne was filled with little creatures, living and post-life.

Most nights, shaken by the engines and the rumble of ship-life, Brightbourne is the last thing he sees before he plummets over the precipice of sleep.

'The deal is, if I find so much as a gecko turd in my room, they get my size-tens,' Kimmie declares.

Each evening Amon Brightbourne leaves the eight P.M. meal early and goes up to enjoy the view from the miradors on Deck 15. From this flying deck jutting out over the water he can see the whole migration fleet. He never tires of the sight. *Ava'utapu* at the centre of the delta of cruise ships, *Ofu* a kilometre to port, *Niua* to starboard. The three patrol boats weave ceaseless patterns of vigilance. The fishing fleet mostly operates beyond the horizon. The open-ocean transfers of catch between long-liner and cruise liner are thrilling exhibitions of maritime bravado.

The flag of Ava'u and the royal standard fly from the staff; half a kilometre up Touia'o Futuna bobs on its tether, saggy and scrotal. It needs to be re-gassed.

Excitement is high about crossing the Tropic of Cancer. There were deck parties, singings and services on the equator. Each evening Amon notices the air is cooler. Above Cancer the temperature changes will become marked, dropping degrees in the course of a single day. There's talk in the restaurants and laundries of a great celebration when the fleet passes through the Bering Strait and crosses the Arctic Circle. Amon doubts that. The resolve and pandemic-spirit of the first days of the migration have already strained. Squabbles break out in the refectory lines. Rages over noise from neighbouring cabins. Complaints about the equity of the water rations. Territory staking on the decks and common spaces. Rumours run the corridors on soft-soled deck-shoes. We're not being told things. *There's a Russian submarine following us ready to send us to the bottom if it gets the order. We're to be shipped off to work for a Chinese uranium mine. Forced labour uh huh. How do you think this is being paid for?* Lord Tanumafil, Minister of Social Policy and Communities, pre-empted this but his deck community workers and corridor committees work non-stop resolving conflicts, settling feuds, refuting conspiracies.

Before Cancer is Hawaii. First landfall since Mua Lagoon. Honolulu! The United States! *Everyone will get shore leave, no one will be allowed off the ship, the US will take anyone who wants to leave, everyone will have to get vaccinated and pay for a biosecurity test. The fleet will sail in to brass bands and fireboat things spraying those big arches of water and the queen will be received by the president and the first lady!* The corridor committees try to damp down expectations. No one knows what will greet the fleet.

Island life was outdoors life and the travellers take every opportunity to quit their airless, smelly corridors and live on deck. A junior brass band practices on the Sun Deck. Women loll in companionable groups on tapa mats taking in the evening warmth. Old men lean on the rail and look to windward. The national rugby team organises morning runs. There is boys' five-a-side football in the tennis court, women's touch rugby sevens on Sun Salutation yoga court. Dr. Timani from Queen 'Ana sets up his telescope and projector for star-watchers. The stars stand strange over this side of the world. There's a competition for the best photograph of the Milky Way. Amon greets them all.

Amon Brightbourne's paseo ends where it began and every night Prime Minister Pohiva is there watching the forward horizon. They stand, they make observations about the lengthening of the day, the weather, the sailing conditions, the day's shipboard novelties. Prime Minister Pohiva invites Amon Brightbourne to his stateroom for evening drinks. Amon takes tea,

Prime Minister Pohiva whisky. The prime minister asks about the geckos, Amon asks about the queen. So prefaced, they can talk around, about and sometimes through the things they can't say in their working days.

Amon always leaves halfway down the whisky bottle.

This night when Amon sets down his teacup and gets up from the chair Prime Minister Pohiva says, 'There's a thing I think you should see.'

He opens the balcony door.

'Please, join me.'

The sky is clear, the constellations brilliant as spear-points, the fleet passes through a bloom of luminescent plankton. Waves of light peel from the bow, the wakes trail neon across the still sea. The fleet seems tiny, *Ava'utapu* a toy, Amon Brightbourne less than a planktonic photon. He is electrically aware of the darkness surrounding every moment of life.

'The world holds wonders yet,' says Prime Minister Pohiva. 'The aurora—the northern lights. I look forward to seeing that. And the ice. Did you know that the first humans to see the Antarctic ice were Māori navigators? Here is another wonder. Look ahead.'

The trick is to soften the focus, unsee to see. Let the eye adapt. His fingers tighten on the rail. The forward horizon glows. Mystery risen out of the ocean. *Ava'utapu* leads the fleet into an endless wall of light.

'What is that?' Amon whispers. Here are the awe and terror of Exodus.

'The City of Lights,' Prime Minister Pohiva says and for an instant Amon sees glowing streets, towers, halls and boulevards afloat on the black ocean. 'The Chinese squid fleet. We picked it up on the satellite. They set out arrays of floodlights to lure squid.'

'There must be hundreds.'

'Two thousand and forty-six,' Prime Minister Pohiva says. As the fleets close the wall of light resolves into individual stars.

'Each ship puts out as much light as an English Premier League football stadium,' Pohiva says. 'It's visible from orbit. Not the Great Wall of China, it seems, but the Great Squid Fleet of China. Do you know what is interesting, Mr. Brightbourne?' The lights move, the wall parts, opening a dark channel. 'There are no squid. Wrong season, wrong current, wrong part of the ocean.'

The fleet sails between shining walls. Patrol boats and long-liners pull close, calves to their mothers.

'Why are they here then?' Amon asks.

'For us to see. We attract the world's attention. You've heard about the submarine.'

'I've heard stories.'

'It is no story. A Japanese submarine has been following us since Tokelau. The Russians will wait until the Bering Strait. The US has its satellite and spy planes. The Chinese have sent their squid fleet. None of them know what to do about us. We're the first great climate migration. A whole nation at once. An exodus. If they stop us there will be an international incident; if they let us pass there will be more of us. Many many more. Tonga, then Samoa. Vanuatu. In the end, even Fiji. Then Africa will stand up and walk. South Asia, South America. Heading north.'

At the end of the tunnel of shining ships, a rectangle of black widens into ocean.

'I don't know what I'm doing,' Amon says. 'Every day I go on, I talk to her, I talk to the Foundation, I talk to PBV, I talk to people I don't know.'

'We make it up as we go along,' Prime Minister Pohiva says. 'This, I have learned, is the Law and the Prophets.'

'That new woman, the project liaison. Nauja Lund. She seems to have some idea. She does think I'm an idiot.'

'I hear she thinks that of everyone. As you say, she seems to have an idea.'

Ava'utapu breaks into pristine darkness. Looking aft Amon sees two squid jiggers break from the ship-walls closing behind him and fall into the fleet's wake. And in one breath-taking instant the Chinese fleet goes dark, horizon to horizon.

'His Majesty Prince Siaosi Vaka'uta's consortium has decided it doesn't want to be a spaceport or a tax haven or a blockchain mill,' Prime Minister Pohiva says. 'He sold his islands to a Chinese venture-capital company.'

'The Chinese government.'

'Correct, Mr. Brightbourne. Beijing has claimed that we are now Chinese citizens. It's nonsense of course. It's simply an attempt to bully the Greenlanders. But this is the open ocean. What is the old seafarers' saying? "South of forty there is no law; south of fifty no God."'

'I'm feeling glad of that Japanese submarine now.'

'Two days to Hawaii, Mr. Brightbourne. US territorial waters.'

For the first time Amon notices that Prime Minister Pohiva's hand shakes on the rail. The backlight from the stateroom casts revealing shadows Amon has not seen before: sagging skin, pouchy eyes, tired jowls, a down-turned cast to the lips.

Amon understands the whisky now. It's his excuse, his disguise.

This is a sick man. A sick man who is afraid.

93

No one in the Inatsisartut, not the premier, not the Naalakkersuisut, not the civil servants, not the ancillary staff know how she did it but Ane Hammeken, minister for trade, foreign affairs and climate, has secured the best office in the parliament house, a corner site with views over Nuup Kangerlua to the western hills and skerries, north-east to great Sermitsiaq, sentinel of the north, still capped with snow.

This morning the minister has arranged her comfortable chairs to respect the view. On the mid-century Kofod-Larsen coffee table stand two cups and a tall, elegant pot.

'No,' says Ane Hammeken.

'I cannot work with her.'

'Yes, you can,' Ane says. 'You did. You turned Qaqortoq around.'

'I shouldn't have promised what was not mine to deliver.'

'That's why you're too good for politics, Nauja. They're getting a box-fresh multi-purpose performance space.'

'PBV branded. And now everyone from Narsaq to Nunap Isua wants a new sports centre or community hall or co-op.'

'I hear their queen is a real celebrity down there.' Minister Ane pours more coffee. Nauja lifts her hand to decline. She feels rustic and booted in the minister's curated space. Road grit in her cream carpet, soil of the southern fjords. Time turns everything into its opposite. In GU Nuuk school, at the volleyball hall, in the mini-mall and the coffee shop and the teenage hang-outs behind the piled shipping containers, Nauja had been the order-giver, the instigator, the organiser, enforcer and occasional emotional bully. That was as high as she would rise in the school hierarchy. As high as she wanted to rise. She'd seen the price of leadership. She understood the weight of a crown. Nauja Lund is content for the wing spiker she screamed at in timeout for fluffing an easy spike in the grudge match against GSS Nuuk to hold the ministerial seal and the corner office and yes the Kofod-Larsen coffee table. She is happy for her now to be the order-giver, the instigator, the organiser.

'She's young, she's smart and charisma shines out of her,' Nauja Lund

says. 'She was a fitness instructor before the coup. She understands moti-
vational.'

'The coup?'

'More an enhanced abdication,' Nauja Lund says. 'It was in your background briefing. You did read it?'

'I did.'

'All of it?'

Occasional emotional bully.

'I may have skimmed some detail.'

'The exercise is to get everyone to see each other as people. Faces, names.
Families and relatives. Shared experiences, shared stories.'

Nauja Lund sometimes thinks her greatest achievement was getting Finance to sign off on the cocaine-expensive satellite calls.

'This can work as long as everyone believes they're involved and that
they're listened to. Zero-sum is a hard mind-set to thaw. The least scent of
partiality and we're back to them and us.'

'We've identified forty disinformation sites in the past five days,' Ane
says.

'Russian.'

'Of course. We've lodged complaints, for all the good it will do. We've
moved the cabinet meeting forward to thirteen hundred. The premier
would like to sit in.'

'Of course.' She had hoped to go home for lunch and see Tuusi. She can
make out a corner of her roof behind the hill where the Hans Egede statue
used to stand. 'You won't replace me.'

'I'm less likely to change my mind now.'

'Well, then replace her.'

'Raisa Hopeland?'

'She doesn't know what she doesn't know.'

'A stýra of the Nýttnorður Foundation.'

'Move her sideways. Uninvolve her.'

'I could consider that.' Ane smiles and Nauja Lund's work is complete.

She hears the metal clear from the Mother of the Sea statue. And there
he is, in cargo shorts and sleeveless T, barefoot up on the deck bent over
the barbecue like DJ Meat at the decks of Club Carnivore. He doesn't see

her crunch up the gravel drive. It is ever the wonder that he can extricate the barbecue from the tangle of bikes, skis, outboard motors, computers and monitors and kids' slide/swing/climbing frame under the house. It never occurs to him to throw out some junk. Nothing in Nuuk ever gets thrown out, just moved further from sight. He dances to his terrible terrible metal, shuffles bare foot to bare foot. She loves to see him do it.

'Hail to the chef!'

Tuusi picks up his phone and swipes off the music. He holds up a warning finger, dashes into the kitchen. Tuusi is a big man, light on his feet. He returns with a large plate covered with a tea towel. He whisks off the towel with a magician's flourish. Two caribou steaks from last year's hunting season. He itches to be done with desk work and Nuuk and be up under the breath of the Semersauq with his brethren on this year's great hunt. He brings an ice bucket with a bottle of champagne. His left hand he holds behind his back.

'Champagne . . .' Nauja Lund begins. Tuusi produces two flutes, plastic, etched with the Air Greenland logo.

'They went for it,' Nauja Lund says.

'Pretzels to petitsfours.' He pops the champagne with the gleeful seriousness of a meteorologist launching a weather rocket and pours two glasses.

'That's . . .' Nauja Lund says.

'Real champagne. I buy real champagne now.'

They touch glasses. The soft tap of printer-fresh plastic. He carries the ice bucket to a low table between two loungers.

'Where are the kids?' Nauja asks.

'Siisi's at a party. Okak is at the Stadion with his crew, annoying the residents.' On his thirteenth birthday Okak declared that he was going to be a rapper. Over thirteen months he has put heart, talent and effort into it with a dedication that surprised his parents. He has a crew and those who know, who made the first Nuuk hip-hop scene, say he's good. On summer evenings they work moves on the sports fields at the Stadion. They're going to cut a video. He hasn't yet told Nauja and Tuusi his crew name. Tuusi drummed with a couple of metal bands and, careful though he is to uphold the rock-dad's disdain for hip-hop, he could not be more proud.

'How was the Inatsisartut?'

She takes a sip from the model glass. Real champagne. *Make it last.* Not even Air Greenland pays enough for more than one bottle of imported champagne.

'The Inatsisartut think I'm a genius.'

'And . . . that woman?'

'Raisa Peri Antares Stormtalker Hopeland. I won't be happy until she's doing promotional TikToks for outdoor pursuits in Qaqortoq.'

'Ane wouldn't move you.'

'I asked Ane to sideline her. Leave it to the professionals. You should see what they're doing down there, Tuusi.' He would love it. Machines and motion. Real heavy metal. 'Every day I wake up there's something new. The speed they work at, I can't believe it.'

'They drill into volcanoes,' Tuusi says. 'In the middle of the ocean. I believe it.' He checks the barbecue, brushes the steaks with his special marinade and sets them on the heat. Caribou gives him terrible diarrhoea but the symbolism matters. Nauja appreciates that he celebrates his achievement with her before his friends. And she is happy at his triumph. There is still not enough work in design to give up the teaching job but Nuuk is a small enough city that every time a flier takes a drink from an Air Greenland coffee cup they will know it's a Tuusi Lund design.

This evening, for a moment, they are both heroes.

'More champagne,' Nauja says, and there is, and the sea is silver, the sky clear to the edge of space, etched with the scrimshaw of transatlantic aircraft. How many are innocent, how many scrying?

She never thought this way before.

She is changing the world. She is writing history. Carving it in stone.

She never thought that before.

She sips her champagne and an old, slow glow lights in her belly and she smiles a secret, woman's smile that Tuusi, intent on his meat, can't see. Yet.

She wakes with a yell and a lunge, out of the twisted quilt, into the shower.

'I'm late!'

Tuusi looks around the bathroom door. His morning attire is the same as his evening wear: shorts, T-shirt, barefoot.

'Why didn't you wake me?' Nauja Lund shouts.

'You hate it when I wake you.'

'Did the alarm go off?' she shouts from under hot water.

'You slept right through it,' Tuusi says as she speed-scrubs her teeth. Something died in her mouth last night.

'Put some shoes on and drive me!' she shouts as she wrestles a bra over wet skin. They both hear the sound of an aircraft passing over the house.

'There'll be another one.'

'Tomorrow,' Nauja says, dressed, backpack and ruggedised laptop ready, hair in some semblance of presentable, plane gone and climbing over the sea. 'Tomorrow!'

'Didn't you say . . .'

Nauja glares at her husband. Now Okak is awake, moving around the house on a preprogrammed feeding loop. He frowns at his mother, then slides off to the refrigerator. He sleeps like a mountain and won't have heard anything coital from the bedroom. Siisi messaged to say she was sleeping over. She is the one with the sharp senses.

'Okay. This one time.'

She makes the call on the balcony. There is time for breakfast and two coffees, then Tuusi puts on shoes and, still hungover—he had most of the beer that sidled in after the champagne—drives her to the airport. He comes into the terminal because he wants to see the Foundation plane close up. Low cloud has moved in over the mountaintops, rain threatens. The tilt-prop comes out of the clouds, turns and reconfigures to land.

'That is some machine,' Tuusi says, big-eyed as a child. 'You are lucky.'

Nauja Lund says. She flashes her pass to security and the woman nods her through to the gate.

94

'And I saw a beast rise up out of the sea,' Marine Toeava whispers. 'Having seven heads and ten horns, and upon his horns ten crowns, and upon his heads the name of blasphemy.'

Murmurs, hisses, muttered invocations on the bridge of the RADF *Nafanua*. Some cross themselves.

'Enough,' Major Fia orders. The atmosphere aboard the patrol boat does not need the Book of Apocalypse and the dragon in the sea. 'Stand off and launch the drone.'

Captain Efi throttles back. The quadcopter lifts from the rear deck and steers towards the monster.

When it received the distress call the fleet diverted to assist. Hails from each of the migration ships were met with silence. Then the radar showed the size of the unresponsive object. Ava'u mobilised its defenders. Out there was a thing beyond the experience of any seafarer in the fleet. *Nafanua* and *Neiafu* took aboard the marine corps and set course. Major Fia whispered an awed *My God* at the first sighting through his binoculars.

A city hovered on the horizon—a floating city. Curtain walls, towers, masts and stacks. Roofs and staircases. The crowns of trees stood over the lower buildings. The two ships drew closer. Naked-eye close. The city rose from the ocean on massive concrete legs.

Closer still and the object shed its supernatural awe. The urban super-structure stood on six oil-production platforms fixed together into a half-kilometre-square grid. It floated unpowered in the water, drifting with the current, small waves breaking against the concrete pontoons. Birds circled over the roofs. A lot of birds. Birds and smoke.

'Sill no response, sir,' said *Nafanua*'s comms officer.

'Take us in slowly, Captain Efi,' Major Fia said.

The drone climbs the rust-stained concrete pontoon, the windowed sea-wall of residential blocks. Glimpses of interiors in taupe and ecru, glass and chrome. Exclusive art. The drone clears the top of the accommodation units and looks down into a plaza of open-air restaurants, big-brand shops, coffee kiosks, cocktail bars. Here is a street gym, here a fountain and some pleasingly bright public sculpture. A small park, a stand of trees, a garden with yoga mats.

'No churches,' says Marine Toeava.

'No children,' says Captain Efi.

'No one at all,' says Major Fia.

Not one window is intact. Not one chair, not one table stands upright. The outdoor cocktail bar is a heap of smashed glass and shredded parasols. Smoke pours from the scorched window frames of a Starbucks.

'Closer,' Major Fia orders. The drone pilot drops the quadcopter to a pavement-height hover. 'Bullet holes,' the major says. Every wall, every pillar and upright, even the pastel paving tiles are pocked with impact craters. 'Closer.' He points to the coffee shop. 'Is that a foot?'

The drone drifts into the dim interior of the Starbucks. The camera closes in on a foot in a Nike sneaker, a body bloated and blackening. Blood pooled, head a mash of bone, hair, fluid.

'I want to see what is attracting those birds,' Major Fia says. The drone drifts out into the light. A dark flash, then the camera spins through sky, tree, pretty pastel tile into snow and nothing.

'What happened?' Major Fia says.

'Something took out our drone,' Captain Efi says.

Major Fia looks long at the towering concrete hulk before him. His officers await orders.

'We go in,' he says. 'Platoon A first. Hostile boarding protocol. Platoon B stand by. Captain Efi, find us a way into this thing.'

Sergeant Anoaʻi moves to cover in the doorway of the smoking Starbucks and signals his squad to close up. Major Fia covers the end of the plaza. Smashed shop-fronts, walkways, accommodation-unit balconies, gantries, stacks. His helmet cam feeds images to *Nafanua*, his helmet HUD— the latest and last piece of technology procured for the Royal Avaʻuan Marines—gives him tactical images from *Neiafu*'s drone, hovering a kilometre overhead. He is acutely aware that he is a man in his early forties on active service with a brawl of lean, mean, superfit kids who spend all day with weights. He knows they call him Toy Soldier. Let them. He is malietoa, the queen's warrior, the only one among them to have seen active service. Helmand, 2012. Tongan, Fijian and Avaʻuan soldiers came in support of British forces. Twenty-five marines from the kingdom joined the alliance of the willing. He is the only veteran still serving. Most went to private security companies in Iraq or the US or floating arsenals in the Red Sea. Some moved to the merchant marine, or international construction. Some went to drink and prescription opioids, some to religion. Isaia lost his fine legs to an IED. Manu walked out one starry night to the blow-holes and gave himself to the ocean. He, Sosefu Fia, was years in nightmares and the roaring of memories, when the sun gave no light and people no comfort and life no warmth.

White men's wars.

'There's a working Wi-Fi network,' Comms Corporal Anesi says, scanning her helmet display.

'Password protected?'

'It is.'

Major Fia casts around among the debris of the coffee-shop floor. Among the shards of broken tile and smashed glass, the MDF splinters and the projectile casings he finds scattered business cards.

'Try this.'

She taps the alphanumeric keypad on her wrist.

'We're in.' Every coffee shop has a card with its Wi-Fi password. 'It's a kind of portal. Welcome to *Oceanea*.'

'Which is?'

More taps.

'A seastead.' She speaks in English. There is no Ava'uan word for this sea-city.

'Explain please.'

'"A sea-going independent sovereign state,"' Anesi reads. '"*Oceanea* is an experiment in alternative polities. A social and technological creative hothouse for entrepreneurship. A laboratory in human potential. Built in Panama and launched in 2032."'

'Dead and abandoned in 2033,' Major Fia says.

They find the body. The blood is hard and glossy. Corporal Anesi takes pictures and relays them back to *Nafanua*.

'Three bullet wounds,' she says. 'Looks like they finished him off with an axe.'

They find the drone, rotors broken, carapace cracked and pocked. With his combat knife Major Fia pries loose a finger-joint-long vaned needle. He comms the patrol ships.

'Call in Squad B. Hostile boarding protocol.'

A red flash on his HUD. *Neiafu*'s drone has seen something. Sergeant Anoa'i gestures the squad to cover. Fia hears the whine of drone engines. Heads turn, crane, trying to fix the shifting engine buzz without catching the attention of the drone.

The Taliban in Helmand never had air power.

The sound closes. Closes. A metre-long black drone makes a slow pass five metres above the squad. Cameras turn and fix. They are seen. The drone stops, turns to align with its cameras. Major Fia sees the barrel slung under the belly of the drone, and the fat cylinder of the magazine, like a spider with her spiderlings cocooned to her body: a flechette gun. No doubt that it's the same weapon that destroyed *Nafanua*'s drone. Its efficacy against hard targets is low. It is designed to shred human flesh. Turn a face to a bloody skull. Enhanced with VX neurotoxin, a scratch can kill. First to move will draw fire.

The drone side-slips closer.

And Marine Tuilagi is on his feet, reaching over his shoulder, roaring the battle cry of House Tuilagi of Ofu.

The flechette gun locks. Tuilagi swings, aims, fires. A Kel-Tec KSG combat shotgun gives the drone one full magazine. It comes apart in a burst of black plastic, chips and shotgun pellets. The KSG is Tuilagi's signature weapon. Still roaring, Tuilagi lunges forward to stomp the plastic scrap into crumbs.

'Marine!' Major Fia yells. Tuilagi freezes. 'As you were.' There could be razor-edged, neurotoxic flechettes among the scrap. Tuilagi flashily reloads his shotgun.

Major Fia orders Squad B to search for who or what controlled the drone. Sergeant Anoa'i moves Squad A out. Smoke and birds lead them to the bodies. They form a smouldering heap in the meditation garden. The attempt at cremation was lazy, hasty. The corpses at the centre of the pyre are char and bone, the outer ones partly burned; a right arm, a head, the upper half of a body, legs. The small enclosed spiritual space reeks of char and rot. The marines pull scarves over their lower faces. Some pray. The garden howls with flies.

Sergeant Anoa'i sets up a perimeter; Major Fia and Corporal Anesi set off to investigate and photograph.

Designer labels. Handmade shoes. None wear any jewellery. Amputated fingers and hands where rings and watches have been taken. Fia and

Anesi work steadily, rifling through blood-soaked clothing for ID. No phones, no cards. Every piece of portable wealth has been looted.

A frigate bird clatters down, waddles close to the pile of bodies, risks a stab of hooked beak at an outstretched foot. Fia kicks at it. It hops back. No eyes as predatory as the eyes of sea-birds.

A shot, another shot. Squad B has made contact somewhere out there among the pastel panels and cloud-painted screens. Rapid fire, a clip emptying. Amateurs shoot like that. A short-burst stutter of automatic. Three shots. Marines returning fire.

'Report,' Major Fia orders.

'We have a hostile down. No casualties among our forces.'

'What's the state of the hostile?'

'White male, mid-thirties. Shot at us with a handgun from a second-floor apartment. We returned fire. Multiple bullet wounds to the lower legs. He requires medical evacuation.'

'Make it so. Does *Neiafu* have the facilities to stabilise him?'

A static-filled pause.

'Major, there will be good medical facilities on this . . . habitat. Better than *Neiafu*.'

'We can't take the risk,' Major Fia says. 'Get him to the ship.'

'Major, I've found schematics,' says Anesi. 'There are panic rooms.' She flashes augmented reality maps to every HUD.

The first panic room is at the rear of a spa and gym. The gym has been comprehensively looted: only the running machines and the elliptical trainers remain. The safe room has been blasted open. Anyone sheltering inside was mashed, then incinerated. Scraps of an underwired bra, a woman's right shoe. The next haven returns no answer when the marines remove the booby-trap grenade, designed to kill anyone emerging from the panic room.

'Who builds paradise with a panic room?' Tuilagi jokes.

'This is paradise?' Toeava answers.

At the third their calls and knife-hilt knocks return a reply. A camera globe turns, a voice answers through a speaker.

'Identify.'

Major Fia steps into the camera focus, delivers his name, his rank, the nature of his service.

'Ava'u?' the voice asks.

'Identify yourself,' Major Fia says.

'I am a sovereign citizen under the law of the sea. You have no jurisdiction here. You are hostile armed forces invading the sovereign state of
Oceanea.'

'We're here to rescue you,' Major Fia says.

'Joinder must be established,' the voice says. An English-speaking man,
with an accent unfamiliar to Major Fia. 'On receipt of acceptable identification I will print out contracts for your signature and notarisation.'

'I don't have time for this,' Major Fia says in Ava'uan.

'Leave him in there,' Sergeant Anoa'i says in the same language.

'I have something on this,' Corporal Anesi says. 'Sovereign citizenship
and Freeman on the Land are some kind of extremist-libertarian pseudo-
legal thing. It doesn't see any government as legitimate. Or law, either.
They have this thing about the law of the sea.'

'Do they now?' Major Fia says. He switches back to English. 'Sir, the
law of the sea requires me to offer assistance and succour to seafarers in
distress. We are a search and rescue operation.'

After a tiresomely long silence the man says, 'I will open the door and
come out.'

'Are you alone in there?'

'The only other occupant is dead,' the voice says. 'I'm unlocking now.'

'Place your hands above your head and await permission to exit,' Major
Fia orders.

Heavy bolts shoot back behind the steel door. Locks disengage. The
door slides open. A short, middle-aged white man, starting to bald, stands
there, his hands on his head. He wears inadvisable cargo shorts, a software
company T-shirt and expensive shoes. Behind him ugly fluorescents light
the interior of the panic room glaring white. Three beds, a refrigerator,
water, a chemical toilet.

'My name is Sindri Ólafursson,' the man says. 'Can I come out now?'

95

At thirteen years old, Ema Maivia is the fiercest dance captain Amon has ever worked with. She bawls out Sam Laupepa, a prop forward from Queen 'Ana Men's First XV twice her size, for an offbeat step.

'Again,' she commands. 'Positions.' Chorus, dancers and principals run to their marks still out of breath. Amon cues up *The Room Where It Happens*, the intro horns stab, the beats arrive and four principals—three boys and a girl who has never soloed before—clasp their hands behind their backs like US eighteenth-century Founding Fathers and skate into the opening hip-hop conversation while the Deck 9 Crew assume formations and factions.

Deck 9 will win the *Ava'utapu* Junior Choir competition. No question. They have the best song. They have the best soloists. They have the best chorus. They have the best musical director in Amon Brightbourne. And they have beyond any doubt the best choreographer and dance captain in the fleet.

Interdeck, intraship competition ignited in earnest after Hawaii. Spirits broke high again. The fleet was made to anchor three kilometres outside Pearl Harbor in Mamala Bay with no one, not even the queen and her lords, allowed off the ship. Hawaii came to the fleet with news cameras and flyby drones and reporters and lifestyle-interviewers and jolly boats filled with waving, cheering sightseers from Honolulu taking pictures and trying to catch the attention of the people on the decks far above them. The evening news showed clips of women dancing, men performing the sipi tau, children singing, teams playing deck volleyball, the queen gracious and adorable and media-friendly.

We have lost our islands, she said. So we must make a new home in the north. Climate change is real.

The news reports interviewed some of the travellers.

We have lost our islands, they said. So we are going to make new homes in the north. And yes, climate change is very real.

For twenty-six hours everyone felt like a celebrity.

Then the fleet sailed around Ka'ena Point and turned north and senators from landlocked states went on the same news shows questioning who these people were, what was the legality of their migration, what was to stop them landing on US soil and disappearing into the hinterland?

Ema Maivia cracks orders to her dancers. Amon brings the chorus together into the ensemble section, makes them drop their voices to a suspicious whisper—what does happen in the Room Where It Happens?—and the gym doors burst open. Kimmie Pangaimotu marches in and bellows over the music.

'Amon Brightbourne! Council!'

'I'm kind of committed,' Amon says but the rhythm is broken. The production stops mid-step. Voices fail. The music plays a beat before Amon kills it. Ema Maivia stomps forward in a cyclone of Ava'uan invective. Amon knows enough of the language to be impressed and intimidated. Kimmie Pangaimotu draws herself up to her considerable height and waits out the storm with fakaleiti hauteur.

'Amon. With me.'

'This has better be important,' Amon says.

'Bloody important, 'ofa'anga.' Amon's long legs can barely keep up with her in the corridors. People press themselves to the walls. Children dart back into cabins. 'We found someone.'

'What? Found who; where?'

In the elevator now.

'He claims he knows you. Well, not you; someone you both know.'

The doors open onto Deck 13.

'Again, who?'

Kimmie hurries Amon across the Atrium to the Kraken's Lair dance bar.

'Raisa Hopeland.' Kimmie taps a key code.

'You locked the doors.'

'Talk to him, Amon.'

'You locked the doors. Is he dangerous?'

'Get to know him. You've got the connection.'

Kimmie opens the nightclub door to a barrage of disco lights. Movers, arrays, chasers, colour changers. The glitter ball scatters dazzle spots around the room. Directly under it a small man in cargo shorts and software company T-shirt sits on the DJ booth steps.

'I turned them on and couldn't turn them off again. Silly.' He gets up. He is barefoot. He advances hand out.

'Hello, Amon. I'm Sindri. I believe you know my fine friend Raisa Peri Antares Hopeland.'

'He corroborates Major Fia's report,' Amon says. The Council of Voyagers has found a temporary venue for this extraordinary meeting in the Hogwarts World of Wizarding Book Nook on Deck 10. The walls of books remind Amon of comforting wet February Sundays at Brightbourne. No hidden doors in this library. Even with a third of the council virtually present there is barely room for members, queen and honorary consul. Kimmie Pangaimotu waits outside, directing young readers to go and make a noise or play a game or something; anything active. 'Reem Al-Waleed caught one of her private security guards stealing. There was a scene, he shot her; the guards turned on their employers. They shot everyone, attacked them with axes, looted what they could. Burned the rest. Sindri didn't see everything, otherwise he wouldn't be here.'

'The other man we brought back?' Lady Tupua asks. 'The one we shot.'

'Regrettably, he didn't survive,' Major Fia says.

Small prayers from around the low children's table.

'Hands and fingers missing?' Prime Minister Pohiva asks. 'Eyeballs gouged out?'

'Biometric identification,' Amon answers. 'Access to cryptocurrency accounts.'

'And they're out there?' Queen Ta says.

'They took the ancillary craft and fled the sea-habitat,' Major Fia says.

'Do they threaten the kingdom?' Queen Ta asks.

'They are heavily armed with automatic weapons and small arms,' Major Fia says. 'We have the advantage in heavy weapons. They have numbers. They could swarm us. If we lose any of the patrol boats, the fleet is in grave danger.'

'Do we know where they are?' Lord Vaea of Niua asks from his ship.

'The bridge reports nothing on our radars,' Major Fia says. 'There is a risk to our fishing fleet. The raiders are in small boats with limited range. They will need to make a landfall or take a boat with longer range.'

'Call the fishers back into the protective envelope of our patrol boats,' Prime Minister Pohiva orders. The cabinet concurs, the command is relayed.

'We need to talk with this Sindri Ólafursson,' Queen Ta says. 'Thank you, Major. Amon, please stay.'

Kimmie brings Sindri to the Book Nook with the air of a torture queen from an HBO fantasy series.

'Please accept our apologies for your accommodation,' Queen Ta says. 'We are pressed for space.'

Sindri takes one of the child-height seats next to Amon. Council and Crown sit with knees almost under chins. Farcical yet potent.

'I owe an eternal debt to Your Majesty and the people of Ava'u for rescuing me,' Sindri says. 'You are my salvation.'

Lady Tupua raises an eyebrow. Sindri knows what words ring with Ava'uan washed with the language of the Bible.

'You are our guest,' Queen Ta says.

'You have been through a dreadful experience,' Prime Minister Pohiva says. 'We would appreciate it if we could hear in your own words. The nation may be under threat.'

'Of course,' Sindri says. He looks at Amon Brightbourne across the library table. 'First, if I might? I have a proposal.'

'He's a cunt.' Raisa's voice booms on the Dolby surround sound. She stands three times life-size in 4K glory on the big screen in the Movietime cinema. Goddess of the North. 'An archcunt.'

'I haven't told you his proposal,' Amon says.

'He offered me a place on that seastead,' Raisa says. She stands on a fresh-wood porch, the pine rail behind her oozing sap from its knot marks. 'I called it the USS *Apocalypse*.'

'Prophetic,' Amon Brightbourne says.

'What did he offer you?' A breeze from off the fjord moves Raisa's hair. Amon notices that he notices it.

'He'd set up a trust, like the Foundation. He'd work alongside the Foundation. He'd make South Greenland . . .'

'Kujalleq,' Raisa interrupts.

'Kujalleq some kind of . . . digital Singapore. Only not crypto. Blockchain. Kind of a blockchain freeport powered by hydro. I don't completely understand what he means. But he still has money.'

'He'll always have money. It's what Sindri's about. Crypto, blockchain;

resource-intensive pseudowork. Also, Kalaallit hydro is not renewable. It's fossil fuel. That glacier melt don't come back.'

'It's melting anyway,' Amon says.

'That's what Sindri'd say.'

'You're saying don't trust him?'

'I'm saying trust Sindri to make money. His foundation will be a success. What it leaves behind; well, that's somethin' else.'

Amon hears her relax into her old London speech. Time circles back to the garden of the Dorling Avenue house. Her in the beautiful dress as blue as eternity. Red tights. Red and blue again when Queen Ta and the Naalakkersuisut met.

'Do you trust him?'

'I told you what it was like when we were partners,' Raisa says.

'I'll inform the cabinet. Thank you.'

'Amon.'

He steps back into the camera focus.

'Let's do dinner.'

His heart veers like a kite.

'I eat in a canteen,' he says.

'Take it to your room. On a tray.'

'What about the time difference?' Scuffling objections. 'I mean, what is it? Eight hours? When it's supper time for me, it's breakfast for you. Supper time for you is breakfast for me. Maybe lunch . . .'

She smiles, shakes her head with old familiarity.

'What?' Amon says.

'You said supper.'

'And?'

'We sit at screens; we watch each other eat. Whenever. It's just an idea.'

'I'd love to.'

'It's a date, tweed-boy.'

He's twenty-seven again. Amy Winehouse sings *Love Is a Losing Game* and the smoke of burning London rises.

'One thing,' he says. 'How are you with geckos?'

96

Thrusters engage. The Ava'uan migration fleet, thirteen ships in close sailing order across five kilometres, puts blue water between itself and *Oceanea*. Marines disposed of the bodies. Engineers tagged the hulk with beacons. The US Coast Guard at Honolulu has surveyed the ghost with a Global Hawk HUAV. National Security cutters *Kimball* and *Midgett* sail to take command of the seastead and secure the sea area. The mutineers are still out there. The Japan Self-Defence Force submarine *Toryu*, now in regular and friendly communication with *Ava'utapu*, reports no contact or sightings of the pirates' small craft. No response from the Chinese squid-fisher spy ships.

The concrete piers descend beneath the horizon, then the pastel-coloured superstructure. The fleet's last sight of *Oceanea*, hope of liberty and entrepreneurship, laboratory for new ways of living human, is the halo of sea-birds.

Ahead rolling black, yellow-edged clouds mark the cyclonic zone where the North Pacific High spills into the Aleutian Low. Bruises and primroses; a liminal place, a zone of transition. The cloud-gates of the north. Beyond lie new waters, new skies, new climates.

Queen Elisiva Ta'ahine Tu'i receives Sindri Ólafursson in her Deck 15 corner captain's suite. Beyond her floor-length windows the edge of the world crawls with lightning. Kimmie Pangaimotu takes her place behind her Queen and stands with righteous haughtiness.

'Mr. Ólafursson, please take a seat.'

'Thank you, your Majesty.'

'"Ma'am" is fine. May I offer you something to drink?'

'Coffee would be lovely, thank you ma'am.'

'We're not a great coffee culture, Mr. Ólafursson, but we'll try our best. Kimmie?'

Small talk is the demesne of queens. Sindri matches Ta's nicety with nicety, politeness for politeness. He leaves the coffee half-drunk.

'Mr. Ólafursson, your proposal.'

'I'm excited to hear your decision,' Sindri says.

'Don't be. I have to disappoint you, Mr. Ólafursson. The Council of Voyagers has discussed your proposal. We've taken advice and we reject it. It is not in the best interests of the nation.'

'I'm sorry, ma'am. I must have failed to communicate adequately the benefits for you. I may have been a little traumatised. If I might be permitted to talk to the council? Better still, if I could address the people directly? A popular vote, perhaps . . .'

'Ava'u is a monarchy, Mr. Ólafursson.'

'Of course, ma'am, but before anything else, it's a community. Community is what keeps these ships sailing. Community is what holds you together. Community is the one thing of Ava'u you will take to the Greenland shore. If I could talk to the community, as a community . . .'

'We have made our decision, Mr. Ólafursson,' Queen Ta says. 'Also, you'll be staying with the leiti Kimmie in her stateroom. And Mr. Brightbourne. One or the other will accompany you around the ship.'

'Am I under house arrest?'

'You'll be our guest until we resupply in the Aleutian Islands.'

'You're going to maroon me on the Aleutian Islands?'

'You've got money,' Kimmie says. 'You can get yourself flown out. I'm not thrilled about having you as a houseguest.'

'Were you talking to Raisa Hopeland?' Sindri says. 'You can't trust anything she says about me. We have history.'

'I won't answer that, Mr. Ólafursson,' Queen Ta says. She rises from the sofa. Kimmie clears her throat to prompt Sindri to observe protocol. 'Now, I have to judge a singing contest. You can come with me or Kimmie will take you to her room.'

'I love singing contests,' Kimmie hisses in Sindri's ear.

'I'll come.'

'Wise choice,' Queen Ta says.

'Amon was right,' Kimmie says in Ava'uan. 'He is a cunt.'

Ema Maivia and her Deck 9 Crew storm the contest with their number from *Hamilton*. Ema receives her trophy from the hand of the queen herself and immediately hands it back. It's needed for next week's Interdeck

Adult Choir contest. The roar of applause in the Dancetime Ballroom, Ema's sheer excitement and the spontaneous dancing come that fraction too late to drown out Sindri's comment of *Well, the master of the queen's music wins the song contest.*

The celebratory dancing and singing continue well past school-night bedtime. Past good-living folks' bedtime. Past any bedtime.

Thirty kilometres due south, twelve small craft appear out of the night, attack and board the two Chinese spy ships. They kill everyone aboard and take control. The two squid boats steer west for the Midway Islands. The submarine *Toryu* intercepts the Chinese distress call and turns back to pursue.

97

Dozens of times she's made this. Hundreds, maybe. She knows the proportions, the timings, the temperatures in her fingertips, in her toes and knees, like a dance. She has brilliant ingredients; she has the necessary ratio of slapdash to precision; so why is she as fretful as a kite in a thunderstorm?

Raisa has a dinner guest. It's a date. Maybe more salt? Extra chillies? Coriander: the veg crate gave her a pot of growing coriander.

She reaches for the knife. Pulls back from the vile herb. Coriander madness.

And there's just enough time for her to change into her dinner clothes and be downstairs to turn on the heat and welcome her guest.

Nauja Lund stands on the threshold, coated, booted, new Naalakkersuisut hard hat under one arm, in the other a bottle.

'I've brought water.'

'Royal Ava'u.'

'Rare now.'

Nauja Lund sheds boots, hat, outerwear and arranges them neatly. She smells of the sea and a softly spicy perfume Raisa can't place. The table is laid; set by the window for light and something to look at that is not each other. Late-summer flowers in a water jug.

She pours two glasses of Royal Ava'u.

'How did you get this?'

'We are not without sophistication in Nuuk.' Nauja Lund takes an uncomfortable sip. 'That smells good.' Raisa recognises the peace offer.

'Hopeland stew. Like our national dish?'

'Raisa, sometimes I have difficulty making you out. You talk so fast; you leave words out . . . Was that a question?'

'Rhetorical.' Raisa opens the lid of the Dutch oven. 'And on-purpose ambiguous. Sorry.' Hopeland stew should smell of Hearth, it should smell of history. It should smell of stars. Tonight it smells of deliberate exoticism, of the casual thoughtlessness of a woman who can fly crates of vegetables in from Iceland on a whim. She ladles out two bowls. 'In our tradition, you don't need rice or pasta or bread. And you eat it with a spoon.'

Nauja Lund lifts her spoon, sets it down again.

'There is something I must say. I know you invited me here to clear things between us. We have not started well. We grate on each other. What we have to do here is too important for that. Let's not eat on a disagreement.'

'Go on.'

'Why did you tell Amon Brightbourne to reject Sindri Ólafursson's offer?'

'Sindri's toxic. He would wreck everything we're working for here. He'd turn this place into some incest-child of Dubai, Singapore and Las Vegas.'

'Some might consider that a good thing.'

'I know Sindri.' Raisa levels the Spoon of Accusation at Nauja. 'I was Sindri's business partner for twelve years. I didn't tell Amon to reject him. I told him what I told you.'

'Please, Raisa. I agree with you. The Naalakkersuisut agrees with you. The point is that we weren't consulted.'

'It was personal. A private opinion.'

'Amon is the father of your son, I know. Raisa, there is no private in this. We are not private people now. You had your chat, Amon Brightbourne went to the Council of Voyagers and Sindri Ólafursson is being put off at the Aleutian Islands.'

'Good.'

'You are entirely unrepentant,' Nauja Lund says.

'This may be a Lutheran country but I'm no Lutheran. We have our own religion. It doesn't do repentance.'

Nauja Lund looks at her like a curious, ground-dwelling bird. She picks up her spoon again.

'I've said what needed to be said. We should eat, this will get cold.'

'Not yet,' Raisa says. 'I haven't said what needs to be said. You make me feel everything I do is wrong. You make me doubt everything.'

Nauja Lund blinks.

'I do?'

'You make me feel stupid.'

'A woman of your accomplishments is not stupid. How can I put this?' Her mouth twitches. 'You're not afraid.'

'There are nineteen thousand people out in the sea, there's millions going into this, billions into the PBV energy scheme and I'm not afraid?'

'Afraid of failure, yes. Of something unforeseen going wrong. You're not afraid of death. That every time you step out of your door, your world may kill you. Raisa, every one of us grows up with that fear. The cold. The sea. Food, power. Helicopter crash, medical emergency . . . One failure could kill me. Out of that fear grows respect. Our universe is stubborn and implacable and what we have we negotiate from it. You have success, wealth, security, a hearth and your own gods wherever you are. Your world insulates you from fear. Ours brings it into our homes and teaches us to live with it.'

'Can I learn it?'

'You can only be it,' Nauja Lund says. 'When you are, you'll know. Now we should eat.'

'It's supposed to be eaten warm, not hot,' Raisa says. The temperature is right but the flavour is off. The vegetables taste of air-travel, the water that went into the sauce has made the consistency different, the heat is electricity not gas and these are not her knives.

'Is this chicken?'

'Lab-grown chicken,' Raisa says brightly. They eat the Hopeland stew. They drink the bottle of Royal Ava'u Water. Night falls and weather moves in and Nauja talks about her family: Siisi, the brilliant, directionless daughter, bored with the sixty streets of small-town Nuuk. Okak, the hip-hop son, bright and running at a dozen things at once. Tuusi: teacher, designer, fierce hunter. Raisa talks about Atli, independent teenager in the yellow house in Vonland, how Hopeland children have their own gender before they choose to be boys or girls or something else, how Atli moved the Hopeland way forward and has two genders, one young male, the other entirely hés own. Nauja Lund tells Raisa about the Nunavut Inuit sipiniit who change physical sex at birth but retain their prenatal gender through life, which leads to the Ava'uan fakaleitis and their position in Queen Elisiva's monarchy which prompts Raisa to mention that Amon Brightbourne says she likes to be called Queen Ta which loops her back to Nauja Lund's scolding. Then Nauja Lund looks at her phone and says it's late, I should, and Raisa doesn't dissuade her but neither does Nauja Lund hurry to get her boots and hi-viz and hard hat. They say good-nights and it's-been-goods. Raisa closes the door and hears the sound of vomiting from the street.

Raisa tastes a spoon-tip of now-cold Hopeland stew. Nothing wrong, nothing off. An acquired taste, then. It'll do for lunch with Amon tomorrow.

98

At twenty-three minutes of twenty-three Atli sets out from the Foundation house on Noorlernut. Hés instructions are clear. Hé may take only left turns. Hé may not bring any iron, steel or magnetic material with him. If anyone asks where hé is going hé must lie.

There are few in the sixty streets at this hour but those that are pause and turn at the vision flowing past them. Angel, demon, anirniq returning to the sea, avenging tupilaq. A pickup stops, reverses. Camera flash. Voices—not threatening. Questioning. Hé doesn't speak Kalaallisut and so doesn't have to lie.

Hé knows the location, a new-build industrial unit on the road east of the marina. Royal blue. Five minutes from the house, twice that walking widdershins. The cliff above Poorsimat shields the small boats from the most ruthless winds but any night at twenty-three of twenty-three there is breeze enough to rattle the sheets and draw organ chords from the piled sea containers. Hé pulls up the hood of hés wrapper to protect hés hair from the squalls of sleety rain.

Hé feels the thrum of power through the handle of the small white door. Hé grins.

Work cubicles and small offices occupy the public front of the warehouse. Atli smells new wood new cement new glass new paint new floor tiles new floor-tile adhesive. And more: the seaside, funfair, subway bristle of ionisation. Hé slides open the doors to the warehouse and steps through. Four electrode spheres mark out a large square sanctum. At the centre stands a Tesla coil crowned in flowing blue corona discharge. A man stands before the coil, hooded, silhouetted against the Tesla-shine.

'Whom has the lightning called?' the man shouts.

The coil ripples with power. Atli feels the electrolytes in hés blood sharpen. Hé feels magic.

'Atli Raisasbur Vega Hopeland. Stormtalker!'

Hé throws back hés hood, lets the wet wrapper fall.

'What do you want, Atli Vega?'

Hé steps forward, tall and lithe in compression gear and boots from which hé has assiduously removed all metal. Hé spent hours training hés hair into stiff braids at the back of his head, twining like tentacles. Hé thinks of them as earth-currents, hés connection to the planetary electrical field, expressed from hé in the white lightning hé painted down the left side of hés face, neck, body, down to hés left little toe. As below, so above.

'To be an Arcmage,' Atli says and the theatre gets hé, gets hé in the throat, in the belly, in the eyes.

'Welcome, paduan,' Finn says and pushes back his hood. 'Enter the circle and we will start on the way.'

The arc dies. The sole light in the windowless warehouse is the blue plasma shine of the toroid. Two days earlier Atli saw the container unship from the Royal Arctic Line. He opened the container to find the tightly lashed crate inside. He guided the forklift into the warehouse. He pushed the dolly bearing the crate into this space. Finn took over then and in a fairy-tale day and a night turned a dockside warehouse into a Temple of Boom!

Atli steps close enough to the coil to feel the down on hés face stir. Primal light.

Hé rubs his eyes.

'It itches.'

'The big coil throws off quite a bit of EM. UV to X-ray,' Finn says. 'I've got eye drops. They help. I'd get some after-sun on your face too.'

Sunburn in Greenland.

'So how do you?'

Finn taps his left eyeball with a distinct click of fingernail.

'Lenses.'

'I like that,' Atli says, though right now the thought of anything touching hé eyes is torment. 'With demon-irises. Or flames.'

'Lesson two.' Finn points at the yellow-and-black foot-switch between his paratrooper boots. 'The scram button.' He stamps on it and the coil dies. Atli blinks in the sudden paint-stenchy darkness. 'Hall lights,' Finn commands and fluorescents stammer up, tube by ugly tube. 'It kills the coil completely and, more importantly, safely.'

'Will I need it?'

'If you do, you do. Okay, let's get you started.' Another command lights up a small room at the office end of the warehouse.

'Ah,' Atli says pointing at the coil. 'Aren't we . . .'

'The big coil?' Finn says. 'You'd toast yourself, paduan. Lot to learn before I let you near the Great Coil.' Finn leads him into a side office. 'This is the lightning lab.' Cold neon glares from Ikea desks, shelves, storage crates. Unassembled flat packs lean against the wall. The room smells of MDF and packing cardboard. Extension leads cable-tied together run along the angle between floor and whitewashed concrete-block wall. Power tools, charging docks. Spools of steel wire. A long wooden dowel wound with the same wire, pliers, bolt cutters but what draws Atli, charge to charge, is the coil on the desk by the window to the main warehouse. A hand-high half-dumb-bell stands on a plastic box of electronics. Atli crouches, eye to toroid.

'This one . . .'

'That one. First . . .' Finn takes a phial from a desk drawer and throws it to Atli. Eye drops. 'And these.' Next across the room come a pair of proper steampunk goggles. Smoked-glass lenses, leather.

'Safety first, safety last, safety always.'

Atli doses and dons goggles.

'Okay,' Finn says. 'Three-stage power up. Scram first.' Atli finds the socket in the scram button and pushes the power cable home. 'Power switch.' Atli hesitates over the small rocker switch on the back of the electronics box. Respect the coil. It is not a toy. It contains elemental forces. Atli taps the switch.

'I can feel it,' hé whispers. This is more than the resonance of body fluids. Every cell in hés body polarises. Hés DNA realigns. Hé has a field; hé has a cardinal direction. Hé is wired into the world-lines of electromagnetic force. Hé understands hés name now.

'You can see it too.' Finn orders out the lights. Ions shine in the darkness, a pale blue nimbus around the head of the tiny coil. 'Reach out to it.'

'What?'

'It won't hurt you. Once afraid of a Tesla coil always afraid of a Tesla coil.'

Atli reaches hés right hand to the toroid. Sprigs of lightning spring to hés chromium-glossed fingernails. Hés grinning face lights blue. The reflecting lenses of hés goggles dance with Tesla-light. Hé wiggles hés fingers and the arcs follow. A single pointing finger, a single flickering line of power; God creating human. Atli Stormtalker touching the universe.

'It kind of . . . prickles,' Atli says. 'Like when you put a triple-A up your cock-slit.' Which he did, in the Burs' House, one long winter night, with Tekla assisting. 'Can I touch it?'

'What do you think?'

It would be like seeing an orca inside a wave and needing to stroke it.

'I don't have to.'

Hé shuts hés hand into a fist.

'Power down,' Finn says. Atli hears satisfaction in his voice. Atli turns off the power. The fluorescents come back on. 'Armour. You need chain-mail. Arcmages make their own armour.'

'I'm pretty sure Raisa didn't.'

'Raisa did not. That's because Raisa is privileged and lazy and leads a charmed life.'

Atli cocks hés head.

'That's true.'

'She'd never have finished it. You'll finish this, link by link. It will be slow and it will be laborious and I advise gloves. Conjunctivitis is bad, conjunctivitis and blisters are worse.'

Finn slides a coil of tight-wound steel wire off the wooden former. With the bolt cutters he snips off four rounds. The steel hoops bounce and ring on the desktop.

'Four-way link,' Finn says. 'It's the basic stitch for chain-mail.'

Atli pulls on a glove.

'I got a question, Finn.'

Finn pauses, rings and pliers in hand.

'It's kind of personal . . . I noticed it in Iceland but I didn't ask. Those marks on your face and hands. The pattern is like those rings in your hand there. Did you get too close to a coil?'

Finn sets his matériel down.

'I got too close to something. Okay. In the kitchen. This is a story for beer.'

99

He tells no one of his coming but the house knows and opens the way for him.

The dust is higher, the potholes in the drive deeper than he remembers. He stops where the conifers give way to broad-leaf wood and a clear space overlooks the meadow. Two sets of goalposts cast early-evening shadows over the browning grass. A dog chases a ball across the parched pitch. The woods are dusty-leaved and tattered in end-of-summer heat and ring with birds. Songs from France, from North Africa, from Spain; birds driven north by the changes, singing through Broighter Wood. The birds, then the people. Then him. He focuses his hearing: a woman calling her dog. A tractor. Wind in leaves. A transatlantic aircraft. Under all: the tintinnabulum.

The Music still plays.

He orders the car to stop again where the track forks to house and outbuildings. The only thing he recognises from the old stable-yard is the walnut tree. Walnuts keep flies away, Auberon used to say. When he lived here these were rotting masonry, roofs stark as ribs, door and windows open-eyed and -mouthed. Here stands a village, longhouses around courtyards, two-level galleries, steep rain-shedding roofs shiny with solar panels. Basketball hoops, a Toyota up on breeze blocks, swags of drying laundry. People at tables, with evening meals. Potted Mediterranean trees. Kids on bikes burst from a court to escort him to the house.

Chatelaine Lorien waits in the porch. At her side, Lisi, and the kid, Nanerl. Two middle-aged men, one tall, one short, hairless and piratical. He remembers them from Auberon's Speedforth. Didn't they build everything? Partners, kids, faces.

A call from above. Morwenna looks down from the porte cochère, a canny bird leaning on two hiking poles.

He adjusts his mask and slowly climbs out of the car.

Everything is slow and breathless now.

Two of the bike escorts rush to help with the oxygen tank.

Hadley has returned to Brightbourne.

He is given his old room and an entourage of kids. It's as familiar as an old piano. The old four-poster, the ship that each night set sail for morning. The aged chapel harmonium. He tries out the keys but the pedals cost too much breath to pump. Ghost suits in the wardrobe. Some might fit him again, now. Airfix model tanks on the dressing table: Churchill, T34 and Tiger, quad and howitzer, Bren Carrier. The tanks have lost their barrels and tracks. Dust is engrained deep in the detail. Cardboard boxes of paperbacks: Bond, the kink of Modesty Blaise, the Lensman books with Chris Foss covers. Further down the stratigraphy, Moomintroll, *The Phantom Tollbooth*. He grins at Molesworth. He finds himself on the wall: with Auberon on the UFO Terrace. What's that in the trees? Amidst the mechanisms of the Music. In swim trunks by a pool on the Broighter Burn, captured in deep boy-play. Maps, family trees, newspaper cuttings, framed and yellowed. There's a baffling scorched patch on the carpet in front of the windows and similar marks on the curtains. What's with the half-melted poker by the fireplace? The mill pool has been cleared. Evening light lengthens beyond Slieve Gallion.

What is that, in the wood?

A dog barks.

The entourage waits outside his door. It becomes obvious that Hadley's exploration of his room will outlast their patience so they bip his phone to bip them back when he needs them. He falls asleep on the bed high as a plateau and wakes, jangled with the easy confusion of age, fifteen minutes before dinner.

Bip, team.

The kids help him with a dandy suit from the wardrobe, help his feet into the country brogues, help him lug the oxygen tank, help him down the Infanta Staircase. They are loud creatures of many colours; more fae than human. Indwelling spirits of Brightbourne, not quite girls not quite boys. Just kids.

The candles are lit, the dogs under the table and dinner guests gathered. The air is divinely still, the candle flames burn tall and unwavering. Every head turns at a sound no one expected to hear: a quadruped tip-tap-tip-tap, the sound of two hiking sticks and two dress heels on the Infanta Staircase.

Morwenna, descending to earth.

Hadley's entourage flurries to help her and is greeted with a bellow.

'I can do it my fucking self!'

Morwenna allows the kids to settle her on a chair and rest her sticks against the wall. She jabs an imperious finger at her wine glass. Only when she has tasted the wine and signalled for the glass to be filled does she circle her finger to signal that dinner may start.

Small plates arrive and are replaced as they pass up and down the table and empty. This is a feast of many hands, many cuisines. Hadley likes this eating, manifold and generous and spun out over hours. The type he is used to in Spain. Yes, he's come from the Sierra de Guadarrama but he's lived in many houses: the Balearics of course, the green north, Catalonia—too expensive. Andalusia—too hot. Madrid—too Madrid. Every year is a burning year now. He watched the fire line move north, season by season. His heart broke to see the pine forests burning. The sky turned orange. Ash rained for ten days. He can't get the smoke out of his lungs.

No, that's not the reason for the COPD.

The samples still bring in money. Someone's always discovering them in other people's music and the licensing wheel turns. He had quite a name in ring-tones, when people used to phone. His entire career has been in bitty bits of things. Pass the fattoush.

The plates circle, the voices flow, the wine pours and the Emanations and constellations rise and wheel over Brightbourne.

100

After dinner Hadley and Morwenna shuffle to the ballroom. He opens the piano, tests the tuning. He stashes his tank under the stool, pats the plump leather to invite Morwenna to join him. She sits with the slow, heavy care of, say, a crane lowering a Tesla coil into a rooftop sanctum. The wallpaper peels a little further, the paradise birds fade a little paler.

'Play me something,' Morwenna says.

Hadley lifts long fingers to the keys. His left hand beats out the ostinato of one of his proudest compositions, a piece of production music that has featured in two hundred shows and ads worldwide.

'Something proper.'

He segues seamlessly into *I Wish I Knew How It Would Feel To Be Free*. On the third variation he becomes distressed, his breath shallow and tight.

'Help,' he whispers, never dropping a semiquaver. Morwenna holds the mask to his face. When he has finished the final, triumphant recapitulation, she slips the straps over his head, straightens them against his long wizard's hair. The late-August moon rises over Broighter Wood and he plays by its light. Morwenna listens, head bowed, eyes closed. When he has finished she rests her hand on his.

'You're back to die, aren't you?'

'I am.' He picks out a right-handed theme that has just come to him. 'I won't be that long.'

'You want to get it done before the rainy season,' Morwenna says. 'It's bloody miserable.'

His laugh turns to a choked spasm.

'Can't even fucking laugh now.' A second theme. Something there. 'I had to see the house.' And the house creaks, clicks, cracks for him. 'Lorien's done good.'

'It's alive. Too alive for me. Kids everywhere. But the house likes it.'

'I'll try not to trash it.'

'Better make it quick then.'

Another half-laugh.

'You terrible woman.'

A shadow across the moon, something vast and dark and silent passing over the house. In its wake the air in the dark ballroom is changed; lighter, differently ionised. Night-scented.

'I know how the trick's done.'

'It took you this long?'

'The late nineties.'

'Yet you stayed away.'

'In my life, believe me, you learn when you're not welcome.'

'It was our lore. Women's magic. The Grace and the Price. All the way back. We have to keep the house safe.'

'From feckless Brightbourne men.'

'Oh darling, you'd have charmed it away. Run it down, forgotten about it. Lost it.'

'We shouldn't have lied to Amon.' A third theme appears. Hadley tries out variations. 'About the Price.'

'It was lies,' Morwenna says.

'Whoever tells the first lie wins.'

Now Hadley combines his three themes, adds bass notes.

'I'd love to see Amon.' Lorien told him over dinner of the adventures of the Ava'uan migration fleet. It can be followed on any shipping-tracker app.

'His son was here,' Morwenna says. 'Just after New Year. What was his name?'

'Atli Raisasbur Vega Stormtalker Hopeland,' Hadley says. Eleven years since Hadley and Atli met in this house, at another dying time. 'Is he Graced?'

'He will always have family he will always be loved he will always have somewhere to go he will always be a man.'

'I wonder if it was working all those years to bring Brightbourne and Hopeland together. Make something new.'

'Mystical shit, Hadley.'

'I am mystical shit. Listen. Maybe he's like the power chord at the end of *Quadrophenia*.'

'Rockism, darling.'

'Hear me out. For once.'

She smiles.

'The central conceit—that Jimmy the Mod's personality is divided into four parts—is bollocks. But everything that was great about the Who is in that album.'

'I have to point out that it should be "Quadroph*r*enia".'

'Each part of Jimmy corresponds to a member of the Who and every band member has a leitmotif and it's all very rock opera. At the end of *Love, Reign O'er Me*, there are nine chords and one immense power chord. And it ends. I always thought that final chord was the four parts of Jimmy coming together. In a titanic crash of sound.' He picks out the song's synth arpeggio. 'Atli is that power chord. Everything comes together. All forces reconciled. History ends.' He bangs out the massive chord, full pedal. 'I should point out that I am on some pretty steep medication.' The chord fades into the paradise wallpaper, the stained glass in the French windows, the plasterwork birds in the ceiling. 'Or maybe it begins.'

'Can you still remember Debussy?' Morwenna asks.

'My memory's not the problem.'

'Fuck the Who. Play me Debussy.'

101

Mist condenses on his mask with every inhalation and evaporates as he breathes out. Dew trickles down the oxygen tank, drips from the tubes. The air is a dank, unbreathable oily fug. Lorien flits from gear train to drive belt, hammer array to chime bar, goddess of carillon and tintinnabulum in hiking boots, fleece, baseball cap, oiling, adjusting with doll's workshop spanners and screwdrivers, slipping new-milled cogs onto spindles, stripping and replacing a wire, throwing an entire section of clockwork orchestra onto a backup drive train as she removes a section for maintenance. She too has an entourage of young people to pass her tools, hold sections in place, follow her directions to small jobs of daily upkeep, take the pieces she has dismantled to the tool shop with her precise instructions. Pupils, apprentices, disciples. Brightbourne surges with young life. Lysander's Music needs a constant flow of water and a constant flow of lives to play its thousand-year score. The Music declares faith in a future.

Lysander brought him here age nine, when this was a mouldy, cobwebbed outhouse clogged with 1940s hydroelectric engineering. His father described something to him, hands dancing, eyes brilliant, face ecstatic, trying to make him see beyond the coils, the turbines, the heavy iron bracings. He watched the work through his father's long absences, the hammering, the angle irons, the arc-light behind the cracked glass. When Lysander did return, his visits were intense inspections of the project interspersed with all-night planning sessions in the library. Hadley, heir of things beyond his comprehension, came to the meetings. Table lamps, raised voices, his father's endless exasperation. Cheques signed.

Tens turned to teens and Hadley understood the absences and what was happening in the old hydro-house. Then his time came to leave Brightbourne, powered by music through the twilight of punk into the midnight neon of Blitz and technopop. Here was a music that had a place for a boy from the Big House in a forgotten corner of Ireland. You could come from anywhere with the right eyeliner, the right Fairlight riff. He bought a keytar. He still has it. He brought it with him the day the Music lived. He can see clearly his father giving interviews to a press, radio and television that had no idea what he was talking about, that saw a rural eccentric with a colourful past who might make an interesting three minutes on the local evening bulletin. Then his father waved the signal flag and up at the pond Hadley cranked open the sluice and ran to beat the water into the hydro-house. The air filled with mist and spray from untested joints. His father ducked under drive belts, sidestepped the spinning weights of governors, tightening connectors, freeing stuck movements, tapping reluctant mechanisms with a small upholstery hammer. The hydro-house shuddered to its bottommost brick. A flywheel spun up; a weight rose. Like a clock chiming the hour, entrained mechanisms turned, meshed, cascaded upwards into more complex devices. Lysander Brightbourne, face prophetic with ardour, pointed to the ceiling. A hammer pulled back and struck a bell, six times. The final note hung, then the hydro-house came to life in chimings, tinklings, flutings, bellings. Music emerged from the cacophony: a perpetuum mobile, circling, exploring.

'A thousand years!' Lysander shouted over the cacophony. 'A millennium of music!'

After the cameras and reporters left, Hadley remained in the hissing, chiming damp, listening until he heard the change. The first variation was complete. When he entered the brick it had been bright noon. When he closed the door behind him it was early evening.

On that same spot on the wet iron grille, in the spray and the rainbows where sun strays through the high, dirty windows, he watches Lorien tend the Music. She has not aged since he last saw her. As if every day working with the Music, its vibrations and harmonics entered her DNA and wound it like a spiral watch-spring.

'We're done here!' Lorien calls through the spinning notes.

'I'll come up in a bit,' Hadley shouts back. She shoos out her entourage and leaves Hadley alone with the Music. He listens deep, pushing through the cycles within cycles, the loops and canons, hoping to hear a change. His father's manuscript—more almanac than score—has the variations timelined for the next thousand years but Hadley likes the idea of synchronicity, stumbling into the right place, like observing a rare bird in the wild. Fifty-two years the water has run from under the mountain, the gears turned, the hammers risen and fallen, the bells spoken. The perpetuum mobile which began that August noon still wheels through its first iteration.

Fifty-two years and he hasn't heard the opening measure.

Hadley takes an autumnal pleasure in that.

He messages his entourage to help him on the mossy steps. The sun has set behind the shoulder of Slieve Gallion and the sky is streaked with purpling cirrostratus.

102

Light wakes him.

The wrong light, at the wrong time, from the wrong quarter. It blazes through the gap in the curtains, throws a slab of brightness across the worn carpet, bisects a discarded shoe, half-lights the oxygen trolley, climbs the door, crosses the flaking plaster of the ceiling, shivering with roused dust. It flickers, a flame blown on other winds.

He reaches for the oxygen mask on the bedside table. Six slow breaths, then he says in a clear voice, 'Come in then.'

A hand reaches through the gap in the curtains and takes an edge. The hand blazes with light and by its light he sees that every clock in the bedroom has stopped at a different time. A second incandescent hand takes the other curtain and parts them. The Brilliant Boy steps cautiously into the room. Cat eyes in a shining face search the room.

'Here,' Hadley whispers. The Brilliant Boy turns to the bed. He burns so bright the air ripples around him but Hadley feels no heat as the Brilliant Boy steps lightly to his bedside and bends over him, so close Hadley feels the stirrings of his honey-scented breath. Sparks swarm in his black, open mouth.

'All right then,' Hadley says. The Brilliant Boy steps to the window, hands out-held. Clothes are not necessary, nor the breathing mask and tank. Sweet radiance fills Hadley's lungs; he feels so charged, so light his feet barely brush the floor.

With his left hand the Brilliant Boy parts the curtains, his right he extends to Hadley. How painless this is. The Brilliant Boy is fur soft to the touch, fuzzy with photons. The windows stand open, the moon rides the streaking clouds above Broighter Wood. The Brilliant Boy steps up onto the air. It's the most natural thing for Hadley to follow. The Brilliant Boy leads him up into the shining night. Hadley pauses to look back at Brightbourne. He marvels a moment at the unprecedented perspective: the chimneys, the leadwork, the roof. Those slates need replacing. From this fresh angle the lives curled up together in this Golden Place shine; their breaths, their wants, their relationships tangled like the hyphae of night-luminous fungi. Connected. He listens a moment to the Music and is satisfied. This is how it ends, not with a power chord but a tocsin.

'Right so,' he says and the Brilliant Boy leads him up through the air into endless light.

103

Seventy-six fireworks. Seventy-five launch with success, accuracy and spectacle. Seventy-six: perhaps a fox brushes against it, perhaps the launch tube was carelessly sited. Perhaps it just fell over.

Rocket seventy-six carrying one hundred grammes of Hadley Bright-bourne, ashed, mislaunches. It draws a line of shrieking fire across Broighter Wood, hits a tree, spins up into the air, a Catherine wheel now. The Hope-lands gathered on the UFO Terrace watch it wheel over their heads to land in the gutter along the east wall of the house. The payload detonates; fragments of burning Hadley spray down onto the ballroom and up onto the main roof. The guttering is clogged with leaves from many autumns, moss dried over a long warm summer. Magically, it has not rained in thirty days. Moss smoulders. Crisp leaf litter ignites. Fire leaps the length of the gutter and licks up the edge of the roof. Flaking paint catches, Victorian soffits blacken and smoke and burn. Flames lick under the slates, smoke rolls out in a breaking wave.

Everyone stares, everyone stands. The fire is high and inaccessible. Lorien calls the firefighters. Jacob and Demetrios, still in funeral finery, rush a ladder from the Hearth, haul it up onto the roof of the porte cochère and from there set it up to the roof. A hose unreels up through a chain of hands to Demetrios. He plays the jet across the slates but the pressure is low and the smoke now shrouds the entire eastern hip of the roof. A new light flickers behind a bedroom window. The fire is in the house. Flames creep around the roofline. Cast-iron guttering cracks, molten lead from melted tie bars drips from the edge of the roof. Loosened tiles slip and the fire, breathing deep, leaps up.

'Where is the fire brigade?' someone shouts. Sirens have been heard approaching, departing, circling. Cookstown Fire and Rescue is only five minutes at emergency speed.

'They can't get in!' Lisi exclaims. 'The gate isn't open.'

Kids on bikes speed to open up the path, but the lost minutes doom Bright-bourne. The bedroom windows crash outwards as the ceiling collapses in burning roof timbers. The rooms behind explode in flame. A mass of tiles and blazing wood slumps onto the roof of the ballroom below. The ball-room roof gives way, the grand piano under flaming timbers. Tongues of fire curl around the fearful birds in the old wallpaper. The spectators move back to the lawn. Lisi shouts a warning to Demetrios on the roof. The fire is outflanking him, creeping along the guttering and through the dry roof vaults. He slides down the ladder as the whole front gutter catches. The east end of Brightbourne blazes. Smoke churns behind every window. Two fire engines arrive and run hoses out to the pond. Firefighters move the people back, back. Further back.

'Is there anyone in the house?' the chief fire officer asks. Lorien looks around, counts heads.

'Everyone's here.'

Smoke ekes from under the doors of the first-floor bedrooms, fills the landing, pours down the Infanta Staircase, gathers in the hall. Seventeenth-century doors hold the fire but the heat builds, boiling volatiles from the wallpaper, the varnish, the oil paint of the portraits of the Brightbournes. A fanlight fails, air rushes in. Landings, galleries, staircases flash over. The watchers howl as the heart of Brightbourne explodes in flame. Every window blows out. The Infanta Staircase is a ladder of hellfire. The firefighters open up with hoses but the blaze has a strong hold and the house masonry is old and frail. The east chimney collapses in an eruption of sparks and embers. Brightbourne blazes from gable to gable. Lisi holds Lorien. The noise, the roar of burning is horrible. Ashes and embers soar in the updraught.

'The Music!' Lorien shouts. 'Save the Music!'

The chief fire officer understands. The house is beyond saving. The firefighters switch to foam and gently lay a carpet of fire-retardant on the hydro-house roof.

In the firelight Morwenna leans on her sticks, smiling.

By four thirty the fire is extinguished. All that stands of Brightbourne is the porte cochère. Some of the old oak roof timbers glow beneath the char for days.

That's how Hadley Brightbourne comes home and by Grace alone destroys the Golden Place.

The Music plays on.

104

The key to dressing for a date is, and always has been, variation. Amon Brightbourne did not agonise over the decision of what wardrobe to salvage from Ava'u: he was wearing it.

At midnight Captain Ruzza will time-jump the fleet two hours into the future as it crosses from North Pacific time to Alaska time. Breakfast date will become second-breakfast date. At the top of the world latitude lines come together and Amon time will converge with Raisa time, late-breakfast by lunch by afternoon-tea by dinner until their clocks meet in Baffin Bay.

Time-signatures and variations. Today Amon's variation in his unvarying wardrobe will be a daring Trinity knot in his tie. The trefoil must look skilled, never effortful. Elegant showmanship. Auberon taught him the seven major and six minor knots in the mirror on the Landing That Goes Nowhere, standing side by side before the glass, close enough for Amon to catch the particular aroma of old-man stubble. These days when the wind blows down through time, he catches a hint of that sweet, oily perfume from the creases of his own face.

He tucks the tail under for the eleventh move of the thirteen-part ritual. Stops. Lets it fall.

A change in the world-song. A voice has stopped singing. A whole line of music has fallen silent.

He leaves the tie un-Trinitied and opens his MacBook. A call. In a preview window above the menu bar he sees Lorien.

Sick with dread he clicks the connect button.

'Amon!' Knock, no answer. She opens the stateroom door. 'Amon!'

He has pulled his favourite chair to face the balcony. Outside is an afternoon of annealed grey metals. Rain lashes the window. The fleet sails cold seas in hard rains through long alien nights. A gecko clings to the back of his chair, blue on beige, pulsing its throat.

'Amon?'

'Do you know trip-hop, Kimmie?'

The voice from the chair kills Kimmie's irritation at having to fetch him again to a Council of Voyagers meeting.

'I don't know what that is, Amon,' she says and closes the door quietly behind her.

'It was a short-lived but influential musical subgenre originating in Bristol in the English south-west in the early 1990s,' Amon says. His voice is high and birdlike. Lizard-voice, Kimmie thinks. The gecko speaks. '"Wandering stars, for whom it is reserved, the blackness of darkness forever". Do you know that song?'

'I know it's a Bible verse, Amon. Jude 1:13.'

He sings a small tuneless tune.

'We're homeless now, Kimmie. All refugees.'

105

Since the Ava'uan fleet crossed North 50 Prime Minister Sionatani Vuna Pohiva has worn rugby socks under his tupenu on his evening walk of the decks. At North 60 he may concede a jacket but it is a matter of national pride that the prime minister be properly dressed.

He meets fewer people on his patrol—the cold, the wet, the lack of warm clothing keeps people on their decks—but they talk longer. Fears. Doubts. Rumours. Problems. This is his constituency office. He listens. He reassures where he can, explains if he may, intervenes if he is able; gives hope.

We will take on cold-weather clothing at Unalaska. It will be PBV branded, and warm.

I will have a word with Moderator Viliami. You're not the only one tired of sermons on the Book of Exodus.

No, we are in no danger from the Russians. Russia is not our enemy. No one is.

Your second cousin on Ofu saw a pod of orcas? I shall look out for that. Orcas would be a thing to see.

And he rolls on in his stiff, rocking gait. At the end is a thankful groaning collapse into the chair in his stateroom and thirty minutes with non-Western spirituality. He has worked through the Analects of Kong Fuzi and the Tao Te Ching, the Upanishads (grazed: there is a lot there, he settled on the Rig Veda), the Bhagavad Gita (short). Next is the Koran (also short), and the Bible (not short). There is nothing Western about the Bible. Then whisky. Most nights he falls asleep in his chair. The bed is too low. He can't get out of it and at his age he needs to; maybe three times a night.

Mrs. Matai. The second duty of a politician is to remember names. From Fu'amotu village on the south-east side of Ava'utapu. Her husband is with the fisher fleet; her oldest son, Taniela, in France, a tight-head prop with Montpellier Hèrault Rugby. She hopes he will join her in the new land. Mrs. Matai, on behalf of her corridor—her entire deck—in highest honorific language, has a petition. Will the prime minister do something about the water rations? She can't remember when she last washed her hair.

The children will have no clean clothes. It's like being back on the island waiting for the water tanker. We sailed away from that, didn't we?

Please be assured, Mrs. Matai. We're two days from Unalaska. We'll take on all the fresh clean water we need to make it to the new land. Thank you for your dedication to saving water, can you keep it up a little longer?

He waddles on. A skirl of northern rain rattles the deck. Prime Minister Sionatani Vuna Pohiva stops, then topples forward onto his face.

For the death of a monarch, the islands observe one hundred days of official mourning. Alcohol is not drunk, kava is taken only on the tenth day after the interment and daily churchgoing is observed. Black is worn, and ta'ovala mats.

The death of Prime Minister Pohiva sends the leitis of the royal protocol into a huddle. His position in their schema dictates twenty days of state observance but many families lost their ta'ovalas to Cyclone Velma. Pohiva was a son of Niua and there is no possibility of his relatives paying respects until landfall in the Aleutian Islands. As for the family bringing the traditional ha'amo of food and drink for ten days after the interment, there can be no interment until the new land.

House Tu'i and House Pohiva confer across five kilometres of choppy, rainy North Pacific. No ta'ovalas will be worn and black confined to a single armband, regardless of kindred or rank. The funeral rites will take place in Unalaska. The casket will hold the small black pebbles of the lanu kiikii laid in the grave one hundred days after interment. *Ava'utapu's* morgue freezers are full, so Prime Minister Pohiva rests in the ice-cream store. The queen declares free ice cream for *Ava'utapu.* Thus the Pohivas of *Niua* fulfil their ha'amo obligation. Choirs practise, ministers of religion amend orders of service, Queen 'Ana school brass band rehearses formation marching on the Sky Deck. Amon Brightbourne composes a toccata, Kimmie Pangaimotu sews him a mourning armband from her old funeral blouse—'because you'll never remember to do it, palangi.'

While the nation of Ava'u prepares for a state funeral Captain Ruzza leads the fleet into the arc of the Aleutian Islands, past the fog-girded volcanic cones of the Islands of Four Mountains, the green cliffs of the Fox Islands, under the snowcap of Mount Makushin into the port of Unalaska. A significant portion of the town's four and a half thousand residents turn

out on Summer Bay Road to watch the big cruise ships navigate the sand
spit to the refuelling depot.

Rain edged with snow swirls into the reception lobby. Amon Brightbourne and Kimmie Pangaimotu are stout as tikis in PBV-branded winter
wear. Kimmie has decreed that Kimmie does not do cold and Amon has
conceded that there are climates for which tweed is not suitable.

They watch the Pohivas in their Sunday tupenus forage the pebble
beach at the shore end of the fuel depot pier, picking up stones and throwing them away. The Ava'uans are restricted to a secure area on Amaknak
Island, north of the airstrip and segregated from the residential town and
the fishing docks to the east. The stones look cold. The Pohivas look cold.
The world looks cold, an entropic cold that can never be warm again.

'Why are we here?' Kimmie asks. She stamps her feet on the now-damp
carpet.

'To make sure he goes.'

'I think you misunderstand. Why am I here? You're the one knows him.'

'I don't know him.'

'Raisa Hopeland knows Sindri Ólafursson, you know Raisa Hopeland.'

'And Kimmie Pangaimotu Hopeland knows me.'

'How are the dinner dates going? Kimmie thinks those are so cute.'

Before Amon must answer, Sindri Ólafursson arrives out of the elevator, a third potbellied godling in PBV cold gear. A black van, high-shine,
blacked-out windows, passes through the gate at the entrance to the docks
and draws up at the foot of the gangplank. Sindri shakes Amon's and Kimmie's hands.

'My offer is always open,' he says. 'Sustainable blockchain is the future.'

'Cunt,' Kimmie says loud enough for Sindri, carefully descending the
sleet-slick gangplank, to hear. A private jet waits on Unalaska's airstrip.
Sindri Ólafursson crosses the short distance from the ramp to the black
van. A door slides open, he slides in. And away. 'Over the horizon, Sindri
Ólafursson. You did right, Amon.'

'My dad did right,' Amon says. 'He came home. Brightbourne burned.'

'The Music survived. The Hearth survived.'

'Sindri was a danger to the fleet. I still am, Kimmie. To the future. The
Grace knows how to wait.'

'Amon, kynnd,' Kimmie says. By tradition the fakaleitis have been able
to say what social harmony denied other Ava'uans. 'The universe doesn't
revolve around you.'

The Pohivas have filled their basket with the right stones. Security escorts them from the shore to the gangway.

'They look like us,' Kimmie says as the security guides the stone-seekers to *Niua*'s gangplank. She tips her chin at the flurries flocking in from Makushin. 'That's snow now.'

'That's snow,' Amon Brightbourne says.

'Fuck snow,' says Kimmie Pangaimotu.

Ava'utapu's siren sounds; seven, eight, nine, ten blasts. A funeral is announced.

Armbands are adjusted. Video relays tested. Children inspected. Bands positioned, choirs marshalled, ministers of religion robed. Aristocrats attired. Mats are laid, speakers checked. Two hours after Captain Ruzza sounds the horn the funeral begins. Everyone thinks the speed and efficiency commendable. The bands play, the Pohivas march the prescribed five-kilometre route through every deck on *Ava'utapu*. People weep and crouch and dip their heads. Choirs sing. Hymns and anthems resound. Ministers read lessons, make long sermons. Family members, politicians, civic dignitaries and sporting celebrities deliver sobbing eulogies. The Pohivas each lay a black alien pebble, polished smooth with scented oil, around the lectern where the black-bordered portrait of the Honourable Sionatani Vuna Pohiva sits. The queen makes a short emotional speech and leads the nation in prayer. Amon Brightbourne starts from his fugue-state doze and with every voice the chapel organ and his electronics can muster thunders out his Funeral Toccata. Each ship answers with their siren. The spectators of Unalaska, two kilometres away across the bay, watch baffled.

Fuelling (both hydrogen and hydrocarbon), watering, provisioning, resupplying take three days. Families model their cold-weather clothes in processions around the decks. This is a down jacket, these are our beanies and we all wear matching PBV fleeces. Layering. That's the thing. Ship visits ship. Aiga visits aiga. Everyone knows that the next time the people call on each other will be in the new land. Captain Ruzza wants to sail the moment the PBV supply ships clear harbour. The weather window on the Northwest Passage closes fast. The Northeast course along the top of Russia, then driving west to East Greenland, pushes the fleet's resources to the limits. And no one can predict how Russia will react at this time when the Ava'uan migration fleet has catalysed political reactions across the Arctic.

Six days after the state funeral of Prime Minister Pohiva everyone is back on the right ship, on the right deck with the right people. Storeroom shelves groan, tanks slosh with water, fuel bunkers are fat with fuel. Captain Ruzza gives the seven horn blasts of departure. Thrusters engage. The patrol boats move into position, the fishers cast off from the mole. As one the three ships push out from the wharf and rotate in formation. It's designed to impress. The PBV ships sound their horns in salute.

Kimmie Pangaimotu and Amon Brightbourne watch the grey dock, the city of hydrogen and old carbon fuel tanks, the green banks and the fog-shrouded cap of Mount Makushin turn away and a new vista of grey mole, fishing detritus, pickups and leaden sea beneath leaden sky swings into view.

'Shithole,' Kimmie Pangaimotu says. 'Tell me Greenland won't be like this, Amon.'

'It'll be warmer,' Amon Brightbourne says. 'It's nineteen Celsius in Saarloq right now.'

'That's not warm, 'ofa'anga.' She frowns, claps a hand to the rail. 'Something's wrong.'

Amon Brightbourne lays hand to rail. He knows every mood and note of the engines by their vibrational harmonics. The thrusters are in full reverse.

'We're stopping.'

Their phones buzz with simultaneous messages.

'Shit,' Amon says. Kimmie is already out in the corridor.

'Out of my way!' she bellows in Ava'uan. Families duck back into their staterooms. The leiti Kimmie in full flight can only mean the direst emergency. Amon arrives moments behind her on the crowded bridge. Captain, bridge crew, queen, Council of Voyagers, military, all talking, all asking questions, in Ava'uan, English, Italian.

Amon pushes through to the window. The fleet holds position in the harbour, the three liners in their arrowhead formation, the fishers flanking, the patrol boats standing a hundred metres seaward. A US Coast Guard cutter blocks their exit from Unalaska deep-water port.

The Ava'uans look to their queen. She wears sports gear, caught out on the way to take a spin class.

'Captain, Bridge Manager?'

'We have been ordered not to leave Unalaska Harbour,' says Bridge Manager Vai Vailahi. 'Captain Alvarez of the USCGC *Friedman* demands that we place our fleet under her command.'

Outrage.

'Silence!' the queen shouts. 'What is this, Vai?'

'We are under arrest by US Customs and Border Protection as undocumented migrants,' Vai Vailahi says and the bridge of *Ava'utapu* erupts.

106

Queen Ta is fit, Queen Ta is fast, Queen Ta leads daily workout session in the Muscle-time! Gym and an overweight, under-exercised fakaleiti like Kimmie Pangaimotu struggles to keep up with her.

'Stand still will you?' Kimmie pleads, trying to pin the pandanus crown of the Tu'is to the Queen's hastily-oiled and plaited hair. Queen Ta adjusts her ta'ovala mid-jog. Captain Alvarez of the USCGC *Friedman* is coming aboard. Elisiva Ta'ahine Tu'i of Ava'utapu, Ofu, Niua and the lesser islands, queen from horizon to horizon, sunrise to sunset, will not be found wanting. Kimmie adds a Cleopatra cat's-eye of kohl to Ta's make-up in the elevator. Leiti Fetuu waits in the elevator lobby with the 'Akau Ta. Ta has thrown regalia over gym gear but she is queen whether in sacred mats or Lululemon leggings. She kicks off her sneakers. Barefoot is honourable. Kimmie and Fetuu fall in behind her. Ta takes her place at the end of the line in the atrium. The fleet has returned to dock. The *Friedman*, 4,500 tons, 127 metres, maximum speed 28 knots, 113 complement, guards the open ocean with a Mk-110 57mm Naval Gun, 20mm Block 1B Phalanx close-in weapons system, four 50-calibre machine guns, a helicopter and drones.

Two cars offload the boarding party onto the rain-soaked concrete. Captain Alvarez is a tall, middle-aged brown woman in a blue ODU, grey-streaked hair tied back severely beneath her cap. With her are four armed coastguard sailors in combat fatigues, helmets, HUDs. Captain Ruzza receives the captain and her party. She surveys the assembly.

'Captain, I would like to inspect your safety certification.'

Alvarez, her boarding party, captain and bridge manager stride past the politicians, past the lords, past the honour guard of marines and their commanding officer, past the royal fakaleitis, past Queen Elisiva Ta'ahine Tu'i. Her grip on the 'Akau Ta does not waver. Only when the elevator lights signal that the lifts have reached the bridge does the atrium explode with voices.

'The insult!' Major Fia rages. 'The dishonour! Ma'am, how can you . . .'

The public address system plays its jingle. Bridge Manager Vai speaks. Under Section 50 paragraph 191 of the United States Coast Guard authorizations, Captain Alvarez has seized Festival *Ocean Adventurer,* Nordic *Aurora* and Nordic *Polaris* and placed them under the command of the US Coast Guard. Passengers must return to their cabins and remain there until further notice.

Every eye is on the queen.

'Go,' Queen Ta says. 'Do as they say. Be safe. I command it!'

In her stateroom she tears off her regalia, flings the pandanus crown to the floor. She sets the 'Akau Ta on the couch and swears long and hard in English. She looks long and hard in the bathroom mirror, daring herself to cry. The internal phones are down, ship Wi-Fi offline. Over the hours information leaks from the public address. Kitchen staff to report at 14:00. Stand by for meal rotas. Rain beats against the glass of her stateroom. Still no phones or Wi-Fi.

A tap at the window that is not rain. Major Fia crouches on her balcony. Ta opens the sliding doors. He steps in, saturated, shivering. 'How . . .'

'I climbed round the outside,' he says. 'It's like a children's playground.'

Ta fetches him a Festival Lines bathrobe.

'Get out of that wet stuff.'

'With permission, ma'am.' Major Fia changes in the royal bathroom. 'Ma'am, my duty is to defend Kingdom and Crown.' Queen Ta sits, the major remains standing. Even in a cruise-line robe he is imposing. 'The kingdom has not faced so great a threat since the cyclone.'

'I agree,' Queen Ta says.

'The Americans mean to disperse us.'

'We will raise support. The UNHCR. The Arctic Council.'

'With respect, ma'am, these ships will be rust at the bottom of the sea before the United Nations acts.'

'Your point, Major?'

'Your Defence Force stand ready for your orders, ma'am.'

'What do you propose, Malietoa?' Queen Ta says.

'We break out.'

'The Americans have a warship.'

'We have three, ma'am.'

'We shoot our way out of the harbour?'

'That would pose an unacceptable risk to civilians. I propose we take their ship. Before our internet was closed down, I took the liberty of downloading information on the Legend-class cutter. I could capture and operate that ship with twenty marines. All we need to do is disable it.'

'You mean, sink it?'

'Make sure it cannot threaten us.'

'And Captain Alvarez? Her troops?'

'We return them to the dock. We do not take hostages, ma'am. Americans always underestimate their opponents. They think we're quaint Pacific islanders. We are not. We are warriors.'

'They would send more than the coast guard after us. They would send the navy.'

'We fight a rear-guard action until the fleet reaches Russian waters.'

'Russia?'

'They're already watching us, ma'am. They'd welcome an opportunity to embarrass the USA.'

'The Russians would no more welcome nineteen thousand Ava'uan refugees than the Americans. We are refugees, Major, whatever we think ourselves to be. No, I can't permit it. The Americans do not forgive. They would blow you out of the water, Major. I can't order you to do that.'

'We are willing to make the sacrifice, ma'am. It's a chance. Against no chance.'

'Leave me, Major.'

'Ma'am. With your permission?'

Queen Ta nods. Major Fia returns to the bathroom. His clothes are still saturated, clinging, abrasive.

'No orders, ma'am?'

'No orders, Major. Thank you.'

He dips his head and returns to the gusty, rainy balcony. A foot on a rail, a hand to the balcony frame and he swings boldly, thrillingly to the next balcony.

Queen Ta goes to the bathroom. The major has folded his bathrobe and laid it neatly at the end of the bath. She locks the door. She turns to the mirror.

'Now, Ta,' she says and this time she cries like a desolate child.

107

The girl goes past on the e-scooter for the fourth time. Atli looks up from his armour-work and catches her catching his eye. She accelerates around the corner of Joint Arctic Command. This town has great e-scooters. Chunky all-terrain tyres. Matt paint jobs. Atli turns back to his steel rings. Four onto one, close up. Four onto one, close up. In the electromancy laboratory his armour smithing was too hermetic, too ascetic. Outside he can hear and smell, feel the movement of air and the tremor of ship engines, see and be seen. Scooter-girl will be back. He hears the hiss of fat tyres on the cracking blacktop and is ready.

He stands, gloved fist raised. Steel rings catch low afternoon sun. She stops, wheels her e-scooter onto the dirt and kicks it shut.

'Okay,' she says in English.

'You're Nauja Lund's . . . daughter,' Atli says.

'You're Raisa Hopeland's . . . son.'

'Bur.'

'Okay.' The girl tilts her chin at his gauntlet.

'Chain-mail armour. Every Arcmage makes their own armour.'

'Arcmage.'

'Knights of the Order of Electromancers.'

'Okay,' she says, flips open her scooter and speeds away.

She's back the next day.

'You haven't done much on that glove,' she says.

'It's slow work.'

Atli sat outside in the hope that she would roll past on her fat tyres.

'Electromancers.'

'We have power over lightning.' She rolls her eyes. Show-off boy. Showing off is what Arcmages do. 'Okay, we're performance artists. Except our art—our medium is Tesla coils.'

'You have a Tesla coil?'

'Several.' Make a small move. 'Would you like to see them?'

'In there? With you?'

Poor move.

'Kynnd Finn is back tomorrow. He's been doing a consultation in Helsinki.'

'An electromantic consultation.'

Why does he feel that she knows much much more than she is saying?

'For a concert.'

'Okay,' she says, hops onto her scooter and away she goes.

Next day she rolls up outside the sanctum to find Finn sitting on the porch in a foldout camping chair.

'You're Finn,' she says.

He looks at her with suspicion.

'I am.'

'I'm Siisi Lund. Good electromantic consultation?'

Atli brings two coffees, then a third. He makes great coffee. Finn asks no questions. Seagulls bicker over the fishing crates down the pier, rising and squabbling and circling.

'I'd like to see them now,' Siisi says. 'The coils.' Finn nods. She tucks the folded scooter under her arm and follows Atli into the warehouse.

'What happened to his face?' Siisi asks Atli. 'Those are burns, right?'

'He fought a demon,' Atli says.

'Okay,' Siisi says.

Atli opens the door from the front office to the main warehouse. The Coil of the North stands at the centre of its array of electrodes.

'This makes lightning,' she says.

'It does,' Atli says.

'Can you show me?'

'I'm not allowed.'

'Not allowed?'

'I'm still a paduan.'

'A what?'

'A student.' He hates saying that. 'A paduan.'

'Did you get that from *Star Wars*?'

'Or *Star Wars* got it from us. The first Electromancers came from Padua.'

'Where's that?'

'Italy, I think. There's something else I'd like to show you,' Atli says. 'It'll be a couple of minutes.' He slips into the lightning lab. When Siisi tries the door, she finds it locked.

'Hey!'

'Mysteries and revelations,' Finn says, running an electroscope over the primary coil.

'I got a low boredom threshold,' Siisi says.

'It's worth the wait.'

A couple of minutes turns to five, to ten. To fifteen. In the kitchen low-boredom-threshold Siisi discovers the yata hanging in the window. She peers close and her breath sets the mirror spinning. Siisi blinks. Something in her eye. She turns to ask Finn *what is that?* but Finn is nowhere to be seen. Instead there is—

'Atli?'

—a wizard wreathed in folds and sleeves of black that seem to float on an electric wind. His—her?—toes don't quite seem to touch the ground. Hair fierce-gelled into a thunderhead. Right eye solid black, the other the seed of an arc of white lightning that forks and reforks across the left side of her? its? face, down the neck, down the arm to the nails of the left hand.

Wow, she says in Kalaallisut.

'I hope that means wow.' Atli's voice.

'Now that's an Electromancer,' Siisi says.

'It's me,' Atli says. 'Another me.'

'Do I call you Atli?'

'That's my name. Same name, different gender. I'd ask if you're talking about me, could you please refer to this one as hé, the other as he?'

'Pronouns,' Siisi says. 'I'll try.'

'Try is enough. Now: You want to see what an Arcmage does?'

'Paduan,' Siisi says as Atli shows her into the lightning laboratory.

Hé swirls her past the toy coil to the paduan Tesla, sixty centimetres high, classic mushroom coil, arrived from Iceland five days ago. Atli throws a pair of goggles to Siisi.

'Ultraviolet,' hé warns.

'What about you?'

Hé taps hés lightning eye with a feather-arc fingernail.

'I got lenses.'

Without seeming to touch any fabric, hé steps out of the robe. It collapses.

Beneath hé wears more mundane compression wear, the base layer for an electromancer's armour. Hé is as lean and taut as a skinned fox.

'Primary ignition.' Hé stomps the foot-switch.

'Good boots,' Siisi says.

'Lights off.' The neons obey. 'Secondary online.'

'It glows,' Siisi says. She grins beneath the reflections of the coil in her goggles.

She suits those goggles.

Atli fetches an Electromantic wand and holds it out to the glowing secondary.

'No armour?' Siisi says.

'This one's only twenty thousand volts,' Atli says. An arc crackles between the coil-head and the tip of hés wand. 'High voltage, low current. That's the secret.'

Atli works hés repertoire of three small tricks. Lightning glitters in Siisi's eyes. Atli adores an audience. Hé kills the coil, turns, bows. Hé knows hé looks cute.

Hé lolls back in an Ikea office chair, one leg casually slung over the chair arm.

'So, any questions?'

'Yes. That thing in the kitchen.'

'Thing?'

'Small, tiny, mirror, thing.'

'A yata,' Atli says. 'Did it move for you?'

'Should it?'

'Depends. Did you look into it? Did you see anything?'

'Like those floating things inside your eye,' she says. 'What was that?'

'This takes coffee.'

'I'm good for a coffee story.'

'Okay then.' Hé goes to the kitchen, cleans out the coffeemaker, sets the kettle to boil. A draught from elsewhere sets the yata spinning.

Hé grinds coffee, rinses mugs.

'First, a warning. Don't fall in love with my family.'

108

Raisa still drives like a nightmare. Nauja Lund clutches her ruggedised laptop.

'Raisa. Put the car on autodrive.'

All are summoned to Nuuk: government, Foundation, PBV, funders and partners. Planes land, load, take off with airlift regularity. Nauja Lund speaks hourly with Minister Ane Hammeken and the parliamentary Ava'u Committee. Raisa fronts PR briefings and press statements, always careful to refer to the incident as the *internment of climate refugees*. 'Unalaska Crisis' is solutionist. These are lives. *Internment of climate refugees* hands the moral burden back to the Americans.

Raisa slaps the autodrive button on the steering wheel.

'What do you think the Nuuk will do?'

'The Inatsisartut will back the Naalakkersuisut and call a full emergency meeting of the Arctic Council. Ministerial, SAO, the Indigenous Peoples' Secretariat. Observers. NGOs too,' Nauja Lund says. 'They will talk for a month, issue a declaration and nothing will be acted upon. No Arctic Council declaration has ever been acted upon.'

'That's a bit cynical.'

'I am not a cynic, Raisa. Do you remember what I said about being afraid?'

'That I didn't know it.'

'And now?'

'I'm terrified,' Raisa says.

'Terrified is different from afraid.'

Scattered pallets, dead cars and abandoned shipping-container sheds line the road; sheds for fishing, quads, hunting, whatever men need big sheds for.

'They're PBV employees!' Raisa bounces her hands off the wheel in frustration.

'The US does not recognise that,' Nauja Lund says. 'They see illegal migrants. Migrants have no rights. If they were citizens . . .'

The two women look at each other.

'Is that possible?' Raisa asks.

'You're building a town in two months,' Nauja Lund says. 'Great things are possible.'

They run from the abandoned car to the plane waiting at the heliport and slide into their seats, the last passengers. The doors seal. Fans unfold into takeoff configuration.

Raisa hunts for her phone. Nauja Lund's is already in her hand.

Nauja Lund briefly took up running at university in Canada. She found that she runs like a penguin. Since then the fastest she allows herself to move is a purposeful walk. She runs now, up the corridor where the premier presses through politicians, ministers, Foundation and PBV and funders to the parliament chamber.

'Mr. Premier!'

Premier Kuko, a short, dark, wolverine of a man, stops.

'Five. Minutes,' Nauja Lund pants.

'We're due to start.'

Nauja Lund nods, wordless. Raisa arrives and has words.

'We need five minutes.'

Premier Kuko nods his advisers to a discreet distance.

'Ane's office?'

'Raisa Hopeland too,' Nauja Lund says. 'And coffee.'

Afternoon August-light gilds Nuuk. The houses smile. The streets relax into their cracks and potholes. Sermitsiaq flaunts a tutu of cloud and a golden tiara. Excellent coffee in an excellent pot on the excellent Kofod-Larsen table. Nauja Lund takes a centring sip and looks at the red roof of her house.

'The USA is undergoing one of its regular strong-border, anti-immigration, Homeland-Security spasms. They see undocumented migrants. They're terrified this is the start of the climate change diaspora. They're right. It is.' She looks from minister to premier.

'Stateless migrants,' Raisa says.

'Give them a state. Make them citizens of Kalaallit Nunaat.'

'Just like that?' Ane says. 'Clap hands and it's done?'

'They're gonna be citizens someday,' Raisa says. 'Why not now?'

'There are procedures,' Premier Kuko says. 'Processes.'

'Too slow,' Raisa says. 'They'd be stuck for the winter—maybe two winters. PBV's Kujalleq field starts cracking hydrogen by November. It needs crew.'

'Probationary status?' Nauja Lund suggests.

'The constitution has no mechanism for that,' Premier Kuko says. 'Nauja, you know that. Creating the legislation for such a thing would take as long as granting citizenship to nineteen thousand people.'

'Is that the real problem?' Raisa asks. 'That it would be, like, your population increasing by a third, overnight?'

Premier Kuko looks long at Raisa before replying.

'There were problems at Qaqortoq.'

'Problems we solved.'

'Problems Nauja Lund solved,' Ane says.

'We convene the Arctic Council,' Premier Kuko says.

'The US will veto anything we propose. And you know that, Premier,' Nauja Lund says. 'No, we apply pressure.'

'Put pressure on the US?' Ane says. 'We are sixty thousand. They are four hundred million.'

'But we have Qaanaaq,' Nauja Lund says.

Greenland has a long sub-dom relationship with the United States. When Denmark fell to Nazi Germany in 1940, the US occupied its Arctic territory for five years. In 1946 the US offered $100,000,000 to buy the island at the top of the world. When that bid—and subsequent bids—were rejected, the US negotiated to expand the Thule Air Base—Qaanaaq Mitarfik—in the high north-west twelve hundred kilometres above the Arctic Circle, far from the sight of Denmark. Here the coldest of cold wars played out. In 1962 Project Iceworm planned to hide six hundred nuclear missiles in four thousand kilometres of tunnels dug into 52,000 square kilometres of ice cap. Lonely tractors would tow trains of Iceman missiles to ever-changing firing positions beneath the ice. Glacial flow terminated Project Iceworm but the exploratory drilling base, Camp Century, supposedly entombed in eternal ice, had its dirty secrets exposed by global warming. Dirtiest of all, its nuclear power plant now threatens to leak decay products into the Davis Strait. In 1968 a B-52 bomber went down burning onto the sea ice south of Thule and lost its load of thermonuclear devices. The conventional explosives det-

onated and spread dirty stuff across twelve square kilometres of North Star
Bay. Seven hundred personnel worked for nine months to remove half a million gallons of contaminated water and ship it back to the US. Greenland
was declared nuclear-free in 1957; the details of the Broken Arrow incident
and Project Iceworm were suppressed and came to light only in 1996 during
a compensation case brought by Danish workers for exposure to plutonium.

The dirty neighbours at Thule transferred the base to Space Force
Command in 2020. Upward of three thousand planes still fly in each year.

Then Greenland becomes the independent sovereign state of Kalaallit
Nunaat. And all leases and licenses on the new nation's territory are subject
to renegotiation.

'Remind me about the length of the US lease on Qaanaaq Mitarfik,' Premier Kuko says.

'Five years automatically renewing,' Nauja Lund says. Kuko knows the
terms as well as she. They both took part in the post-independence rene-
gotiations. Hydrocarbon licenses were rescinded, mineral leases redrafted,
fishing licenses auctioned, geothermal and wind-power licenses sold and
the lease on the Thule Air Base set on a new, more equal foundation.
'Unless . . .'

'Either party raises an objection,' Ane says.

'Kalaallit Nunaat would find the United States' detention of nineteen
thousand future citizens objectionable,' Nauja Lund says.

'Grossly objectionable,' Premier Kuko says with a grin. 'I think the US
values its polar base a lot more than three boatloads of climate refugees.'

'How can we make this work?' Nauja Lund asks.

'I'll talk to the president.' Premier Kuko stands, takes a sip of still-hot
coffee.

'I'll propose it to the Inatsisartut,' Ane says. 'I'll press for a vote today.'

Nauja Lund messages Tuusi in the corridor. *Defrost the steaks.* The po-
liticals crowd into the chamber. *Get beer.* She pulls on her coat. The sky is
clearing into a limitless evening. *Send the kids somewhere.* Raisa is already
out in the courtyard zipping up her outer layer.

'Good work, Mrs. Lund,' Raisa says.

'Good work, Ms. Hopeland.'

Nauja takes the right-hand path down to the shore. She breaks into her ugly penguin jog. She takes the steps up to her porch two at a time and her thoughts run in rhythm with her feet on the wood.

You. Are. So. Getting. Sex. Tonight.

Raisa takes the left path, up the ridge to the Nýttnorður House. She'll surprise Atli. Her feet quicken. Back in Nuuk, back in the Hearth. Socks, candles. Wine. Get Atli to cook something. He's a lazy fuck but he's a good cook.

She bangs open the door and there is Finn crossing the living room from the shower, towelling dry his hair. He's naked, dripping, shiny clean.

'Finnevar Mikael Hamal,' Raisa says. 'What are you doing here?'

Shiny clean, dripping, naked. Before he can answer she throws herself on him, knocks him onto a sofa. She bites his shower-wet right earlobe, whispers.

'This is me forgiving you.'

109

Amon never gets used to the Ava'uan way of calling unannounced. It runs from schoolchildren to prime ministers. The door will burst open. *Eimoni, whatever you're doing stop it.*

'Kimmie.' After the lock-in of the US occupation he's just reacclimatised to having the stateroom to himself. Stretching into space. Filling the room with his choice of music.

'Amon.'

Not Kimmie. Amon spins his chair, jumps to his feet.

'Ma'am.'

Queen Ta glides past Amon to open his balcony door. She beckons him outside.

'Sorry to call on you like this, Amon,' Ta says. 'I'm without my dear prime minister.'

'I'm not sure what I can offer,' Amon says.

'It's not what you offer, Amon. It's what you are,' Queen Ta says. 'An outsider. I have told you things I could not tell anyone else.'

'What do you want to tell me, ma'am?'

'Kalaallit Nunaat threatened to refuse to renew the US Space Force's lease on the base at Qaanaaq Mitarfik. It's a masterstroke. We are free to leave. But we will not leave as the Nation of Ava'u.'

'I don't understand ma'am.'

'The US cannot be seen to capitulate to a nation of sixty thousand people. They must be seen to let us leave out of goodness and compassion. To that end, they can't be seen to have arrested us illegally. We were classed as illegal migrants, illegal migrants we must be. And illegal migrants have no nation, no government. Illegal migrants have no Queen.'

'No,' Amon whispers.

'That is the price, Amon.'

Queen Ta grips the cold metal rail with two hands. She surveys the slick-wet dock, concrete shining pewter under high, hard floodlights. Wind draws low notes from the pylons.

'The Fale Alea must dissolve. I must abdicate. What do you advise, Amon?'

'I'm not in a position . . .'

'You are in the best position, Eimoni.'

'Then I'll tell you what I think. You, Ta, have always done the best for your people. It's always cost you. It cost you your family. It cost you the Kingdom. But it was best for your people. You can't not do what's best. You'll give up the crown.'

'That's what Pohiva would have said.'

'Wise Old Turtle.'

'First queen of Ava'u and last. The Council of Voyagers has agreed on an abdication letter. It's quite short.'

'The Hopelands have a saying. All departures should be sudden.'

New rain, keen from the west and hard with the promise of ice inside each drop. Ta opens the balcony door and waits in the stateroom for Amon to join her.

'Thank you, Amon.'

'Ma'am.'

She catches on the word. 'You won't have to call me that. After.' At the stateroom door, she turns and says, 'Do you want to come with me?'

'I'm a coward, Ta.'

'It's a shame I won't get to escort Captain Alvarez off my ship.' She shakes her head. '*This* ship.' As she speaks, in his ankles, his shins, his hip bones, Amon feels the thrusters power up.

The instrument of abdication waits in Star Dressing Room 5 backstage of the Showtime Theatre. One sheet. One pen, on the table in front of a mirror haloed in LEDs. Name in lights. She should ask Kimmie how it works. This is her domain. Kimmie's the dressing room, hers the changing room. Footlockers to footlockers.

Queen Ta turns the sheet of paper to her.

Instrument of Abdication

I, Elisiva Ta'ahine Tu'i of Ava'utapu, Ofu, Niua and the lesser islands, do hereby declare my irrevocable determination to renounce the Throne of Ava'u for myself and my descendants, and my desire that effect be given to this Instrument of Abdication immediately.

In token whereof I have set here my hand this September 2nd, two thousand and thirty-three, as witnessed by those whose signatures are subscribed.
Signed at Festival *Ocean Adventurer*

_____

Elisiva Ta'ahine Tu'i
Witnessed by

_____

Moderator of the General Assembly of Ava'u

_____

Lord Tupou of Hunga and Nuapapu

_____

Captain of Festival *Ocean Adventurer*

She cries with the emotion and dignity of a queen, careful not to let a tear dimple the paper. She takes the pen and signs the instrument.

Ta opens the dressing-room door and asks the witnesses to enter. Each signs, each thanks her, dips their head. Kimmie Pangaimotu enters to take the instrument. She dares not look near Ta. The last part of the last protocol calls for Ta to linger a few moments in the dressing room while Captain Alvarez inspects the instrument and leaves the ship.

Are you sure you want to meet us on the bridge? her advisers politicians friends defenders said. *You might need time alone . . .*

No Ava'uan finds solace in solitude. Ta collects a few pieces from her stateroom. The engine pitch shifts, a deep tremor runs through the ship. The fleet is under way. She feels no triumph in that to set against her loss. The only economics are those of necessity. She enters the bridge and chokes back a swell of pride. They are all here. They applaud and cry praises and alleluias. Everyone is in tears.

Unalaska's wet concrete slips past. USCGC *Friedman* clears the mole; she will escort the fleet north through the Bering Strait into the northern ocean. The Aleutian incident has shaken the geopolitical dice. The Arctic powers mobilise ships, task aircraft, repurpose satellites. A giant is emerging from the melting ice.

Ta lays the regalia of the Tu'is on the chart table one piece at a time. Tupenu, ta'ovalas, neatly folded and placed with respect. The three necklaces of the islands. The pandanus tiara. Last she lays the 'Akau Ta across her robes of office.

'No, ma'am.'

Major Fia takes the staff of authority in his two hands.

'This belongs to the defender of the people.'

Ta takes the 'Akau Ta in her two hands. She looks at it as if she has never before seen the acts of her ancestors inscribed on its shaft.

'Carve my deeds with pride then,' she declares, raises the staff and strikes its heel on the soft rubber flooring. Cheers, tears. The national anthem breaks out, then a hymn, then the songs of love and heroism and home that men sing at their kava parties, that everyone knows, and *Ava'utapu* turns north and sets course for the open ocean.

The rupture in the laws of the universe climbs the tether line from *Ava'utapu* to Touia'o Futuna like lightning. The sleeping, snoring gods of old Ava'u shock awake from semi-hibernation. They scramble for space to look up and out. Wrong-winds rock their temporary home. A wave of aghast fear races around the worldlet.

Another line has broken. Their connection with the world of people through House Tu'i has severed, the end flailing free in the wind. Only this one cable now binds them to the nation and they cry out and cling together as the ship turns in to a different wind.

Storms are coming.

110

So she sits with hé, scooter folded up beside her like a weapon, boot-heels in the dust, and hé links loop to loop, one to four to five, one to four to five, with patience she hasn't seen in men (men?), not even her dad when he works at his Wacom tablet. And hé tells her about hés family, always growing, always connecting, so big you can travel from relation to relation without ever coming to the end of it. A family where what's important is not who gave birth to you, or who en-spermed you, but who cares for you. Where children are passed around like clothes and carry the names of stars. Where you can shine with light of any colour and brilliance.

Hé tells her about Vonland, how hés mother grew a forest around hé and inadvertently set up a major energy company. Hé tells her about being a kid, how children are their own gender and can be whatever they want to be as long as they want to be. Hé tells about hés yellow house.

'I'd love a house of my own,' Siisi says. A house near water. Away from these sixty streets. Away from church, university, friends, parties, boys; a house by water, on a road that goes somewhere.

Hé tells her about the two Atlis who lived in the Burs' House, the man and the other-than-man. More-than-man. Language and theory cannot describe that Atli. Nor does hé have to be described, named, tagged. Orthopraxy, not orthodoxy.

'Means?'

'What you do, not what you believe.'

From there is an easy crossing to what she might have seen in the yata. How world, life, thought and practice shape the universe and can sometimes be glimpsed in mirrors. Hé'll show her their constellations; stars she's known all her life connected differently, with different names. And the Emanations. What she saw in the mirror, that curl of gelid light, was that an Emanation? Maybe. They change constantly. What is important is that most people see nothing. She saw something.

Now it's dark and getting cool and her phone is asking her if she's coming back for food. She kicks open her scooter and rides back up over the

ridge and she's done what hé warned her against. She's fallen in love with
his family.

The next days and nights are dense with cloud so instead of the new constellations Atli shows Siisi the books. From Vonland, from Sherguard
Storage, Beckton; from Fournier Street, Finn has collected the archive of
the Arcmages and brought it to Nuuk.

In the hundreds of plastic storage boxes Siisi finds wonders. Whale-
speakers and sky mages. Socialites and revolutionaries. Thieves and pilgrims. Star-crossed lovers with whole skies between them finding each
other over a lifetime, swinging from constellation to constellation. Secret
societies and sisterhoods of the moon. Divine architects and demonic
builders. Reformers, educators; heroines and heroes who save but a single
soul. Faces and hands of all colours and sexes and genders and aspects.
Reading about Karl-Maria Lindner in the Pacific she understands why
Ava'u and why they are coming.

'Why do you live like this?'

'Why would you live any other way?' Atli answers. 'Come up to the
house tonight. I'll cook.'

She comes up to the house.

There she meets Raisa.

111

The ships pass through the Bering Strait and into the high north. Captain Alvarez hails the fleet.

'Migration fleet, this is the Arctic Ocean.'

At North 72 the fleet turns east onto its four-thousand-kilometre journey across the Beaufort Sea, through the needle's eye of the Prince of Wales Strait between Banks and Victoria islands into the Parry Channel, through Lancaster Sound into Baffin Bay and a great southward run through the Davis Strait to the open waters of South Greenland. Racing winter. Racing re-forming ice. Racing geostorm and geopolitics. A long, cold, fear-filled passage without sun or stars.

Once-loud decks are muted and sullen. People pass without conversation, without greeting. Tensions build into arguments. Old resentments are remembered and sat over. Deck wardens break up more than one fight between the young men. Children are quiet and there is no comfort in song or faith. The wind blows hard and unrelenting, the sea runs slate and foam. The ships judder and creak and every line and rail howls. The corridors are cold, every piece of metal beaded with condensation and the calls of the sea-birds are the voices of the drowned.

On a night one and fifty hundred kilometres north of Prudhoe Bay an anti-cyclonic front pivots in from the high north and sweeps the sky clear. The Aurora Borealis stands over the fleet. On every ship, from *Ava'utapu* to the labouring long-liner *Luna Malia*, people go on deck to stand under the shining sky.

Tongues of green fire speak across heaven. Streamers of light become curtains become murmurations of luminescent green starlings, turning as one with breath-taking speed into new forms. The zenith stutters and glows. Before human eyes wondered, these lights danced above the high north. Before ice, before life itself. They will only fade when the planet's magnetic field winds down and winks out, hundreds of millions of years, millions of sky-struck generations from now.

'Pohiva told me he wished so much to see this,' Amon says. He stands at the rail of the royal stateroom balcony.

'He was a serious man,' Princess Halae says. On their evening meetings they speak a fusion of Princess Halae's idiosyncratic English and Amon's hobbling Ava'uan, yet they understand each other. 'He would bring me presents when he came to the palace. Ice cream mostly. Something sweet.'

Shock can travel in a snail's shell. Loss may come creeping slow. For almost a week after the abdication Ta played the royal show, visiting the dining rooms and laundries, talking to the school kids, teaching gym classes and leading Women's Walks of the decks. (Down coats and good socks, ladies! It's cold out there!) Then she cancelled spin sessions, skipped the Women's Walks, visited the Neptune's Table restaurant less frequently. Sent apologies for missed council meetings, then not even apologies. Ta Pilolevu withdrew to the stateroom she shared with her sister, then to her bedroom. Kimmie Pangaimotu's instructions were to leave the tray at the door, collect it an hour later. Kimmie reported this to Amon, who, perennially guilty, made it his duty to talk to her, outsider to outsider, exile to exile, bereft to bereft. His excuse was daily short compositions for Princess Halae. She saw through his pretence at once. Ta remained in isolation, a wounded animal lying up, breathing, staring, mourning, healing.

Up on the edge of the exosphere a sudden bombardment of solar particles kicks out a wave of photons and the sky flickers and shifts to a spiral curtain of green. Rays shoot upward from the high reaches of the lights, up into the edge of space. Aurora becomes corona: the crown of the north. Princess Halae gasps.

'Do you hear it, Eimoni?'

Ship thrum and boom. Sea seethe and rush. The wind in the wires. Amon has trained himself to listen: He heard the music inside the Spitalfields coil and gave it to Raisa in her duel with Finn. He listens for the hiss of cascading particles. The harmonics of magnetic resonances. The sub-bass of the planet's iron core spinning faster than the mantle that entombs it.

'I don't, Halae.' The sky-spiral flickers, shifts chirality in an instant, back again. The fleet sails into the mouth of a labyrinth in the sky.

'I wish you could,' Halae says. 'It says: We are so small. These ships, the ocean. The cold. The sky-light. There's always something bigger. That goes on for longer.'

'That's wise music, Halae.'

'I think so.' Her face clouds, she leaves the balcony. Amon follows. 'It's good you couldn't hear it, Amon,' Halae says. 'If you had you might have put it into your own music. It's wise music but it's not happy music. I'm glad I heard it but I don't want to hear it again.'

He closes the stateroom door and hears a bedroom door open. The fleet drives east. Above it the sky spasms with electric fire and old stars connect into new constellations.

At West 141 the *Friedman* signals that it has reached the limit of its jurisdiction. Captain Alvarez bids the migration feet Godspeed and turns back to Prudhoe Bay. The fleet sails deeper into the Beaufort Sea. Its navigators receive ice reports. The Northwest Passages close by the hour. Nor'easter season along the Atlantic seaboards of the US and Canada starts earlier, lasts longer and pushes deeper and higher. A low-pressure area two hundred miles south of St John's in Newfoundland draws in cold air from northern Canada and fattens it on North Atlantic Circulation heat for a week. Then decaying Hurricane Justine rolls by. They flirt, they kiss, they dance. They feed each other, they merge, they monster. They waltz past the coast of Labrador, drawn into the corridor of the Davis Strait. The summer in Kujalleq has broken records for warmth and mildness. Constrained by cold landmasses, gorged on the heat of the north-eastern branch of the disintegrating Gulf Stream, the low-pressure area grows into a synoptic-scale extratropical cyclone.

Big words, but dry.

The 1991 Halloween Storm was a synoptic-scale extratropical storm. That was the Perfect Storm. This is the Immaculate Storm. It doesn't have that title yet. It will. A spiral of the worst weather in the world twelve hundred kilometres across, wind speeds rising beyond hurricane, seas averaging at fifteen metres, peaking at thirty, punishing rain, sleet, August blizzards as cold air floods down from the Greenland ice sheet: this beast is worthy of a title.

In fifty-two hours, the Ava'uan migration fleet will meet it in Baffin Bay.

The Council of Voyagers convenes. Wall screens open and fill with the faces of the fleet captains, the councillors aboard the other ships and maps and satellite images of the Western Arctic. The projected course draws a yellow thread through the archipelago at the top of the world. Another image shows that same geography as a composite of weather images. A claw of cloud curls over eastern Labrador, talon hooked into the Hudson Strait.

'There's no doubt?' asks Lord Tupou, former acting prime minister, now council deputy chair.

'There's always doubt,' Bridge Manager Vai says. 'The storm may change course. It may make landfall. It may blow itself out. It may grow into a hyperstorm. It may fade away.'

'Can we go around it?' Lady Tua of Ofu says from the screen.

'If we knew where it was going, perhaps.'

Heads turn to the door. Voices rise and fall silent as one. Heads dip. Princess Ta enters the bridge. She wears a long dress in a dark floral print, sleeveless the better to display her tattoos. She holds the 'Akau Ta like a magician's staff.

'Madam Chair,' Lord Tupou says. 'Princess.'

'Continue,' she says.

Vai Vailahi lays out the options. The Prince of Wales Strait is narrow and, under storm conditions, dangerous but it is the most efficient transit of the Northwest Passages. A blue line on the map: The southern route runs nine hundred kilometres east-south-east by Queen Maud Gulf under Victoria Island, another seven hundred north along the coast of the Boothia Peninsula and through the Peel Channel between Prince of Wales and Somerset Islands to Lancaster Sound and the open waters of Baffin Bay. The way is long, choked with islands, and would leave the fleet without reserves of fuel or water.

Now a white line. To the north the M'Clure Strait opens on a straight run of the Viscount Melville Sound and Parry Channels past Resolute to Greenlandic waters. The western end of M'Clure is an iceberg graveyard. A solid scrape across a sub-surface berg could snap thruster pods from its hull and leave a cruise ship helpless with winter and the refreeze closing in. The waiting storm shifts air across the Western Arctic: at any moment a change in wind direction could send a zombie-fleet of rotting bergs hundreds of kilometres east, blocking the north end of the Prince of Wales Strait and approach to the Parry Channel.

'There is another option,' Vailahi says. He expands the map to include the entire Arctic Ocean, centred on the pole. Another click highlights a red course, along the north coast of Russia, south of Svalbard, close to the PBV geo-hydrogen plants at Jan Mayen, through the Denmark Strait between Greenland and Iceland, turning north to make final landfall in Kujalleq. 'The Northeast Passage remains open for three weeks later than the Northwest Passage.'

'Could we make open ocean in time?' Ta asks.

'West of Severnaya Zemlya there is no sea ice,' Vailahi answers. An overlay appears on the map, showing historic sea-ice ranges, year upon dwindling year.

'How much longer is the eastern passage?' Captain Efi of *Nafanua* asks.

'Almost three times as long.' Cries of dismay on the crowded bridge. 'We'd have to backtrack thirteen hundred kilometres. The total distance is nine and a half thousand kilometres.'

Cries become invocations of Jesus. This is a distance equal to what they have sailed from Ava'u to the Beaufort Sea. Amon has the musician's gift for numbers but this calculation is simple. The migration fleet travels at the speed of its slowest member: the venerable *Luna Malia,* which maxes at fifteen knots: twenty-seven kilometres per hour. Multiply and divide and everyone arrives at the same deadline. Allowing for breakdown, repair, refuelling and resupply the fleet will arrive three weeks later than the Northwest Passage route, on the edge of winter.

'We will need to refuel at Prudhoe Bay and Murmansk,' Vai Vailahi says.

Captain Ruzza whispers to Amon Brightbourne. The captain's accented English is incomprehensible to Ava'uans. Amon speaks a little DJ-Italian.

'There is another option,' Amon says. 'Return to Unalaska and wait a year.'

Voices shout; outrage on the bridge. Ta lifts the 'Akau Ta high and there is silence.

'I think you have your answer, Captain.'

'I had to ask,' Ruzza says in his heavy English.

'Of course you did. I have a question. This storm: How dangerous is it? Compared to Velma.'

Vailahi clicks a fresh satellite image onscreen. The talon of cloud is fatter, tighter, more opaque, centred over Ungava Bay. Amon thinks he sees a dark seed folded into the arc of the claw. A black eye.

'At present it is a threat to the fleet. And it's still deepening.'

'Could we lose ships?' Ta asks.

'The fishing fleet is old and vulnerable. The patrol boats are rated to Severe Tropical Cyclone. The cruise ships are the most seaworthy but they are not invulnerable. Anything more than superficial damage could be disastrous. We are a long way from rescue. As I said, it could move inland, it could dissipate. Or it could get bigger. And it could come straight for us.'

Ta studies the two screens.

'I propose the eastern route. Seconder?'

Lady Tupua gives her aye.

'Vote?'

Hands rise in the bridge and on the screens. Amon finds his hand up. The proposal is carried.

'Captain, plot a course,' Ta orders. 'Lady Tupua, talk to the Americans and Russians. Amon, talk to the Foundation. We will need their money. Again. We reconvene in two hours.'

The ship shivers as the thrusters swivel and slowly bring Ava'utapu onto a new bearing.

112

From the smart wooden painted houses straggling up a hillside Amon guesses Raisa is at the Nýttnorður House in Nuuk. Saarloq is still foundations and steelwork, with dispersed public buildings like savannah trees. Amon's Greenland—no, Kalaallit Nunaat: council policy is to call the new home by its Kalaallisut name—is a sense of prowling elementals and the arcs of background that lie between Raisa's shoulders and the camera frame. Chords of Saarloq, crescents of Nuuk. In those spaces today he sees a citadel of cloud along the western horizon, like a high Rajput fortress. Raisa ties her wind-tousled hair back and squints against the south-light. Her eyes are in hiding, in a cave, tired and old and hunted.

'I'll go to the ráðh,' she says. 'Get me a budget, Amon. I'll need it fast.'

Time is short, time is shorter, time runs out at the end. Leave a thing undone, unasked, it will go unanswered forever, carried away on the meltwater torrent of final moments.

'Raisa.'

She frowns.

'Raisa, I have to say this. I think I made the biggest mistake in my life . . .'

His phone pings. Council message.

'Raisa . . .'

In the spaces beyond her shoulders a figure moves across decking. A man, half seen, tall, striking. Comfortable in outdoor wear the way that Amon never can be. The man ducks away again when he sees Raisa is in conference.

'Who's that?'

He knows. His phone pings again and it's the excuse he needs to dodge the answer.

'Amon, I need to talk . . .'

'I have to go.' Still he hesitates. 'Emergency.'

'Amon,' Raisa says as he steps out of the camera focus. She says to the closing door, 'You have to know: I have always loved you.'

'I need a fuel and supply budget,' Amon says, arriving on the crowded bridge. One by one the ship commanders appear in their windows.

'You don't, Amon,' Princess Ta says.

Amon feels the ship quiver. Thrusters slowing. Captain Ruzza and a full crew occupy their bridge stations.

'Can everyone hear?' Princess Ta says. The faces in the screens nod. 'Lady Tupua.'

'Russia will grant us passage only in return for territorial concessions from Kalaallit Nunaat,' ex–Foreign Minister Tupua says. On this bridge Amon has heard elation, despair, anger, resolve. Never rage like this. Here is the true storm. Tumult. Roaring voices. Kimmie's eyes are white with fury. He doesn't see the leiti Pangaimotu, the un-crowned Mz Starshine, the almost-star of *New Zealand's Got Talent*. He sees a warrior enraged. It is a fearsome thing.

He hears his nasal, up-and-down voice squawking, *what? what?* into the tumult like a petrel tumbled in a squall.

The 'Akau Ta rises above the highest head and comes down with a bang on the floor. Three times Princess Ta calls for silence. The anger, the shock is a slow-settling sea.

'Continue, Lady Tupua.'

'There's little to explain. The Inatsisartut unanimously rejected any concessions to Russia.'

The Immaculate Storm creeps forward, winds tighter on the screen.

'I will not retreat and lose a year at Unalaska,' Princess Ta says. Mumbles, rumbles of consent. 'Do we agree that our only option is forward?'

Rumbles become ayes.

'I propose the Prince of Wales Strait route without delay,' Princess Ta says.

'Second,' Lady Tupua says. 'Ayes?'

The vote is unanimous.

'Captain, take the fleet by the Prince of Wales Strait route,' Princess Ta says. 'God save Ava'u.'

Slowly, truly, like magnetised needles on water, the fleet turns. Looking through the bridge windows Amon imagines a great charcoal smear of darkness lying between sky and sea.

113

The house moves and creaks like a ship in the storm. On the heights it bears the full force of the nor'wester. Bunting beats, the fairy-lights Atli strung along the porch rail dance. The steel struts of the platform thrum. The roof groans and strains.

Finn turns down lamps, lights up candles. He scatters cushions and does things with aromatic oils. He puts on his music. Raisa doesn't get his music. Raisa doesn't get music.

That's not quite true. Raisa gets her music. Amon Brightbourne's Raisa music. Twenty-three years since she first heard it in the Dorling Avenue tree-house. She's never stopped hearing it, she realises. It's the neural drone at the base of her being: Brightbourne's long music.

Now Finn opens wine. He's in full hunker mode. She doesn't want to hunker amid cushions by candlelight and shiver blissfully at the rain on the windows and the lamp-posts bending in the gale. A storm stole the roof from polytunnel 8 at Vonland. She spoke the name of the storm on the pitching deck of *Los Ascending*. A storm fretted along London's western ramparts the night of the duel of lightning above Spitalfields. Lightning Woman stepped from a storm into her bivvy under the electric oak. Storms are gods, storms are chaos, storms are change.

'Finn.'

She catches him about to take his shirt off.

'Where's Atli?'

Armour-piercing mood-killer.

'At the sanctum.'

'And his girlfriend?'

'She's . . .'

'Not his girlfriend. Where is she?'

'I don't know. Does it matter?'

'Nauja Lund's daughter matters.'

Finn pours wine.

'No wine, Finn. Could you turn off the music?'

The yellow digger on the vacant lot across the road rocks on its treads. A beast surely comes. Finn taps off his music. The wind-shriek leaps close.

'Finn, I need to talk to you.'

He does up his unfastened shirt buttons. She sits at the end of the sofa, hands clasped between close-pressed knees. He gets up from the hunker-nest to sit on a chair; right-angled to her, the therapist's seat. Field of vision but not full eye contact.

'You and me, Finn. We're more than kynnd. Have been for a long time.' She can see him about to speak so she raises a hand. 'We always end up together. I found you with Óðinn in Reykjavík. I was angry.' His mouth is open, again the hand. 'I know I know: kynnd. And it was like the shot that jumped me out of Iceland. And I know you: There's been gods-amount of others. But we always come back to each other. Don't we? Through time, across the world. Field lines. We get drawn to each other. Can't break away. Okay, speak now.'

'If it wasn't us, I'd say you were proposing marriage.'

'Oh no. Gods no.' The Rasmussens next door, seal-slick in weather gear, hunch along the road and battle their front door open in the gusting sleety wind. She wonders again about Atli. 'What I'm proposing . . . what I want . . .' She bites her lip. 'Gods why is this so difficult? Okay. You know this. I talk with Amon every day.' She expects interruption. Finn keeps silence. 'It's become more than talk. It's like a date. God I hate that word.'

'Do you love him?' Finn asks.

'I do, Finn. Oh, he makes me so angry and he's stupid and entitled and he has no sense about anything. All that. But I've never . . . stopped . . . loving him.'

Something beyond the range of human senses sets candle flames wavering.

'What I want, Finn. Oh gods. What I want is both of you. I want him and I want you. I love him and I love you.' She risks eye-to-eye contact with him. 'Can I have that?'

'Okay,' Finn says. 'Okay.' He lifts his full wine glass, sets it down again. 'Have you had this little chat with him?'

'Fuck's sake, Finn; "little chat"? That's like "bless her little head". No. I haven't.' The air throbs to a shift of pressure. The sleet-smear across the window changes angle. The Immaculate Storm is fractious. 'Maybe I sort of said something.'

'Do you think he'd understand it?'

'I don't know. Hopelands and Brightbournes have been wound around each other so long now. His people were halfway to us anyway.'

'It needs to work for him,' Finn says.

'Does it work for you?'

'There are boundaries. I have history with him.'

'He's got history with you too.'

'And he is absolutely, completely, not my type.'

'I'm not asking that.'

'And you know me, Raisa. There will always be others.'

'I know.'

'Does that work for you?'

'I can live with it.' She bites her lower lip. 'I know I want something that works better for me than anyone else.'

'You always did, Raisa.'

The wind drops. The sleety rain breaks into flurries. The storm is moving away, drawn to a new quarter.

'I'll take that, Finn.'

'Be careful with us, Raisa.'

'I will.'

'Because you get what you want and then you don't know what to do with it.'

She turns Finn's words over.

'He always said I never finished anything. So I decide to finish something. To complete something. And then you tell me I won't know what to do with it.'

'I want this to work. For all three of us.'

'This isn't how I saw this playing,' Raisa says.

'This is not how I saw this playing,' Finn says. He offers wine and this time Raisa doesn't refuse. 'To us. All three of us.'

'Three stars. A little constellation.' Raisa sips the wine. 'We haven't finished this but you can put your horrible music back on again.'

Tuusi sprawls across the sofa like a walrus. Nauja nestles in the twelve percent of unoccupied upholstery. Storm-force gusts beat the windward wall like a drum. The house has carried many lives through worse. Screen-shine lights their faces football-pitch green. Tuusi is an avid follower of the

English Premier League. Blue is the colour; Chelsea Chelsea is the name. He wears a new-season first-team shirt. Nauja thinks he should have bought it two sizes larger but let him enjoy his middle-aged delusions while he can.

'Where's Siisi?'

'At the Foundation house.' He passes the plastic bowl of kettle chips. Nauja Lund waves it away.

'I don't like her staying there.'

'You don't like her seeing that Hopeland boy.'

'Not a boy.'

Tuusi tenses, surges, hisses on the sofa. A sweet cross into the box, a shot over the bar.

'Sometimes a boy, sometimes something else More. I don't understand it. Siisi does. I trust Siisi. What this is is, you don't like his mother. Hés mother.' Tuusi eats crisps like a digger, scooping up open bucket-loads.

'We understand each other.'

'Message her then,' Tuusi says through crunching. 'Say you want her back. Weather and everything.'

'And how would that make me look up there on Noorlernut?'

'So you'll trust Siisi then.'

'These Hopeland people arrive and change everything.'

'It was changing anyway.'

'I know, I know. Just . . .'

'Just?'

'If it would just stop, even for a moment; just let me catch my breath.'

Rain swirls, rattles over the roof, bangs the screen door that Tuusi hasn't got round to fixing three years after Nauja complained.

'Sounds like it's backing north,' Tuusi says.

'Shit. The flight will be going tomorrow.'

'Do you have to be on it?'

'In ten days the fleet sails up Qaqortoq Fjord and drops anchor. And we are not ready. I need to be there to make it less not ready.'

'Will one day of less-not-ready make a difference?'

'Everything makes a difference now. North?'

'North.'

'I hope it misses the fleet,' Nauja says, as close as she gets to a prayer. Tuusi rolls over it with an exasperated roar as Liverpool gain possession in their box, counter-attack down half the pitch pass pass pass and smack it into the top-right corner of the net. Nauja picks up her phone. 'I might message Siisi anyway.'

Atli opens the long leather case and with care, reverence and violation lifts the twin electrode-staffs of the Grand Primary. Hé carries them into the hall of the Coil of the North. Finn's armour is too long, too tight on hé but all hé has knitted of hés own is a left gauntlet. Hé sets the staffs in the sockets in the polished concrete floor and turns to Siisi, who has unfolded a chair by the kitchen door.

The rain drums a hi-hat beat on the metal and the wind calls demon voices from the eaves. Siisi glances up. A night for high electromancy and forbidden power.

'These are the staffs of office of the Grand Primary of the Order of Electromancers.' Finn commissioned a Vík metallurgist to reforge the brass globes damaged in the Battle of Spitalfields. Atli walks to the centre of the triangle formed by the Great Coil and the two staffs. Hé pulls the coif over hés head, swirls into hés wrapper and raises hés arms. 'Watch!'

Hé stomps the foot-switch. Power throbs louder than the storm. Fluorescents flicker. The steel columns drip tongues of St Elmo's fire and the secondary coil roils with actinic light. Hé lifts one staff, draws it close to catch an arc and sets it back in its socket. Hé takes the second staff, catches the arc from the first with it, moves it close to the Great Coil to complete the magic circle, draws the lightning out and sets the staff back in its socket. Atli stands in the centre of an Arcmage's Triangle, ringmaster of the lightning show. Hé holds up hés right hand in the Sign of the Generator, hés left in the Sign of the Motor.

'Atli Raisasbur Vega Stormtalker!' hé yells over the seething voltage, the drum and bass of the storm.

Siisi applauds. Atli moves hés foot to the kill-switch and stops. Hé's not alone in the Arcmage's sanctum. Something says hés name. Something in the fizz of the plasma, the resonance of the chain-mail covering hés body, the cracking of the triangle of power. Siisi can't hear it, no one outside the triangle can. To hés ears it's clear and plangent. The lightning called hés name. Hé's not afraid. How can hé be? The caul falls from hés trepanning. Senses open.

'I thought it was shit,' hé whispers.

No, says the storm. *Oh no never no.* And in telling that it tells hé another thing: its own name. Atli says that name. Power crackles from the arc-lightning in hés eye, across hés face, down the field lines drawn so carefully over the left side of hés body. The storm hears. The rain beats as hard, the wind as long and monstrous but Atli feels it turn, like magnetic particles realigning in the brain of a migrating north-bird.

'It's true,' hé says. Hé stomps the coils, sweeps back hés hood, tears off hés coif, gasping, wide-eyed.

'Okay?'

Hé can hardly walk from the Electromantic Triangle. Energies, forces murmur around hé.

'Okay?' Siisi asks again. Finn's warning about the Great Coil hangs like electric ghost fields.

'Yes,' Atli says. In the library hé struggles out of the heavy, awkward armour. Hé hasn't the strength to arrange it on the cross. 'No.' Atli hadn't believed the legends, the lore and mythos, the rituals. The magic. Electromagnetic fields can induce hallucinations and mystical trips in human brains. Tesla coils are electromagnetism in motley. Something said hés name. Hé said the something's name and felt the storm turn. 'You know my name?'

'You have too many names,' Siisi says.

'Stormtalker.'

Siisi rolls her eyes. Having a thrash-metal father breeds little tolerance of rockisms.

'Maybe it's not . . .' Hé takes the words no further because hé isn't sure they can say what hé felt. Siisi's phone has sent her a message. Another eye roll, widdershins this time.

'Mom's wondering where I am.'

'You're all right.'

'I know. She isn't.' Siisi collects her backpack. 'Not so bad,' she says, opening the warehouse door. A swinging wind swirls rattles of rain across the harbour road and through the cones of yellow streetlight. 'She worries.' She pulls up her hood. 'Atli Stormtalker. I have a thing to ask you.'

'Ask.'

She flicks open the scooter.

'How do I join your family?' She steps onto her scooter, twists the throttle and rattles off, dodging between the rain-filled potholes. Storm-clouds tear into long fuligin ribbons and roll up to the north. Above them stars realign.

114

On its seventy-seven thousand two hundred and twelfth orbit, monitoring satellite *Huangjing 2J* passes over the Labrador Sea and south-west Greenland. It sees: neat nets of roads with street-lights. Longer sperm-tails of highway reaching to each other over the hills and around the fjords. Jetties and piers, ro-ro ramps. Fuel depots and hydrogen tanks. Reservoirs, water and hydro systems. Power lines and electrical distribution centres. Community buildings. The foundations of apartment blocks. Rows of hydroponic farms glowing life-pink in the thermal spectrum. Construction-villes, earthmovers and cranes and temporary cabins piled on top of each other to maximise space on the cramped sites. Blooms of sewage discharge into the fjords. Ships in those fjords. The main settlement at Saarloq is the closest to completion: Nanortalik and Alluitsup Paa are intentions gouged into turf and stone.

Huangjing 2J also sees a storm departing Kujalleq, tracking north-west over Ellesmere Island at forty kilometres per hour.

The godlings of Touia'o Futuna sense it first. With something like but not exactly smell they become aware that the storm has turned and is coming for them. With something like vision, which not only sees heat but tastes it at the same time, they have enjoyed the flavour of unprecedented ice-cap melting in Greenland and Baffin Island; exa-joules of solar energy locked into meltwater and water vapour returned in spectral walls of fresh-flavoured indigo as rain pummels north-eastern Canada. This beast eats energy. Latent heat spins the Immaculate Storm up to a deity-level event.

Not that they understand any of this. Wisdom is not a necessary quality of a god. They smell/feel fear, taste/see terror, link arms and scrum down.

The order of the passage of the Prince of Wales Strait is this: The three patrol boats range twenty kilometres ahead on ice-watch. Ten kilometres behind them the fisher fleet's four most robust ships will look out for shifting or tumbling ice. Rapid melting moves the centres of gravity of these zombie ice slabs; they can roll and abruptly change orientation. Then come *Avaʻutapu*, *Ofu* and *Niua* in single file followed by the rest of the fisher fleet.

The passage will take ten hours. If the strait is clear. Church leaders call the people to pray for fair weather and no ice. Clergy preach Matthew 7:14: "strait is the gate, and narrow is the way, which leadeth unto like."

Nafanua enters the Prince of Wales Strait at 19:12. Sunset is 20:14; sun rise 06:08. The fleet will pass through the narrow way in darkness. Yet on each ship the people take mats and bedsheets and quilts on deck and find places where they can sit and bolster themselves against the cold and keep watch through the night passage. They hold their children close. Banks and Victoria Islands smudge the horizon: stone and slate water, grit and green. The sun drops south-west like a wedding ring lost in the ocean. Time is broken here: days race from endless light to bottomless darkness, each an hour shorter than the one before, the sun more reluctant to leave the southern horizon. A pod of narwhals paces the fleet, *Niua* to *Ofu* to *Avaʻutapu*, then breaks away into open water. Horned fish. The sun is afraid and the gods of Touiaʻo Futuna fall silent, outmatched.

Into the darkness: a line of red, green, white lights threading the needle's eye.

Princess Elisiva Taʻahine Pilolevu keeps vigil on *Avaʻutapu*'s bridge. Captain and crew watch the radars, the sensors, the weather-satellite images. The storm is currently punishing western Greenland. Blow long, blow fierce. Blow yourself out.

Twenty kilometres north-east, Major Fia on *Nafanua* stands radio in hand, scanning the dark for a thing he cannot quite comprehend.

Father Isaaki walks *Avaʻutapu*'s upper decks, greeting parishioners, listening, offering a word, a prayer.

Moderator Viliami walks *Avaʻutapu*'s lower decks, listening, offering words of strength and comfort from the Bible.

Lady Tupua stands at the rail of her stateroom balcony and pulls a tapa mat closer around her. It's no defence against the cold of the Prince of Wales Strait but the family mats were the precious thing she chose to save of her family treasure. Their patterns, their images, their histories hold ancient warmth.

West of Banks Island, Dance Captain Ema Maivia turned fourteen. Now with four girls from her troupe she too tours the decks, encouraging the women to join them in the old dances. Heads, hands, hearts.

Amon Brightbourne sits at his MacBook, MIDI keyboard connected, software open. By lamplight he tries to make music. There is no music in him tonight. He goes up on deck. The people greet him.

In the bathroom of the stateroom she shares with Amon, Kimmie Pangaimotu peers into the mirror and starts making her face. Cleanse, degrease. Refresh pores. Foundation, stripe and blend. Cheekbones. She grimaces at the turkey-skin on her throat. Work it. Lips. Eyes last. She regards herself long and deep. Flawless. The Prince of Wales Strait shall have the perfect leiti.

Eight hours and twenty-five minutes into the passage. Two hours from light. The watch changes on *Nafanua*'s bridge. Major Fia keeps his post. He looks up. He smells something. Everyone on the boat smells it. Captain Efi orders a searchlight. Marine Toeava sends the beam seeking over the black water. A ripple: something submerging. A splash, something surfacing. Alien noises from the unseen land. The beam quests forward. A low line of grey white lies between dark sea and dark sky.

Ice ahead.

Words goes back and the fleet drops to a slow idle. The patrol boats venture into the ice, seeking open-water leads, chains of cracks and slush. How far? How fast? Ice never stops moving. Canadian Coast Guard at Resolute Bay confirms drifting, rotting ice at the north-east end of the Prince of Wales Strait and offers the services of their icebreaker, CSHC *Resolute*. Forty thousand dollars per day. Per ship.

The patrol boats edge between slushy slabs of decrepit pack ice. The lead seems wide and open. Resolute Bay and satellite data are unclear on how far the ice stretches. There is a delicate balance here: too cautious and the lead may refreeze. Too eager and the cruisers could ice-in if the lead turns into a dead end. And the wind is rising, setting the ice field rocking. Slabs lift and settle on the rising swell, drifting.

An hour after entering the lead Major Fia reports. Open water at twenty kilometres. *Ava'utapu*'s bridge crew looks to Princess Ta. There is only one command that can be given. *Ava'utapu* moves into the lead, followed in the unvarying order by *Ofu* and *Niua*. The smaller, nimbler fisher craft take up the rear. The rising sea breaks the decaying pack ice into unpredictable, shifting slabs. Floes grind against hulls; every bang and squeal and shudder brings the helpless dread that a submerged strike will send a thruster pod to the bottom of the strait. The cruise ships' searchlights light the lead and the ice fields. The cold is outrageous. No one leaves deck. This is ice and it is terrible. On every side stretch grey discs of gently undulating ice-plates, rippled, sometimes pressure-ridged as high as Deck 6, some pooled with melt ponds. Cracks and leads jostle with ice-balls set bobbing by the ships' wakes. Where the ice-balls—shuga—touch they freeze together. Fresh nilas—the first grey skin of ice over open water between floes—crack and break as the plates move against each other, piling up into rims like plates.

Jesus was wrong. Dante Alighieri was right. Hell is not the burning trash-pyre of Gehenna. Hell is the locking of water into ice, ice, ice. Most of the Ava'uan travellers have not read Dante but all who see the lift and tilt of the moving ice understand that this is their harrowing. This is the Ninth Circle.

An hour before sunrise *Ava'utapu* emerges from the lead into the open water of the Parry Channel. Forty minutes later the chugging *Luna Malia* breaks out and the fleet resumes sailing order.

'We're clear,' Princess Ta tells the people. 'We have passed through the ice.'

The sun rises low and sullen from the southern expanse, barred by tracks of purple cloud, and by its thin light Princess Ta sees the thing she forgot in the fearful passage through the ice. East by south-east a behemoth rises from the sea. From a curtain wall of grey towers an anvil of white cloud, swirled in bands of whipping cumulus, the hammer of God raised over the Northwest Passage. The storm has turned.

Reports arrive. Peak winds of 120 kph. Gusts up to 55 kph. Wave-height average ten metres. A thing like this has never been known north of the Arctic Circle before. It's the storm crow of planetary change. The people of Ava'u know this beast well. It didn't end them the first time. It's returned to pick their bones clean.

'Can we ride it out in Resolute Bay?' Lord Tupou asks.

'It will hit us before we arrive,' Vai says.

'Back?' says Lord Vaea from *Niua*.

Captain Ruzza mumbles to Amon Brightbourne.

'The Prince of Wales Strait is closing,' Amon interprets. 'Berg ice is moving east from the M'Clure Strait. The way is shut.' Ta's grip tightens on the 'Akau Ta.

'Then take us in, Captain.'

115

It's death. This is how everything ends and he hates it and fears it and he can't look away.

He could hide from Velma. In the shelter all he sensed were the distant sounds of destruction. There is no shelter in Parry Strait. No hiding. Mountains of water thunder-hammer the hull. Wave trains roll in forever, capped with white tungsten and steel foam-scab. Endless energy. Endless annihilation. Spray sweeps his stateroom window, twelve decks up, to freeze on the rail. Balcony wires shriek. The sliding door bulges and shivers. Water seeps through the loosened seams to pool on the polished wood. Above the tormented fleet stands the citadel of the Immaculate Storm.

He can't look away.

Ava'utapu plunges and rolls. He reels towards the glass, puts out his hands to stop himself. He imagines the glass shattering into spangles, plunging through. The rail won't save him. Falling into the spray-lace hollow of the killer wave.

The glass holds. The ship rights.

Deck committees have stationed carpenters on every level with tools and wood to board up breaches. The first demon of terror is flooding; sheets of water running the width of the ship, pooling until she can no longer right herself. The Ava'uan voyagers have prepared. Kitchens are closed, swimming pools drained, common areas declared off-limits. People stay in their rooms. Deck committees have posted medics and set up a network of runners to pass orders up and down the corridors should power fail. Total power loss is the second demon of terror: a big cruise liner without thrust or steering, without systems or comms, turned by the storm and rolled over. In their rooms, each family listens to the boom of the sea, watches the waves break and the skins of rime build up over the windows and feels the ship tilt and lurch and remembers the *Princess 'Akusita*.

They thought they knew the sea.

The Pulotu Road boys have hauled down Touia'o Futuna and deflated the abode of the godlings.

Kimmie Pangaimotu rolls and vomits profoundly in her bedroom. She is not a quiet patient. Pleas, prayers, oaths in three languages, pleadings for Amon to do something if only kill her. The stench of vomit punches Amon low and hard. The geckos found a place to hide hours ago.

The stateroom furniture waltzes across the floor as the ship plunges by the head and rolls. The crew hold *Ava'utapu* right to the storm. The strait is only sixty kilometres wide and the storm has moved south over Ellesmere Island. Soon the fleet must tack to take the seas abaft. Turning broadside to the Immaculate Storm is the moment of greatest danger. This is the third demon of terror. Any one of them can send a ship to the bottom of the Prince of Wales Strait.

And still he can't look away.

He follows the wave aft to watch *Ofu* breach the crest, pitch, roll, right slowly: 180,000 tons lifted like a toy. He feels *Ava'utapu* rise to the next wave. The floor tilts. The furniture slides. Kimmie, voice weak with exhaustion, swears in soft Ava'uan. Wave after wave.

Brightbourne's library held an 1818 edition of Blake's *For the Sexes: The Gates of Paradise*. Twenty-one plates, each the size of a postcard. Forty words between them. Worlds and eternities within. Each unforgettable. An arm reaches out of whitecapped waves, a face half-submerged, upturned. The hand open. The plate is named 'Help! Help!'

That book is ash now, together with its library, and Brightbourne.

He sees the arm out there, reaching up from twenty-metre waves, swept further and further away from help and light. He sees death out there. He can't look away.

Princess Ta has held the 'Akau Ta for eleven hours now. Her arm aches but if she lets it fall from her grip, disaster will swallow the fleet. It's only half superstition. In the dark hours before the storm-wall, lit only by screenshine, she swore a binding vow upon the staff of kings, by gods older than Jehovah and his Christ, than the divine flotsam clinging to a deflated weather-balloon. Gods who came before Biki and Maimoa'o, Fonuavai and Fonua'uta, Hemoana and Lupe, before names could constrain their pure creative wildness. By them: not one soul.

She has led the people through the gates of the North, under the aurora sky. Through nightless days racing into lightless dark. Through ice into the storm at the top of the world, the storm that never ends, that has spun them into its gyre, an endless voyage through waves and wind and ice. Until water and food run out and she is Queen of a fleet of skeletons and storm-zombies, cursing for eternity from their cells.

'Ma'am.' Fetuu brings a pill and a glass of water. Ta has never been a good sailor—a secret shame for a Tu'i. Fetuu dosed her with Dramamine to get her onto the royal war canoe for the annual Mua Lagoon regatta. Princess Ta pauses, pill to tongue. The voices on the comms channel have changed tone.

'What's happened?'

'We've received a distress call from *Luna Malia*,' Vai says. 'She's lost engine power and steerage.'

'Where is she?'

'Eight kilometres east-north-east,' Vai says. '*Neiafu* is diverting.'

'Is there anything we can do?' Ta asks, knowing there isn't. The plan is that the faster, nimbler patrol boats aid any ships in trouble. The screens show *Neiafu* five kilometres ahead of *Ava'utapu*, changing course in monstrous seas.

'Captain Vuna has it in hand.'

She swallows her Dramamine. A twenty-metre wave rolls towards *Ava'utapu*. Its trough, as deep as the wave is high, is the black gullet of the northern ocean. The bow pitches up, water breaks high above the bridge. Spray freezes on the ice-slicked foredeck.

Not one soul, Princess Ta whispers in the heart of the great sea wave.

You can look at death only for so long because death is boring. Death cosplays great but has only one trick. The waves come, the ship rolls. Amon lets go his handhold. He finds he can balance. He has found the still eye of the Immaculate Storm, as small as a black poppy seed, a molecular knot of air. From that point of equilibrium, Amon sees what to do.

He steps deftly around the sliding furniture. He pauses at the door, deciding what to do with his satchel. He doesn't want it joining the general dance but it can't come with him. He hangs it over the framed evacuation notice on the back of the door.

Kimmie Pangaimotu may be the most seasick leiti in Ava'uan history but her hearing has been sharpened on palace gossip.

'Amon?' she calls from her vomit bed as Amon opens the stateroom door.

Fuck.

'Amon?' He steps into the corridor and closes the door on his name.

The second click is the deciding click. Kimmie rolls from her bed. Space-time reels around her. She catches a whiff of reek. How can so much pau'i come out of one leiti? She pulls on a shrug. She sees the soft leather satchel hanging on the back of the door.

He left his bag.

The world is ending.

Into the deserted corridor.

'Amon?'

There isn't time for him to have reached the aft lobby. Left to the forward elevators. She arrives at the golden doors to see the indicator light climb to Deck 15 and stop.

'Come on come on come on,' she hisses at the second elevator. In the lift she discovers there is much worse than lying in your own bed afloat on a sea of vomit and that is being in a metal box grinding up a steel tube by fits and starts, whines and jolts as the ship moves around it.

What if she gets stuck?

Gets stuck and the ship capsizes and she's on her side in this metal box in a metal ship racing to the bottom of the cold cold ocean?

Gets stuck in a metal box in a metal ship, in an airtight bubble at the bottom of the cold cold ocean, with all the air she'll ever breathe?

'Fuck up, Kimmie,' she says in English and the elevator announces Deck 15, doors opening.

116

The automatic doors to the Sky Deck have jammed shut. He remembers—somehow—a corridor safety briefing on where to find the emergency handle.

The assault of sleet drives the breath from him. He gasps in the stunning cold. Tweed is suitable for all occasions save polar gyre-storms. The wind punches him back into the elevator lobby. Black ice slicks the decking. The ship dips, sways to port, spray flies fifteen decks high. Amon grabs for the safety rail and hauls his way along the superstructure to the leeward side. Brogues too fail as appropriate storm-wear. The potted palms are lashed down tight, their tattered fronds coated with ice. Deck furniture is a spider-orgy of black legs. Grey slush slops from the ocean-view spa-pools.

At the top of the staircase to the pool deck he finds a sheltered corner. He thrusts aching hands into armpits. A wind-eddy slaps his soaked hair across his face. He claws it away. He looks down the length of the ship. The empty pool is a grave of sun-loungers and cushions. Beneath a black sky of boiling cloud he gazes upon primal chaos. To his right *Ofu* and to the left *Niua* weather titanic seas. Between waves the height of houses he glimpses a patrol boat making best speed against the fleet's direction of travel.

That bodes ill.

It has to be now.

He steps to the rail. A slip almost sends him down the steps. He grabs the railing and cries out. It burns. It burns blue.

'I'm back,' he shouts.

This again? The storm turns its eye on him. *You still don't know my name.*

'I don't need to!' Amon shouts. The agony in his hands fuels his voice. 'But I will tell you my name. My name is . . .'

'Amon Brightbourne!'

He recoils and almost loses footing on the ice. He braces against the frozen aluminium railing to look around. Kimmie Pangaimotu, a lifeboat in a storm, hauls herself along the safety rail towards him, hand over scarf-wrapped hand.

'What the fuck are you doing?' she bellows.

'Kimmie, shut up!'

His hands, his hands are dying. Cell by cell, his fingers, then his palms, his wrists, forearms freeze.

'Come away from there.'

'I have to do this!'

'No I have to do this. Again, Amon. Every fucking time.'

'Leave me.'

'I will not.'

'Stay there. Do not come near me!' He turns back to the apocalypse-sea and shouts into the lull, 'My name is Amon Oisin Attica Brightbourne. I am the Brilliant Boy. I am the Graced. Mine is a charmed life. You have no power over me!'

The ships, the waves, the walls of cloud hang in time. Then the storm crashes in again with a murder of hard-frozen sleet and a gust that sends him to his knees. Storm, sea, sky turn upside down. The ships float in heaven. His nerves have been pulled through his skin and stapled to the wind, the killing cold, the spray, the sea. The Immaculate Storm plays him like a piano. He sees the heart of everything.

'Leiti strength, 'ofa'anga,' Kimmie whispers, rips Amon from the rail and hefts him over her shoulder.

'I talked to it, Kimmie,' Amon burbles as they ride down in the halting, jolting elevator.

'Fuck up, Amon,' Kimmie Pangaimotu says. The cold has got into his palangi brain.

By the time she reaches their stateroom and roared for the corridor nurse the wind has dropped a Beaufort-point, the waves have dwindled three metres.

He leaves two mittens of skin where his hands froze to the railing.

117

By nightfall the storm has dropped to Beaufort 4. Satellite images show it doubling back on itself, south by south-east. It defies meteorological sense. The fleet sails out into choppy Baffin Bay. The crew of the *Luna Malia* took to life rafts at the height of the storm; the ship foundered thirty minutes later. By the time *Neiafu* reached the sea area the storm had diminished to Force 7, low enough to attempt a rescue. By 17:00 all crew from the *Luna Malia* were reported safe and in good health.

Princess Ta slips from her chair. She leans, bends, tries to push life back into concrete joints, rusted muscle fibres. Finger by finger she releases her grip on the ʻAkau Ta and leans it against her seat.

Not one soul.

She jogs on the spot, bends one leg at a time up behind her to stretch out joints, tendons, muscles.

Not one soul.

Moderator Viliami, Father Isaaki and Methodist President Fakatou announce a joint service of rejoicing and thanksgiving: all ships. Whatever god you call upon in peril on the sea.

118

Atli brings two coffees from the machine at check-in. He sits beside Siisi, stretches his legs out, hands her a paper cup.

'She just called her a cult leader.'

Their seats are on the line of sight with the office's window. Nauja paces, storms, jabs an accusing finger. Raisa stands, arms folded, a head taller and everything deployed to occupy maximum space.

'We could go,' Siisi says.

'We could,' Atli says. Neither of them will for the same reason that neither of them could refuse the summons to the airport.

'You: with me,' Nauja ordered as she picked up her travel bag from the place by the door where the boots and coats and sticks lived. Tuusi backed the pickup out from its berth among the family archaeology. 'And get the boy.'

'He's not a boy.'

'Get the whatever.'

Nauja threw her bag in the back seat beside Siisi. She held her laptop prim and proper on her lap on the short, grimly silent drive to the airport.

Siisi Lund had not expected her announcement to go without comment. She had passed a white night working out what to say at breakfast, rather than give that sleepless night to Nauja and Tuusi by telling them when she came home on the tail of the storm. She thought that wise and considerate. Tuusi looked up from his phone and raised eyebrows. Nauja turned her full, slow hawk-stare on her daughter.

'You what?'

Okak decided it was time to start a moisturising regime and slipped to the bathroom.

'I think I want to join Atli's family.'

'Do you hear what this girl is saying?' Nauja Lund said and Tuusi tried to muster as much concern as he could without ganging up against his daughter, which Nauja saw and was about to open up about when she noticed the wall clock. 'I don't have time for this now. I have to have time for this. Now I have to catch a flight.'

She didn't talk to Siisi in the car and marched right past Atli, straight
to Raisa at bag drop.

'I'll wait if you want,' Tuusi said in the drop-off area.

'I'll be okay,' Siisi said. Her father reached over and squeezed her arm.
Her mother was already in full-blown argument. Airport staff moved in
quickly to divert the row to a less public place. The Inatsisartut liaison
and a Nýttnorður stýra slap-fighting at Nuuk Airport check-in was not
good PR.

'Your mom's not doing much,' Tuusi says.

'Raisa. We don't do parent titles.'

'Raisa's not doing much.'

'Passive-aggressive is her thing.'

Raisa throws her hands up in the air and bursts out of the office.

'Put me on the next flight,' she shouts to the check-in operator.

'Everything is booked up,' the operator says.

'Then charter me something.'

'There is nothing,' the operator says. 'Not until tomorrow.'

'Tomorrow?' Raisa says.

'There is a Foundation plane due out of maintenance in two hours.'

'I'll take it.'

'Whoa. Entitlement,' Siisi says.

'You still want to be one of us?' Atli says.

'We will talk,' Raisa calls to Atli as she marches past and out into the
early light to wait for the Foundation plane. Nauja Lund leaves the office,
nods to Siisi and passes through security.

'Oh I think so, Atli Stormtalker,' Siisi says. 'You are agents of chaos. I
like that.'

It's not two hours. Not three. Four and a half hours later the plane rolls
out of the service hangar. And there's another problem. There are no pilots
rostered on.

'It's self-flying?' Raisa asks the service engineers.

'It is,' they say.

'I'll take it.'

Raisa waits another impatient forty minutes for the plane to be fuelled,
preflight-checked and programmed. She buckles in. The ground crew push

it back, Nuuk Control gives clearance. Raisa has taken many self-guiding flights but she's never lost the little catch of eerie as the plane gives its safety drill, moves out onto the strip, unfolds its lift-off rotors and slips into the sky without human intervention, as free and mindless as a dragonfly. She used to read the displays but found that she had no idea what they meant and ignorance summoned doubts. The plane folds its auxiliary fans away, circles over Nuuk and turns south-east. The fjord-land of Kujalleq confounds her sense of geography—never strong: She hasn't forgotten losing herself within fifteen kilometres of her own home when she walked away from Vonland. If she had known where she was going she would not have found the Cave of the Papars and the stone forest. Humanity's greatest talent is its ability to make shit up as it goes along. She looks across inlets off inlets off inlets. Islands off islands off islands. Fractal. Green and grey, grey-green; to the spill of glaciers, scarred and fractured like hands, and beyond them, above them, the frontier of ice, the horizon to an older shining world.

'Fuck fuck,' she says. Again with heat because no one can hear. 'Fuck fuck fucking fuck!' Just as the truce between her and Nauja Lund grows into peace, it falls apart. At check-in. In front of everyone. In front of their burs. Now she knows what to say. Now from seven thousand metres she sees the answers; l'esprit de l'avion. Maybe talk to your daughter about what she wants? Maybe she knows better than you? Because you never once asked me anything about my people. You had your answers: a cult, a tribe, a secret society, a commune. Now listen to me. It's two-hundred-thousand-and-counting humans of all races and genders and neurologies and histories and ages across gods-know how many hearths because it's always growing. You can voyage across it for a lifetime and never reach the end. Open door leads to open door. It's a nation within all nations, a religion with no belief, a family with no marriage, no mother or fatherhood, no siblings. Only and always kynnd. Because Western/Eastern/Southern families have done such a great job. It's not perfect. Nothing made by humans can be. It works because family is whatever works.

She remembers her vision in the summer woods, of Brightbourne burned, the trees fallen, yes, but of a human institution with the hope of enduring ten thousand years. A family that might outlive the Anthropocene. Gods and whatever comes after gods knew what it might be by then.

Let her make her mind up. That was what she should have said. You can't hold people. You're not losing a daughter; you're gaining ten thousand years of kynnd.

The plane shakes. It advises Raisa to buckle up. She loves flight turbu-
lence. It's the cage-rattle of mortality. Another shake, this one with a small
stomach-lifting drop. Then a big drop and this she does not love. ATC
comes on the line with an extreme-weather warning.

'What?' Raisa says to Qaqortoq Tower. The plane rattles hard enough
now to refute her doubt. Qaqortoq sends satellite images to the plane's
HUD. The Immaculate Storm hit a wall of meteorological carnage over
Ellesmere Island and shattered into a host of whirling storm-shards. Most
spun their energies away to nothing. Some fed on the heat gradient of the
Arctic's warmest ever summer and sent five separate micro-storms shrieking across the North from Qeqqata to the Hudson Strait to Ungava to
Kujalleq; fast moving, fierce. Chaos-gods. Saarloq is under snow; dangerous crosswinds have closed Qaqortoq and Narsaq. Qaqortoq is diverting
her to the nearest landing site inside the AIs safety parameters, a disused
airstrip at Qoquaq from an abandoned Cold War–era uranium prospecting
expedition.

'Where?' Raisa says. The plane banks. The AI shows her a pin six kilometres north-west of Saarloq. There doesn't look enough there to put
a gull down safely but the plane is decided. Raisa plunges into white-out
and drops into a hole in the air. Everything not fastened to the cabin goes
into free fall, then the plane climbs out and up. Raisa's fingers hook the
armrests. Useless. She is helpless here. The little plane bucks. Raisa hears
a thin whistling keen and realises it is coming from her lips. Death smiles
in the seat beside her.

Ten thousand years. No.

The plane flies out of the bottom of the storm. Land beneath her, snow-
scabbed grass and cold stone, closer than she thought. Much closer. Sleety
snow whips across the world. Auxiliary rotors unfold, the wings recon-
figure. She feels landing gear open and lock. Wind shear slaps the plane
towards a bouldery shore, sea running hard and fast, whitecaps sliced flat
by the veering wind. The plane claws landward, wings dipping, settling
in a series of tilting bounces. The propellers slow, the plane loses grip on
the air and Raisa drops a spine-jarring five metres to ground. Mechanisms
bang and crack.

Down. Alive. Raisa unbuckles her seat belt. The last word on her lips,
she realises, was not Amon or Finn or Atli. Just a short, exhausted 'shit'.
She peers through windows crusting with snow. There was an airstrip
here? The plane has come down one hundred metres from a half-glimpsed

shore in a shallow valley. It leans at an anxious angle that suggests broken machinery.

The AI broadcasts a distress call.

They'll find her. They'll find her soon.

How will they find her? Nothing is flying. Cars. ATVs. Can't move for four-wheel drives. Can they drive in this weather? They're Qaqortoqers. They drive in every weather. Six kilometres, ATC said. Well, that's half an hour, say an hour in this. She's getting cold. She fumbles her outer layers from her travel bag and struggles them on. Gratings and wrenches where there should not be. The snow is piling up, the windows tiny portholes in the rime. The wind gusts, the plane lurches. A thing that had creaked now cracks.

What if it flips over?

Sit it out sit it out sit it out.

The planes settles deeper to port. Then the cabin fills with spinning red warning lights.

119

Nauja Lund is a kilometre down the road from the Eqalugaarsuit micro-hydro-plant in a PBV Land Cruiser when the alert comes through. She pulls over to let the AI check location. The car rocks in the swirling wind. Snow skitters across the road, gathering in the tussocky grass of the verges. She knows who's down. She's in the best position by three minutes. Three minutes can be everything.

'Qaqortoq, this is Nauja Lund. I will attempt a rescue.'

A kilometre past the two stacked green container-cabins the service road becomes ruts. Slush fills the potholes. The headlights illuminate a globe of whirling white. Then the ruts are gone.

A screen message and a measured AI voice tell Raisa there's a hydrogen leak.

Raisa knows hydrogen. She knows how to crack it from water with geo-power. She knows how to turn it into useful fuel, she knows how to store it and how it's different from hydrocarbons and what it does when something goes wrong.

Hydrogen has no odour, colour or taste. Tainting chemicals that might identify a leak also contaminate fuel cells, so the gas in the carbon-fibre tanks in this VoltAer V17 is pure and invisible as djinn. Hydrogen flashes in as little as a 4 percent mixture with air and requires ten times less energy to ignite than hydrocarbon fuel. A static spark from a human wearing, say, artificial fibres such as those found in outdoor clothing could trigger an explosion. Hydrogen flashes hot and fast. It forms a cloud over a wide area, resulting in a fuel-air explosion. Fireball.

Hydrogen safety drill: get out, get away, stay away.

Raisa reaches over to open the passenger door. Ice crusts fall from the window seals. The wind beats snow into the cabin. The cold blinds her. Move slowly, move surely. She grips the edges of the door frame and lowers herself to the ground, careful not to rub a static charge from any surfaces.

Hydrogen has no smell but she imagines it like this snow, this wind. Wet cold that reaches through every pore into the spaces of the bones. She presses close to the fuselage, keeping away from the propellers. Gods know they might suddenly spring to life. Shredded. Incinerated. Frozen. Gods know. She whispers the trimurti of hydrogen blasts. *Hindenburg Fukushima Uno-X.*

The plane stands nose to shore, left-wing down. It dropped hard against a rock. The landing gear is bent and pushed up through housing and the wing.

She should check her location. She's still connected to the plane's satellite link. Her finger hovers over the app. No. Tap tap boom. *Hindenburg Fukushima Uno-X.* She walks around the tail. Out of the shelter of the plane the hunting wind strikes from every direction. The snow scissors in like a ring of blades; the world opaques. She can't see the nose of the plane now.

Hindenburg Fukushima Uno-X. She walks in what she thinks is a straight line until the tail too disappears. Now the pecking uncertainties arrive. How far is too close? How close is too far, that the rescuers might find the plane and not her in this white-out? She's too numb to think about that, or how long it might take rescue to find her and where it might come from and how good layered outdoor clothing is at keeping her core temperature up and hat yes she has a hat! She hauls out a silly woolly bobble hat and pulls it down as far as she can tug it. Her phone tumbles to the snowy grass (grassy snow?). She stares at it dumbly: What is this thing, like a black window in the grass now, like that black slab from that old sci-fi movie she never got?

Phone. Phone help. She crouches to pick it up with stone fingers. Cracked things grate and splinter. She taps at it, taps at it, pokes at it, stabs it, nothing is happening why is nothing happening then she realises it's gone to screensaver and she hold it up to her face and it comes to life—Atli! It's Atli! She's calling Atli, then remembers he and hé are her wallpaper. There's the phone. Phone help!

Call. The little green dumbbell thing jiggles. What is that supposed to be anyway? Iggle jiggle wiggle.

White. Light whiter than snow smashes her forward like a stone fist, smashes her into the stony ground. A boom followed by a high white whine. Those things inside her that felt cracked break like a porcelain vase struck with an axe.

The car gives Nauja Lund a fix on Raisa's location and ratchets up the arrival time as the weather deteriorates. Autodrive is sure but autodrive is slow. She shuts down all AI except collision avoidance, grips the wheel and steps on the accelerator. Only when you drive across open terrain do you understand that the world is rocks. Big rocks, little rocks. All rocks. The car jolts and jars hard enough for Nauja to clamp her mouth shut for fear of biting her tongue. Terrifying killing shapes lurch out of the lashing white. Nauja blazes with dread and adrenaline as she wrenches the car away from a mission-killing boulder. The wipers merely relocate the freezing sleet. She yelps as autodrive whirls the wheel through her fingers with a force that would have broken both thumbs if the first lesson of all-terrain driving wasn't branded into her cortex. Thumbs on the outside. The AI spots the subtle murderers: the hidden streambeds, the tilted slabs sloping up to axle-cracking drops, the secret scarps. She daren't glance at the map. She can only hope it's dwindling fast.

A blossom of brightness in the shrieking greyness. Instinct stamps on the brake. Insanity. The laws of reality are breaking out here. Then she hears a distant flat detonation, an onomatopoeic blast.

Nauja Lund takes her foot off the brake. Far, she can't be far. Near, she must be near. Another white light, extended, moving, then it bursts. And then another, like a door, a vulva, a figure in the storm-snow.

She drives towards the light.

First seeing: too many rocks too close too snowy grey. Next hearing: the whine opens into wind roar and the infra-bass of close, unseen waves. Then—then then then—the cold. It knocks her awake and aware. Behind it comes the pain. She tries to get up from the spidery sprawl into which the hydrogen blast threw her. Her left side feels as if every bone has been wrenched from every other.

She can't move.

She has to move. To lie here, to lovely lie here without effort or thought or need for anything but pulling the whipping snow over her like a quilt and rolling up in it and snuggling down in it, is death.

A black hole in the grey. Her phone. She drags herself to the black rectangle.

Last seeing: a face in the black mirror of her phone. The face of a boy, mouth open with mystery, brow furrowed with puzzlement, ablaze with light. Cat-pupil eyes. She looks up.

The Brilliant Boy stands over her. His face shines with kindness and wonder. Light seethes around him. Raisa feels her skin and hair bleaching. She looks up into the blessing face.

'Fuck you,' she says and grabs her phone and drives its edge between the Brilliant Boy's eyes. Those cat-eyes slits open into black holes. His mouth becomes an O of surprise. With all her strength, Raisa shoves the phone into the Brilliant Boy's face. His substance is soft but resistant, like a cornstarch paste. Raisa clenches her teeth against the grating pain, pushes with two hands. Deeper. A line of black division opens from his forehead down the edge of his left eye socket to cleave cheekbone and lip. The Brilliant Boy offers no resistance, shows no pain. He is incapable of pain.

'I thought we done this,' Raisa hisses. She forces the phone all the way into the Brilliant Boy. A black fissure cracks him from skull to sternum. Raisa grabs the edges of the black rift and wrenches them apart. The Brilliant Boy splits in her hands, top to bottom, tears like ripped clothing; falls apart. Inside, the same dark, the rent in the world. Deep in the black beyond the world a new light sparks to life. It moves towards Raisa and she sees a rhythm to that movement, the swing of a woman walking. A shining woman marches up the long dark rift in the universe and steps out into Qoquaq, Kujalleq.

'You're back,' Raisa murmurs. The Lightning Woman lays a finger to her lips. An actinic aura burns around her; a thousand nano-arcs flicker from her skin. She kneels before Raisa and reaches out a hand. Raisa lays her palm to Lightning Woman's. Power bolts through her. Raisa spasms, cries out, jerks back. Lightning Woman turns the hand palm up. Raisa takes it. Again, an agony of power blazes up her bones. Lighting Woman beckons. Tugs gently, encouraging. A third time the lightning burns through Raisa and this time she understands. She struggles to her knees. Lightning Woman rises to a crouch.

'Okay,' Raisa says. 'Okay.' The wind tugs and punishes, the snow gathers in the creases of her outdoor clothing. Her core temperature is fading. She should be dying. She puts down a balancing hand. She feels no cold.

You don't, they said in the survival training courses.

She pulls herself to her feet. Every time her strength fails, the pain wails, her resolve wavers, a charge of energy flows through her from Lightning Woman. They stand clasping hands in the driving storm. Lightning Woman takes a step away. Raisa can't walk the way of the Lightning Woman, orthogonal to the universe. The clasp slips, fingers brush, separate in sprays of feather-arc. From far away, Lightning Woman turns.

'You don't need to say it,' Raisa says. 'I don't have to hear it.'

Lightning Woman lifts a hand. The way beyond the world closes forever.

Raisa's phone falls out of the other place to the snow. She bends to pick it up. Easy. Empowered. She crackles with energy. It glows in her eyes. She slips the phone into a wrist pocket of her parka.

A third light shines in the whistling grey. A light of this world, that divides into two lights, then becomes the snow-scattered headlights of a PBV car.

Nauja Lund staggers through the wind to Raisa.

'Come with me, come on, come.'

She throws a guiding arm around Raisa's shoulder and jolts back with a cry. She felt a shock.

'I'm okay,' Raisa says dreamily. 'I'm okay.'

The snow doesn't settle on her.

'In here in here.' Nauja opens a rear door. 'Lie down, there's a blanket. It'll heat up fast.'

'I'm warm,' Raisa says and Nauja feels a wave of heat as Raisa moves past her onto the seat, swings her legs up and curls in like a foetus. Nauja lays in the course to the Qaqortoq medical centre.

'I've got her,' she calls on the radio as the car turns round and picks a sensible course back over the streambed and around the rocks. Nauja glances in the rearview mirror, then hangs up the microphone to take a longer look behind her.

A soft glow shines from the rear seat of her car.

120

Flights have been booked out for days. The ferry is at capacity but Atli manages to get three tickets south. Finn shoulders the bags and goes to find a nest among the dignitaries and reporters and camera gear while Atli frets at the top of the ramp. The ferry sounds its horn. A pickup races through the gates and pulls up at the foot of the ramp. Siisi jumps out and heaves her bag across her back. Atli sees her father wave, then lean across to nod to him.

The passage south is surly, sleet scoured and Septembral. The lounge is crowded, noisy; insomniac Atli wakes from a white sleep to find Siisi gone. He meets her on deck. The flaws and buffets of passage clear from the east. Beyond the black mountains the day breaks clear and high. The ferry sounds its horn, warning the fleet of construction vessels in Qaqortoq Fjord. Saarloq blazes under perpetual light and energy. The din of community-building carries clear across the water.

'This is real,' Siisi says. Atli hears the breath of wonder in her voice. 'All this just from goodness.' He makes his small, nervous move. He slips an arm around Siisi's waist.

'My mother would hate that,' she says but leans against him.

'Your mother isn't here,' Atli says.

'She is. That's the point.'

'Siisi, I have to ask you something. Well tell you, but it's an ask. Eventually. When I was in Ava'u, seeing Amon, I met a girl. Tiwa. She was American. She was a post-grad. Social sciences. We went travelling around the islands.'

'You have to tell me this right now?'

'We kind of had a thing. I say "kind of" because it didn't work. She liked hé but not him. I think she resented him. But that's not me. I'm both.'

'Yes,' Siisi says.

'Yes?'

'Yes. I like both of you. That was your question? And it's not two yous. Not to me. There's one Atli Stormtalker who has two Emanations.'

'Oh.'

'Is that all right?'

'That's all right.'

'Good then.'

The engine pitch changes, Qaqortoq arrives in view beyond the headland, ferry mechanisms clank and vibrate. Passengers emerge from the lounges on deck and quickly, in the huddle of bags and weather-wear, Siisi takes Atli's face between her hands, brings it to her, and kisses him.

Qaqortoq is being invaded. The heliport buzzes with aircraft. Every Airbnb was reserved weeks ahead. Households rent out mattresses and floor space. Stores, bars, restaurants have stockpiled supplies. Batteries, bottled water, bottled gas. Families hire out their cars, pickups, even diggers and mopeds. The Kujalleq government brings a school bus in from Nuuk. Afterwards, it will serve the two communities of Saarloq and Qaqortoq. The ferry docks and news crews, politicians, influencers, observers surge ashore. With them, Team Arcmage. World news heads for accommodation or shoot GVs. The electromancers wait for the surge to subside, disembark at their leisure and ask directions to the medical centre.

Amon's fingers turn red and glossy, then swell into bloated yellow blisters like the tubers of a toxic plant. They hurt like fuck.

'That's good,' says Chief Medical Officer Dr. Ma'afu. 'The nerves are alive.' He doses Amon on revelation-grade painkillers. Kimmie Pangaimotu tends the raving wounded: feeds him, toilets him, dresses him, cleans him.

On the third day after Amon Brightbourne defied the storm, the doctors lance the blisters.

'I'm seeing this,' Kimmie insists. 'You owe me.'

He has not been a gracious patient.

The needles go in and a stupendous gush of thin yellow serum flows out, each a kidney dish's worth.

'I'm impressed, Amon,' Kimmie says. 'I never knew you had it in you.'

He holds up his hands. Drained, wrinkled, baggy skin. Hands of horror. Freddy Krueger fingers.

'Will I be able to play?' Amon asks.

'I hope so,' says a voice from the door. 'I fired my master of music but my sister says you take private commissions.' Ta is diminished and sagging, muscles drained. Her skin is dull with fatigue. 'We sailed out singing, we must sail in singing.'

'Try them first,' Dr. Ma'afu says.

Ex-queen, leiti and chief medical officer accompany Amon to the multi-faith chapel.

'Would you mind?' Amon asks at the door. Turn on the organ. No problem. Select voices. Easy, with a slight tug of drying skin. *It will slough off*, Dr. Ma'afu said. He is a slougher now. He settles on something standard yet stretching. Bach: *Sleepers Awake*. Bach is always a chord of eternity. He barely manages the first theme. He leaves yellow ichorous smears on the keys.

Ex-queen, leiti and chief medical officer wait with expectation.

'It's going to be a cantata,' Amon announces.

It's not much of an intervention. Raisa is already dressed and waiting in the lobby when Finn, Atli and Siisi arrive.

'We're busting you out,' Atli says.

'This is a hospital, not a jail,' the nursing officer says. 'And hypothermia is a serious matter.'

Finn kisses Raisa.

'Doesn't feel cold to me.'

'I'm just here for the show,' Siisi says.

Raisa calls in a PBV car and drives it with glee and abandon over the hill and down to Saarloq. The site fizzes like a kicked beehive. The nearer to Arrival the less ready the project seems. Pallets and piles, cones of aggregate, concrete-stained shuttering. A galaxy of welding arcs. Half-clad walls, prolapsed insulation, headless ducts.

Raisa installs her guests in her apartment. The insulated walls hardly diminish the noise. Power tools, warning beepings, engines engines engines. There is hardly room in the mooring for the supply ships, let alone six fishing boats, three patrol boats and three cruise liners.

'Siisi, you can stay here or with Nauja.'

'I'd like to stay here.'

'Sure. You get the couch. Atli, floor. Finn, with me.'

Finn collapses onto the bed like a calving berg and it's two more sleeps to Arrival.

Only the oldest of the gods of Touia'o Futuna remember what rituals and celebrations marked the arrival of the great navigators on Ava'u. Thanksgiving there was—the navigators set sail with the purpose of finding new lands and homes—and pride. Relief, anticipation, excitement: long passage ended, storms weathered, stars followed, land sighted.

The Pulotu Road squad re-gas the balloon and send Touia'o Futuna back to its proper place between heaven and ocean. From divine altitude the godlings watch the migration fleet navigate Baffin Bay to the Davis Strait to the Labrador Sea. Warmer days, longer days. To north, west and south they see the Immaculate Storm's hobgoblin children thrash Nunavut and Kalaallit Nunaat before they run shrieking into oblivion but the fleet sails quiet seas and gentle winds. And in the lull, they hear voices. They strain their unworldly senses. Ava'uan voices singing. Simple, heart-rousing melodies, mighty harmonies. *Saying, what are they saying?*

Storm and sea, courage and unity. Gratitude and grace. A green land before them.

The godlings nod. The kids will be all right.

Amon drops his burning hands. The massed choirs fall silent and immediately break into chatter.

'People!' he calls in Ava'uan. The Immaculate Storm heeded him but not the singers of *Ava'utapu*.

He felt naked and exposed without hands to make his music. No keys, no apps, no dots on paper. Only the ideas in his head, his voice and the common tongue of music theory. But when he stood before the sections and sang each their parts, they listened and his voice and confidence grew and they gave his song back to him so much greater and richer.

This was the pure music, the muscle music, the cell music. The lightning inside.

'Okay, from the third measure,' he says and the storm of voices ignores him until he raises his hands. The passage of air over them is like fire but he imagines it dries, toughens, heals. 'Measure three,' he says and opens his hands and the voices answer.

The rub of the Arrival is this. Some will arrive first and the rest will arrive after. Who is first and who comes after fuels a deepening cyclone of rumour and speculation across the migration fleet. Questions of precedence delight Ava'uans. A lottery is proposed, to end all dissent. The churches veto it. Randomness offends God's perfect will. All agree that the first footfalls must be from all three islands. That there must be dignity, courage, respect. Beyond that, lords, commons, religious and sporting bicker and clash.

South, out from the panoply of the aurora to nights peopled by strange constellations, an upturned moon. Then, on the 60th parallel, the long-awaited turn, due east, towards the coast of Kujalleq. In the way that the Kalaallit say they can smell ice, old Ava'uan mariners declare they can smell land. The godlets know for sure. Not by smell or geographical senses. They hear the new land. It is full of voices. Creatures of the same substance as them, some alike, some very unlike. No divine rulers, no hereafter judges. No holy mother, no sun-father. Sea-dwellers and changelings. Women of power, women of fear. Spirits, geniuses. Benevolences and antipathies. Some powers the denizens of Touia'o Futuna hold are divided not among these ancient divines but among humans: powers of healing, sewing and joining, weather-talking. As they hear, they are heard.

The gods of Touia'o Futuna can't wait. Someone new to bicker with.

She's tired of news and updates and drone footage of the fleet out in the Labrador Sea and glossy reporters in glossy fresh outdoor wear and their gross simplifications and grosser misrepresentations and downright lies about Greenland—they call it Greenland because not one of them can pronounce its Kalaallisut name and it won't be news long enough for them to learn. But what boils her piss are three letters. M. L. Z. EmEllZee. Migration Landing Zone. Ugly. Patronising. She would stamp down on it if she were in a position to stamp on anything—which she isn't because Stýra Raisa Hopeland is out of the PR loop, partly because she is still under medical supervision for hypothermia and partly because she has form in swerving off-message.

She closes the screen. It will only annoy her. She looks out of the window and sees the one thing that annoys her more: Nauja Lund approaching through the long evening shadows. Raisa steps out to meet her on the porch.

'They're sleeping in there.'

'They want to talk to us,' Nauja says. 'About the Foundation. CNN, MSNBC. *China Daily.*'

'You could have called me,' Raisa says.

'I wanted to bring you this.'

Raisa hadn't noticed the Fjällraven backpack. Nauja Lund sets it on the rail and produces a bottle of champagne.

'It's the real thing. You deserve it, Raisa Hopeland.'

'I so do,' Raisa says. 'So do you.'

'Tuusi is keeping one for me,' Nauja Lund says. 'I am on duty for a while yet.'

'She's fine,' Raisa says. 'Siisi. That's why you came.'

'Yes, and to say I have no objection to Siisi joining your family. If that's what it is.'

'It's whatever she wants it to be.'

Nauja Lund sighs in exasperation.

'Is it always going to be like this with you Hopelands?'

'Yes,' Raisa says. Nauja Lund steps past Raisa to open the door. She looks for a long moment. The roar of working Saarloq rushes in past her like boisterous dogs. It will only fall silent at two minutes to anchors-down.

'They're exhausted,' Raisa says.

'We're all exhausted.' Nauja Lund regards Raisa with one of her discomfiting gazes. 'You crackle a little less.'

Nauja Lund closes the door and shoulders her backpack. She wipes her eyes.

'I hadn't thought it would happen so suddenly.'

'You won't lose her, Nauja.'

'I know that now.'

'The party will be good.'

'I know that too.'

'She'll be a star.'

'She is already.'

Nauja Lund turns at the foot of the steps. A lifter carrying a bundle of plastic piping from its arm reverses past, beeping.

'About CNN, MSNBC. *China Daily.* Do you want to do it?'

'Fuck no,' Raisa says.

'Me neither. Let it go undone.'

'Nauja.'

The short woman turns back again.

'I know what you meant now. About the fear.'

Nauja Lund nods her head.

'I will see you at Saarloq Wharf, Raisa. Tomorrow.'

121

Princess Elisiva Taʻahine Pilolevuʻs speech to the nation of Avaʻu. September 22, 2033.

The Showtime Theatre of *Avaʻutapu*, relayed to all ships of the Avaʻuan Migration Fleet.

Tomorrow we arrive in the new land. Our new home. Our voyage has been long and hard. We have faced storm and ice, violence and injustice, treachery and peril. Dear souls, great souls have passed over the horizon. Eighty days ago, I stood before you in this same theatre. I was your queen then. I was dressed in the regalia of a queen. Today I am dressed in the way of the new land and I am no longer a queen. It may wear a glove, but this hand still holds the ʻAkau Ta. I swore a vow on it that I would keep the nation together. I could not keep that vow. I gave away the nation so that we could remain a people. You forgave me. You kept faith with me. I have no greater honour than that you granted me in leading you. All you travellers, all you workers, all you families and teachers and carers. All you community leaders, all you religious, all you children. All you navigators, all you brave marines, all you fishers out there in your small craft. You held together. We arrive tomorrow as a great people. Do you remember what I said? We are not refugees. We are not migrants. We are not asylum seekers. We are voyagers. And now our voyage is done. Fair winds and safe harbours. God has sailed us safe to morning.

122

She can't sleep and after an hour of listening to the construction noise she decides she shouldn't sleep and gets up. Clothes. Clothes are good. She glances back at Finn starfished across the mattress. The man could sleep through a nuclear bombardment. His net of scars stands bold in the slot of construction light falling through the half-closed blind. Siisi, by somnambulism or design, has slipped off the sofa and lies curled like a kitten with Atli in a floor-nest of quilts, cushions, sleeping bags.

06:03.

She opens the porch door to noise and a light that blinds the tentative dawn and goes to the rail. White helmet with a red volcano: PBV. Nýttnorður green and white, Kebec Hydro red and black, Norges Statens Pensjonsfond blue, Nunavut Infra white and black. Arctic Council white and sky blue, ARCAN rave-orange and pink. The Naalakkersuisut: sky blue with polar bear, rampant.

And she finds tears pouring down her face. Incomprehensible, free-flowing tears. Her belly catches in an eddy of emotion. She smiles, she sniffs, she laugh-weeps. Joy, loss, exhaustion, sadness, hope, determination, blazing passion, loneliness, insecurity. Inner meltwater.

It's all grown up. It doesn't need her now. She can let it go. Walk away. That's what Raisa Hopeland does. Walks away. From Arcmage House, from Brightbourne, from salad veg, Sindri Ólafursson, from PBV. You never finish anything, Raisa Hopeland. A will-o'-the-wisp, a flibbertigibbet. Now, convulsing with ecstatic racking sobs, she understands. This is her great gift: to start a thing and know when to take her hands off it, to let it go, to walk away. To leave it to others. Saarloq will be fine without her. She can stop being extraordinary.

Today the Ava'uan voyagers arrive in the bay. And the day after, when they take up the tools and the farms and the jobs to make it their own, she can do anything she wants.

She howls into the fore-dawn and the great work swallows it. She laughs, she sniffs. Tears, snot, phlegm: the lot. She's wrung out. She feels released. The terrifying vertigo of the life unplanned.

She could go back to the forest. She came here to green the south and abandoned the work after one video call from Amon Brightbourne. Abandonment is the soul of forest. Blessed neglect. Maybe call in to see what direction it's grown without her. Or maybe not. Walk away and let it grow. There's a Starring to arrange, or maybe not. There's talk to be had with Amon Brightbourne, or maybe not. She's unnecessary.

The great things can go unfinished because they can never be finished.

She holds out her hand, fingers lightly up-curled. It's only a faint bass drone now, a salty tingle in the blood. She brings thumb and fingers together, an open flower. A wavering blue flame pulses lazily in the space between them. Raisa throws her arm outwards, flings open her fingers. The last fire of Lightning Woman flies out into the working-light glare and fades to nothing.

Heads turn in the street, on the John Deere cranes, on the wooden scaffolding. For an instant Raisa wonders if the workers heard her, saw her. Their attention is turned not to her but to the new road from Qaqortoq. A stream of headlights reaches the top of the pass and winds down into Saarloq. Car after car after car; grey hulks in the pre-dawn. Under the floodlights they take on identity: pickups, SUVs, ATVs, a couple of quad bikes, the school bus. Vans and tractors.

Qaqortoq has come to witness the Arrival.

123

Everyone wakes before dawn on Arrival Day, those who have slept. The spirit on the twelve ships is solemn, excited, apprehensive.

Amon Brightbourne rises late, brain lagged by Dr. Ma'afu's painkillers, and has to send runners deck to deck to deck to assemble his choir for a final practice. The prime places at the rail have already been claimed. Some have been there all night. After ice-watch in the Prince of Wales Strait, night on the Labrador Sea is merely chilly. Arrival Day breaks flat calm. An eerie fog lies on the approaches. There is not a whisper of wind. Ava'uan flags lie limp and dank against the flagstaffs. Touia'o Futuna rises proudly perpendicular. Ships' foghorns call to each other across the approaches. Out there, unseen, lies the fractured coast of Kujalleq.

'Sopranos by the soft-play area, basses in front of the coffee dock,' he orders. 'Kimmie?'

Kimmie Pangaimotu uses the twin threats of leiti snark and leiti muscle to bully the choir into position. She unleashes Ava'uan profanity on daw-dling altos and lazy tenors. Amon takes his place at the front. He will have his back to the new land. He takes the singers through a vocal warm-up. Coughs and spitting and phlegm. Mist dews hair, clothes, skin. The sea is poured pewter. He lifts his scarred hands and the choir opens an oceanic C-major chord.

And shapes materialize in the mist; grey on grey, summoned by song. Awe rolls across the voyagers like far thunder. The sea holds one last terror. A city of towers rises from the glass ocean. The fleet closes on the ranks of pillars and they resolve into the columns of wind turbines, shading to grey in every direction, a forest planted in the ocean. The fleet threads between the towers. Blades turn sluggishly high above, half-hidden by the fog. Each turbine shaft carries the PBV logo.

Amon drops his hands. Choir, ship, fleet fall silent. In that stillness and silence everyone hears a great rushing, beating, rumbling. High notes pierce the mist-wall, whispering half-heard and triumphant braying. It is uncanny, alien, unfathomable.

'Amon.'

Amon Brightbourne startles from the grey trance.

'I'm going to get ready.' Kimmie stands at his shoulder.

'It's over an hour yet . . .'

' 'Ofa'anga; still you don't get it.'

'You'll be a star, Kimmie Pangaimotu.'

'We are stars, Amon Brightbourne.'

'See you in the new land.'

'In the new land.'

Amon raises his hands again.

'Part two. First measure. Basses, you're not coming in with enough presence. I want to *feel* this.'

Raisa dithers so long over what to wear that she must run to make her place in the line-up. Every street is clogged with vehicles from Qaqortoq, the empty plots crammed with pickups and SUVs. Qaqortoqers and site workers press three deep along the bay road. Raisa mutters hasty greetings to site manager Angunnguaq Lyberth, Nive Taunajik the water engineer, Mikivsuk Nappaattooq in ecosystems: the talent that built Saarloq and Alluitsup Paa and Nanortalik. And here are her personal guests: Lisi. From Spitalfields Rev. Hope, Coil of the East. Finn. Atli, swathed and coiffed and made up like lightning walking which is what hé is, and no one paying the least attention to hé because the spectacle is all out in the bay. Siisi at hés side. From Vonland, Tante Jebet, wavering on two sticks, supported by Signy and Óðinn; from Reykjavík, Tekla. Raisa greets each, hugs Atli, kisses Finn long.

'You all right about this?' she whispers.

'I will be,' he says. 'Now get down there!'

She presses through the reporters and news workers and takes her place at the end of the line of Foundation directors. To her right stand the representatives of the Inatsisartut. From President Egede to the small woman beside Raisa, all wear traditional dress.

'Great morning,' Raisa says to her neighbour who wears a magnificent beaded collar and cuffs, embroidered short sealskin pants and long kamik boots.

'Yes it is,' the woman says and only then does Raisa realise she is Nauja Lund.

'You look different,' Raisa says, embarrassed.

'You don't,' Nauja Lund says. Raisa settled on fleece, hiking leggings, journeywoman boots.

'I mean, amazing . . .'

'Thank you. My great-grandmother made the collar and it's our family tradition that each generation adds to the beadwork.'

'Your work is wonderful.'

'Thank you but not my work. I am quite quite handless. Tuusi is the crafty one.'

Raised voice among the reporters. Raisa and Nauja turn to see Siisi trying to push her way through the line. Nauja says a word in Kalaallisut. Enough understand it to make passage for Siisi. She goes to her mother. They touch foreheads. Eye to eye, more intimate than any embrace.

A pulse of anticipation runs along the bay road and down the pier as news corporation camera drones take to the air. Camera crews film the crowd for GVs and close-ups of people their viewers might have heard of. In the night the Foundation fleet withdrew east towards Qaqortoq. Saarloq Bay lies open under a cobalt sky but sea fog stands heavy at the mouth of the fjord.

All at once the roar of Saarloq ends. All is quiet, all is still. Every eye and ear turns to the wall of fog across the western approach. Ships' horns out of the grey, growing louder, closer. Air and earth resonate to the pulse of massed marine drives.

What's that sound? Singing?

Then as one the prows of three great ships emerge from the fog. Three thousand breaths catch. And the ships come, bigger than anything Raisa can imagine: floating cities bearing down on Saarloq. Now the smaller craft appear, the patrol boats, the fishers. A wall of ships fills Saarloq Fjord.

Singing, yes singing. Voices from the highest deck of the centre ship. A choir in white, and a thin figure like bound twigs in front of them.

Along the bay road on the rocks and hillsides, the piers and scaffolding, the people cheer and applaud and blare car horns. The great ships answer with their sirens. Drones dart and skim like sea-birds around *Ava'utapu*, *Ofu* and *Niua* as they churn water and slowly spin in bows to shore; compass needles finding true north.

'That I should live to see this,' Nauja Lund says, voice shaking.

The decks are full to the rails with people.

Engines power down. Anchors roar to the seabed. Horns, hands and voices fall silent. The reception party moves into position, Raisa stays back in the place proper to a stýra of the Nýttnorður Foundation. A tender appears from behind the centre ship and curves in to the pier. A new sound crosses the water; children's voices talking, shouting, laughing, a joyful racket growing louder as the tender approaches landfall. Ava'uan sailors jump ashore to make the boat fast. These things always take longer than expected. Longer still, by Ava'uan time.

Children burst from the boat onto the dock, a benign noisy invasion. Boys Sunday-smart in radiantly white shirts and best tupenus. Girls and fakaleitis in long tupenus and ta'ovalas. Hair and skin oiled, beads and bracelets. Barefoot all. The smaller children look around uncertainly. Major Fia, tall and very handsome in full dress, reassures them. And here are the leitis of the court, Leiti Fetuu and Leiti Kimmie Pangaimotu; made-up, coiffed and dressed to conquer. Here is Princess Halae, looking around her in delight, beaming. Last, a woman in white steps from the boat onto the dock. The children encircle her. Leitis and Malietoa step in behind her. The Ava'uans wear formal attire, but she is dressed in Western outdoor wear; layers, hoodie, weatherproof. Like the others her feet are bare. She wears the three necklaces of the islands and carries the staff of her people. She plants the 'Akau Ta firmly on the decking. The children look to her. Princess Elisiva Ta'ahine Pilolevu nods, tilts the 'Akau Ta shoreward, and as one they walk down the jetty to the new land.

The second boat arrives. Major Fia returns to the jetty to greet a contingent of marines, unarmed, in traditional dress. A command, and they line up, stamp forward as one and perform the sipi tau, the dance of challenge and transition and of guards changing.

The cameras love it.

The third boat brings the Council of Voyagers, the Twelve Lords and the powers religious, sporting and community. By now the carefully stage-managed Arrival is chaos. As with any enterprise involving a mob of kids, the decorum and gravitas of the Arrival—President Egede welcoming the newcomers, Princess Ta accepting in the name of the people of Ava'u—lasts until boredom arrives. Reporters try to snag interviews, civil servants try to process documents, Foundation managers try to explain the settlement process—key workers first, then large families into the completed homes, late March before Nanortalik and Alluitsup Paa come online. Children run around; someone gets lost, someone is in tears. Qaqortoqers press forward to shake hands with the aliens. Ta disappears into a mob of voices. Major Fia attracts much admiration, the leitis Fetuu and Kimmie amazement. The woman who argued about services at Raisa's public meeting in Gertrud Rasch looks at Leiti Fetuu with bafflement; Siisi Lund solemnly shakes Kimmie Pangaimotu's hand. Princess Halae is enchanted by Atli.

Another boat arrives, and now the other two ships are putting out tenders. Raisa darts left, right, trying to get a line of sight on the new wave of arrivals. Among the white shirts and black tupenus she thought she glimpsed a scrap of colour, a weave of tweed.

'Here.'

Finn lifts her onto the hood of a pickup. She scans the faces pressing down the jetty. There. There! Him. Oh him! Oh him! The Ava'uans are half-a-head taller than the Kalaallit norm, but he rises above them. So pale. Thinner than when she saw him on screen, thinner even than she remembers. Gaunt. He has grown his hair out, the red streaked with grey. It could be the exact same suit he wore when she called him up to the Soho rooftops. She has no doubt he's shod in brogues. He clutches his great-uncle's satchel to his chest like a loved one's heart. He looks round him, lost, confused.

'Go to him,' Finn says. 'Go on. Go!'

Their fingers brush, then she jumps down from the truck. The crowd's brutal tide drives her back two steps for every three she takes towards him. She loses him, finds him, loses him again as the crowd pushes her into a new flow of bodies.

'Amon!'

He can't hear her.

'Amon!'

She's lost him.

Raisa climbs up on a plastic-wrapped bale. She sees him.

'Amon!'

He can't hear her, can't see her. She takes the yata from around her neck and holds it high. The wind from beyond sets the mirror spinning. Low sharp northern sun flashes across the surge of bodies.

The yata light catches him. He blinks, turns to see what dazzled him. He sees her.

He shouts. She can't hear him over the clamour. He presses towards her, swimming against the current, she towards him, neither of them looking away for fear that if they lose eye contact, they will lose each other for another wandering time.

His hands. What has happened to his hands?

She jumps from the bale and his arms are there and they come together and at the centre of the chaos they find a small stillness, the exact size of both of them. 'Oh, you you you you you!'

After the shuttle boats dock.

After the speeches are made.

After the health checks and the documentation. The assignments and the meal tickets.

After the photographs and the selfies and the Instagrams.

After all this, the rowdy boys, the useless boys who once hung around the Pulotu Wharf and made nuisances of themselves in the Chinese bars on Pulotu Road; who troubled the police and were thundered at from pulpits; who won't be off the ships any time soon, but have jobs and responsibilities in the new land: these boys go up to *Ava'utapu*'s Sky Deck and untether the saggy, stained weather balloon. With a laugh and a cheer they set it free. It climbs lazily through the still air until, at the edge of sight, it catches a higher wind that sweeps the old gods of Touia'o Futuna eastwards to the great plateau of ice and meetings and matings and adventures beyond the imagining of mortals.

And after the gods go rolling east, after the unitings and the reunitings, Raisa leads Amon Brightbourne gently by his wounded hand up the wooden steps of her house.

'Come on,' Atli says to Finn. 'Siisi says I can bunk at Nauja's place. I'm sure she can find a quilt for you.'

Finn turns back to look at Raisa and Amon.

'Skinny fucker.'

'Are you all right?' Atli asks.

'I will be.'

After all, we have a woman and a man in a wooden house at the top of the world, with years and oceans between them.

'For a while,' he says. 'I'll have to leave.'

'Awhile is enough,' she says. 'No one ever really leaves.'

He lays the old satchel against the sofa. The leather has been worn to such softness that anything inside leaves its impression on the skin. Such as a movement. A quick darting movement upwards, then motionlessness. Then another subtle bulge, travelling up the inside of the bag. A gecko pokes its head from the gap between the flap and the body of the bag, tastes new air, new land, new life. The second gecko joins it. They freeze for a throat-pulsing moment, then scuttle down the bag, across the floor on their soft, adhesive feet, and vanish into the warmth of the walls.

ALL IS FULL
OF LOVE

124

They come from a thousand Hearths, from the great cities of the north-lands: Nunatsiavut and NunatuKavut and Nitassinan; Inuktitut and Kebec; Alaxa and Kolyma and Taymyr. From the ring of ocean islands, from the forests of Klaalit and Iseland. From System, across months of infrasleep on the long loops in from the Auras out at the Lagrange points to distant Earth. From Mars. Not many: the cost of intra-System travel will always be exorbitant and those that want to send witnesses—or just go—are either group-funded or rich or driven. The event has been timetabled for a thousand years and orbits are precisely calculated so that even if travellers spend months in flight, they will arrive in good time. They spin down the space elevator, re-tool their biomes and physiologies in the vertical city that has accreted around the lowest ten kilometres of the elevator, then source planetary transport. Many can't make the adaptation—the peoples of the Moon's underground cities, the greatest and most glorious in human history—and occupy machine avatars or virtual presences.

Those that come are not all human. Machines, intelligences, the de-extincted. The uplifted. The trans-human, the post-human. All the many shapes of intelligence.

By air, by sea, by wheels or in some instances by foot, they come to Eirin. To the big lake in the north-east corner of the island, to the country at the north-west corner of the lake. No matter how they come, no matter how far they have travelled and in what wondrous craft, no matter their bodies or manifestations or abilities, they all must enter through the one gate in an ancient, crumbling stone wall. Otherwise, they cannot enter because there will be no gate and no path. For eight hundred years the great forest has stood at the centre of Eirin and in this golden place in the shelter of the hills it grows deep and dense and warm and brilliant with birds. They follow an ancient way, often more signal and a sense than a track. Unseen animals flee from the motion, setting leaves and branches astir. Silhouettes of great ungulates, breath steaming, move in the deep glades and marshes. All is rot and damp and frantic growth, silver moss and the drop of fat, spinning leaves and the bright colour of parasitic flowers. An ancient Hearth stands here, though, like the gate, you have to know how to see it. Houses and courts sprawl under and through and over trees; here are pavilions and refectories and workshops, power houses and information centres, libraries and ballrooms and staircases and skywalks grown into living wood.

As they approach the pilgrims listen for the first sound of tintinnabulation, carillons, chimes from a universe away, the bells of Elfland.

The Music still plays at Brightbourne.

Not for much longer. This is why they've come, Hopelands and friends and lovers and kynnd from across System. Brightbourne has set up air-conditioned tents and pavilions for the visitors and over many days the listeners arrive. In the long, insect-loud nights they gather and feast and drink and dress up and laugh beneath their own private constellations: Enion the Mama, Ahania Leader of the Starry Skies. Enitharmon with her guitar. Fyn Fights-With-Demons and his two staffs. Emen the Brilliant Boy, his bag full of stars. Rai Lightning Woman, the Unfinisher.

The next morning they go down to hear the Music end. The old brick turbine house was replaced long ago by a hall of immensely strong, clear glass so that those who came—generation upon generation—could watch the wonderful mechanisms whirring and ratcheting and ticking inside, wrapped in spray-scattered rainbows. The mechanisms have been rebuilt several times; now a patrol of tiny robots climbs and swings around the mechanisms but Lysander Brightbourne's design is unchanged. Unchanged also is the motive power: water from the pond spins the wheels and drives the belts. The flow under Shliv Galeon has never failed, not even in the terrible years.

The Music stands in a clearing in the rainforest. The kynnd gather. Some are not recognisable as human, animal or machine. The sun beats down, the notes spin out through the open louvres. The music mill whirs away, cycles within cycles.

Everyone knows the time but the Music leaves no doubt. Monthly, annual, ten-year, fifty-year, hundred-year measures come together. A high escapement never used before, built a thousand years ago purely for this moment, spins to life. A belt jolts into movement, a toothed wheel turns and plays out the final theme. All themes come together. Cease. A hammer rises and falls to strike a single high chime.

The Music ends.

At the head of the mill race the sluice drops. The machinery falls still. Water drips from cogs and springs, ratchets and cams.

But the kids are bored. They drift off, form friendships and gangs and rivalries, explore. They look for entertainment, for mischief. A pond! They wade into the blood-warm water. They find the sluice. Laughing, they lift the gate. The water gurgles into the race. The wheels turn.

The Music begins.

ACKNOWLEDGMENTS

First to the Arts Council of Northern Ireland, who awarded me a grant to research and write this book. They have long been supporters and encouragers of my work and that of many other writers, musicians, actors, visual artists, dancers—the whole spectrum of the arts in the north. Fund the arts!

To Bruno Puelles, a fine, fine writer and good friend who read and gave valuable notes at a very early, very rough, very partial draft of the first two sections of this book.

To my patient agent, John Berlyne, who both batted and fielded for this book so many times. Hope it's worth the wait.

To Cheryl Morgan, who read this for gender issues and made suggestions full of insight, wisdom and fun.

To all of you who've supported this project down the long years it's taken to make it here. You know who you are.

To the staff and keepers of Lissan House, Co Tyrone, the Golden Place.

To the people of Iceland, Greenland, Tonga.

Last and most of all, to Enid, whose tales of her and her mother's time working in the Kingdom of Tonga were filled with delight and subtlety and humanity and paradox and moved me to look oceanwards. It breaks my heart that you won't get to read this. But all was full of love, and all is full of love, and all will be full of love.